the
Locked
Away
Life

BOOKS BY DREW DAVIES

The Shape of Us

Dear Lily

With or Without You

the Locked Away Life

DREW DAVIES

bookouture

Published by Bookouture in 2022

An imprint of StoryFire Ltd.
Carmelite House
50 Victoria Embankment
London EC4Y 0DZ

www.bookouture.com

ISBN: 978-1-83888-666-0
eBook ISBN: 978-1-83888-665-3

To Marios.

Thank you, my love.

PROLOGUE I
BRUNO (21 JUNE)

He'd never felt so powerless in all his eighteen years – a mixture of dread, panic, and the realisation that he could *actually* die. What if they kept him locked in here for days? How long would he last without food or water? Bruno imagined his parents, his two younger sisters – and oddly, Dominic – mourning his untimely death, faces white, frozen in grief, but he pushed the images away, berating himself. Self-pity wasn't going to help. Bruno was entirely to blame for his situation. He'd brought himself here. Even with Esther's warning not to march himself into the hands of the enemy, he had, willingly...

No, it was too late for regret.

Esther. What Bruno wouldn't give for one of her badly typed text messages. He heard Esther's voice then, 'Dear heart, the mind is fallible, but at least you get to keep it with you.' Don't put all your trust in things, she'd meant. In a phone. A device which could be broken, corrupted or stolen from you. '*Everything of value is already* here.' Bruno almost felt Esther's finger tap the side of his head.

There were other sensations in the growing darkness. His empty pocket buzzed with phantom phone syndrome. His brain kept firing off queries to search online: 'How long can a person survive in isolation?' 'Ways to pick a lock?' 'Where is the closest police station?' Bruno yelled in frustration, but his voice was already hoarse from shouting and the only thing to escape his throat was a stulted cry.

He couldn't just *sit* here. Without his phone, he felt like a limb was missing. There must be *something* he could do?

Launching himself off the bed, the old mattress springs creaking angrily, Bruno tried the handle again, as if this time it might miraculously open. He banged his fists against the door until they throbbed. At the window, he pulled at the bars with all his might, but they didn't budge, and anyway, the window seemed nailed shut. In a fit of frustration, he knocked over the bedside chest of drawers, sending the Bible which had been sitting on top scattering to the floor. Guiltily, he picked it up again – however angry he was, Bruno couldn't wilfully damage a book, especially *that* book. Placing it safely out of the way, he turned his attention to the bed, heaving it up with all his strength, the old mattress springs jangling as the metal frame hit the wall with a satisfying thud. The cloud of dust made Bruno cough and shield his eyes. Was there anything under the bed that might help him? The light from outside was fading, and there was no electricity in the cabin, he'd checked. Soon he'd be in absolute darkness, with not even the torch on his phone to guide him.

Peering at the exposed floorboards, Bruno searched for a paperclip or a scrap of metal, something, anything. He recoiled at the shape of – was it an animal? A rat perhaps? As he watched, it still hadn't moved – maybe it was dead? Bruno came closer and gave the small mound on the floor a gentle nudge with the toe of his sneaker, ready to jump away if it stirred. The animal gave a squeak, but not the sound of a rat or a mouse; it was the artificial squeak of a children's toy. In any other situation, Bruno would have laughed. After closer inspection, he could see it was a small plastic frog with protruding eyes and a broad, dopey grin. He picked it up and dusted away the grime and cobwebs – having to ignore his impulse to immediately and thoroughly wash his hands.

Reaching back to the wall behind him, Bruno lowered himself to the floor, still clutching the toy. As he sat there for the many hours to come, he would squeeze this newfound companion whenever he became too sad, too caught up in his own misfortune. After all, that's what had brought him here in the first place. His whole life, he'd been waiting for someone else's permission to transform, to become his real self. To *start* living. Bruno had held himself back in so many ways, distancing himself from people who cared for him – his sisters, his parents, even Dominic – only Esther had managed to break through his defences. Bruno had locked himself away, for far longer than he'd ever been in this cabin. Perhaps that's why Esther understood, because she'd done exactly the same.

Everything of value is already here.

But Esther was wrong about that – what mattered most didn't reside in his mind...

Squeak, squeak.

And in the darkness, and the pain, Bruno felt something lift.

PROLOGUE II

ESTHER (22 JULY)

Esther was as close to the cliff edge as she dared, which – considering what she was potentially intending to do – seemed laughable. Too late for self-preservation now, she thought. The impulse to save herself from harm was redundant. And yet, she felt it keenly. The strong easterly wind was in full force, it whipped her hair around her face, into her mouth, and in her eyes. Her clothes fought her body for emancipation, to be blown around these Scottish hills in perpetuity. She glanced down at the drop beneath her but pulled herself back sharply. It would do, that's all that mattered. What happened afterwards was none of her concern.

Whose was it, then? Her daughter's. It would fall on her shoulders. And Bruno's too, Esther's dear heart. He'd blame himself. Would a dark shadow be cast over his young life forever?

Pride! That she mattered so much! Esther was a footnote, a decrepit nuisance, a drain on their resources. She was freeing them of the burden. All the dark memories began crowding into her mind again; the loss of Thackeray, the public shaming, the decades of isolation. Release! And she was choosing to exit on

her own terms, not in some nursing home, force-fed stewed
fruit...

A gust claimed the folds of her clothes, lifting her up out of
the wheelchair, her small frame held aloft, levitating – or so it
felt – in mid-air, and Esther imagined she was about to be flung
out of the wheelchair for good. *This is it*, she thought – and at
that precise moment, Esther realised she was terrified.

'I'm not ready,' she cried, ridiculously – because what else
was there to do? The elements had claimed her. But there were
so many things left undone. To thank her daughter. To throw
another dinner party. To read a page of a book, any book. For
Bruno to show her one more confounding, yet extraordinary use
for his Inter-Net. How little time there was when we were only
ever renting these bodies.

And just as swiftly as the wind had lifted her, teetering on
the edge of hope and understanding, Esther began to fall.

ONE

BRUNO (23 APRIL)

Bruno walked up the steep pathway, approaching the house. Already he could see it was unlike any of the others in the village; his dad called it a 'manor house', but Bruno wasn't sure what that meant exactly, except it implied *grandness*. The trees and shrubs alongside the path were overgrown, and Bruno had to brush stray branches away as he went, but he kept his eyes fixed on the building – yes, it was grand, but it was also weirdly misshapen, especially the windows, as if they'd been added by completely different builders, with differing ideas of what a window should look like. As children, they'd called it the witch's house. A word came to him then: *chovahauni*. He paused on the path to google it on his phone, as he often did when a Romani word from his childhood popped into his head. It meant 'enchantress' or 'witch'. Bruno felt an impulse to make the sign of the cross, like his uncle – his dad's brother – might have done, but he rolled his eyes. Instead, he slipped the paper advert out of his back pocket and read it again for courage:

> *Help with Internet required. Complete Beginner. Paid position, please enquire at the address below.*

It was the word 'paid' that had made Bruno, uncharacteristically for him, unpin the advert from the wall – after checking no one was watching – and stuff it into his bag. Steal it, is what he'd done. It was only a piece of paper, he'd reasoned, with no value – and he'd wanted to make sure no one else applied before he could. Window-washing only brought him eight pounds a property in the village, and he had to wait for them to get sufficiently dirty again, which could take weeks, even with all the grime from the motorway. Bruno also helped his mother out at her salon, sweeping hair, cleaning the mirrors, doing her basic book-keeping, but he needed to bring more money into the family, not take a cut from his mum's earnings. There was always the option of working in the local dispatch warehouses, preparing retail stock, or delivering it across England by truck, but this was only a last resort. You could get trapped working at the warehouses, he'd seen it with older kids he'd been at school with, they'd go away for a few months or a year, come back for Christmas, and before you knew it they were trudging through the underpass in January, to start a life sentence. Not one seemed to get out again. And Bruno wanted *options*. That's why he had his own *secret* reason for earning money, that not even his mum knew about...

Folding the paper again neatly, he slipped the advert back into his pocket and made his way to the front door. It was late April – sunny, yet cold, when washing windows still froze him to the core; his fingers often felt as if they might fall off. Around him, new leaves were emerging on branches, but he could see some of the trees and bushes had already started to flower, as if they were too impatient to wait any longer. He knew the feeling well.

When he reached the door, Bruno was momentarily unsure what to do – he'd never encountered one as ornate and as expensive-looking as this. On the side, he noticed there was a bell, partly obscured by a vine, but underneath it was an ancient rectangle of water-stained paper which read 'DOES NOT WORK' in faded block handwriting.

Square in the middle of the door was a metal aeroplane. Bruno had assumed it was simply decorative, but then a thought dawned on him – maybe it was functional, some kind of fancy rich-person knocker? The Merlson family, who were managers in the warehouses, had a showy gold one on their door in the shape of a lion's face, but Bruno had never used it because he worried about being blamed for leaving grubby fingerprints.

He tried the plane now, experimentally lifting the tail. It could be raised with some effort, he discovered – it needed some WD-40 – and it came down again with a loud 'tok' that seemed to reverberate through the massive door and caused birds to leap from nearby trees. Repeating the process twice, Bruno waited expectantly. Out of habit, he scanned his body, going to his wrists and hands first – always first – mentally willing them to relax. He smoothed down his brown hair, which had grown darker over winter, but would become mousier again in summer, before ruffling it up again, and smoothing it once more. He clenched his buttocks and tightened his jaw. Remembering his clothes, he glanced down at what he was wearing – grey sweatpants with a green line down each leg. Black T-shirt. Dark grey jacket. His cream sneakers weren't as white as he'd like them to be, but he had to make concessions. Overly cleaned sneakers might draw attention. Everything about his attire was carefully chosen, as if he was creating a 'teenager' character in a computer game. Bruno wanted to convey 'male, teenager, normal' to the viewer, and have them quickly move on without any question or comment.

He waited. And waited. Bruno was about to bang the knocker again when he heard a woman's faint voice inside.

'Yes, hello?'

'I'm here about the ad,' Bruno called through the door.

'You're what?' came the voice. 'You'll have to speak up.'

'The ad. In the library.'

'You're from the library?'

'No, I saw your *advert* there,' he was basically hollering now. 'It's the community library. In my mother's hair salon. Where people can swap books. It was pinned on the notice-board. You wanted help with the internet?'

There was the crunching grind of what sounded like a medieval lock being turned, and then the door opened slightly.

'Ah, that's much better, don't know why I didn't think of that before.' A slice of pale face appeared at Bruno's waist height, one bright amber eye, almost coppery in tone, regarding him inquisitively. 'I have relatively good hearing, in my left ear at least – emphasis on *relative* – but this door absorbs sounds like a black hole. Now, how can I be of service?'

'You wanted to learn about the web?'

'The what, dear?'

'The web,' Bruno repeated louder, trying to enunciate. His cheeks were growing hot. 'You know, websites and stuff?'

'Ah, yes... What's it called?'

'The internet?'

'No, that's not the one I'm thinking of.' The amber eye swivelled in its pink socket. 'It will come to me.'

'But you did put an advert in the library?' Bruno asked, even more confused. He stopped short of confirming it was a paid position; it felt rude to mention money so early on.

'I did. Or more accurately, it was Mary, my neighbour, as my surrogate.' The eyebrow shot up. 'The *On-Line!* That's what I meant to say. I told you it would come to me.'

Good, they were getting somewhere.

'So... you'd like to have lessons in how to get online?'

'Not particularly,' came her pithy response, 'but with the way the world has gone, I don't seem to have much choice in the matter. Let me look at you.' The door opened even further to reveal an elderly woman sitting in a wheelchair, her long grey hair pulled back into a bun. Uncharitably, Bruno's initial thought was, 'I hope she doesn't smell bad' – all his grandparents had died by the time he was a small child, and so he wasn't used to being around old age, it unnerved him. The seated woman seemed so frail; what if he hurt her by accident? There were veins in her face, and wrinkles of course, but her cheeks and forehead were inexplicably smooth. Her hands were the most alarming, the fingers like long hooks. 'Oh, aren't you lovely?'

Bruno felt the inquisitive eyes regard him, and his cheeks blushed deeper.

'Come here...' Hesitantly, Bruno leant towards the old woman, and was relieved to find she smelled of talcum powder. She raised her hands, placing them on either side of his face. 'I won't hurt you,' she told him, as he instinctively pulled away. Her fingers were icy against his burning cheeks. She started to manoeuvre his face side to side and up and down to see him at different angles. Bruno hated being gazed at like this, it was taking all his self-control not to sprint away down the path.

'If I'd known someone so handsome was coming today, I would have dressed up, and forgone this ratty old cardigan.' She let go of his face, and he stood up again, smoothing his hair anxiously. 'I'm not always in *the chair* either,' she indicated the contraption she was sitting in. 'Just to be clear, I *can* walk. I had a stroke. Eight years ago. Left me with funny legs. Not ha-ha, unfortunately. Some days I have to acquiesce.'

Bruno wasn't sure what 'acquiesce' meant, but he nodded politely.

'Dear, dear heart...' She dropped her hands into her lap, still staring at him with what seemed like delight. 'Where *did* you come from?'

'Down the hill, from the village.'

'And tell me, are you a radical?'

Flummoxed by this question, Bruno scratched the back of his neck.

'I don't think so...' he stammered.

'What a shame. What *do* you believe in?'

'You mean God and stuff?' It wasn't exactly the line of questioning Bruno had imagined from the job ad.

The woman shrugged her bony shoulders to her ears and then let them go again.

'In life? In the world?'

Bruno considered her question.

'I don't know,' he replied, feeling slightly defeated.

'Anything?' she prompted again, hopefully.

He hated being put under a spotlight like this; it was school all over. There was so much blood pumping to his face, he could feel his pulse throbbing in his temple.

'Let me help you,' she suggested. 'Do you have a mother? Sisters?'

'Both. Two younger sisters.'

'Are you kind to them?'

'Yes...?' Bruno realised he didn't sound particularly convincing. He wasn't *always* kind to his sisters, they often annoyed him, but he did love them, and wanted to be a good older brother. And his mum was his mum, of course he loved her, but it felt odd saying as much to a stranger. Weak, somehow.

The woman's copper eyes scanned him some more.

'Do you believe in the Holocaust?' she asked.

'Believe in it? It happened... didn't it?' All a sudden he didn't feel so sure, even though they'd spent a term on it at school.

She nodded.

'Can you play an instrument?'

'A musical one, you mean? No.'

'Shame. Neither can I. Although, in the late seventies, I managed a five-piece improvisational jazz and experimental music ensemble called the Feminist Avant-Garde Group. They were never very good unfortunately – although that wasn't really the point – but I loved to watch them perform. One final question, my dear heart – you are humouring me so. Tell me, do you think I *will* be able to learn about your *Inter-Net*? Is it possible? I know we've only just met, but first impressions. Am I a lost cause?'

'I don't think so,' Bruno stuttered. 'You like asking questions, and that's what it's really good for.'

'And how do you know if you're asking the right questions?' she asked.

'You get the right answers,' he replied quickly.

'*Exactly*,' the woman's eyes twinkled with satisfaction. 'You'll have to turn me round, I'm afraid,' she said, wheeling herself backwards so Bruno could enter the house. 'Do you mind?' She tapped the handle behind her left shoulder with one of her long fingers, and Bruno dutifully swivelled the wheelchair around. It was easier than he imagined, she was so light, and unlike the plane door knocker, the wheelchair seemed well oiled.

'Let's retire to the kitchen,' she called over her shoulder. 'Through the hallway, onwards!'

Bruno kicked the door closed behind him and started to wheel the woman into the house. The wallpaper in the hallway was blood-coloured. Bruno had never been in a house with red walls. His mum had redecorated two years ago, before his father became ill, and she'd painted every wall a uniform off-white.

'First on the left,' the woman announced as they approached the doorway, 'it's a strange place to have the kitchen, I know, but it was modernised in the sixties – not by me, I can assure you. The original kitchen, the dairy, was on the other side of the house nearer the paddocks.' As she continued to talk about cows, and churning butter, Bruno glanced down and noticed that the woman's scalp had a bald spot – no, the hair was simply thin, the way it was scraped back only adding to the effect. He felt terrible for her, this shameful part of her body exposed to him, a stranger, and he wanted to find a comb and fix it.

The kitchen was bright day to the hallway's macabre night, flooded with light by large windows.

'Let's set up over there,' she instructed. Bruno dutifully wheeled her over to the table, careful not to bump into it, and sat beside her in a rickety wooden chair. Motes of dust swirled in the sunlight, but the tabletop was spotless, which Bruno appreciated, and he allowed himself to rest his elbows. In the centre of the table was a collection of handsome jars filled with buttons, milk tops, paperclips, rubber bands, and the tie-bands from bread, normal, useful things, somehow made special in the reflection of the sun.

'Now you may ask, why do I want to explore the On-Line if I'm so averse? And I would say to you – we used to have a Post Office in this village. Do you remember?'

'It was part of the newsagents?'

'Exactly, they shut it down. Banking and mail, poof. There was a grocer too – there one day, gone the next. I remember a time, long ago, there was a butcher. Before that even, a slaughterman with a van, Eddie, always with a pristine apron, which I found a little suspicious, but he would drive right to your door, came here every Thursday. Not my door, of course, my path was too steep for his van. He walked up with a basket, complained every time. So, you see, it's a necessity. And when I ask anyone, where has everything gone in the world, they tell me – *On-Line*. It's some magical place they created when I wasn't looking. The promised land. No one explained the ramifications until it was too late. Or maybe they did, and I wasn't listening.'

'Don't you have anyone to help you here?' asked Bruno. Who dusted the jar tops? They gleamed bright.

She waved away this question. 'Too many people – my trusted neighbour Mary, my daughter Jane, the doctor, all the nurses – I can't get a moment's peace. But the problem is I'm not a very good student, in general, but especially when I am to learn something so... ethereal, if you see what I mean? When I grasp at straws, it can make me hot-headed. Mary has tried, bless her, my daughter too, but it feels very much like physics, and I never enjoyed physics.'

'I don't like physics either.'

'Good, so we are on the same page. How do we begin? Can I fetch us pens and paper?'

Bruno laughed as if she was making a joke, and quickly realised his mistake when he saw her blank expression.

'Do you have a phone?' he asked.

'Of course, it's the hallway, on the occasional, you can bring it in here, the cord reaches.'

'Ah,' Bruno said, realising the issue instantly. 'Not a land-line, a mobile phone.'

'Oh, one of *them*,' she replied, sniffily. 'I hear they cause cancer.'

He winced at hearing the c-word, thinking of his dad.

'Do you have a computer?' he asked, trying a different tack. 'A laptop?' he suggested, not very confidently.

'How would I know if I had one?'

'What do you mean?'

'Where would it *be*?' she asked, impatiently. 'What would it look like? If you describe it, I can try and think if I've seen it before.'

Bruno had an idea.

'You'd probably know your router?'

'You'd be surprised, dear...'

'It's a box with lights that blink and flash, they would have set it up when they came and connected your broadband.'

'My what?'

'They have turned on your internet, haven't they?'

'Of course not, that's what you're here to do, or am I getting something completely muddled?'

'You have to ring the phone people, and they connect you.'

'Connect me how? To what?'

'To the cable, although I don't know if you'll get high speed up here.'

'Am I to understand it is a physical thing, this inter-net? We need to buy some before we can start? If I give you some petty cash, can you run and get enough for our lessons?'

Bruno paused at the mention of money. A thought sidled into his mind: how much was lying around the house? Unused notes stuffed in old jam jars? Forgotten, outdated even. Could money become outdated? What business was it to him, Bruno mentally reprimanded himself; his parents had brought him up better than to covet an elderly woman's money.

'It might be easier if we use my phone, for the time being.' The instant he'd said this, Bruno regretted it. Although he was always extremely cautious not to leave any breadcrumbs on his phone – he used private browsers for anything even mildly incriminating, and constantly viewed his web presence from the eyes of someone peering over his shoulder – what if he'd missed something? He tried to remember the last thing he'd googled and it came to him quickly – *chovahauni*. Witch. Perhaps the pen and paper were a better solution after all...

'Dear heart, if you don't possibly mind, could we reconvene again tomorrow morning? I suddenly feel exhausted by all this new information.' The spark in her eyes *had* seemed to disappear, and she did look tired. 'I told you I'm not a very good student.'

'Absolutely,' Bruno replied, relieved – he could do a thorough cleansing of his phone's search history before then.

'Before you go, do you have any questions for me?'

Bruno considered this. 'Only... what's your name?'

'Oh, my boy,' she chuckled, and it was a sound like glass being tapped by metal. 'Esther, very pleased to meet you.' She held out her spindly hand, with the long, pointy nails. Bruno stared at it for a brief moment, before taking it carefully in his and gently shaking. He needn't have worried, it seemed much stronger than he'd imagined, the grip matching his. 'Till tomorrow then.'

He was almost home by the time he remembered that he'd totally forgotten to ask about payment.

'How was it?' his mother asked, as she placed Bruno's dinner down in front of him. It was mince and potato wedges for the second time that week. The quality of food was plummeting in direct correlation with the number of cut-out recipes stuck to the fridge that read: 'Feed a whole family for under a tenner'.

'Brief,' Bruno replied truthfully. 'But I'm going back tomorrow.'

'What's the old Jewess like?' his father asked, taking his plate of mince. Even with the perky expression on his face, he still looked grey and not quite himself from the chemo.

'Filip, we don't say that word,' his wife admonished.

'Why not, it's accurate?'

'No one describes a person by their religion. We don't call Reg and Sylvia the Roman Catholics, do we?'

'Not to their face...'

'The kids, Filip.'

'Fine. What's the old *hermitess* like?' Bruno's dad prided himself on his vocabulary. The longer and more antiquated the word, the better. If you were ever unsure what to buy him as a present, you could always fall back on a trivia book he could read in the bathroom.

'What does "Jewess" mean?' asked Bruno's youngest sister, Daphne, who was already chomping her way through her fifth potato wedge. She had recently been prescribed glasses for astigmatism, toying with them constantly as she ate, pushing them up and down the bridge of her nose.

'It's a woman who is Jewish.'

'Like I'm vegan-ish but I like chocolate eggs too much?'

'Sort of. Eat your special mince, the stuff's not cheap you know.'

Bruno pushed his oily authentic mince around with his fork and considered asking for the vegan alternative.

His dad cleared his throat.

'She was involved in some scandal in the seventies, Reg reminded me – it was in the tabloids. People said she fled here.'

'Did she ever come down to the village?' Bruno asked after swallowing a stodgy mouthful and taking a big sip of water. 'Esther was talking about when the newsagent had a Post Office.'

'Years ago now. She always stuck out. A lot grander than our lot. The last time I saw her, she had one of those mechanised chairs, like a popemobile.' Bruno's father winced, as if he'd been struck by an invisible force.

'You alright?' Bruno asked him gravely.

'I will be.' His dad smiled wanly. 'It will pass.' He patted his son's hand.

'Did you go inside her house?' Megan asked. She was six years older than Daphne, and four years younger than Bruno, and had completely made the transition from sweet sister to annoying teen. Her current rebellion was to wear her hair over as much of her face as possible, but you could still feel the glower of her eyes, even if you couldn't see them.

'I did, and there's old stuff everywhere. Books and furniture and lamps. On my way out, I saw a stuffed animal.'

'What kind of animal?' squealed Daphne.

'I'm not sure, but its eyes were watching me.'

Daphne screeched again, bits of vegan mince flying onto her plate.

'Alright, let's keep food in our mouths, please,' their mum warned.

'How come Bruno gets to go up there and we don't?' Megan complained.

'Maybe he'll take you one day?'

Bruno ignored this suggestion.

'She's paying you, right?' his dad asked.

'Uh-huh...' replied Bruno, taking a big mouthful.

'What are you saving for, anyway? You've become a bigger penny pincher than your mother.' Bruno chewed, keeping his eyes down – his mouth conveniently too full to answer. 'Probably going to spend it on some secret girlfriend he has tucked away, am I right, girls?'

Daphne giggled so much her glasses almost slid off her face.

'Mum, is a hermitess a woman who wears a helmet?' she asked, brightly.

'It's someone who lives alone for a very long time, who wants to be left by themselves.'

'But why do they wear a helmet?'

'*Hermit*, not helmet.'

'What does a hermit mean?'

Her mum sighed.

'Eat your wedges before they get cold.'

'So it means *eat your wedges before they get cold*?' both sisters laughed. 'You're a hermitess,' they said, pointing to each other with wedges. 'No, you're a hermitess.'

Daphne started to fake cry, with real tears. 'Mum, Megan's calling me names!'

Megan rolled her eyes – the flash of whites could just be seen through the fringe of hair – and continued to pick at her food.

'Mum!' Daphne cried louder.

'I'd like to be a hermitess sometimes,' Bruno's mother mumbled under her breath.

The next morning at 10 a.m., Bruno walked down his street and through the village towards Esther's house. 'Village' made Whittleham sound much cutesier than it deserved, situated right by Junction 18 on the M1, a main distribution hub for large chains like Argos and Marks & Spencer because of its prime location in central-south Midlands. Almost all of the adults who lived in the village were connected to the warehouses in some way – sorting and loading the pallets of stock, or as lorry drivers, transporting the pallets around England. Whittleham, in west Northamptonshire, six miles east of Rugby, was pretty unexceptional – with its small medieval centre surrounded by a utilitarian mish-mash of housing estates – except for one thing. In the 1960s, Romani travellers had started to arrive for seasonal work, mostly around Christmas – and some of them, uncharacteristically for travellers, had stayed. Bruno's grandfather had been one to settle. Over the next fifty years, the travellers had assimilated into village life, many becoming long-haul lorry drivers. If there had once been any cultural tensions in Whittleham, they seemed to have mostly been resolved over the years by camaraderie in the warehouses. There was still a well-used site for caravans at the west of the village, and some Angloromani had slipped into common usage, but most second-generation offspring like Bruno felt relatively removed from their ancestry – until they were bussed to Rugby to attend secondary school, that was, and found themselves mercilessly bullied about it.

The main street of Whittleham was home to Bruno's mum's hairdressing salon, called 'Snips', a fish and chip shop named 'Fins', 'Terry's', a bakery – which was trying to replicate the look of the chain bakery Greggs but had failed, a betting shop and a newsagent. Five years ago, there was talk of a Tesco Metro opening, but it had never materialised. The villagers had to drive ten minutes to do a proper supermarket shop in Rugby; ironic, considering most people in Whittleham spent their days sorting shopping for the rest of the country but couldn't get much locally themselves.

As Bruno walked along the main street, quiet after the mass migration of day-workers to the warehouses before 9 a.m., he noticed his ex-classmate Dominic smoking outside the corner shop.

'Slacker,' Dominic called to him good-naturedly, but it made Bruno flinch. He felt conspicuous in the town during the workweek when almost everyone else had gone through the motorway underpass. 'Come here, I want to show you something.'

Sheepishly, Bruno wandered over, reminding himself to relax his wrists and hands. They had never been friends at school. Dominic had been unarguably the coolest kid from the village. Their townie classmates called the Whittleham students – whether they had traveller blood or not – 'gypsies', 'caravanners' and much worse, but Dominic, who was proud of his traveller heritage, even wearing a silver pendant of a wagon wheel around his neck, seemed impervious to their insults. He never reacted, letting the jibes slide off him effort-lessly. He was easy-going, hugely liked – especially by the girls – and even the meanest townies grew to begrudgingly respect him. Bruno, on the other hand, felt constantly awkward at school. But something weird had happened since the end of final term. Dominic, like Bruno, was one of the few classmates not to start at the warehouses, or – if their families could afford it – to go away on a gap year. The two had been left in a limbo of 'what next?' which had strangely equalised their status.

Taking a drag of his cigarette, Dominic indicated that Bruno should watch something on his phone. Bruno took off his backpack and leant against the stone wall beside him, a good distance apart, mostly to avoid the plumes of smoke, but also because it felt too intimate so close together and Bruno was aware of passers-by. Dominic shuffled closer, tucking a strand of jet-black hair behind his ear, and held his phone nearer to Bruno. On the screen, a woman was taking a shower. Bruno felt instantly uncomfortable – what if it was porn, and he was watching it in public, and only a few metres from where his mum was setting up the salon for the day?

'It gets better,' Dominic promised ominously, snorting smoke out of his nose. Bruno tried not to cough. His eyes moved from the screen to Dominic's hand, noticing how the hairs on the underside of his wrist were dark against his pale skin. He was wearing a white short-sleeved shirt buttoned up over a black Ramones T-shirt, that didn't exactly scream 'I'm at work'. Along Dominic's left arm there were drawings and scribblings in blue ballpoint pen, a smudgy ying-yang symbol, a robot short-circuiting, and six games of noughts and crosses.

'Who are you playing noughts and crosses with?' asked Bruno.

'Myself, mostly,' Dominic replied, not taking his eyes off the phone, 'I ask everyone who comes into the shop but I don't get many takers.' He nudged Bruno. 'This is the part.'

Reluctantly, Bruno returned his gaze to the screen just in time to see the naked woman, who'd finished rinsing herself, draw back the shower curtain to reveal a hideous face with pointed ears and long, sharp teeth. Bruno practically jumped out of his skin.

'Good, right?'

'Yeah,' Bruno replied, enough cortisol pumping through his veins to lift a bus.

'The eighties were the best for horror films. All in-camera effects, no CGI.'

'The best.' His heart was palpitating.

'Did you know that mirrors used to be made of silver – that's why vampires couldn't see their reflection? Silver was used in old-fashioned photo processing too. But modern mirrors are made of aluminium, and now we have digital cameras, so these days vampires *would* be able to see their reflection and show up in photos.'

'Great if they're influencers.'

'Yeah, exactly,' agreed Dominic with a laugh, scrawling through the video, obviously trying to find another jump scare. This was the longest conversation Bruno had ever had with Dominic – he'd never realised he was so... geeky. 'Oh,' Dominic looked up from his phone. 'I heard you're giving lessons to the old lady on the hill?'

Bruno was startled.

'How do you know about that?' he asked quickly.

'Think her neighbour told me,' Dominic jabbed a thumb at the newsagents behind them. 'This place is gossip central.'

That made sense. Bruno had worried his dad was telling random people.

'Speaking of,' Bruno said, changing tack, 'are there any shifts going here?'

'Coming for my gig, huh?' Dominic said, nudging Bruno again. 'Don't you work for your mum? And wash windows? You always seem to be rushing around with a bucket.'

'It's still not enough. My dad's on sickness benefits, and I want to contribute more now school's over, but I'm also trying to save money...'

'To get out of this place, huh? Sorry about your dad, too. I can ask about shifts, but the pay's terrible and it's so boring, I

sleep between customers most days. Have you tried Fins?'
Dominic nodded at the fish and chip shop.

'They said I didn't have the dexterity to man the deep fryer.'

'Harsh. Terry's?'

'They only hire girls.'

'Sexist. And the betting shop smells like feet, you don't
want to work in there.' Dominic took a long drag on his
cigarette, making it crackle. 'What's the old woman like?'

Bruno considered how to answer this. He could make a joke
at Esther's expense to try and impress Dominic, but that didn't
sit well with him.

'She seems nice, actually,' he replied.

'Nice,' Dominic repeated, nodding and stubbing his
cigarette out against the wall before throwing it onto the road. 'I
better get back.' He turned so his face was very close to Bruno's.
'We've got to stick together, you and me. Otherwise, we'll just
become another one of those drones in the warehouses.' He
leant even closer, and Bruno could feel the heat of his breath. 'If
you ever want any weed...'

'I think I'm good... at the moment, thanks.' Bruno had never
touched an illegal substance in his life. His dad had to badger
him to even take a sip of beer before his eighteenth birthday.

Dominic nodded, and headed inside the store, the bell
bleating a 'Baa-baa'. When he was gone, Bruno walked over to
the road, took out a tissue from his pocket and picked up the
cigarette butt, wrapping it up before placing it in the bin.

'Dear heart, you returned!'

Bruno wasn't sure what to say to this – had Esther not
expected him to?

'Mum wanted me to give you these...' he took out a large
Tupperware container of scones from his backpack, which his
mother had baked in the early hours. 'Stomach fillers', she called

them; 'door stoppers' was their nickname behind her back. Bruno had wanted to say 'scones' to Esther – as in, rhymes with 'cons' – but stopped himself, thinking she might pronounce them, to his mind, the posher way, as in rhymes with 'cones'.

'How delightful, what are they?'

Esther was standing today, supporting herself on a wooden stick, but she wasn't much taller out of the chair than in it. She was wearing dark green twill trousers, a pink woollen jumper that was so baggy it was almost shawl-like, and her hair was in a much looser bun, tendrils escaping and falling down around her shoulders.

'Sco-ones?' Bruno replied, uncertainly, trying to approximate a blending of the two pronunciations.

'Ah, scones,' she said, in the regular clipped 'con' way. 'Thank her profusely. I once had afternoon tea in a desert with an Arabian prince, clotted cream, perfectly chilled. The only thing that stood out as unconventional was the lack of sweetness in the food. I was told afterwards that the prince was a diabetic, so all the preserves and jams were made especially without sugar, which made them eye-wateringly tart. Lots of polite wincing. Shall we try the library today?'

Esther clutched Bruno's arm for support, her grip strong, their progress a slow one through the house. It seemed she couldn't walk *and* talk; it took all her concentration to keep her legs moving, and every now and then she would squeeze his wrist, which meant stop for a moment. 'I'm not normally like this,' she explained. 'Much sprightlier on the whole.'

'Do you want me to get the wheelchair?' Bruno offered.

'We don't need that old thing today. Very nearly there!'

Bruno had never been in a personal library before, and instinctively he reminded himself to whisper. Books lined every wall, interspersed with oil paintings of intimidating people, but what struck Bruno the most was the network of spiderwebs across the ceiling. Once he'd safely deposited Esther into a leather chair, he felt like running laps around the house – to dispel the built-up energy from walking so slowly, and to get away from all the cobwebs.

'Tell me all about yourself,' she said, leaning forward to look at Bruno intently, as if she was trying to memorise the contours of his face.

'Don't you want to start on the internet...?'

'That can wait. And why are you whispering? I want to know about *you*.'

'Qualifications, you mean?' Bruno thought he might have to prove himself worthy of teaching Esther. Maybe yesterday's lesson had been so underwhelming, she'd had second thoughts?

A bony shrug. 'If you like?'

'I just finished my A-levels. English, History and Geography. Do you want to know my grades?' Another impartial shrug of the shoulders. 'Two Bs and a C,' Bruno tried to put on a brave face, which was difficult under Esther's X-ray stare. 'Which is... It's not... Geography was... with everything...'

'Grades,' Esther said, shaking her head, 'are utter unequivocal horse manure.' Bruno sat stunned. Was she saying his grades were *shit*? What did unequivocal mean? He felt dazed, as if he'd been slapped around the face. 'That's unfair,' she went on. 'At least horse crap is nitrogen rich – makes lettuces grow into absolute monsters. Grades do no such cultivation. Abolish them, I say.'

Bruno at least felt relief she wasn't condemning his grades. 'But how would people get into uni?' he asked, genuinely intrigued.

'Don't get me started on *that* institution.' Esther leant back in her chair. 'Is university where you want to go?'

'Eventually... maybe,' Bruno stammered. 'I don't know what I'd do though, and uni is very expensive. I'm taking a year out.'

'To travel?' Esther's eyes brightened.

'To work.'

The light dimmed. 'In the warehouses?'

Bruno sidestepped the question. 'I have my own window-washing service. I help in my mum's salon.' *And this, teaching you*, he wanted to add.

'You still haven't told me anything about *yourself*. I don't particularly care what people *do*.'

'Aren't we just the things we're doing?' Bruno answered, giving a self-deprecating smile.

Esther looked aghast.

'Dear heart, *no*. That's destructive thinking.'

It's all right for you, Bruno thought, perhaps unfairly, *sitting up here with all your money, doing nothing*.

'What was that?' Esther asked, snapping her finger and pointing at him.

'What?' Bruno shook his head guiltily. The old woman couldn't read minds, could she?

'Your expression, something pushed to the surface just then. The mask came off.'

'It was nothing.' He hated being put under a spotlight, called out like this.

'You can tell me, you must.'

'I was thinking it's *easy* for you,' he said reluctantly, but Esther seemed to draw the words right out of him.

'I'm a spoiled old woman, out of touch with the world. Sitting here in her gilded cage.'

'Not exactly. Not in those words. But there's so much pressure. It's stupid.'

'You're right, it's horrid.'

'I studied really hard, but my dad was sick, and my brain didn't work. All the information kept sloshing out of my head. They said I could take some time out, but I'd have to do the A-levels next year instead, and that seemed worse. I wanted to get them over with.'

'I'm sorry to hear your father was sick. Is he still unwell?'

'He has – had – prostate cancer.' Bruno usually wouldn't say the 'prostate' part. 'They say he's in remission.'

'That's very good to hear. Thank you, dear heart.'

'For what?'

'For being so honest.'

'I didn't like it.'

'I know, I push.'

'You can't force things out of people,' Bruno said, in almost a growl, which was unlike him.

'You also can't wait until everything aligns on its own. We all need a gentle shove sometimes.'

'What did you do to me?' asked Bruno, shaking his head. 'I feel... weird.'

'I knocked us out of "nice". Once you've left nice, even for a moment, everything changes. Sure, nice is nice. It's scones, and afternoon tea with princes, and being a good son, a good person, and you do this, and I do that, and we're all playing the *game*. A lot of my friends and acquaintances were taking psychedelics in the sixties. I never touched the stuff. My brain was enough on its own. What interested me wasn't the trippy lovey-dovey stuff, when they'd come up to you all googly-eyed and say that we were all part of the cosmos. It was the day after, when they crashed. That's when you saw their real mettle. Your family is from Romani traveller stock in the village, am I right?'

'My dad's side.'

'That explains your incredible dark eyes. And when did his family arrive here?'

'In the seventies, his dad became a manager in the warehouse. Only supposed to come for a season but they sold the horses and stayed.'

'Do you have much connection with your traveller heritage?'

'Only a little. The other kids make fun of us at school mostly. My dad doesn't like talking about it much.'

'Assimilation. Who can blame him? And your mother, you said she owns the salon?'

He nodded. 'She didn't grow up in Whittleham, she met Dad in Rugby.'

'What do they want in life, I wonder?'

'For Dad to make a full recovery, I guess. For my sisters and me to be okay.'

'But then what?' Esther shook her head slightly. 'One day, not too long away, you and your sisters will have grown up, and then what will your parents want to do? Retire? I've never understood retirement. A consolation prize. But again, I'm not typical, as you have already pointed out. So, I *try* to understand. I might be clumsy sometimes in my questioning, but I'm interested. There's too much disinterest in this world already. I don't have any truck with it.'

'My mother loves books, I think she'd be happy reading every day.'

'A woman after my own heart.'

'I don't know about my dad.'

'Your face just blackened, dear heart. You worry about him, of course. There's a lot on your shoulders; the eldest son. The only son.'

Bruno blinked back tears.

'I just want them to be proud of me.'

'Don't, that's a trap. You'll do yourself more harm that way. Take it from me. Up here, in a huge house, all alone.'

'Everything I say, you just say the opposite,' Bruno responded, with a confused chuckle.

'You've found me out, that's what radicals do. You have greatness in you, Bruno. We all do. But yours is just under the surface. I'm only scratching.'

'Do you even *want* to learn about the internet?'

'I do. I mean, I must. It's a matter of survival. The hunter doesn't necessarily enjoy gutting the rabbit, but there's no rabbit stew without it. Have you met my daughter?' Esther watched for his response carefully.

'No,' replied Bruno.

'She has the best intentions, put it that way. But those intentions are to take me from my home, and I will not let that happen. I have to get smarter. That's where you come in. You're my secret weapon.'

'How will learning about the internet help you with your daughter?'

'You couldn't understand – at your age everything is a possibility. It's a paralysis of choice. When you get to my age, those choices start to fade, which is annoying at first, then sad, but soon it becomes a matter of survival, and you'd better learn how to skin some rabbits quick. My body is becoming more and more dependant, so I have to work smarter. I don't want to become obsolete. But really, I truly am a very terrible student. I don't like new things, especially not after so many years of living here all by myself. Therefore, I'm inviting you to teach me in a place of "not nice". You saw how I was yesterday – stubborn, uninterested as soon as I'm tested. Most people wouldn't have come back today to this tyrannical old windbag, but you did; why?'

Because of the money, Bruno thought instantly. But no, that wasn't completely true. There was something about him, a stickability, a stubbornness. He did show up for things.

'You genuinely want to help,' Esther continued, 'and that's not something that can be learned in a classroom or graded in an exam.' Bruno didn't know if this was correct exactly – he was *very* interested in the money aspect – but he preferred this line of questioning to the one earlier. 'I need a lot of help, my dear. It may get ugly, and it most definitely won't be nice, but I think together we might just do it? What say ye?'

What could anyone say to such a rousing speech? It was therefore quite the anti-climax to actually start the day's lesson.

'We'll have to use 4G,' Bruno explained as he took his

phone from his pocket and held it between them on the table, 'we might get better reception up here than I do at home.'

'What's wrong with it?' Esther asked when she saw his phone.

'Nothing,' he replied nervously. He'd scrubbed the phone the night before, rubbing it with a cleaning wipe, and purging the search history completely. 'What do you mean?'

'It has a massive crack down it.'

'Oh yeah.' Bruno had dropped his phone two weeks after getting it. It wasn't typical for him to leave something broken, but he was trying to save money, and there had to be sacrifices. 'You don't notice it after a while.'

'Doesn't the cracked glass cut you when you brush your finger over it?'

'Not if you're careful,' he replied, slightly defensively. 'It might not be nice,' he added, pointedly, 'but it's all we've got.'

'I should keep quiet,' Esther replied, her eyes sparkling at his moxie. 'Noted.'

'What do you want to learn about first?'

'You tell me?'

'Let's do a basic search.'

'The baser, the better.'

'What are you interested in?'

'Most things, to some degree.'

That wasn't helpful.

'We need something specific. How about planes?'

'Why did you suggest that?' Esther asked, warily.

'Because of the one of your front door – the metal knocker?'

'Oh yes. I'd almost forgotten it was there. You lose sight of the things you see all the time. Most of the things in this house are invisible to me now.'

'Like the crack on my screen.'

'Touché.'

'See here, this is the box you type in your query.' Bruno started to enter 'plane' in the search box.

'It's not simply a "plane", dear heart, it's a Spitfire, given to me as a memento.'

'Spitfire,' Bruno typed instead dutifully, before showing Esther the image results. She seemed underwhelmed as she peered at the screen.

'Pictures. I could find them in a book, much larger and easier to see. In fact, I'm sure I have one in here. In the encyclopaedia at least.'

'You choose something then,' Bruno replied, agitated but trying not to show it. 'What do you love?'

He saw it then, a flicker on Esther's face. He wanted to snap his fingers and point at her in the same way she had earlier.

'Look around you,' exclaimed Esther, collecting herself, the flicker subdued, 'this room is brimming with the things I adore.'

Confidently, more confidently than he was actually feeling, Bruno stood and walked to the closest bookshelf, taking a book at random and returning to his seat.

'*The Feminine Mystique*,' he said, reading from the cover, 'by Betty Friedan?' He had trouble saying the surname and experimented in three different ways. The jacket cover must once have been a hot red but had faded to a magenta. It always felt like stepping back in time, holding a hardback. His mum only read paperbacks, or her Kindle. Bruno wondered – secretly – how much some of these old, expensive-looking books might be worth... 'When was Betty born?' he asked.

'She must be about my age, if she's still around.'

Bruno checked the author page.

'Doesn't say here,' he said, showing Esther.

She gave him a look that read: *Well, this is a great waste of time.*

Picking up his phone, Bruno tapped away for a couple of seconds.

'Born Bettye Naomi Goldstein on February fourth, 1921 in Peoria, Illinois.' His pronunciation was suspect throughout.

'Again, books, dear, books. Your device isn't new technology. It's just repackaging information in a less – to my eye – pleasing way.'

He was losing her again.

'A library is limited. No offence, but most of these books are pretty old.'

'No offence taken. Books are *meant* to get old.'

'This phone carries more information than all these books put together, and I can take it anywhere, and the information is constantly being updated and added to. Who's the guy on the island?'

'What man? Which island?'

'He gets stranded? We talked about it in English.'

'Robinson Crusoe?'

'Yes! If you're Robinson Crusoe and you're trying to survive on a desert island, do you choose a knife or a device that can tell you everything about surviving on the island? How to make a knife, even?'

'To skin the rabbits.'

'Exactly.'

Esther nodded thoughtfully, processing this.

'Is she dead? Betty Friedan?' she asked at last.

He checked his phone, scrolling down.

'February fourth, 2006.'

'She died on her birthday.' Bruno checked the dates, Esther was right. 'Does it say what she died of?'

'Congestive heart failure.'

'Does it mention if she managed to eat her birthday cake first?' He scanned the text and shook his head. 'Did she like her presents? Does it say if she was surrounded by loved ones? Was she ready to die?'

Bruno read: 'The *New York Times* obituary for Friedan

noted that she was "famously abrasive", and that she could be "thin-skinned and imperious, subject to screaming fits of temperament".'

'Sounds like fun at a party,' Esther said, *sotto voce*.

'You can find out anything you want.' Bruno placed the phone on the table again, his voice a little too cheery, trying to paper over the emerging cracks of his argument.

Esther was silent, thinking.

'There was a man, long ago. Could your device find information on him?'

Nodding, Bruno picked up the phone again.

'His name is... Thackeray Conroy James.' She spelled it for him.

'Did he write the novel *Vanity Fair*?'

'If so, he kept it especially quiet.'

'There's actually a lot here...'

'Stop!' Esther yelled, one hand up, much too loud for any library. 'I've changed my mind. I don't want to know. Do you hear me, Bruno? Get rid of it! Please.' She looked wild – her breathing heavy, eyes bulging.

'Okay, it's gone, it's gone.'

'Can you remove it completely from the device?'

'I can clear my search history, if that's what you want?'

'Please. And promise me you won't look for him again. Promise me?'

'I promise.' She was still breathing heavily, as if she'd been running up a great height. 'Are you okay?' he asked.

'I'm fine, a little tired. I think that's enough for today.'

He'd failed, Bruno knew it. All her talk of grades not being important, this had been a test – her test. He stood and glumly put *The Feminine Mystique* back in its place on the bookshelf.

'When can you next return?' Esther asked, her voice much less strained.

'You want me to come back?'

'Of course, how else am I to learn?'

'I'm washing windows tomorrow, but the day after?'

'Dear heart, it's a date.'

As Bruno headed down the hill, the strange energy Esther had infused in him began to dissipate, seemingly with each step. It was like a spell losing its power the further he went. He'd forgotten to raise the question of money again, he realised, as the sun appeared, both warming and momentarily blinding him – but he shouldn't worry, the advert clearly stated, 'paid position'. Esther was obviously wealthy, living in such a big house. Maybe she'd settle with him by the end of the week?

What did trouble Bruno was Esther's reaction to the name Thackeray – what was it? Corbin? – James. Bruno felt an impulse to google him again but stopped himself. Let Esther have her secrets – it wasn't as if Bruno didn't have his...

He glanced at the time on his phone, and realised it wasn't even lunchtime yet – his sisters were at school, his mum was working, his dad was probably at home, watching TV, convalescing. Bruno felt a pang of guilt when he thought of his father. He should be keeping him company, but instead he wanted to think of a reason not to return to the house. Perhaps he could pop to his mum's salon, answer the phone for her? But it might make him look like he had nothing better to do, and the unspoken question would hang heavy in the air: *why haven't you applied at the warehouses?*

No, he would head home and continue to investigate other ways to make money. There was learning to code, but that seemed even harder than physics to get his head around. Trade in bitcoin? Bruno would have to invest the money he'd already saved, at the risk of losing it. It felt like he'd researched every conceivable – legal – way to earn extra cash online. Perhaps he could ramp up his window cleaning service, expand to the neighbouring villages? To transport his equipment though, his parents would have to drive him, and Bruno wanted to be less of a drain, not more. He should learn to drive then. Lessons cost money. How could he earn more money? And round and round Bruno went in a never-ending loop.

As expected, his dad was holed up on the sofa watching a sports highlights show when he arrived.

'Anything good on?' asked Bruno, the official family line whenever the TV was on.

'Never is,' his dad replied, which was always the favoured response.

'Can I make you a sandwich? We have some ham slices?' The good thing about a newly vegan sister was a slight surplus of processed meats.

'I'm not up to lunch today.' His father did look slumped and grey and defeated. It killed Bruno to see him like this.

'Are you nauseous?'

'Only when I laugh,' his dad chuckled sadly. 'How's it going with the Spitfire Princess?'

'Esther, you mean?' Bruno made the connection then, with the plane-shaped door knocker.

'That was her nickname back in the day, according to Reg. He popped over to see me earlier, did you know he used to work at the papers in London when he was a lad? Back when all those feminist women were burning their bras and growing their armpit hair out. Nothing wrong with a bit of bounce, but not shaving? That seems a bit extreme...'

Bruno ignored this remark.

'Did Reg say what happened to Esther?'

'He couldn't remember *exactly*, he was going to have a poke around in his old stack of papers in his back shed. It was during the time of the Cold War, maybe she was a spy?'

'But why did she come to Whittleham?'

'To escape the press, most likely. They had it in for her, Reg said, he remembered that at least. And because property is cheaper up here, especially back then. She'd have picked that house up for a song.'

So, Esther might not be rich after all, Bruno thought worriedly.

'I'm going to do some stuff on my laptop,' he announced, making for his bedroom.

'Bring it in here, if you like?' replied his dad.

'I can't concentrate with the television on,' Bruno fibbed, glancing at the football on the screen. He softened his voice. 'When's your next chemo appointment, Dad?'

'I have to have another MRI first. To see how I'm getting on.'

'Mum never told me about an MRI.'

'She doesn't want you to worry.'

That's *all* I'm doing, thought Bruno.

'Do they think it has...'

'They're not sure,' his dad answered quickly. 'That's why they ordered the test, just to be on the safe side.'

'You'd say if anything was... wrong?'

'No secrets,' his father nodded.

'Dad...' Bruno began, trying to formulate the question in his head. 'When the girls and I leave home, what sort of things would you like to do?'

'What do you mean? When I retire? I don't know... Buy a campervan, travel about? Your mum wants to go to Machu Picchu, but that seems a bit out of the way.' He wiped his eyes. 'This is a turn-up for the books – no one asks about long-term plans when you have cancer.' He sniffed. 'I'm not crying, honest. It's my sinuses. Fetch me a tissue from that box?'

Bruno did as he was asked.

'You know, we're in no hurry to see you go,' his dad said,

wiping his nose with the tissue, his eyes still wet. 'Money's tight, but this is your home, as long as you want it. I know you've put your life on hold, because of...' he pointed to his hairless head.

'Dad...'

'I want to see you happy.' He took Bruno's hand. His father's skin was reminiscent of Esther's – papery soft, as if the skin would rip if he moved too quickly.

'I am,' Bruno replied, with as much genuineness as he could muster.

His dad smiled a sad, sweet smile.

'Good boy.'

In his bedroom, Bruno flopped face first onto his bed. Why couldn't he be the kind of son who enjoyed watching football with his dad? There might be a time – soon – when Bruno would literally do *anything* to watch TV with him. He remembered he had a word to ask about too – 'unequivocal', the one Esther had used, but he didn't move from the bed.

Reaching for his laptop on his bedside table, Bruno loaded a private browser and typed a URL from memory. The resulting website showed smiling teen faces. 'Voices from across the UK' 'Our Stories!' 'Transformed by Love' 'Empowering You!' He'd watched all the videos by now, so he clicked through to the section titled 'Residential Workshops'. The next one was in a few weeks – the cost was £1,800 for three days. Bruno had just over a thousand pounds. Impulsively, he brought up his bank to make sure the money was still in his account – of course it was. For a second, Bruno imagined what the money might do to help his family. He could catch a bus to Rugby, withdraw the thousand pounds at the bank and give it to his dad tonight, or maybe he could buy his parents a trip to Machu Picchu? Bruno pushed away these fantasies. He had to stay focused. They would thank him one day.

He closed the browser and deleted his search history again, just to be safe.

'I have a surprise,' Esther said two days later in 'the study', which was cluttered and stuffy, despite it being cold outside. She manoeuvred herself out of the armchair – no stick today, but she still used the furniture for support as she crossed the small room. Maybe that's why it was so cluttered, Bruno thought: for extra strategic handholds. A nurse had been at the house when he'd first arrived, but she'd been quickly dispensed with.

Esther picked up a white plastic bag from a side table, and carefully returned with it to her armchair, placing the bag on Bruno's lap before stiffly sitting again.

'Open it,' she encouraged.

Bruno pulled out a brand-new boxed iPhone.

'My daughter bought it,' Esther explained, beaming.

'It's...' Bruno was lost for words. He'd never owned an iPhone in his life – they were too expensive and so he always settled for a cheaper smartphone.

'Jane's been trying to force one on me for years. When I told her yours was worse for wear, she jumped at the chance to buy me one.'

'Oh-h,' stammered Bruno, realisation dawning on him. 'Yes, this is for you.'

'I asked her to make sure it came equipped with all the bells and whistles. Will it do?'

He nodded, trying to mask his disappointment. 'I can set it up for you now if you like?' Why would Esther buy him a brand-new iPhone? Bruno reasoned, using his nails to rip into the plastic wrapping. Anyway, it wasn't even the latest version, he noted pettily.

'I haven't forgotten you either.' Esther reached into her

pocket and presented him with an ancient flip phone. 'I would like to gift you this. It's hardly been used – I could never remember to charge it – but I thought you could maybe keep it as a backup or spare?'

'Wow, thank... you,' said Bruno, with fake enthusiasm. He flipped the phone open and closed a couple of times – it was such a strange movement, almost violent, the loud 'clack' as it snapped together – before stowing it away in his backpack.

The unboxing of the iPhone itself was also anticlimactic.

'A lot of faff,' Esther complained, 'they're trying to be too smart with all this packaging.' When the phone was revealed, however – a shiny black lozenge with plastic coverings to protect the screen – it didn't disappoint.

'How do we make this tiny monolith work?' asked Esther, bouncing it in her hand to gauge its weight.

'It needs to charge first, I think,' but when Bruno experimentally pushed the button on the side, it sprang to life.

'Ah,' Esther said, nodding, 'The apple – original sin.' She pointed at the screen. 'Old Testament. "One of ours" as my father used to say.'

'It's their logo,' replied Bruno, not really following.

'Wonderfully cunning,' said Esther, tapping her nose.

They spent a better part of an hour setting it up, huddled together, shoulder to shoulder. Bruno did most of the heavy lifting, it would be too slow otherwise, but occasionally he'd pass the phone to Esther to complete a single action. She struggled with the cursor – the location and how hard to tap the screen.

'Where's it gone?' was her regular frustrated refrain, but by the fifth attempt she'd almost mastered it.

'We should set you up an email,' Bruno suggested.

'Why would I want one of those?'

'So you can contact people.'

'Can't I call them?'

'Email is like an electronic letter,' he explained. 'You'll need one to do anything online, really.'

'If I must.' She gave one of her resigned, stubborn shrugs.

'What do you want your email handle to be?'

'Dear heart, a lot of your words are gibberish to me.'

Bruno struggled to think of a way to explain a 'handle'.

'It's like your address.'

'Can we not use my current one then? Or will people steal it? My daughter is terrified I might be taken advantage of. People ring all the time, saying there's an issue with my online bank. Scammers, apparently. I go along with them. Log this, do that. Yes, yes, I say. Can you give us your mother's maiden name? I fabricate one. Can you tell us your passcode? I make one up on the spot. They get very muddled by the end, before I laugh and hang up.'

'Everyone you communicate with should know your email address,' explained Bruno. 'It's your password you need to keep secret.'

'Can I not even tell you?'

'You shouldn't give it to anyone. For safety.'

'What if I forget it? Can I write it down?'

'If it's memorable, you won't forget.'

'You'd be surprised.'

Bruno took a deep breath.

'Fine, you can tell me your password. I'll memorise it so it's not written down anywhere.'

'Wonderful, dear heart. Two brains are better than one. And yours is considerably stronger than mine on these matters.'

'Let's take it one step at a time.' It was getting much warmer in the study. 'This is *my* email address.' He typed it in the phone for her.

'Did you make a mistake there?' She pointed to the 'at' symbol.

'They all have those squiggly "a's",' Bruno clarified.

'Whatever for?'

'I don't know,' he admitted. This was harder than he'd envisaged. 'Yours could be your name.'

'Try "Esther" then?'

'It needs to be unique. Someone else probably has Esther.'

'I see; I'm late to the party. How about Esther 2?'

Bruno tried this, but it came back as taken.

'What about Esther 3?'

'How about *Esther on the hill*?'

'That makes me sound like Humpty Dumpty, only useful if I want to contact all the King's men.'

Focus! Bruno wanted to yell but didn't. Esther may have encouraged him to not be 'nice' but it was difficult to break the habit of a lifetime.

'What's your full name?' he asked, instead.

'Esther Rebecca Alona Saul.'

'Esther Saul then?'

They tried but it was taken.

'I'm getting a sense of déjà vu,' Esther announced suddenly.

'Are you okay?' Bruno asked, concerned. 'Do you want me to open a window?'

Esther held both hands in the air, as if she was a conductor about to make an orchestra play. 'I already have an email!'

'You do?' Bruno was shocked.

'It's all coming back to me. My daughter, Jane, set it up for me years ago.'

This revelation changed everything.

'Can you ring her and ask what it was?'

She held up a spindly finger. 'I have it written down!'

'Where?'

'Now that is a very good question...'

'Let's call your daughter.'

'I'd rather not have her involved. She's meddlesome. It will come back to me.'

Bruno didn't want to lose their momentum.

'Can you remember anything about your email address? Did it have your name in it? Was it Gmail, or Hotmail? Or Yahoo?'

'Say the last ridiculous-sounding one again?'

He repeated it.

'That sounds like it.'

He brought up the Yahoo email page – but soon realised guessing both the correct email address and the password would be impossible. He navigated to the email recovery section, but that needed a recovery mobile number, or – ironically – an alternative email address.

'I've got it!' Esther yelped, finger in the air again.

'You've remembered the address?'

'Not quite,' she replied, eyes glinting, 'but I remember where I wrote it down. In the library, check the E encyclopaedia, see what's written beside the entry about the Enigma Machine.'

Bruno jumped up and ran out of the study and towards the library. He'd never actually run inside Esther's house – because of her lack of mobility, he always seemed to travel much slower, as if he was in treacle – and it was thrilling. He returned a few minutes later, holding the thick tome.

'Is it there?'

'I haven't checked yet.' Bruno opened the encyclopaedia and started to flick through the pages, searching.

'You know, I was evacuated during the war as a baby, and the family I stayed with were distant cousins of Alan Turing...'

Bruno gave a howl of triumph. He showed her the page – beside a black and white illustration of the Enigma machine, was neatly written:

saul.esther.2005@yahoo.com

'It must have been the year it was created, 2005, otherwise I don't have the foggiest reason as to why it's there.'

'There's no password.'

'Try "Abigail" – that was my sister's name.'

The combination didn't work.

'Add her birthdate after her name.'

Bruno did what he was told and hit Enter.

'Why are they asking if we're a robot?' Esther asked, peering at the screen.

'Extra security.'

'Are robots really that much of a risk?'

He didn't have time to answer, because the next moment they were through.

'We did it! We're in!' Bruno cried jubilantly.

'How exciting,' Esther replied, more reserved in her reaction. 'What does it contain?'

Bruno scrolled through the inbox.

'Spam – it's like junk mail.'

'How did they know to contact me, this "spam"?'

'They just email everyone in the hope of a response,' Bruno explained.

'Ah, so I'm not special, then...'

'Here's one from an actual person. It was sent eight years ago. Someone called David.'

Esther froze with a look of, what, fear? She grabbed the phone from Bruno and stared at the screen intently.

'Such ridiculously small letters, how does anyone see anything *properly*?'

'Would you like me to read it to you out loud?' asked Bruno.

'No!' Esther snapped. 'Can't we print it, somehow? A physical copy – is that possible?'

'I'd have to go to my mum's salon and use her printer.'

Esther considered this, holding the phone to her chest.

'I don't want this to leave the house.'

'I can try and make the text bigger on the screen?'

'It's fine! I'll make do.' Bruno could see Esther's eyes were beginning to well. She stared at the iPhone screen, blinking back tears. 'It's no use, I can't *see* anything. Please read it, dear heart.'

Bruno took the phone and cleared his throat.

'*Dear Esther,*' he began. Glancing up, he noticed a stream of tears running down her pale cheeks. '*I am writing with the sad news of my father passing. He died in his sleep after a short illness at Aberdeen Royal Infirmary on the second of April. Dad had hoped it would be the day prior, just so the lawyers might think it an error and not deduct inheritance tax. Such was his humour. I have tried to contact you directly, but unfortunately Dad's only phone number for you seems to have been outdated. I found your email address in his address book; as you know he was a Luddite, so it stood out. I understand you and my father were very close at one time, and I know it pained him you were no longer in contact, although – as you might know – he would have denied missing anyone. But as his health deteriorated, he would often say your name, and seemed to want to talk with you, even when, in the latter stages, he was not as responsive as he once was. Approaching death, it seems, absolves us of our bitterness, and leaves us cracked open. That's how he was in the final twenty-four hours, he seemed to let go completely, and not only accept his fate, but welcome it. I've never seen him more at peace, and when he did pass on, it was with a lightness of energy I did not know he possessed. There is hope for us all, I suppose (sorry, channelling Dad's gallows' humour).*

Yours faithfully,

David James'

Bruno didn't need to ask who the email was about – Esther's reaction made it clear it was someone very important to her, and he remembered that Thackeray's last name was James. David's father, Thackeray, had died, and Esther had not known about it for years. Wouldn't there have been a note about in a newspaper? Bruno wondered. An obituary, he remembered it was called... Bruno hadn't seen a television in the house, or even a radio for that matter, but that didn't mean there wasn't one somewhere. But he felt instinctively, however, there wouldn't be, that Esther had purposefully cut herself off from the world, to avoid the pain he had now so quickly helped to unleash.

Esther cleared her throat, neck long, her head raised. She looked very dignified to Bruno.

'Could you help me write a response?' she asked, evenly.

'Of course,' he replied, pleased to have a task.

'Dear David,' dictated Esther, 'I'm sorry to hear of the passing of your father, and for not responding sooner.' Bruno typed as quickly as he could, trying not to make any mistakes. 'For many years, I did not keep communication with the world, so I have only myself to blame for not sending my condolences sooner. I am so pleased Thackeray found peace, there is hope for me yet.' Bruno snuck a look at Esther – she had her eyes closed. 'It would please me very much if we could speak by telephone,' She recited her number. 'I realise now, how many things I would like to ask. Yours faithfully, Esther Saul.'

A single tear ran down her left cheek.

'Would you like me to send it?' Bruno asked.

'Please, dear heart.'

He checked it again for mistakes and then hit the send button.

'How long will it take to arrive?' asked Esther.

'It's instantaneous.'

'I see.'

'We might have to wait for him to receive it.'

'Very good,' she replied, looking towards the window, and the low clouds outside. 'I have become very accustomed to waiting.'

. . .

They continued their lessons, in a much more subdued manner, over the next few weeks. At the start of each one, Bruno would find a reason to open Esther's email, hiding his disappointment when there was no reply waiting inside. She, however, seemed hardly to register the lack of response. Esther would take a cursory glance at the inbox, and then ask about something that was vexing her – how to move around in Google Maps (this had been a revelation to Esther, the ability to drop a virtual pin onto a street location anywhere in the world) or an issue filling in an online form. Bruno was much more impatient, formulating next steps in his mind – they could send a follow-up email to David or find another way of communicating with him? Secretly, Bruno had searched 'David James', but it was a common name and nothing useful came up, even after adding 'Scotland' and 'Aberdeen'. Including 'Thackeray' would have refined it even more, but he'd promised Esther he wouldn't search for him, and he dutifully kept his word.

Although a spark seemed to have gone out of Esther, Bruno realised he shouldn't do anything to try to cheer her up, which was his natural impulse. He simply let her be instead. On some level, he recognised that she was in mourning, just as he had been in a state of deep grief after his father was diagnosed with prostate cancer. Morose Esther was a much better student anyway – less combative, more focused. She was very motivated when she put her mind to something, stubborn to get things right even, completing the homework he set at the end of each lesson, and improving quickly.

Esther cheered up the most when it was dry and warm enough outside to sit in the garden.

'This wild jasmine bush is for my dear friend Genevieve,' she explained one afternoon, as they sat side by side, Esther in her wheelchair, Bruno perched on a chair from the kitchen. She had picked their spot, beyond the lawn and close to the grove of fruit trees, 'to get the most of the sun and see the beautiful apple blossom', but Bruno soon realised it was because Esther wanted to do some light weeding as they continued their lesson. Every now and then, she would shoot out of the wheelchair to pluck the offending plant with her bare fingers, and have to negotiate herself back up, rubbing her soily hands on her legs, before returning her attention to the phone Bruno was still holding.

'Genevieve was also my lodger for many years in London,' she continued, after one such dive. 'She was constantly lighting jasmine incense, almost burned the house in Swiss Cottage down several times. I remember, one evening we were eating dinner together and the fire brigade bust open our front door – all these burly men, it was wonderful. Ash from her incense burner had fallen onto some sheet music and set it on fire, and fortunately a neighbour noticed the smoke before it got too out of hand. Genevieve, however, was furious with our poor saviours: "How dare you break into our house, with your *phalluses*." I think she was in shock, but it came out in unbridled anger. One of the younger firemen, spooked by Genevieve, accidentally soaked her with his hose. To be clear, that is not a euphemism. At least, I think it was accidental. He might have had a death wish. Either way, burly though they were, I've never seen men move so fast in my life. It was as if there was a fire somewhere!' She laughed, wiping her hands together to get rid of the last of the soil. 'My dear Genevieve. She's dead now too, in the late nineties. A rare blood disease.'

Bruno didn't know what to say. It seemed getting old was outliving everyone you knew and cataloguing the depressing ways they died.

'Shall we try something new?' he asked, trying to bring her attention back to the phone.

The concept of online shopping was easy for her to grasp in theory but more difficult in practice, while social media was a bust – she couldn't, or wouldn't, see the point.

Weirdly, Esther was also very resistant about text messages.

'Why, when I can just pick up the phone? Or email? How are there so many different ways to do the same thing?'

'For convenience,' Bruno explained, receiving an icy glare from his student. 'You choose the right way of communicating for the right task.'

'But how do you know which is the correct one to use?'

'Experience. Practice.'

'Hmph.'

Three weeks after their first lesson together, Bruno received a visitor.

He was in his bedroom, playing The Sims on his laptop, but the game was so laggy, he had to keep stopping to let the frame rate catch up. He was trying to build a replica of Esther's house, the parts he'd seen at least – he hadn't been up to the top floor at all.

'Bruno, can you come here, please?' his mother called loudly from the living room, making him snatch off his head-phones and feel instantly guilty. Mum was off on Mondays, and Bruno had wanted to make them lunch, but he'd completely lost track of time – it was already a quarter past one. He also felt a general remorse about playing games on his laptop when he should be working, or looking for work – but it was stressful worrying about money all the time, didn't he deserve *some* downtime? Bruno's most recent plan was to learn a digital skill – film editing or Photoshop – so he could earn money as a freelancer, but he was undecided on what to focus on. Most of the software was expensive to buy, complicating the choice. He could download it illegally, but Bruno didn't even watch pirated movies and TV shows, he felt so guilt-ridden afterwards.

'Where's Dad?' he asked, when he came into the living room, not at first seeing the woman sitting at the kitchen table.

'On a walk,' his mum replied quickly. 'Bruno, this is Jane, Esther's daughter. She's here to see you.'

'Hello, Bruno,' said Jane, with a flat smile. She stood and extended her hand across the table. 'Good to finally meet you, I've heard a lot about you.'

Nervous energy surged through Bruno, creating enough adrenaline to make him leap clean through the ceiling. Why was Esther's daughter here? Had he done something wrong? *Hands, wrists*, he reminded himself, panicked. He squeezed both fists, his palms already clammy.

'Bruno, are you alright?' his mum asked, giving him an odd look.

'Ah yes,' he replied, discreetly wiping his sweaty palms on his thighs before shaking hands with Jane. There was a definite family resemblance; she had the same high cheekbones as Esther, hair pulled into a tight bun, grey-blonde not grey-white, and she had the same inquisitive eyes, but unlike her mother, there was none of the warmth and mischief in her expression. In her smart navy suit she seemed all business – she reminded Bruno somehow of a parole officer.

After shaking, Jane indicated for him to sit down opposite her at the table, as if this were her house and he was visiting.

'Jane's a barrister,' his mother said, her voice in a slightly odd pitch that put Bruno even more on edge. Instead of leaving them to it, as she might typically, she stayed, hovering just behind him. 'Are you sure I can't get you something to drink?'

Jane shook her head.

'Is everything okay with Esther?' Bruno asked, worried suddenly.

With the same shallow smile, Jane nodded.

'Mother is fine. Well... as fine as someone can be in her situation.'

'Jane lives in Coventry,' his mum explained.

'I moved fifteen years ago from London, to be closer to her.'

'Coventry's lovely,' Bruno's mother added politely.

'And Whittleham, what an *interesting* community you have here.'

'It's nothing on Coventry. Lovely big houses. Do you have children, Jane?'

'No,' she replied matter-of-factly. Jane studied Bruno's face for a moment. 'And you're the one who's been giving Mother lessons – on the internet, no less. I applaud you. Many have tried before. All have failed.' Jane interlaced her fingers on the table. 'She seems to like you.'

Did he imagine a slight tone of accusation to her voice?

'Yes... I, ah... Esther is...'

'Can I ask how your arrangement... came about?'

'There was an advert in my salon,' his mum replied, quickly. 'Wasn't there, Bruno?'

He nodded, adding, 'I think she asked her neighbour to post it for her.'

'Do you give other lessons?' asked Jane.

'What do you mean?'

'Is this something you do for *other* elderly people in the neighbourhood... or simply my mother?'

'Bruno is extremely proactive,' his mum began, 'especially for his age. You're an entrepreneur, aren't you?' she patted his shoulder. 'Has his own window-washing company, won't stop. Half the windows aren't even dirty by the time he comes back round.'

'Mum...'

'We're very proud.'

Jane's smile remained unchanged. It was like a copy of a poorly rendered smile, overly pixelated.

'How old are you, Bruno?'

'Eighteen.'

'On the cusp of adulthood. I wonder, when you're helping

to set things up for Mother online, are you privy to her personal details?'

'Yes,' he answered truthfully. 'But I never write anything down, if you're worried about passwords and things.'

'It had crossed my mind,' there was a gleam in her eyes then, but it held no cheerfulness. 'My mother is a vulnerable older woman with health issues, so it falls to me to ensure not simply *anyone* turns up at her door.'

'Bruno is not *anyone*,' his mum replied, a slight sharpness to her voice.

Jane took a deep breath.

'Of course. Mother always did prefer men over women. Ironic for such a staunch feminist. In the past, there have been *issues* with younger males she befriended, nothing torrid I assure you, they simply weren't the *type* of person to be surrounding oneself with. I can see that's not the case with you, Bruno. Can I ask, how often are these lessons?'

'Three or four times a week?'

'And is she paying you?'

Bruno paused. He'd still not been able to bring up the question of money with Esther – it was almost impossible after she received the email from David, it felt insensitive to broach it when she seemed so sad. Each lesson he told himself he was going to break out of 'nice' and raise the issue, but every single time he either forgot, or couldn't find the appropriate moment.

'It was advertised as a paid position, but we haven't sorted out the details yet. I think we will by the end of the month...' This wasn't completely untrue – Bruno had given himself until the end of April. Esther would *have* to pay him then, surely?

'Do you have any qualifications?'

'I passed my A-levels.'

'In computer science?'

'In English, History and Geography. Two Bs and a C.'

There was a slight twitch in Jane's expression, one that Esther might have called out.

'Will you go on to university, or is that not an option?'

'Of course it's an option,' Bruno's mother replied, curtly. Bruno cringed internally. It was the constant elephant in the room. *Would* he go? Would they have enough money? Not to mention, what would he study? – he had no idea. 'Bruno's taking time to figure his future out, aren't you, honey?'

'Seems you have a lot reckoned with already. Multiple businesses. The window washing. Now, the tutoring. What would you read?'

'Read?' Bruno asked, puzzled by what Jane meant.

'At university?'

Bruno was stumped by this; did she mean – books? How would he know already?

'Whatever they gave me,' he said with a self-deprecating shrug.

'Is there anything Bruno can help you with, specifically?' asked his mum, even more brusquely. It was rare for her to talk like this to a stranger, she was usually much bubblier, especially after years of owning a salon. It was clear Jane was rubbing her up the wrong way. 'We should really be thinking about lunch soon.'

'I'll cut to the chase. Bruno, my mother is eighty-two years old. She should not be living in a large house by herself; anything could happen, and I dread with every phone call that it will be from the hospital to say she's had a fall. As you probably know, Mother is exceedingly stubborn. I have tried negotiating with her – bringing in help over the years, someone to cook, to clean, to take care of the garden, but she always sends them packing. Ultimately, I would like to sell the house and get her into an apartment closer to me. I obviously can't do anything legally without her permission, I can't even send estate agents around to value the property. Mother is terrified that I will put her in a care home, and despite all my assurances, she is vehement she will not leave the manor house. She has barricaded herself away for years, so I can understand the fear of returning to society, but the harsh truth is she will only get older and frailer. Did she tell you she's had a stroke?' He nodded, and Jane seemed impressed by this. 'Bruno, you are one of the few people Mother seems to trust, so I ask that you become my eyes and ears. She hides most things from me – how much pain she's in, how difficult she finds everyday tasks like bathing and cooking for herself. Every time I bring them up, we have an argument. I love my mother dearly. It falls on my shoulders to take care of her. If she does not get some type of adequate support, she *will* hurt herself, and then a home might be unavoidable. So, for her sake, can I depend on you?'

'You want me to spy on her?'

Jane shook her head, a disappointed expression on her face.

'Bruno, I'm asking for you to *help* her.'

'What sort of things do you want to know?' he asked, warily.

'Anything that puts her at risk. Have you seen anything that might be worth bringing up now?'

Chewing the side of his cheek, Bruno mulled over her question. He felt like he was breaking Esther's confidence, but then her daughter made a very strong case.

'If Bruno helps you,' his mother interrupted, placing her hand on his shoulder again, 'would there be *compensation?*'

Jane raised an eyebrow.

'More than what Mother is already paying?'

'Doesn't seem like there's been much in the way of payment yet. He isn't running a charity.'

'I would be open to a discretionary fee, dependent on the information.'

'Did you hear that, Bruno?'

He nodded, but even with all his financial pressures, he

didn't like the idea of taking Jane's money; it felt much more like he was ratting out Esther for cash.

'Is there anything,' prompted Jane, 'anything at all?'

'Only...' Bruno sighed. 'Esther gets forgetful where she's left things. It frustrates her, she complains the nurses keep moving things around, but I don't know if that's the case.'

Jane nodded.

'Is she taking her medication each day?'

'I don't know.'

'Does she complain about pain?'

'Esther doesn't really talk about it, but I can tell when she's struggling. Her concentration's off. Early last week she was up and walking around without her stick even and then on Friday she was in her wheelchair, and I think it was pretty bad.'

'Mother has an alarm she's supposed to keep with her in case she falls or if there's an emergency. It's a cord around her neck.'

'I've never seen her wear one,' replied Bruno.

'And will you give me Mother's logins and passwords? As a safety?'

He hesitated again.

'Can I tell her you have them?'

It was Jane's turn to pause.

'It would only anger her, she thinks I'm too interfering already. The protection of my mother's sensitive information isn't really up for debate. I'm her daughter, she's only known you for a matter of weeks.'

'Esther has a right to privacy, though. She allowed me to know her logins and passwords. If I lose her trust, she'll just get rid of me like she did everyone else.'

'A good point,' conceded Jane. 'You could go into my line of work, one day.'

'Told you he was clever,' Bruno's mum said proudly.

'Fine, we'll shelve the conversation about passwords for the

time being, but I want to touch base with you regularly, Bruno.
The web can be a dangerous place for someone like my mother.
I'm not only speaking about nefarious people. There are things
from Mother's history that are best to stay hidden. She seemed
to turn a leaf on her eightieth birthday, becoming more outgo-
ing, less insular, but her mood has darkened again recently.
That's another reason I wanted to meet with you, I was afraid
you might be stirring up the past.'

The email from David flashed into Bruno's mind, but it
didn't feel right betraying Esther's trust. He had to give Jane
some explanation though.

'Esther almost did a search on Thackeray,' he revealed at
last.

Jane exhaled heavily.

'This is what I was worried about, opening up old wounds.
Can you help persuade Mother it's foolish to go down this
path?'

'I can't force her...'

'No, encourage her.'

'To be honest, I don't think she's interested any more. Whatever happened is still too painful.'

'What *did* happen?' His mother asked, 'I mean, I've heard
the rumours...'

'Maybe Bruno can tell you, I'm sure he's investigated it
himself, online.'

'I haven't actually,' he admitted. 'She asked me not to.'

'You must be the only person in this village not to know
some of her business then.'

'Everyone just leaves her be,' Bruno's mum said, bristling
again. 'No one's interested in what happened decades ago.'

'Explain that to her.' Jane sighed again. 'I can only tell you
my side of the story. Mother, like many women of her generation, came into her own during the sixties. My father was an
academic, but she never loved him, and as soon I was old

enough to walk, they separated, and shortly after that I was sent to boarding school. When the scandal broke, all the other girls wanted to know what she was like, my infamous mother, but I didn't really know. She was a shadow in my life. Then she disappeared for several years, until one day a letter arrived to say she had bought a house up here. I rushed to visit, but I discovered she was in a self-imposed exile. We all thought it would be a phase, she would come around eventually, but she never did. And now I take care of her. A thankless task, most of the time. But she's the only family I have; my father passed years ago, we were never exactly close. I do love Mother, however, even if that's not always reciprocated.'

Bruno's eyes were wide with so much information on Esther revealed.

'I'm sorry to hear all that,' Bruno's mother said.

'Thank you, but I'm not here for your sympathy. I want to help Mother. And so I'm very pleased, Bruno, that you have agreed to assist me.' Jane stood, the chair whining on the linoleum. 'I've given your mother my card already. We shall stay very much in touch.'

Maybe it was just Jane's naturally bossy manner, but to Bruno this sounded like a threat.

'Whatever's the matter with you, dear heart?' Esther asked at their next lesson, a day later. They were in a small room she'd called 'the solar' but in fact was very gloomy inside and contained piles of fabric and what seemed like half-finished embroidery and knitting projects. Still confined to her wheel-chair, Esther had asked Bruno to swivel round an overhead lamp for a 'bit of brightness'. 'You seem heavier,' she announced. 'Heavier than normal.'

'Nothing's wrong,' he responded, scanning his body reflex-ively – how he was sitting, the position and placement of his hands and feet, was he giving anything away unknowingly? Or could Esther tell he'd spoken with Jane, yesterday – was it written all over his face? 'I didn't sleep well last night,' he added, truthfully.

'Why ever not?'

'Lots of reasons.'

'How someone your age can have so many causes for insomnia, I'll never know. My not sleeping – after eighty-two long years on this earth – I understand. There's your poor father's health, of course, let's not forget, but I thought the MRI came back optimistic?'

Bruno nodded. He'd been showing her emojis as a break from setting up her online banking – mortifyingly, Esther had asked what the aubergine emoji was for – he thought she might find the concept fun, but she seemed less than thrilled. 'Insipid' is how she'd described them: 'and if your aubergine's purple coloured, I suggest a full course of antibiotics,' she'd added, with a huff.

'Dad's getting much better,' Bruno explained. 'Slowly but surely.'

'A cause for celebration?'

'If you think too positively about something, I don't know, it's like something worse might happen. You jinx it.'

'That's very fatalistic.'

'It's hard to explain.'

'What's hard, dear heart, is you – on yourself.' She seemed thoughtful for a moment. 'I was wondering... how do you get an email address from a person you'd like to contact? One that you've never written to before. Am I saying that correctly, do people write emails or are they only typed?'

'You write them,' Bruno replied, nodding. He reached up to turn the overhead light in another direction, but the lamp was hot now and burnt his fingers. He flapped his hand to cool it, and then realised how this might look, and stopped. 'You could search for the person online, see if they are on social media, like Facebook. We could do it now, together, if you like?'

Esther seemed wary of taking the plunge, but Bruno was excited they might finally find another way to contact David.

'It's the brother...' she said, not stating the brother of whom, but of course, Bruno knew. 'His name is Edward... James.'

'Edward James,' he repeated, typing it into the search box in a browser on Esther's phone, and showing her the results. There was an estate agent, a consultancy, an actor, musician and a photographer in the long list of results.

'I'm not sure at all,' Esther admitted, after she'd scrutinised the phone for a long time. 'Do you have to know their employment, is that how it works? He could be retired, for all I know.'

'Is there anything we could add that might help identify him?' Bruno wanted to suggest adding his father's name but hesitated. He didn't want to give away how close he'd been to making a similar search – on the brother David – several times over.

'Edward's middle name... It's the same as his father's given name...'

'Like the author of *Vanity Fair*?' Bruno asked coyly.

'Exactly,' she replied.

Bruno typed Thackeray into the search box and hit enter – it gave him a satisfying chill down his spine, finally completing this action.

'The first result is a business consultancy,' he clicked through to the 'our team' section and Esther gasped. On the page, staring back at them, was a bald man in his late fifties or sixties, Bruno guessed – he wasn't particularly good at assigning the ages of people over twenty – in a suit and tie, his arms crossed. Maybe it was the fault of the romantic name 'Thackeray', but Bruno had imagined the father and his sons as having long, flowing hair, a delicate bone structure and foppish waistcoats. This Edward James looked more like a boxing coach.

'He's the spitting image,' Esther exclaimed, touching the screen gently with her fingers. 'How uncanny.' She seemed quite shaken.

'We can send an email – it's listed here – or we can call?'

'No,' she replied quickly. 'I'm not ready to speak to him directly.'

'Let's email then,' offered Bruno, not wanting to lose momentum. He brought up her inbox. 'What would you like to say?'

Esther seemed momentarily unsure.

'What if we start with "Hi Edward,"' Bruno started typing. '"My name is Esther Saul, I was a friend of your father". Should we mention his brother messaged you?'

Esther took a deep breath, as if she was building herself up.

'Dear Edward,' she began reciting, Bruno quick to scribe her words. 'You might not remember who I am. We only met twice when you were a child – once at the air show in Edinburgh and briefly at a picnic at Portobello, but you have always stayed with me because of your sprightly energy – it was so like your father's. Forgive me for not writing sooner, your brother David sent me an email several years ago about Thackeray's passing that I've only recently received. I had not heard of his death, having cut myself off from the world for decades, I must be honest with you, to avoid any news on him. Now, as I am approaching my final years, I feel foolish for many reasons, but largely because I did nothing to try and mend the old wounds while there was still time. Instead, I let them fester. Please see this as a small gesture that I would like to make proper amends. Yours faithfully, Esther Saul.'

As she finished speaking, she kept her eyes shut tight, her forehead furrowed, as if waiting for some unseen force to pass.

'Shall I read it back to you?' Bruno offered when Esther finally opened her eyes again.

'Please send it before I change my mind.'

Bruno made a few checks on the spelling and considered what he should add as the subject heading but decided to simply leave it blank.

Esther seemed emotionally exhausted after composing the email, and so Bruno started to wind down the session, when the phone dinged with an alert.

'What's that noise?' asked Esther.

'An email,' Bruno replied, excitedly.

He opened the inbox, but the moment he saw it, his stomach dropped. 'Oh...' he said, scanning the message.

'Read it, dear heart.'

'Maybe we should wait...?'

'Is it from Edward – did we get the right address?'

'Let's take a look at it tomorrow, I'll come early. Actually, I have window washing in the morning...'

'We must read it *now*, Bruno.' He passed her the phone, but she pushed it back to him. 'Out loud, please.'

She looked so anxious, how could he not do as she asked? – even with his whole body screaming for him to take the phone and throw it safely out the window.

'Esther,' Bruno read, '*I'm sure my sweet brother, may he rest in peace, would NEVER have written to you if he'd understood the full extent of your manipulations. How you have the gall to contact me after everything that has happened, especially considering THE LEGACY, is utterly beyond me! How fortunate that you were able to hide from responsibility. My father lived in CONSTANT shame and died miserable and alone, but still beholden to you, it seems. I DO remember you from the picnic, and the air show, although at the time I wasn't aware of the FULL ramifications of your company. My poor mother, how she must have felt, knowing about that pantomime. I'm glad YOU are healing but I'm afraid I cannot afford any such comfort, especially when you continue to rob from my family—*'

'That's enough,' Esther said, her voice high and somehow

far-off, as if she had fallen from a height. 'What does he mean,' she asked, wide-eyed, 'what *legacy*? It was all in the past. He makes it sound like it's still happening now, after everything... How can that be?'

'I don't know,' stammered Bruno, his cheeks burning bright.

'I can't... I can't...' She seemed terribly frail and old all of a sudden, shaking her head, as if she'd aged a decade in only a few minutes. The lost expression on her face worried Bruno. What if she had another stroke from the stress? Should he call Jane?

'Esther,' Bruno tried to focus her attention. He stood up and turned her wheelchair around to face him. 'Esther, please.'

'I simply can't!' she continued to protest, gazing past him.

'Look at me, Esther.' Her watery eyes fixed on his face for a moment, bulging in their sockets. 'Don't get lost.'

She looked quizzically at him.

'Where am I?'

'You're here, in your house, with me.'

'Oh, dear heart,' she said, taking his shoulders and squeezing them with surprising force. 'Why must it be like this? Why?'

'I don't know,' Bruno replied, earnestly, 'but remember what you told me about the "not nice". That was *not* nice of him to send that email – he sounds hurt and angry, and I'm sorry for him, but you made contact, Esther. You were brave.' Tears started welling in his eyes.

'He hates me,' she replied in almost a whisper.

'Then he doesn't know you,' replied Bruno firmly.

'What if he does? What if he knows me better than anyone else left alive?' Bruno didn't know how to respond to this. 'Will you take the phone away,' she pleaded, 'until I see you next?'

'But... it's yours...' he stammered.

'I don't want to be near it!'

Bruno thought of Jane; if she found out that he had Esther's brand-new expensive iPhone at his house...

'Okay,' he promised.

'And please, dear heart, I don't want you to hide from me any more.'

'I'm not hiding.'

'You are, you are!'

'Let's go into the kitchen,' Bruno suggested. 'Get you a drink. It's warm in here. When was the last time you had something to eat?'

'But you'll take the phone?' she asked, ignoring his other questions.

'Of course,' he replied, starting to turn her wheelchair around.

'I was wrong, I don't want its secrets. They're a curse!'

'You're doing fine,' said Bruno encouragingly.

'No, you don't understand. I am the author of my own tragedy. I brought it all on myself.' Esther was taking jittery breaths in now, which worried him anew. Bruno felt he should find a paper bag to help stop her from hyperventilating, like they did in movies. '*I'm* the reason it happened. I did this to myself!'

'Esther,' Bruno said reassuringly, 'it's going to be okay.'

'I wish that were true, but all that's left is my ruin.'

As soon as he arrived home, Bruno carefully placed Esther's phone with his secret stash in his bedroom, beneath his chest of drawers. To access the space, he removed the bottom-most shelf completely and then hid away the phone – carefully turned off – next to the brochure he'd ordered a few days ago, and only after making sure it would be delivered in a 'discreet envelope'. He flicked through the brochure now, keeping alert for footsteps outside his door.

Camp Change! promised to be 'a radical journey of self-discovery' – the word 'radical' underlined – with integrated workshops, trust circles and keynote speaker 'Dr Allan', a developmental psychiatrist and transformation expert, who would 'change the way you see yourself *forever*'. The doctor was tanned and smilingly handsome, crinkles around his eyes, his teeth almost blue they were so bright. Bruno imagined being in the same room as Dr Allan, seeing that smile first hand – only yesterday, he'd asked his mother if they could buy whitening toothpaste instead of their regular sort, but his mum rejected the request; it was twice as expensive.

The other draw was the location – *Camp Change!* was in Great Yarmouth, two and a half hours drive away on the coast, in a 're-purposed' holiday camp with individual sleeping 'chalets'. The rest of the brochure was filled with the same smiling, youthful faces as on the website, only here there was more sand – a teenage boy and girl sitting on a dune laughing; a group perched around a campfire on the beach, one of them strumming a guitar; a solitary teenager gazing towards a horizon, seagulls soaring majestically behind him.

Bruno hadn't been to the seaside in two years, not since their last family holiday, when they'd stayed in a rickety cottage up in Scarborough, a resort on the North Sea, and it had rained the whole trip. This had been a long hard winter, with his dad – Bruno imagined the sun on his face, wading into the tumbling waves, the sensation of feeling completely submerged in water. He let out a long sigh – he'd been holding his breath, he realised – before stowing away the brochure, and replacing the shelf.

'How's Esther?' Mum asked that night during a dinner of spaghetti and (regular or vegan) meatballs. They had decided to keep Jane's visit between them – Bruno's dad was already overly curious about how the lessons were going, so it was best not to fan that fire.

'I think she's getting the hang of online,' replied Bruno,

truthfully. He still hadn't decided whether he should tell Jane about what had happened earlier. Esther had seemed almost back to her regular self by the time he'd left her house.

Megan was glaring at Bruno through the parting in her hair. She always seemed to be angry with him these days for some unknown reason. Maybe it was because he hadn't taken them up to visit Esther yet, but it was his job, it wouldn't be professional to bring his kid sisters.

'How can you hang on to something if it's invisible?' asked Daphne, a vegan meatball bulging in her cheek, making her glasses askew.

'Hang "of" – not hang "on",' her mother replied.

'Beetling,' his dad announced, before chomping on a regular meatball. His appetite definitely seemed to be returning.

'What's that, Dad?' asked his youngest, taking the bait.

'It means "overhanging" – you can have beetling brows.' He wiggled his eyebrows comically, or what was left of them – he used to have bushy brows that went with his thick hair. Dad seemed to make this connection too and stopped wiggling.

'Will they grow back?' Daphne asked, innocently – cheek still bulging.

'Course they will,' he replied, brushing the comment off with a wink, but Bruno knew he was sensitive about the hair loss. 'Are you eating that meatball, or storing it for later?'

'For later!' she giggled, popping another one in her other cheek.

For no apparent reason that Bruno could see, his other sister pushed herself back from the table, and ran to her shared room, slamming the door behind her.

'Hormones,' his mother whispered to Bruno and his father.

'Was I as moody at that phase?' asked Bruno.

'*That* phase...?' his father said under his breath, arching a practically non-existent eyebrow. 'By the way,' he added, at normal volume, 'Reg at work found a paper featuring our lady on the hill, a couple of them, in fact.' He turned to his wife. 'Did you know, Reg used to work for the tabloids?'

'When?' she replied. 'He never told me that.'

'It was one of his first jobs. He was a junior copywriter or something, in London.'

'Why did he work at the warehouses here then?' Daphne asked, after finally swallowing the last of her left-cheek meatball.

'Don't say it like that, as if it's a punishment. Reg's a manager, on good money. Anyway, he was working for one of the red-top newspapers, and not only did he remember the old girl's story – he was even there when it was reported.'

'What?' Bruno replied, shocked.

'Apparently, some woman comes in, wanting to talk to a journo about a story. Reg sits her down with a cup of tea, she has this black case with her, he jokes about it having a machine gun inside. This hippy woman, he can't remember her name, tells him it's a *flute* case, and he should come and see her play a gig on Friday. Reg assumes they're flirting, so he agrees, and off she goes with the journalist. On the Friday, after work, he goes along to the place she told him about, and very quickly he realises he's the only man in the venue. Not a big deal, he might even be able to use that to his advantage, except the moment they start playing, Reg realises it's some radical feminist performance-art spoken word type-thing, and he's sitting bang in the front with a full pint. He said he'd never seen anything like it. And to add insult to injury, the flute player wasn't even very good.'

'Why did she invite him?' wondered his wife.

'If I know Reg, he was flirting like mad, she probably wanted to teach him a lesson.'

'Dad, what is Esther's newspaper story about?' Bruno asked, exasperated.

'Oh yeah, I buried the lead. Nothing about spies, she was a scarlet woman...'

Bruno gasped. 'What?'

'Filip, not in front of...' His wife nodded towards their youngest daughter, who was listening intently as she masticated her right-cheek meatball.

'I'll ask him to bring over the papers, if you like?' Bruno nodded, eagerly – it wasn't breaking Esther's trust because he wasn't searching for information on the internet, he was accessing the actual archival documents themselves. 'Honestly, I can't stop picturing Reg sitting in the front row like a goon. The violinist even took off her top and waved her bare—'

'Eat your meatballs,' commanded his wife, cutting him off, and obediently, he popped one into his mouth, still sniggering at the mental image.

Window washing, the next day, did not go well. Bruno's squeegee broke at the second house while he was doing the transoms; he managed to hit a mailbox with his ladder, causing a very slight lean, and when he was cleaning the bedroom windows at the Boswell place, he surprised a naked old Mr Boswell, who was getting dressed after a shower. Mortified, Bruno apologised profusely, but the elderly man only seemed to find the whole thing hilarious.

He also couldn't stop thinking about what his father had revealed the day before – especially about the woman who went to the papers. It couldn't have been Esther herself, she'd told him that first day she couldn't play an instrument; but didn't she mention being involved with a band? Bruno wanted to discuss all this with Esther – maybe there was something important she needed to know – but what if she felt he'd snooped? He was afraid of upsetting her, or worse, making her unwell.

Back home with a disappointingly small wad of soggy notes

– the cleaning had stalled after the broken squeegee, and he would have to spend at least twenty pounds to buy a replacement – Bruno wolfed down a sandwich, showered and, at a loss for what to do next, decided to take the phone back to Esther's early, instead of waiting for tomorrow's lesson.

At her front door a short time later, Bruno banged the spitfire door knocker, but there was no sign of Esther. He even tried the broken doorbell, but of course that didn't work. A sense of foreboding started to descend on him. At the back of his mind, since starting the lessons – what with Esther's advanced age – Bruno worried that he might be the one to find she had... passed. He pushed this ghoulish thought to one side and used the knocker again. When there was still no response, he considered what to do next. He *should* call Jane, but if he did, Bruno understood instinctively that his relationship with Esther would change forever. She would see him as her *keeper*. Remembering her iPhone in his pocket, he turned it on. There were no alerts, good. Esther's landline! Juggling devices, he found her number on his phone and called it, hearing it ring through the heavy door in the hallway. There was no answer. He tried again. Still nothing. What if Esther was simply out, or in the bath? She wasn't expecting him today after all...

The house felt ominous, the mismatched windows like many watching eyes. Bruno decided to walk around the place, just to be safe – maybe Esther was outside and hadn't heard him banging on the door. He rounded the front of the house, moving overhanging branches out of his path as he went with the back of his hand. There was not much actual forest around Whittleham, so close to the M1 motorway, and Esther had explained that her surrounding land was a small ancient woodland, kept as a windbreak and not ploughed up for agriculture like the rest of the nearby countryside. Strangely, this remnant of something old and long-lost didn't seem menacing to Bruno at all, it felt almost welcoming. The garden itself was small before it merged into woodland; there was an old, rusted wheelbarrow that was displayed more like a feature than an oversight and the grass was longer than lawns down in the village – Esther apparently allowed Jane to send someone around to mow it no more than four times a year.

As Bruno approached the kitchen windows, he felt guilty to have not cleaned them. He itched to take warm soap to the panes, to see how beautifully they'd come up. He swiped the glass with his finger and found it was black with grime. Behind the glass, in the kitchen, a movement caught his attention, refocusing his eyes. Cupping his hands, he peered through. There was no one there – maybe he'd imagined it – but then he noticed a pile of old rags on the floor near the pantry. Maybe it was Esther's laundry? As he watched, the heap moved. Bruno jumped back from the windows in shock. Was it a rat, he wondered? – he'd heard them before, scurrying about in the walls, but never seen them. He peered closer. The blankets or clothing, or whatever it was, moved again, and as Bruno watched, its form came to him – it was a body, a person, lying on the floor.

Esther! Maybe she'd fallen – his impulse was to ring an ambulance and pound on the windows, but something stopped him. The more he looked, the more the heap of blankets – and pillows too, he realised – appeared to be a makeshift bed. But why would Esther sleep on the floor? There was something shameful about this act – homeless people did it! – made worse in that he'd witnessed it, without her knowledge. What if Esther had hurt herself? She wouldn't have gathered the pillows and blankets in that case; they were premeditated. He couldn't see the wheelchair. As he continued to peer through the glass, he watched Esther's form gently rise and fall, so she was breathing, good. Why hadn't she heard his banging or his phone calls? Perhaps she did and chose to ignore them. Her hearing wasn't the best, in one of her ears at least, he remembered. He often slept through multiple alarms when he had to wake up for school.

Bruno was conflicted about what to do next. He knocked lightly on the window, but Esther still didn't stir. He considered knocking again, louder, but he didn't want to scare her, that might cause an even greater issue. And then he decided – he'd return in an hour to see if Esther was still on the floor, and if so, he'd call Jane straight away, without question. He didn't feel completely confident about his choice but it was the best he could come up with.

Not wanting to return home to wait, Bruno roamed around the outskirts of the village and ended up through the motorway underpass by one of the main warehouses. It began to rain – the drops would streak his newly washed windows, he thought gloomily – the grey sky making the large metal buildings even grimmer. Two forklifts were unloading a lorry, and Bruno watched as they took turns, how expertly the drivers manoeuvred the vehicles. He'd researched how much it cost to get your forklift licence – it could be up to £750. It seemed much more complicated than driving a car. Not only did you have to think of forwards, backwards, left and right, but also up and down – like a dance.

'Hey,' came a voice, behind him.

Bruno jumped in surprise, almost leaping off the tree stump he was perched on. He turned to see Dominic, trailing smoke from his lit cigarette.

'What's up?' Bruno said, trying to sound as normal as he could after the scare.

'Nothing much. I'm on a break.' Dominic leant against the fence. Today, he was wearing a long-sleeved black T-shirt with 'Suspiria' written in red above a screaming blue mouth, the wagon-wheel pendant around his neck catching the sky as he moved. His fingernails were painted a chipped lime green, Bruno noticed. 'How's your dad?'

'Better.' This was always the family response – if anyone asked, always 'better'. It dawned on Bruno that for the first time in a while, this was actually the truth.

Dominic nodded and flicked his cigarette butt, still smoking, near the mouth of the underpass. It was all Bruno could do not to fetch it immediately. He also felt an urge to take out his phone; it was too weird – too intimate – to be in another person's company, especially another male, without at least one device to anchor him.

'How's Esther Saul treating you?'

At Esther's name, a ripple of panic passed through Bruno.

'Good, she's good. She's well,' he answered nervously, recalling the image of her lying on the kitchen floor, how uncomfortable that must be: she was all bones. What if she *had* slipped and fallen? The blankets, he reminded himself, the pillows. He should have banged harder on the glass, he was a coward. He would go back soon... 'How do you know Esther's last name?' he asked, the thought occurring to him.

'I know everything in my line of work,' replied Dominic. 'What are you planning on doing once you get out of here?' he nodded in the direction of the village behind them.

'Don't know yet. Uni? Money's tight though, and it's going to be a while until Dad's back driving.' He felt nervous about revealing such personal information to Dominic, but seeing Esther so vulnerable had made him reckless. 'They need me to contribute more. I *want* to, it's only...' He studied the warehouse. 'If nothing changes, I'll start on a seasonal shift. I'll have to.'

'No man, that's how they trap you. You'll wake up in twenty years, with a mortgage, a wife and six kids.'

'Doesn't sound too bad. It's what everyone wants, right?'

'The walls close in on me every time I look at that corrugated prison.' Dominic shuddered. 'We're not meant for this life, we should be on the road, like our ancestors, not chained by the ankle.'

'I guess. I just want to be... regular.'

'*Regular?*' Dominic gave a hoarse smoker's laugh. 'My nan wants to be regular, she eats Liquorice Allsorts. Swears by them, a pack a day, sorts out her intestinal issues. If you mean normal, normal's the enemy. Normal bungs you up.' Dominic looked thoughtful. 'We never really talked at school, did we?'

'Not much.'

'Why was that?'

This was an impossible question for Bruno to answer – it was too loaded. *I wasn't cool enough. I was intimidated by you.* Deeper reasons too, that Bruno didn't even want to admit to himself.

'We should hang out some time,' Dominic suggested, not waiting for an answer.

We're hanging out now, thought Bruno, *and it's very uncomfortable*. Why would he want to do this again?

'We're part of the resistance.' Again, Dominic nodded towards the warehouses where the unpacked lorry was now making a broad circle to return to the main road.

Bruno wasn't exactly sure he wanted to be part of a petty drug dealer's gang. Outsiders. The left behind. He realised he hadn't spoken for some time.

'You didn't like me. At school...' Bruno clarified. He hadn't meant for it to sound like an accusation, and he frowned at his own words. 'Sorry,' he added weakly.

'It wasn't that I didn't like you...' Dominic shrugged. 'It was about survival. We were always on the back foot with the townies. You always acted like school was too lame for you, anyway.'

Bruno snorted. '*You* were the cool one!'

'I guess. Cool in school.' He took out another cigarette from a packet and expertly lit it, blowing out smoke with a whistling chuckle between his lips. 'That'll be on my gravestone: "Dominic Patterson. Cool in school". Oh, sorry – your dad...'

'He's getting better, really,' Bruno replied.

'Good,' said Dominic between puffs. 'You like him, your dad?' Bruno nodded. 'That's lucky. I'm not a huge fan of mine.'

Dominic's father was infamous in Whittleham, a lorry driver with a secret family in Manchester, who – when it was revealed – packed up his stuff and drove off, never to return.

'Do you miss him?'

'Not hugely.' Dominic kicked the fence. 'What are we like, the pair of us? We should be making sweet love to goddess women and taking psychedelics, not moping around a warehouse loading bay, getting depressed about our dads. Want a cigarette?'

'No, thanks.'

'Have one.'

'I don't want to give money to Big Tobacco.'

'You think Big Tobacco are going to care if you have a single cigarette?'

'That's how it starts.'

'It's my money, anyway.' Dominic shook his head. 'Have you ever done anything radical in your life, Bruno?'

This sounded like something Esther might ask. It was also weird hearing Dominic say his name out loud. It twanged a very personal string deep in Bruno's chest, underneath his organs, the sensation reverberating down his limbs.

'Smoking a cigarette is about the least radical thing you can do. They've carefully constructed an image of smoking via film and television over the years to make it seem that it's counter-culture, when in fact it's the complete opposite.'

'Gets the girls though.'

'The ones who like stained teeth.' Bruno was getting braver speaking to Dominic, he realised.

'My teeth are fine. I take them out before I do any proper

kissing.' Dominic mimed removing false teeth, covering his real teeth with his lips. It was so dumb, Bruno had to laugh. 'Go on, one puff.' Caught off guard, Bruno took the cigarette offered to him. It smouldered between his fingers. 'Exactly how big is Big Tobacco?' Dominic was asking. 'Are we talking normal human sized, or like one of those Japanese fighting robots...?'

There was a shocked high-pitched squeal from the direction of the underpass, and both boys turned. It was Daphne and Megan. What were his sisters doing here? Bruno wondered, panicked. He remembered the cigarette he was holding and threw it on the grass behind him.

Megan marched up to them with her hands on her hips, Daphne following close behind.

'What were you holding, Bruno?' she demanded. Even though it wasn't that cold, she was wearing a woollen hat jammed down to her eyebrows, and a scarf was wrapped around her neck that covered her mouth.

'Why are you girls here?' he asked, trying to change the subject.

'We came looking for you.'

'You never watch television with us any more,' Daphne said, pouting. 'When you were studying for your exams, you told us as soon as you'd finished you'd be spending more time with us, but you lied.'

'Alright, girls,' Dominic said, grinning at them. 'Looks like you're on the warpath.' Megan glowered at Dominic but didn't say anything. 'I'll leave you to it. But for the record, he was only holding the cigarette for me.'

'They'll give you cancer.'

'Message received.'

He headed off towards the underpass, Bruno watching him go, feeling like some opportunity for connection had been lost.

'Are you hanging out with him now?' demanded Megan.

'Not really. He just showed up.'

'Are you friends?'

Potentially, thought Bruno. And the fact pleased him, he realised.

Daphne plonked herself down in front of Bruno, sitting with her back to him.

'Can you plait my hair, please?' she asked.

'Right here? Do you have a band?'

She gave an exaggerated nod.

Bruno took three strands of Daphne's chestnut hair, careful not to knock her glasses from behind her ears.

'How tight do you want it?'

'Really tight.'

'You got a headache last time, remember?'

'Why are you always out of the house, or in your bedroom?' demanded Megan. 'That old lady sees you more than we do.'

'I'm around all the time,' he replied, exasperatedly.

'Not really,' said Daphne, turning her head slightly as he plaited. 'You're different.'

'I'm *exactly* the same.' That's the problem, Bruno thought to himself.

'You never ask about us,' Megan spluttered. 'You never want to talk about *anything*.'

'I'm getting older. You'll understand when—'

'Don't lie!' she yelled.

'Megan, stop shouting.'

'We've needed you. You aren't like other brothers, you were *better*. You'd play games and show us anime and we could talk to you. But then you just *went*.'

'It is a bit too tight now,' said Daphne, calmly. 'Ow.'

'I'm here *now*,' he replied to Megan, matching her volume, and then more quietly to Daphne, 'sorry.'

'All you think about is making money.'

'We can pay,' offered Daphne. 'I've saved almost thirteen pounds. You can have it, if you like?'

'You don't have to pay me to be your brother...'

'What do you need it all for?' Megan demanded.

'For board. To help Mum and Dad. So, eventually, I can leave...'

'Leave *us*, you mean?'

'I'll come back.'

Megan started to cry. Bruno stopped braiding Daphne's hair – his sisters were expert weepers, and it didn't always mean they were actually emotional. 'I heard Mum and Dad say they think you have depression.'

'What? I'm not... Why did they...? They never said anything to—'

'Your room is so neat,' Daphne said over her shoulder, as if that was proof.

'Did you go into my room?' Bruno gently tugged the braid he was holding.

'... No... Ouch.' There was the smallest tell-tale delay in her response.

'Keep out of my room! Both of you!' It was Bruno's turn to bellow.

'I hate you!' cried Megan, running away to the underpass.

'You can finish now,' Daphne said, taking a hair tie off her wrist to give to her brother. He dutifully tied her hair. It wasn't a very good job – he was rusty. Daphne sighed. 'I better go after her. It's not just you – she's worried her arm hair's too dark. And I accidentally ate a baby sausage at my friend Alana's yesterday. Accidentally, on purpose.'

'Don't tell Mum I was holding a cigarette.'

'Okay,' agreed Daphne. 'Megan did go in your room. But she didn't touch anything.'

'I knew it.'

'She thought you might have a secret girlfriend.'

'That's so dumb.'

'That's what I said.'

Daphne shrugged again and ran in the direction of her sister.

Bruno's first impulse was to run home to make absolutely sure that Megan hadn't been rifling through his stuff – what if she found his secret hiding place? A lock on his door, that's what he needed – but even more importantly, he had to check on Esther. He sped off in such a hurry, he even forgot to pick up the two cigarette butts.

Back at Esther's, out of breath, he banged using the knocker, not expecting a response. But only a few moments later, he heard the sound of the lock turning, and Esther, holding her stick for support, opened the door, wearing a yellow mohair jumper under dark green corduroy dungarees, the button missing on the left strap, and held in place with a large safety pin.

'Oh, dear heart, it's you! Are we supposed to be meeting today? I was just coming to check the mail – late in the day, I know. What perfect timing.'

'I brought back your phone,' Bruno replied, breathily. He was so relieved to see her in no apparent danger, he had to stop himself tackling her with a hug.

'I've been looking for that everywhere. I must have forgotten it was with you. This really is good providence, as I've had a brainwave, about *the Legacy*. I think I know what it's referring to.' She started to turn slowly. 'Would you be so kind as to pick up the mail on the floor and take my elbow, we're in the sitting room today. It used to be called the high kick room, but as you *can-can* see, we've had to change it.' After entering the hallway, Bruno closed the door behind him, and bent down, picking up the envelopes on the floor as requested, before taking her arm. 'And if the legacy is what I presume it to be, it's very exciting news indeed. It means if there's land, there's still a house, or at least part of a house, or maybe only the idea of one – but greater than the possibility of actual foundations is the intention behind them, or their preservation, *his* intention, if you see my meaning.' Bruno didn't, but he was encouraged that Esther seemed in much better spirits – her spark was back. As they passed the kitchen, he discreetly poked his head through the doorway, but there was nothing on the floor, and no sign of any blankets or pillows – had he imagined the whole episode?

He could smell woodsmoke as they shuffled deeper into the house.

'I made a small fire,' explained Esther, patting his arm. 'I hope it will help to illuminate things.'

The sitting room was toasty warm – which confused Bruno even more, when did she start it? There was a basket of branches and small logs next to the fireplace – one or two looked quite heavy – who fetched those, and from where?

He helped Esther into a thread-worn armchair closest to the warmth of the fire and perched himself on a footstool in the same faded green fabric beside her.

'Did you make this yourself?' he asked, nodding towards the fire.

'Of course, didn't I say before? I keep it relatively manageable, I worry about sparks. People did used to spontaneously combust, you know, back in the day. I wonder why they don't do it so much any more? Fewer candles, I suppose. We could look it up, on my smart little...'

'How did you get the wood?'

'How does anyone get it?' An edge of annoyance was creeping into Esther's voice. 'A man comes and delivers it. How do you get your firewood?'

'We have central heating.'

'Bully for you. Now, I must tell you all about my *realisation...*'

'Your bedroom – is it here, on the ground floor?' Bruno asked carefully.

'That's a bit forward, dear heart. They're all on the first floor, naturally.'

'And you can get up there?'

Esther held his gaze with not even the slightest flinch.

'Of course. Whatever's gotten into you? Let me tell you about—'

'How do you get the firewood into the basket?'

'I fetch it from the wood store next to the kitchen, and bring in in here, like anyone might. Those of us who don't have *central heating* at least.'

'Some of those logs look heavy.'

She gave him a flabbergasted look.

'Are you suggesting I'm lying to you?'

'I'm only wondering how... someone like you...'

'Someone *like me*? I'll have you know, *dear heart*,' she spat the last two words, 'I am perfectly capable of getting around. If I need more wood, I fetch it a piece at a time, or I load my wheel-chair and then empty it in here. Happy?'

'You shouldn't be doing it – that's heavy work for someone...'

'...in my condition? You sound like my daughter.'

Bruno felt his face twitch involuntarily, but he tried to cover it.

'Maybe I could get the firewood for you?' he offered. 'And I could help you make a proper bed, take a mattress from upstairs, even bring down the whole bed frame if I have help...'

Esther held up her hand, making Bruno falter.

'How I take care of my affairs is none of your concern.' He began to protest. 'Thank you,' she added firmly.

Bruno thought of her lying on the kitchen floor, so vulnerable and alone, and it spurred him on, despite her insistence.

'You said we should be truthful, stay in a place of not nice.'

'I think you'll find there is a difference between not nice and not *very* nice.'

'If you had a proper place to sleep...'

'I *have* a proper place...'

'Where is that?'

Esther displayed another flabbergasted expression.

'Anywhere I so choose.'

'But a bed? A proper bed?'

'Where I do or do not sleep is my own business! Too many busybodies coming into this house, spies for my daughter.' Bruno felt another twinge of guilt at this. 'Nurses, doctors, gardeners, cleaners, reporting back to her.'

'Maybe your daughter's only trying to help?'

'She's meddling, that's what. And be warned. I don't take kindly to meddlers *or* spies. I know she will have been in your ear, it's her way. I have my spies too.' Esther smacked her legs. 'You have quite ruined this for me. I had so much to tell you...'

'I'm trying to help...'

'Help? Is that what you're doing? What is it they say, about altruism being but a subtle form of violence?'

'I'm only thinking about your episode yesterday, when the email came through...'

'I did not have an episode! It was shock on hearing bad news. Everything gets pathologised as you age. *Oh, the poor dear.* Can't I simply be upset? But good, you've reminded me, I was about to talk about that despicable email, the legacy, but now I think I will mind my own business, as you should mind yours.'

'I didn't mean to—'

'I sleep where I choose,' Esther interrupted, 'dependent on how my body is behaving. I don't *like* a mattress; once I'm in one, it feels like I'll never get out again.'

'Then maybe we could install some handles to help you up.'

'I don't need *handles*.'

'Not now maybe, but...'

'Tomorrow, when I'm even more decrepit, you mean?'

'There are so many things we could do to make your life easier...'

'I'm not sure you understand...'

'Like moving the kettle onto a lower table so it's easier for you to fill...'

'It's fine where...'

'Putting covers over all the uneven surfaces on the floors – they have these rubber mats in the warehouses, so you don't trip on wires and things. Dad has some at home. It will make it easier for you to get around in the wheelchair.'

'I don't want my hardwood floors covered in rubber!'

So many great ideas were firing off in Bruno's brain, he was practically deaf to Esther's protestations.

'There's no real reason to have everything spread out around the house,' he continued. 'We could move the furniture you really need and use into two or maybe three rooms at the most, and—'

'That will do!' Esther practically roared, snapping Bruno out of his machinations. 'This is my home. Everyone is always waiting to pounce, a handle here, a ramp there, and before you know it, you're wrapped up in bubble wrap or worse, they can then say: "Oh, it didn't work! To the nursing home with you. For your own safety." I would also suggest you get *your* affairs in order before you start giving advice to other people. I have absolutely no problem with your being the other side of the coin, but as you've failed to bring it up, I'm constantly tip-toeing around the fact.'

Bruno lurched back on his footstool, almost falling off it.

'What...?'

'I've had plenty of gay and lesbian friends over the years, it doesn't matter one jot to me. You have it much better these days, some of my friends were arrested before it became legal, and then of course a lot of gay ones died in the eighties. My dear friend Mateo, he was a ballet dancer – his legs! – came here when he was sick for several months before he was hospitalised. So, you see, this is a perfectly welcoming space, and I would prefer it if, in future, we—'

'I have to go...' In an instant, Bruno was up and heading out of the room, Esther calling after him. It was a relief to get out of the hot sitting room, but her words still rung in his ear, searing. How did she know? What had given it away? His hands, his wrists? Panicked, he ran towards the front door, and hurtled down the hill, catching his foot on a stone and twisting his ankle – his body betraying him a second time – before unceremoniously falling into the shrubbery, the world spinning around him turbidly, as if some dark spell had been unleashed, never to be undone.

TWO

ESTHER (19 MAY)

Mere seconds after Bruno had fled the sitting room, she felt her righteous indignation start to melt into regret. She'd been in such a good mood after her inspiration too – squandered! And Esther wanted Bruno's help – now that she had a hunch about what the legacy might be – he was always so ingenious, his brain worked instinctively in the language of the internet, while hers simply did not. Still, she had her phone again, she could make some headway herself. Perhaps it was better to keep her theories to herself, especially if Bruno was to judge her. Anger swelled in Esther's chest again. Not anger; pride, and seconds later, regret. The process was almost comical. Oh, well – the boy needed a nudge, that was obvious. He held so much potential. Was it her place though? And was it a simple nudge, or a shove from a cliff-edge? Esther remembered one of her psychiatrist friends from the seventies once telling her, 'You can be "right" or you can be happy', but what exactly was happy? The sensation was fleeting – a birthday cake and balloons: the balloons deflated, the cake eventually rotted.

Another pang hit her. The poor boy! Her inexcusably despicable self. She must go after him. Esther heaved herself up to standing on her stick but slumped back down in the chair with a cry – she was in quite some pain today, and her nap on the floor hadn't helped as it usually might. She tried again, rocking herself up to standing using momentum, but once she was on her feet again, Esther realised she'd never catch up with Bruno, and so she plonked herself unceremoniously down again, with an 'oof'.

To keep her mind busy, she leant over and picked up her phone from the footstool, where Bruno had left it behind, swiping to allow herself into the device. Her inspired idea about the legacy had come in the early hours of the morning, just before sunrise. Esther was in the garden with a torch and her walking stick, as she did sometimes when she couldn't sleep and it wasn't too cold out. There was much to enjoy in the darkness, the moon for one, the stars, and the change in flowers – the red, burgundy and purple ones disappeared, and the white and pastel shades, glorious early spring irises in this case, glowed as if by magic, while grey and silver leaves become almost iridescent. There were the foxes – shooed away so they wouldn't dig up her beds but respected nonetheless – the swooping tawny owls and bumbling hedgehogs. It was a show not to be missed. Kicking some of the stone edgings back into place, Esther had a brainwave, bright as day. She even turned off the torch. Could the legacy be the parcel of land near Glasgow that Thackeray had begun to build their house on? That might explain his son Edward's anger. 'This will be a place for us always,' Thackeray had promised her.

Frustratingly, Thackeray had never told her exactly where this new home would be. 'A stone's throw from Glaschu' (the Gaelic name for the city) is all she'd got from him. It had been shrouded in mystery, another of his romantic gestures, to be one of his long line of great achievements. To materialise the perfect house – poof!

The idea had stuck with her all morning, and now she

brought up the 'search browser' – such perfunctory names – and typed in 'house foundations', but the results were all to do with modern brick houses. Things must have changed since the seventies, and Thackeray had been very proud that their home would be constructed in local stone, so as not to be 'blown off the hill' by the Scottish gales.

'Why build it there then?' Esther remembered asking, incredulously.

Because he did not want their house anywhere but his homeland, of course, and only with the finest view.

'What if I hate it?' she'd complained all those years ago, mock annoyed, but really quite delighted. Revoltingly so. Didn't every girl dream of having a home built especially for her? She felt excited again, despite her guilt over Bruno – oh why did today have to be ruined? Even back then, Esther's delight at the idea of the house had troubled her younger self. The idea of a man taking care of his woman, so entrenched in her psyche, so limiting, so powerful, so tantalising. Was he building her a castle on a hill so that she would finally be domesticated? Thackeray might try! If anyone could, it would be him though, her opposite in so many ways – a self-made businessman, conservative in everything except making money, solid, unflinching, rugged, unaffected, he seemed to absorb the knocks of the world. Handsome in his confidence and disregard for how he appeared to other people – his bald head and hairy shoulders were attributes to be proud of, although tempered by an attractive square jaw and piercing blue eyes.

Sometimes Esther allowed herself to imagine how Thackeray might fare in today's modern world. Would he have struggled? To be frank, she wasn't an expert on what *today's world* felt like. She'd made her own castle, locking herself away on her own hill. Completely alone.

No, Esther promised herself, she would not spiral, she'd felt so uplifted only a short while ago. Should she send an email to

Bruno, or a 'text' message even? And say, what? The cat was out
of the bag, his reaction had sealed the deal. They could no
longer ignore his sexuality, but now Esther understood she had
probably lost Bruno forever. He would never come back, she
realised, too late.

No, no, no. She could feel it, the dread. The pain. The
decades of sadness. It was Thackeray. She should never have
uttered his name! She should throw her phone into the fireplace
and be done with it. And yet, something held her back...

What if her hunch about the house was right? Did it prove
Thackeray had still loved her, even after what happened?
Perhaps it even meant he forgave her?

With some concentration, pushing her guilt over Bruno
aside, practised as she was at casting it away from her, albeit
temporarily, always only temporarily, Esther was able to bring
up the son's hateful email on the phone.

The words stung her eyes:

'*...the full extent of your manipulations...*'

'*...THE LEGACY...*'

'*My father... still beholden to you, it seems.*'

'*...you continue to rob from my family.*'

How was Esther still robbing from the James family – that
had been the question? Why had the younger son been so kind,
while the elder son was so vicious? Esther gritted her teeth at
the unfairness and inaccuracy of Edward's accusations. She had
sacrificed *everything* – her reputation, her freedom, her future –
and taken *nothing*. What had happened in the intervening
space of time, between the two emails? But of course – the will.
Thackeray's estate. Though, if he had left Esther something, she
would have received it by now – many years had passed.
Lawyers would have reached out. It must be something else.

Her eyes darted back to the phrase 'the legacy', all in capitals. Buy a piece of land, Thackeray had said. Land was always
a good investment outright; they weren't making any more.

Build a home that would withstand the elements and sit for centuries. Be happy in the fleeting moment you have before death. *Ha*, happy. There was that word again like a shiv in her side.

No. She would not give into the sadness – she was stronger than this. Was she though? Esther was only better than most at hiding the pain. And to think she'd lectured Bruno not to tell *others* how to live their lives.

Concentrate. If there was a house, or part of a house, however unfinished – and especially if there was land – it would have been left to the sons, most certainly?

What if it hadn't? It would be left to someone else, another relative, Esther reasoned. Why then did Edward seem to think *she* had some part to play in his family's fortune? 'The full extent of her manipulations?' The last time she'd corresponded with Thackeray was in the 1980s. But still, behind his son's harsh words, something excited Esther – that Thackeray had continued to include her in his life, in some unknown way. She must learn more, but the only person to ask was Edward, and that would not go well. If she could find where this piece of land was... How ridiculous for Thackeray not to tell her – but that was him all over, he alone pulled the strings in their relationship, until she had unceremoniously cut them...

How could she go about finding it? Search for the deeds online? Was the information publicly available? All these thoughts crowded Esther's mind futilely, now her dear heart was gone.

Why, old woman, must you get yourself caught up in this? Because, she answered immediately, it was Thackeray. The unequivocal undeniable truth was, after all these decades, and so much betrayal – and even his death – Esther, much to her chagrin, still loved him. And maybe – yes, it was hope she conjured, the deadliest of curses held in Pandora's jar – telegraphing it beyond the grave by a means only Esther would be able to interpret, Thackeray loved her still, and wanted her to know.

She awoke much later, and as she often did, unsure of where exactly she was.

As Esther's body ached if she lay too long, she seldom slept or napped in one spot, ranging nomadically around the ground floor level of the house, moving from armchair to sofa to chaise longue and back again, and sometimes, when the pain was especially bad, to the floor. She felt at peace on a hard surface; maybe it was having the firm ground beneath her, or perhaps she preferred the bruising ache in her body as she woke, a dull pain better than the sharp one from her bad hip. A self-inflicted discomfort could not surprise you. Her daughter called it *penance*: not the sleeping on the floor, Esther hid that from Jane, but the lack of a proper bedroom, an actual bed. What her daughter could never understand was the whole *house* was Esther's bedroom, the ground floor at least. The upper floor was a vague memory; it was years since she'd been up there.

There was another reason too, which Esther kept hidden, even from herself. The Lodge. Strapped on a too-soft mattress, the restraints cutting her wrists, as well-meaning eyes looked on – no, it was too horrible. She jerked herself up onto one elbow, and away from the memory.

Esther realised she was still in the sitting room, lying on an ottoman. The fire had gone out completely, and it was cold. Pushing herself up to rest her back against the wall, she could see by light filtering through the curtains that it was morning. Alive to face another day, she felt a familiar mix of gratitude and foreboding.

Scanning her body, she waited to see what pain would emerge, and where. A throbbing in her joints, the gnawing in her stiff hip, a general ache in her spine, shoulders, back? The pulsations of a headache, or a dreaded migraine. Her doctor had given her seated exercises to help her mobility and flexibility that she seldom ever did. Two different physiotherapists had materialised, but she'd sent them packing. They seemed to arrive at the crack of dawn – one poor nurse whom Esther had never before seen in her life turned up at 6.30 a.m. with the instruction that she was to give her a shower. Who needed that kind of 'help'?

Locating her stick close by on the floor, Esther heaved herself up, and stood hunched, one hand on the ottoman, wary of a headrush. They could get you. When she was ready, she began the processes of the day: teeth, washing in the sink, medication, a light breakfast of toast – she'd never been a food person – and then out into her garden. This was her favourite part of the day, the sting on her cheeks in winter, the warmer breeze in the summer – *like a lover's breath*, she thought, making herself grimace. How would she know what that felt like after all these years? Thackeray hadn't exactly been one to whisper sweet nothings. Today, she felt relatively pain-free, but at the thought of Thackeray, she was hit by a moral hangover. Bruno! How unjust she'd been to that dear, sweet boy. Esther felt a keen sense of repentance. What a beast she was.

The garden might have also seemed unruly to the uninitiated, but nothing in it was haphazard, from the carefully cultivated wildflowers to the rugged thicket Esther had allowed to creep back from the surrounding remnants of ancient forest. The more conventional lawn was overgrown, but she kept the paths well-trimmed to help with her wheelchair. She enjoyed these contrasts, the brightness of colourful blooms, but not at the cost of dense vegetation for the birds and insects. The typical neat English garden, whatever that was, did not interest her. Instead, she always tried to imagine what the trees might like to look down upon – they had been here long before her and would continue long after she was gone, it was only natural she considered their pleasure first.

Her challenge, then, was how to garden, because there was always plenty to do, without making her changes too apparent. Age had helped; her borders were no longer as straight, her banks less weeded, wildness was constantly overtaking, however much Esther snipped and pruned and gently pushed back. As such, she almost exclusively wore clothes for the garden, trousers for kneeling at the very least, so she could step out from the kitchen and pick up the branches that had come down in the winds.

As she watched the trees sway around her, she mulled over her findings from the night before. If there was a house, or land, they would be close enough to the city so he could get to the airport easily, and yet remote enough for his precious views. Esther had spent at least three hours scrolling around the electronic maps of the Glaswegian countryside, but what did she expect to find? A cross with the words 'here marks the spot'? A babbling brook renamed 'The Esther'? Babbling was about right...

Bruno. Another wave of remorse hit, stronger than the first. She would write to him, apologise at least. What if her dear heart made some terrible decision after her improper cajoling? This chilled Esther. Taking out her phone from her pocket – she tried to keep it judicially in her pocket with varying degrees of success – she attempted to create a new email, but it did not cooperate. She'd never sent Bruno one before – what was his email name and where was it stored? He'd told her, written it down for her, but she couldn't remember where. Esther considered calling his house on her landline and asking to speak to him, but would he answer? Probably: he was polite to a fault. Then what should she say? *I'm sorry for stating* – to her at least – *the obvious*? For simply addressing what he was not brave enough yet to? That would not go over well. Especially as it seemed he was not ready to hear it. Esther was still deciding how to proceed when the house phone rang. She knew instinctively it would be her daughter – somehow, the ringing sounded more agitated, more impatient whenever Jane called.

'Mother, it's me,' came Jane's voice, inevitably, once Esther had shuffled inside. 'I've been ringing, I was about to try you on your mobile.'

'I was in the garden,' Esther replied. 'And I don't have the mobile switched on.' It was best to make her daughter believe she wasn't contactable on the device, otherwise she'd never stop calling the thing.

'You must. I bought it for *emergencies*.' Esther felt the biggest danger to her existence was her daughter impinging on her life more than she already did. 'I have a grocery delivery coming for you this afternoon, don't forget. Make sure they put the bags on the countertop, so you don't have to bend down to lift anything off the floor.' Esther grunted in acknowledgement. 'There was one other thing...' There always was. 'I was chatting with a fellow at the office who knows a thing or two about property law, and he suggested the house might be underinsured because it's been so long since it was last valued, so I was thinking it would be prudent if we—'

'Jane, if I've told you once, I've told you a million times, I'm not interested in the value of this place. I'm never selling.' It was a familiar argument they'd had almost every week for years now, and they knew their parts well. 'If you send your estate agent henchmen, I will dispatch them in the same way I did the electrician you sent to quote for rewiring.'

'Mother, please do not flash anyone else. It's lucky we didn't get in trouble after that... incident.'

Despite her frustration at her daughter, Esther couldn't help but chuckle, remembering the poor electrician's face.

'You have been warned,' she said, sincerely.

'What am I going to do with you, Mother?'

'Absolutely nothing. Let me be.'

'Except I can't,' replied Jane, with a sigh. 'If I don't organise your deliveries, or take you to your doctor's appointments, or get someone over to check your fire alarms, who will? The place would be a massive responsibility for a large family, let alone one woman in her eighties.'

'This house is *my* life,' Esther snapped back, and very soon she would be confident to do many of those things herself, on the internet. Would she, though, without Bruno to help? Another pang of remorse – her dear heart! 'Tell me, where would I put everything if I moved?'

'Storage.'

'Ah yes, a holding pen to incarcerate my worldly possessions until I finally drop dead.'

'I don't like you talking so morbidly,' Jane replied. 'I love you, Mother. For *years*, I've humoured you there, even after the stroke, which was my biggest mistake...'

'Coming back to this house was the one thing that made me strong again. It's my will to live. If you cart me off into an old person's home I will perish, but perhaps that's exactly what you're hoping for.'

'Mother! Please don't talk like that.'

'Then mind your own business!'

Esther hung up the phone, and stomped furiously through the house, crashing about for something to keep her mind off things, muttering angrily to herself as she went, but each room she came to only held further annoyances – a vase of dead hellebores and pink nigella flowers she'd forgotten about, the smell of damp in the library that hadn't been there before, a new crack in a wall. Today, the house was not making a case for her to stay. Everywhere she laid her eyes, Esther could only see decay. To hell with her daughter, and Bruno and especially Thackeray. She didn't need any of them. Busying herself with chores for most of the day, until fatigue – and the dust –

caught up with her in the late afternoon, she just managed to make it into the garden with a thick blanket around her shoulders, to sit in the one surviving lawn chair, before her energy was sapped completely. It was cold, even for mid-May, and so there was no risk of mosquitos; but there were plenty of other flying bodies, a mating swarm of gnat-like creatures, quite boldly, coming to flirt right over her head. Esther loved watching the shadows grow longer, as the night creatures began to appear...

She must have dozed off, because when Esther opened her eyes, it was not long before dusk and the sky had gone from a grey blue to a deep purplish amber.

Movement caught her eye. A man was standing at the corner of the house looking very sheepish. He was perfectly bald, and for a moment Esther thought – Thackeray! He was the right height too, although much less stocky...

'I'm sorry,' the man called, as he crossed the lawn – in a local, not a Glaswegian accent, of course. 'I rang the bell.'

'It doesn't work,' Esther called back, 'and I wouldn't have heard it out here even if it did.'

'I'm Filip,' the man announced, as he drew closer. The name didn't ring a bell either, but there was something so familiar about his face... 'Bruno's dad,' he added.

'Ah, yes! Now it all makes perfect sense.' *Bruno!* 'How is the dear boy?' she asked, her face crumpling with concern.

'That's why I'm here.'

'What's happened?' asked Esther, panicked.

'Oh, he's fine,' Filip replied. 'It's only a sprain.'

'What on earth?'

'Bruno managed to twist his ankle yesterday, not badly, but he's hobbling about. I'm surprised he hasn't told you. Don't you have another lesson this week?'

'Hopefully,' Esther replied vaguely. 'The poor thing, he's been in the wars, that's terrible.' But she was relieved too, reassured it wasn't anything more serious, and that she had no part to play in it.

'I'm not supposed to be here,' Filip admitted, 'don't tell my wife, she'd clip my ear if she knew I was plodding up hills.'

'But Bruno's fine, apart from the ankle?'

'He was on his laptop when I left the house. Seemed as good as a teenager *can* be. The thing is, with Bruno you can never be totally sure. That's what I wanted to chat with you about.'

'Then shall we go inside? I'll make us a hot drink and we can talk at my kitchen table. It's a real honour to have Bruno's father at my house. What a splendid young man you have in him.'

'Thank you,' Filip replied with a bashful smile. 'He's a good lad.'

'The finest.' Esther was still trying to banish her guilt about how she'd treated Bruno the previous night.

'It's lovely to hear you say so. Obviously, *we* know he is – the missus and I – only, we're not sure if he believes it himself.' He glanced around the garden. 'I don't mind staying out here, it's peaceful amongst all these trees – if you're not too cold?' He nodded towards the grove of wild cherry, field maple and hawthorn – Esther imagined they were listening intently to the human conversation, but maybe that was arrogance, they most likely didn't care one jot.

'I have my woollen blanket to protect against the elements, a practice I brought back from my Nordic travels. This one is made of Icelandic wool, a consolation for not being able to see the northern lights on my third attempt. In fact, I no longer believe they actually exist, they're simply a ruse to attract the witless foreigner to buy their wonderful blankets. Shall I fetch you one?'

'I think I'll survive. Can I sit?' He indicated an upside-down wheelbarrow that was rusted through but too heavy for Esther to move, although she'd tried to right it many times. 'The walk took it out of me.'

'Please. Bruno told me you've been unwell. I'm very sorry.'

Filip lowered himself unsteadily onto the upturned wheelbarrow, testing it first for weight. A male robin flitted between them. 'I'm getting better. That's the general decree, at least – tests and what have you.'

Esther kept her measured gaze on him.

'You don't *feel* better?'

He shrugged, running a hand over his bald head.

'I'm not sure. Not in my bones, yet. Maybe I'm waiting for the other shoe to drop.'

'It's not easy getting weak. Skirting the bounds of death. Until you experience it yourself...'

Filip nodded gravely. 'The nights are the worst.'

'They're a horror. When you're too afraid to close your eyes because you're unsure if you will open them again.'

'How do you do it, in this big house, all alone? I have the wife next to me, and kids everywhere, and I might as well be on the moon for all the help it does.'

'Practice, that's what.'

'Hopefully, I'll get enough time to become better at it.'

'I'm sure you will.' Esther folded her hands on her lap and took a deep breath. There was only so much death talk that even *she* – spitfire though she was – could cope with before becoming morose. 'Tell me, what's brought you here to my garden, Filip?'

'You've been seeing a lot of Bruno in the past few weeks. He likes you.' Another pang of guilt hit Esther, but she didn't let it show. 'The boy's a closed book. We worry, my wife and I. He's a self-starter, I'll give him that. I don't know many people who could wash windows all through winter – he freezes to death half the time, but he still gets out there each week.' He chuckled fondly. 'Otherwise Bruno's on the internet, and I know that's every teenager with their phones and computers and social media, but you read about young men online, the dark web and forums and stuff. I want to make sure he's not getting involved in anything – I don't know, *extreme* – only he clams up the moment I ask anything. Teenagers don't want to talk to their parents – I understand. I wasn't always the best father either, learned everything from my old man, unfortunately. I was hard on Bruno when he was younger, but he's turned out well, despite me.'

'I'm sure that's not the whole truth. The apple and the tree, and all that.'

'That's one silver lining of my illness, it's softened me up. I used to be a stickler about school, homework, chores, sport, about everything really. Don't know why, he was such a good kid. Why was it so important that Bruno got up at a certain time and played football and kept his bedroom clean? He was seven, for Christ's sake. Let him stay in his pyjamas and eat cereal, honestly! Do you have any children?'

'A daughter. I definitely didn't win any best parent awards either. Regret is a dish served cold, with plenty of leftovers, lasting you for decades.'

'That's the thing. I don't want to have any regrets if I can help it. It's just finding the way in with Bruno. He won't talk to us, and there's something eating away at him, we can tell that much. He's not the same kid he was a few years ago. Obviously, there's my cancer, what he's going to do next, how we'll afford university if he does decide to go, but it feels like there's more going on. It's *deeper* somehow. He's up all night, hardly sleeps. I'm worried we're losing him.'

'How can I help?'

'He trusts you. Maybe just keep an ear out for anything that sounds... off.'

'I can't promise to spy on him.'

'We're simply keeping a lookout for him. I hope you'll agree he's worth it. Drugs or bad affiliations or... self-harm... or anything like that.'

Should Esther divulge her hunch about Bruno's sexuality? No, even she – gung-ho as she was – knew better than to do that. Without knowing for absolute sure – and even if she did – it was not her information to give. It could only make things worse.

'Here's my mobile number.' Filip hunted in his pocket and found a folded piece of paper. 'One last thing, Bruno doesn't know I'm here, so let's keep it hush-hush from both him and my missus.'

'I'm the picture of discretion.'

Bashfulness flitted across Filip's face, making him seem very much like his son.

'You know, I was nervous coming up here. The famous recluse. Do you know how many stories there are about this place?'

Esther rubbed her hands together.

'I'm sure. I half expect pitchforks and torches some nights.'

'I can see why Bruno likes you.'

'Filip, you'll make me blush. I'm afraid I'm a cantankerous old woman most of the time. I could learn some of your son's patience.'

'Couldn't we all.'

Esther was quiet for a moment, choosing her next words carefully.

'This is not advice, because I do not feel qualified to give any, especially on the subject of parenting. It's more a reflection. I wish I could have sat without judgement, and allowed things to be drawn out, rather than forcing another's hand. It sounds like you're already doing so with Bruno, and bravo. Now you have to trust that when he's ready, he will open up to you. It's the waiting that's so hard – I'm impatient, I demand, I always have. I fail people that way.' *I've failed Bruno already,* she thought. 'I don't think he's in any danger of extremism, in the way you're suggesting, at least. Not that I know much about a dark web, it's all pretty dim to me. But there is something troubling him, I agree with you there. You can't take that burden away from him, however – from anyone, unfortunately. He's discovering who he is.'

'And who he doesn't want to be, I suppose. He's terrified of ending up at the warehouses like his old man.'

'I've only just met you, but I think Bruno could do much worse.'

'I'm not sure, I look back and it makes me feel bad. Dad's family were all travellers, so I grew up with lots of traditions, lots of rules, especially about being a man. I thought I was breaking the mould, but I ended up upholding them.'

'In my experience, travellers don't have the monopoly on doing that.'

'Maybe not.' Filip cocked his head. 'Met my wife when I picked up my cousin after a haircut. I worked very hard when we were dating to prove I wasn't one of *those* guys. Soon as she got pregnant though, I flipped. I told myself it was my protective caveman side. Do you think there's something to that?'

'I can't give you any guidance there, either, I'm afraid. I've never been an expert on men, cave or otherwise.'

They both smiled.

'Mind me asking, why *do* they call you the Spitfire Princess?'

'Ah, that is a good story, a sad one, but the good ones always are in their way. Another time, I promise. You'll have to come back for tea.'

Filip heaved himself off the wheelbarrow.

'Fair enough. Cheeky of me to ask. Let's make a pact, the next time you're having an existential crisis about your own death in the middle of the night, you drop me a text. I mean it. We're in this together.' He stuck out his hand.

'Deal,' Esther said, shaking it again, firmly.

'Two people on the moon is better than one.'

'I couldn't agree more.'

She didn't hear from Bruno all that week or the next. In the intervening time, Esther had scoured a twenty-mile radius around Glasgow using the map on her phone. It was incredible what you could find if you peered closely enough. Using Google Earth, she could stare down at the aerial photography like God, roaming over roof and tree, often giving herself more than a touch of vertigo. With the street view, she could whizz down country roads, overtaking tractors and weekend cyclists. She found a car going the wrong way down a one-way street, what looked like a badger sunbathing by the Ballagan Burn, and an altercation between two men on the footpath in Shettleston. What she could not find, however, was any sign of her far-fetched theory – there seemed to be no legacy of 'the legacy' anywhere Esther searched. That did not stop her though; in fact, it only spurred her on.

What did make her pause was the discomfort in her hip, which grew steadily. By the weekend, Esther was back in the wheelchair, and a day or two after that she was really beginning to struggle.

There was only one thing for it – the bat signal.

Dominic had named it thus, and although Esther hadn't seen any of the films which referenced it, she understood the concept, although she argued 'smoke signal' would have been more apt.

'That's cultural appropriation,' Dominic had countered.

'Appropriation? Of whom?' Esther asked.

'Indigenous Americans.'

'I don't think Americans – Indigenous, Native or otherwise – invented sending messages with fires. I remember ancient

Chinese soldiers would use different coloured smoke to tele-
graph how big an invading army was.'

'Appropriation of Chinese culture then,' he'd answered,
with a wink.

Fetching the slip of paper hidden in the crack beside the
telephone, where the walls joined – Esther knew her daughter
snooped when she was over, even in her phonebook, especially
her phonebook – and taking the phone off its cradle, she dialled
the number using the rotary wheel. It struck her, as she dialled
the last few digits, that this action could be done with one push
of a button on her new 'phone'. No, not even a push was
needed, as there was no button. To stab one's finger in the right
place on a screen, that was all.

The phone to her ear, Esther let it ring twice, and then hung
up. Waiting a beat, she repeated the process to indicate
Dominic should bring weed. One was a request for something
from the shop he worked at, something legal at least. Three was
reserved for an emergency, although Esther had raised concerns
when the idea was hatched.

'If it's an emergency, how will I have time to call you three
times and hang up before the murderer finds me?'

'You'll find a way,' Dominic had replied, unhelpfully.

After the second call, she put down the phone. Now all she
had to do was wait. But even after all her years, waiting was still
the hardest pursuit.

It was almost ten o'clock when Dominic finally showed up.

'The cavalry has arrived,' he said, grinning, with his two
slightly crooked front teeth Esther always found adorable,
holding up the plastic bag with the cannabis inside. They were

not to call it marijuana any more apparently as it was insensitive to Mexican Americans.

'The prodigal son returns, come in, come in. You must be cold. Let's warm us both up, I have a fire going in the great room.'

'Treat all your delivery boys so well?'

'Only the ones I like.'

'You'll get a reputation.'

'I'm sure I already do. Did Mary peek at you through her curtains?'

'I didn't notice. Want me to go back and check?' Dominic pretended to start leaving, waving the bag of weed.

'Come in, you rogue,' Esther insisted, slapping him with the back of her hand as he entered the house. 'How's your brother?' she asked as Dominic wheeled her down the hallway, once they'd shut the door.

'Alright, I think. Don't hear much from him. Fourth baby on the way. All credit to him though, he got out of this place. He's driving trucks near Sheffield.'

'They grow up so fast – it feels like ten minutes ago he was at my door instead of you.'

'Generation after generation selling weed to a distinguished older lady. They should make a documentary about it.'

'No, they shouldn't. And who are you calling *older*? And distinguished, for that matter? You're careful not to mention to anyone I'm a customer, aren't you? Loose lips.'

Dominic laughed. 'Loose what?'

'Lips.'

'That's what I thought you said.'

Esther didn't know what he was finding funny, but it could only be smutty.

'We're in here,' she said, pointing towards an ornate door.

'How come we've not been in this room before?' Dominic

asked, staring up at the stuffed boar's head above the fireplace. Great though the room was, it was swamped by a large table and chairs for ten that took up most of the space. 'This has some serious haunted mansion meets Sherlock Holmes meets Nosferatu vibes.'

'I like to keep some surprises up my sleeve. And less of the vampire comparisons, please.' Dominic parked her by the fire, and pulled out a chair himself, placing the bag of weed, and all his paraphernalia from his pocket, onto the table with a clatter.

'How bad is the pain?' he asked.

'The severest.'

'Have you spoken to your doctor?'

'So he can get me addicted to opiates? No, thank you. Conventional medicine barely works on me anyway. The doctor would only tell my daughter, giving her more ammunition to make me homeless.'

'Don't they have a Hippocratic Oath?'

'Hypocritical, more like. You can't trust anyone once my daughter has had her hooks in them.'

'And what did you do to Bruno?' Dominic was preparing the papers to roll the first joint. They could still call them joints, apparently; that name hadn't yet become problematic.

'What do you mean?' Esther replied, defensively.

'He's limping around, from what I've seen. I wondered if you'd whacked him with your stick.'

'You know I'm a pacifist,' she said, relieved Dominic only meant Bruno's ankle and not her harsh treatment of him.

'All that cloak and dagger stuff you had me do – vetting him, checking to see if Bruno was badmouthing you behind your back, drilling me about his family – it would have been easier if I'd taught you how to use the internet.'

'That would never work, my dear. I don't think your patience, let alone your short-term memory, would allow it.'

Dominic nodded in agreement, as he crumbled tobacco.

Esther didn't particularly like adding it, but they'd be far too strong otherwise.

'You actually did me a favour,' explained Dominic. 'I quite like Bruno now. We're in a gang. *The rebels.*'

'Bruno's about the least rebellious type I've met.'

'I didn't say we were a good gang.'

'I think I might have offended the dear boy.'

'You?' Dominic was mock horrified. 'Never!'

She ignored his sarcasm.

'Do you think Bruno...?' Esther paused, not sure if she should divulge her hunch about him. But she needed to talk to *someone* about it. She missed Bruno, terribly – there was a void in her life now. In some way, Esther wondered if the physical pain she was in was also partly psychosomatic, or at least made worse by her guilt. No, she couldn't gossip about him, even to her trusted confidante.

'...is a serial killer?' replied Dominic blankly.

'Why on earth would you suggest that?'

'It's always the quiet ones.'

'I thought you liked him?'

'I do. Bruno's the type of person who would only murder drunk drivers. Or war criminals. Also, unrelated, but I think he's probably gay.'

'Why so?' asked Esther, surprised he had guessed correctly. She was not making it up then, she thought, relieved.

'It's a vibe thing.' Dominic often spoke about vibes and energy in a similar way to Esther's hippy acquaintances from the sixties. It was back in fashion, or maybe it had never completely gone away. 'I'd feel someone watching me at school,' he continued, 'and I'd realise it was Bruno. He was never looking directly at me, it was always in a reflection when he thought no one could see him. Not in a creepy way. A bit creepy, perhaps. Another reason I thought he was a serial killer, I s'pose.'

Esther decided to come completely clean with Dominic.

'I feel like I may have forced Bruno out of the closet, and he hasn't come back to give me a lesson since. Would you keep an eye on him, report back anything you see?'

Dominic moved on to crumbling the cannabis into the tobacco.

'Yeah, sure. He was bullied at school, you know? The townies were relentless, but they really picked on Bruno. He didn't do anything to make him a target like some of the others either – he wasn't nerdy, or spotty, or short or too tall, or any of the reasons they'd find to torment you. It's almost as if there was nothing, like Bruno wanted to be invisible, but that was the thing that attracted them. Him being gay makes a lot of sense.' He picked up the unrolled joint, licked the edge and rolled it expertly. 'One,' he said triumphantly, holding it up for Esther to see his handiwork.

'My daughter is talking about estate agents again, this time for "insurance purposes". The worst is how it offends my intelligence – if you want to sell my house from under me and plonk me in a nursing home, at least come up with a better excuse.'

'A nursing home sounds great. Get fed all day, no sodding work. I'd take one any day. Hook me up.'

'You'll think differently when you're older.'

'And maybe...' Dominic was lining up the papers for a second joint. 'Maybe it would be good for you to have a little bit more care. You're looking – how do I put this nicely? – emaciated.'

'You charmer.'

'Esther, you're one of my favourite clients. And people. I don't like the idea of coming over one night to find you... not exactly fighting fit. Much less lively.'

'I can't promise I won't eventually die, I'm afraid. I can leave a door ajar just before I do, if you like, so the animals eat me up. I'm no one's responsibility then.'

'It's only the police will ask questions if a young, handsome man with a pocketful of illegal substances happens upon your corpse.'

'You are dreadful. It's not me we should be worried about anyway.'

'Who then?'

'Bruno. I can't figure him out.'

'What a surprise, your new favourite, *Bruno*. What does he have that I don't?'

'Those doleful eyes, for one.'

'I get it. You want to mother him.'

'Definitely not, but I want to make sure he doesn't self-immolate.' She considered briefly telling Dominic about her conversation with Bruno's father, but decided against it. 'Do you think he's in with a bad crowd... online?'

'Doesn't strike me as the type.'

'Do you think he's suicidal then?'

Dominic considered this, his eyes darting to the ceiling as he did so.

'Possibly.'

'That's not very reassuring.'

'I know his dad's unwell, but there's always been a cloud over Bruno.'

Picking up one of the rolled joints, he lit it, took a puff and then passed it over to Esther.

'It's not too strong?' she asked warily.

'It's just perfect – wait and see.'

He was absolutely right about that: after one puff, the aches and pains, both literal and mental, seemed to begin to melt away with the heat of the fire.

'You know,' Esther said, staring at the flames, 'I wonder if I've made the most of my life.' Dominic had gone back to his rolling but was listening keenly, she could tell. The joint smoked away between Esther's fingers. 'I loved someone, very much, but it all fell apart. I had to live with the consequences, the ostracism. It didn't matter to anyone else how much I lost. To have loved and lost is rich horse manure. It's infinitely better to be none the wiser.' She took another drag. 'All those ripples. Wider and wider.' She circled with her hand. 'I wish I could have spoken to him before he died. It's too late now, even with all this technology. You can't search a memory. You can never say sorry. You can't even delete the pain...'

'Whoa, little lady, don't drop the joint. This whole room is kindling.'

'You've never asked me about it, the scandal.'

'Not my place,' replied Dominic, dispassionately.

'Did your brother ever tell you anything about me?'

'Only that you were kind, beneath it all.'

'And what do they say about me in the village?' Esther took another long drag.

'Where would you like to start? That you murdered your husband, and he's buried in the garden. That you were part of the Symbionese Liberation Army. You're actually a ghost, haunting this place.'

'I feel like a ghost sometimes,' she replied, her eyelids drooping.

'Looks like it's bedtime for you.'

'Leave me here tonight. I want to sleep in front of the fire.'

'You're the boss.'

The last thing Esther thought of before her delicious annihilation was a Spitfire flying over a crimson sky.

When she heard the banging on the front door the next morning, Esther's first thought was the shopping delivery her daughter had organised. Panicked, she made a start. One had to be quick to respond, otherwise the drivers gave up waiting, abandoning the heavy bags on the doorstep, and Esther would have to ask her poor long-suffering neighbour Mary to come up the hill and carry them into the kitchen for her.

'I'm coming!' she yelled, wheeling herself out of the great room, and into the hallway. Her joints were stiff, and her head was murky from the cannabis – her mouth tasted like an ashtray too. Esther had nodded off in her chair, but later she moved to the rug by the fire and back again, as the aches and pains drove her, restless moments blinking into her memory in fits and starts.

When she opened the door, however, it was not a shopping delivery person at all, but Bruno.

'Dear heart!' Esther cried, in surprise and joy. 'You came back! How's your poor ankle doing?'

'How did you know about my ankle?' he asked, brow furrowed.

'News gets around,' she replied, brushing off his question, realising her mistake. 'Please – come in, come in.' She ushered him inside before he could escape again. 'Isn't it freezing today? Where is the promise of summer, I ask? Let's head to the great room, there's still the remnants of a fire.'

'I can't stay long,' replied Bruno, not able to meet her gaze.

'Stay as long as you need to, my dear – it's just such a pleasure to see you.'

When they entered the room, Esther was painfully aware that it still smelt of smoke, and not the charming smell of woodsmoke either, but the heavy, noxious combination of tobacco and weed. The room was warm though, or at least warmer than the rest of the house.

Bruno wheeled Esther next to the fireplace, just as Dominic had the previous evening, before sitting in the same seat as he'd chosen too. It was only then that Esther remembered the rolled joints, which were on the table just behind Bruno. Had he noticed them?

'Tell me, how are you, my dear? It's so good to see you!'

'Not great,' replied Bruno, his eyes still on the floor.

'You're angry, I can tell – and you have every right to be. I'm a villain, I should never have been so blunt with you. I would like to offer you my sincerest apology. Can you ever forgive me?'

'I'm still deciding who I am,' he said, carefully, deliberately, as if his words were walking a fine tightrope, 'and who I want to be.'

'Of course, it's your prerogative. I had no right, none! I'm simply thrilled you've come back to me.'

Bruno's voice dropped even lower, as if he was afraid someone might be listening. 'Have you spoken to anyone? About me... about those things you said?'

'No, of course not,' Esther said earnestly, before remembering she had, to Dominic only last night. Filip flashed into her mind then too, but she hadn't discussed Bruno's sexuality with him at least. 'Your secret's safe,' she promised, and she meant it – Dominic might be many things, but he was honest, and she trusted him not to tell anyone her business.

'It's not my secret.' Bruno glowered at her feet. 'I told you, I don't know yet, about anything.'

'And you should take all the time you need,' she said calmingly. 'I've so missed you, missed our lessons.'

'That's the other thing I wanted to talk about.'

'Anything, please.'

Bruno took a deep breath.

'The advert for lessons said they were paid. I've lost the paper ad, I think it went through the wash in my trouser pocket, but I remember it clearly.'

Shaking her head, Esther tried to comprehend.

'Didn't we organise all that in the beginning? Aren't I paying you at the end of the month, or the beginning of the next? I can't remember now...' the fogginess of last night's cannabis wasn't helping matters either. 'We agreed, surely?'

'No, we never did.'

'Dear heart, all this time... You should have pestered me about it!'

'I didn't want to be rude.'

'My dearest boy, rude? You know how I am with rude. I eat it for supper, it only makes me stronger. But I barely know what day it is, let alone if I've settled all my debts. That is an easy problem to solve – but can you promise me something? You'll come back? I miss you, and I miss your lessons, there's still so much for me to learn. The internet is a veritable hydra, and that horrible email from Thackeray's son...' She paused, considering whether she should tell Bruno her crazy hunch about the plot of land. 'Let's just say, I've had a few *ideas*, but I need your help with them. Promise me?'

Before he could answer, Esther's phone, which was on the chair next to Bruno, made a strange vibrating noise.

'It's never done that before,' she exclaimed, looking at it in horror. 'Is it unwell?'

Bruno picked up the phone to pass over to her.

'I think it's a text message,' he said, glancing at the screen.

'Who could be sending me that?'

When she opened the phone, she found a staggering eight text messages waiting for her. Esther's first instinct was to hand the device back to Bruno and have him sort it out, but something made her hesitate. There seemed to be two senders, and she brought up the message from the first one:

What's this? Texting at 4am? Lovely to see you last night, old girl. Will call around for the money. Don't worry, I'll keep an eye on Bruno.

There was no name attached, but that couldn't be anyone but Dominic. Why was he text messaging her, he never had before – did he even have her mobile telephone number? As a matter of fact, did Esther even know her number to give? She then noticed an earlier message in the same thread, which read:

Thankyou you wonderful rogue

It seemed to have been sent at 3.56 a.m., obviously by her. Esther was the culprit! Recollections started filtering back – she'd woken in some pain, smoked another one of the joints, but instead of sending her back to sleep peacefully, the nicotine perked her up, and – under the influence – she must have begun toying with her phone. Dominic's number was on the slip of paper by the telephone in the hall, though. It was then that Esther noticed, amongst the detritus on the table, what looked very much like that slip.

'Who's it from? Is everything okay?' Bruno asked, concern in those dark eyes of his.

'Yes, it's Mary, my neighbour, checking to see if I want anything bought.'

'You're sending text messages now?' He seemed impressed.

'Seems so,' replied Esther, trying to bring up the next message.

Having one of those nights we discussed, she'd written at 3 a.m.

It's almost a full moon, that's why, a response had come five minutes later.

You're awake too?

Can't sleep. Think Bruno is up as well.

Filip! The back and forth had gone on for an hour before they'd finally signed off.

Guiltily, she turned off the phone – although she was never exactly sure if it was off completely, often it would illuminate randomly, and seemed to be constantly making strange sounds – and stuffed it between her knees.

'So, you'll do it, you'll take up your lessons again?' she asked. 'Now I've promised to reimburse you for your time?'

Bruno's face tightened, and Esther prepared herself for rejection.

'Sure,' he said, with a self-effacing shrug. 'Shall we start again tomorrow?'

Even though he did return the next day, it was clear Bruno had changed. Not only was he more guarded than before, but he was simultaneously jumpier – as if she might spring another terrible surprise on him – and considerably sullener. Avoiding the trap of trying to make him change, Esther let him be this time. She was glad Bruno was coming over at all. After a week, though, her patience – what little there was – began to wane. She also had the distinct impression, which perhaps was unfair, that Bruno was only there to make sure she didn't say anything about his 'secret' to anyone. He was keeping an eye on her.

Surprisingly, Esther's quest to find information regarding the whereabouts of 'the legacy' became their new bright spot. At first, she was wary of telling Bruno too much about her wild hunch, but it soon became apparent he couldn't properly help unless she did.

'You've been searching Google Earth for the remnants of a house that was abandoned over forty years ago?' he'd asked, bewildered. 'How do you know the foundations are still there?'

'I remember there was an issue with the truck, getting the sandstone up the hill. They almost had to call the whole thing off, until Thackeray kicked up enough fuss. If he didn't sell the land, the stones are likely to be there, as they'd be too cumbersome to get down again.'

'That's what we have to go on, a pile of rocks on a hill?'

Esther took a deep breath. She didn't enjoy her hairbrained idea being debunked.

'The foundations were set; we drank champagne on their completion, so they'd be *organised* rocks on a hill.'

'Even if they're still there, wouldn't trees and plants have grown over them?'

She had considered this.

'Possibly, but it's infamously windy around those hills, the Scottish gales can bend, break and uproot even the sturdiest of foliage.'

'Doesn't sound the best place to build a house.' *The views though!* Esther wanted to cry, but she'd never seen them, how could she know for sure? 'And he never told you exactly where it was?' Bruno asked, as if reading her mind.

'The surprise was part of the fun...' Until it wasn't. Esther felt the syrupy sickliness of regret. 'This is exactly why I was afraid to tell you,' she snapped. 'Metal detectorists search farmlands from above and find buried treasure, I read about it on the Google, why not the vestiges of a building?' Esther sat taller in her chair. 'If you're not going to help...'

'I didn't say that,' Bruno replied, quickly. 'I'm sure we can find it...'

'If it exists at all, you mean?'

He nodded at her gravely. 'It's going to be much harder, if it doesn't.'

Esther snorted at this. She could never be sure if the boy was being earnest or sardonic. Either way, she approved.

'What did... *he*... do?' Bruno asked, choosing his words carefully. 'It might give us some clues,' he clarified.

'Thackeray owned an aeronautical company.'

'Building Spitfires?' he replied quickly.

Esther kept her voice steady.

'No, they stopped making those after the war. He made high performance parts, and not only for planes, other vehicles...' Weapons too, she'd discovered, to her chagrin, when it all came out.

'So would *Thackeray*,' Bruno spoke his name cautiously, as if it might contain a lit fuse, 'have wanted a strip to land a plane on?'

'That's a very good question, I'd never considered it.' The boy beamed. He looked so handsome when he smiled, which was far too infrequently – there was even a dimple in his left cheek. 'Thackeray was interested in local politics too, if that helps, he was planning to run for mayor of Glasgow in 1974, which was a year after he began the house.' She skipped over the reason why ultimately, he never ran. 'It's one of the traits I liked best about him, his connection with the community. Thackeray had grown up very poor, and was always looking for ways to give back. People sometimes thought us an odd couple – he was very much a product of his time, a captain of industry with all the privilege that entailed, but he had a gentle heart...' A lump had formed in Esther's throat.

'It's important we find the foundations then,' said Bruno with determination.

'Thank you,' Esther replied, discreetly wiping her eyes.

As hoped, Bruno came up trumps almost immediately – a Scottish website that allowed them to search the Land Register to find property owners – only if you had the property postcode or title, and of course they had neither. Crucially, the site also permitted you to search on a map, giving information on the land wherever a pin was dropped. This was quickly added to Esther's evening routine, as she juggled both Google Earth and Scotland's Land Information Service into the wee hours each night. She was beginning to know the surrounding Glaswegian countryside like the back of her hand, every line, every spot, every craggy fold.

'We could email Edward again?' Bruno had suggested, for maybe the eighth time.

'And ask him what? There's no coming back from his scorched earth response.'

'What if we asked another relative?'

'It could get us into even deeper trouble. No,' Esther replied stoically, 'we have to use our own tools, limited though they are.'

Deeper Google searches was a logical next step, although she still felt extremely wary of what she might find there. But after a few more nights of fruitless scrolling on Google Earth, developing a strange ache in her scrolling finger, Esther decided it was time. Surprisingly, she found the process cathartic, sitting beside Bruno as they worked together on searches – 'Thackeray James property Glasgow', 'Thackeray James unfinished house' – the conjuring of old demons.

'I don't want anything to do with newspapers,' she warned.

'No problem, I'll make "newspaper" a negative search word, that way they won't show up.'

Bruno also came up with clever suggestions she would never have thought of, such as changing the date range of searches to coincide with the time David James had sent his email telling of his father's death – while acting with a patient solemnity, which made Esther love Bruno even more.

At one point he suggested an image search.

'Will I see him?' she asked, hesitantly. 'Thackeray, I mean?'

'Maybe,' came Bruno's response. 'Probably,' he added, after thinking on it some more.

'All right, let's try,' replied Esther, preparing herself.

The images, when they appeared, took her breath away. Bruno had brought in his laptop – it made everything easier to see, but how you used it was a complete mystery to Esther – and now there was a small grid of pictures containing Thackeray, glaring steely-eyed back at her through the screen. How long had it been since she'd seen him? She'd burned all his photos, back in her anger, many moons ago. She spotted an image of herself too, used by the tabloids, her head down, walking away from the courthouse, dressed head to toe in black – as if she was in mourning for her life. *The Spitfire Scandal.* How young she seemed at thirty-seven, how beautiful. The press had made her out to be a wizened harpy, but she was a mere child.

'Can you create an image search for Thackeray and me both?' she asked quietly, and of course Bruno could.

One of the squares caught her eye instantly.

'That one,' she said pointing, accidentally touching the screen, even though Bruno had reminded her several times she should not. He clicked on the square and Esther gasped, covering her mouth.

'I remember this,' she muttered into her palm. They were having a picnic, beside a river. It had rained, a sun shower. She'd lost a shoe running for shelter, and ended up with a sodden foot, which they'd all found hilarious. 'My friend Genevieve must have taken this, but I don't think I've seen it before. Can you make it bigger?' Esther asked, transfixed by the image.

Bruno did so, clicking. Thackeray looked so handsome with his square Cary Grant jaw, his linen suit, and brown Oxfords. She'd forgotten how much thinner he was earlier on, although she'd preferred him with more meat on his bones. 'How can we find where this photo is, physically, I mean? Where does it reside?'

'It's uploaded onto an old Flickr account. People don't really use those any more. Here's a description – *scans of photos from the boot sale. Written on the back, Esther and Thackeray, April 1972.*'

'Are there others in the series?' asked Esther, taking away her hand again.

They scrolled through the related images.

'Oh, here's another of you two...' Bruno began, faltering. It wasn't Esther standing beside Thackeray after all, but another smart woman, this one darker-haired. The couple were dressed

in black tie, smiling stiffly at the camera, and the text read
'Royal Edinburgh Military Tattoo Gala, 1971'.

'His wife,' Esther whispered, almost to herself.

'His ex-wife?' asked Bruno.

In one fell motion, she snapped the laptop closed, almost
trapping Bruno's fingers inside.

'I think that's enough for today. But, dear boy,' she locked
eyes with him, 'could you make a copy of the photo, of Thackeray and me?'

'I guess so. I can print it out somehow.'

'Thank you, dear heart,' and then again, almost as if Bruno
wasn't there: 'Can one paper over the cracks with better memories?' She looked at him again. 'And you'll take your machine,
and scrub it down?'

'Of course,' he promised.

'I know I can always trust you,' she added, tenderly.

It wasn't completely accurate to say Esther let Bruno be without
any interference – she wanted him to know he would be
accepted whatever his persuasion. She tried casually leaving
books around by E.M. Forster, James Baldwin, Armistead
Maupin and Oscar Wilde, and when those were ignored, she
upped the ante with Haring, Hockney, and finally,
Mapplethorpe. Still nothing. Esther even considered leaving
the Mapplethorpe on an open page, but she didn't want to scare
the boy.

The matter had been very confusing whenever it came up
with Dominic. Everything was to be accepted, and the correct
terms to be used, naturally – words held power after all – and
yet 'labels' were not appreciated, which seemed counterin-
tuitive.

'How do you know what you want, and if they have it?' she
asked, rather crudely one night, when Dominic was dropping

by more of his wares. She was smoking almost every evening now, partly to help with the pain, but also for the way it made her brain wander, allowing her to access memories without the hot pang of remorse. She was anesthetising her past; the only catch, apart from the dreadful smell the next day, being that it left her brain more muddled and forgetful than usual. And grumpier.

'Defining yourself is powerful,' Dominic replied. 'Labels are limiting.' Esther didn't know if he was teasing her with his answer or not.

'How do you define *yourself?*'

'Well... All of the above,' he'd said with a rakish wink, the tip of his tongue expertly tracing its way down the rolling paper.

'In my time, there weren't any labels to begin with. You were categorised by default. We had to fight very hard to be seen any other way. Did I tell you I was supposed to be part of the protest at the 1970 Miss World Pageant at the Royal Albert Hall, but I was late because my bag of flour split on the bus?'

'Yes, but tell me again,' said Dominic, 'I like that you're delving more into the archives.'

'I always did,' Esther replied, slightly stumped by his response. 'I bored you with it, I must have?'

'I don't get bored,' he replied, lighting the joint. 'But you seem to be getting more from the telling.'

'Perhaps,' she said, taking the joint offered her.

The night-time texts with Filip continued too. There was nothing clandestine about them, Bruno's mother didn't have to be worried, but it was fascinating to communicate by short, instant sentences. It felt like you were sending your words directly into the other's mind. They mostly wrote about their experience of being awake when everyone else was asleep, their worries for the next day, their aches and pains, the weather

outlook, interesting words they'd stumbled upon, small inter-
changes that nonetheless felt weighty in the darkness of night.
But then, didn't everything? She even asked Filip if he had any
idea how to find a lost piece of land – all help was welcome,
after all. Esther considered many times mentioning Bruno's
confusion, but as Dominic might have said, he hadn't yet
defined himself, and who was she to impose her own label on
him? Importantly too, she'd only just got Bruno back. She didn't
want to risk losing him a second time.

Two weeks after Bruno's return, Esther's daughter made an
unannounced visit.

'I called first,' Jane said breezily, by way of explanation,
dangling her set of keys. 'You don't always hear the phone,
Mother.'

'Leave an answerphone message, then.'

'You never check them.'

'Because they're all from you,' scoffed Esther.

Rolling her eyes, Jane fetched a mug, sat down at the
kitchen table, and poured herself a cup of tea from the pot.
Esther tried to remember if there was anything incriminating in
the house to be stumbled upon – the joints were tucked away,
fortunately; she'd learnt that lesson.

'In the wheelchair again?' asked Jane, as she poured.

It was cloudy outside, making the undergrowth beneath the
trees darker, more mysterious, and casting a dull, almost
metallic light through the windows.

'Today, guilty as charged, but yesterday I was doing hand-
springs around the garden.'

'We could get another physiotherapist to come in?'

'And do what? *Stretching exercises*?'

'They might help...?'

'My muscles are too set in their ways, what's left of them.

Which reminds me, have I ever told you about the time I almost drowned in the Dead Sea? Quite a feat, considering how buoyant the water is, but I was happily swimming along when my leg spasmed; "stoker's cramp" they used to call it, a lack of salt, ironically. The most painful experience of my life, short of childbirth. Of course, I couldn't *sink*, but I was very far from shore, and it was an effort to stay upright, especially as I grew tired. I must have swallowed at least a pint of lake water in my panic, which was exactly the sodium my muscles needed, and eventually I made it back in time for drinks.'

'What an adventure, Mother.'

Esther's expression darkened even more than the undergrowth.

'Jane, save your sarcasm for your clients.'

'I mean it. You never talk about... the past. It's usually locked away in the vault. That local boy is loosening you up.'

'Yes, well – loose lips sink ships,' Esther spluttered, nonsensically.

'Not if they're on the Dead Sea, evidently.'

Jane took a wry sip from her mug.

'You're making fun.'

'I'm deadly serious. I like this side of you.'

And indeed, Jane looked hungry, cradling her mug in her palms, eyes round and hopeful.

'What do you want to know?' asked Esther carefully, as if she was being led somewhere against her better judgement.

'Everything. Your travels. About Dad. My grandparents.'

'I've told you all that, surely?'

'You might have, in snippets, in passing, over the years, but nothing cohesive, nothing prompted by me.' Esther considered the validity of this. 'I didn't want to push,' Jane added.

'What's changed now?'

'You seem more receptive. Your phone lessons, the internet... I've never seen you learn something new before. You've always been the expert on life.'

Esther guffawed.

'Far from it,' she scoffed again, before going silent. Outside, it darkened even more, signalling rain, and sure enough, a few drops began to streak the glass. 'What do you remember of Thackeray?' Esther asked, not noticing the change in weather.

'I liked him,' Jane replied.

'You did?'

'Why is that such a surprise?'

'You were so hard to read as a child. So guarded.'

Jane gave Esther a look, eyebrow ever-so-slightly arched that signalled: *and yes, why was that?*

'I only met him a couple of times, if you remember,' Jane explained, 'but Thackeray was always kind. He didn't talk down to me, which I appreciated. I was excited.'

'Excited?'

'You seemed happy. It was by far the longest you'd stayed in the UK, even if you were jetting back and forth to Glasgow. Staying at the house in London was the longest time I'd spent with *you*.' The rain ceased again in the garden as quickly as it had begun. 'How did you meet him?'

'That is a story,' replied Esther, smiling at the memory. 'I was supposed to join the protest at the Royal Albert Hall against the Miss World Pageant in 1970.'

'Really? That's famous, Mother! You were there?'

'Except I wasn't. I was already late, and on the way, my bag of flour sprung a leak on the bus and started haemorrhaging everywhere, and I missed my stop. By the time I arrived, it was all over – police were outside, a bomb squad, the whole area cordoned off. I couldn't see anyone I knew from the Women's Lib, and I was afraid I might get arrested holding my sad sack of flour, so I hightailed it. Thackeray was drinking a pint outside a nearby pub, and I was so lost in my thoughts, wondering how my friends had fared, feeling guilty for having abandoned them, that I walked right smack into him, releasing a huge plume of flour all over his expensive suit.'

'Oh, Mother!' Jane laughed.

'It wasn't funny, there were police cars racing by, sirens everywhere. I was terrified they would think it was another attack. Thackeray calmed me down, getting me a whisky for my nerves. He found the whole thing hilarious; he'd been inside the Royal Albert Hall watching when it happened, felt Bob Hope deserved everything he got for not being particularly funny as a host.'

'I can't believe you've never told me about this before. The two of you covered in flour, it's so romantic...'

'Perhaps. Or maybe it's the moment I sold out.'

Jane rolled her eyes gently at this. 'They don't make men like Thackeray any more.'

'No, they don't,' agreed Esther, staring into her cup. 'For good reason.'

'It must have been devastating when...'

'That's quite enough reminiscing for one day,' Esther said, tapping the table with her fingers, the vault slamming shut. 'Have you spoken to Brian at all?'

'No,' Jane sniffed. 'He has a girlfriend now. I saw it on Facebook. Oh, Facebook is...'

'I know what Facebook is,' interrupted Esther. 'It's socialled media.' Jane took a discreet sip of her tea. 'Do you imagine I had anything to do with it? Your divorce? Not having children?'

'What, Mother? – no. Whatever's made you say that?'

'I wasn't exactly the best role model for marriage and domesticity.'

'Maybe not...' Jane conceded, 'but Brian and I broke up for many reasons. And I never wanted kids, it was made simpler by the fact you never expressed an interest in grandchildren. If anything, having you as my mother made those decisions easier.'

'I wonder if I would have rather liked grandchildren,' Esther said, with rare wistfulness. 'Do you think about your father?'

'Sometimes. Mostly on my birthday.'

Esther was quiet for a moment. 'William was another one. Seemed modern, supportive even – an academic, a thinker, not exactly radical, but open to ideas. Until I became pregnant, of course, and then I was marched down the aisle in an apron. At least Thackeray didn't hide who he was.'

'Except he did, quite spectacularly...'

'I don't want to talk about that,' murmured Esther.

'Fine.' Jane swirled the tea in her cup. 'I had fantasies he'd become my father, that we'd be a happy family together, the three of us. I was crushed when it all came out.'

'Perhaps that was my fault too.'

'How, Mother? You didn't know.'

'Thackeray asked that I keep our relationship secret.'

'Exactly, and why was that?'

'I presumed it was because he didn't like people knowing his business. It was mutually beneficial; I didn't want my lot of activists and anarchists knowing I was in love with...'

'...Someone like him.'

'He represented everything we were fighting against. And yet, I loved Thackeray, still do. That's my shame to bear – to go through it all and learn *nothing*.'

There were tears in Esther's eyes suddenly, but she blinked them away defiantly.

'Oh, Mother.'

'Don't "Oh, Mother" me. It's too late now, everything is. All I have is this house and my garden. If it's taken away from me, what was it for? The pain, the heartache, the sacrifice?'

'Maybe you can finally let it all go?'

'I don't want to. Can't you see?'

Jane was uncharacteristically silent. The rain returned, a patter on the kitchen windows.

'I should go before it buckets down.'

'You only just arrived,' Esther said, feeling strangely put out.

'What did Thackeray used to call you?' Jane asked as she rose and took her used cup to the sink.

'His spitfire...?'

'No, that wasn't it. Something in Gaelic?'

'Oh yes! What was it? How could I forget that? It had completely left my brain until you mentioned it just now.'

Esther was still pondering this as she waved her daughter goodbye, the car reversing down the driveway, when her phone did its angry vibrating.

It was Dominic:

Sorry to be the bearer of bad news, but your daughter's car was outside Bruno's house about half an hour ago when I walked past. Coincidence?

Esther slammed the phone down so hard on the wheelchair armrest, it was a miracle she didn't break it.

THREE

BRUNO (16 JUNE)

He found the front door ajar, which was the first sign something might be off.

'Hello?' he called, 'Esther?'

'In here,' came her voice.

Bruno pushed the door open after wiping his wet feet on the rug, and stepped into the hallway.

'Is everything okay?'

'The sitting room,' she called, primly it seemed.

Today he'd brought the photo Esther had asked him to print – he'd uploaded it to a virtual printing website, and they'd mailed it to his address – he was excited for her to see the result. Bruno had also brought the invoice with his suggested hourly fee of £10, and reminded himself to show it to her, and broach the subject of payment for the lessons again. He'd not pushed – they had a verbal agreement – but there was only so long he could wait, especially when he kept tallying up a range of potential sums and mentally adding it to his savings.

'It's dark in here,' Bruno said as he joined Esther in the sitting room. 'Do you want me to turn on another lamp?'

'No. Sit, if you would.' Her expression was one of intense concentration.

Bruno did as he was told, seating himself on the sofa – he could feel the wonky springs under his buttocks. Esther was sitting very upright in her armchair – her posture reminded him of a court judge.

'How are we today?' she asked, the royal 'we'.

'Good, I've had some ideas about how we can—'

'Bruno, have you met my daughter?'

He was momentarily speechless.

'I... er...'

'It's a simple question. Have you and my daughter met?' She was enunciating very clearly, as if Bruno was hard of hearing.

'Eh... yes.'

She smiled, but only with her mouth. Her eyes stayed exactly as they were. They had a glazed look about them.

'On how many occasions?'

'Twice.'

'And why did you never tell me you'd met Jane?'

Bruno wished he was more capable of lying, but when he was keeping such a deep secret about himself hidden, the truth almost rose out of him by itself, like a counterweight. On some level, Bruno always felt that the more trusted he was in everyday life, the better protected the question of his sexuality would always be.

'I thought you wouldn't like it,' he replied, honestly.

'Now, that is interesting. You thought I wouldn't like it and yet it seems you did it anyway. *Twice.*'

'Jane came to my house...'

'Yes, I know. What did she ask of you?'

'She cares about you. Jane only wants to make sure...'

'*What did she ask?*' Esther's voice boomed, startling Bruno.

'If I'd keep an eye on you.'

'To snoop, you mean? To come into my house, gain my trust, and *spy*!'

'No! Esther...'

'Perhaps she put you up for the job in the first place? Are you a mole, as well as a devious spy?' She didn't wait for him to answer. 'I trusted you.' Picking up her phone, she brandished it at him. 'With all my private information. You're worse than a scammer. You ingratiated yourself fraudulently, and the whole time you were reporting back to my daughter to give her the ammunition to throw me out of my *home*! How could you?'

'It's not like that at all! I didn't tell Jane anything! I wouldn't! Nothing personal, at least. Nothing you didn't want me to. It was just to get her off my back. She wanted to make sure you were okay, and weren't in pain, and were taking your medicine – but I was never on her side, I was on yours.'

'So that's better, is it? Playing us both? Is she paying you? Jane does that, you know. A gardener once. A nurse. To keep an "eye on me". Did she offer you money?' He was silent. 'I asked you a question, Bruno.'

'I haven't taken a penny from your daughter because I haven't *told* her anything...'

'Don't offend my intelligence.'

'You can call Jane and ask her! You both dangle money in front of me, but I've never received anything from either of you, even though I've been coming here for *weeks* now.'

'What do you mean? We organised payment.'

'Talked about it, but that's all you did. Here in your big fancy home, with your brand-new iPhone, and you tell me to not be nice, and then *you're* not nice, and you... talk about *things* I don't want to! And still I come back and do your bidding each time.'

Esther leant forward, jabbing a finger at him.

'Who is this speaking? Who is *he*?'

'What's that even mean?' Bruno practically yelled. 'I'm me!'

'This version of you with a bit of grit, that's who. I'm interested to learn more about *him*.'

'Stop trying to get into my head. I don't like it at all. You push, and you're mean, and then you act as if it's some kind of *lesson*.'

'It is a lesson. All of it. Don't you see?'

'I didn't ask to be taught by you.'

'Well, I don't want to be taught by a sneak.'

'Stop calling me names!'

'If the shoe fits, Bruno. Now, tell me *everything* you told my daughter.'

He laughed, mirthlessly. 'See, you've changed the subject away from payment already.'

'If it's the money you want, it's money you'll get, my boy. Fetch my cheque book, it's over there on the table by the door. A pen too.'

Bruno sat paralysed. 'I didn't mean... Not right... We can...'

'Fetch it!' she barked, and Bruno jumped up, locating the cheque book and the pen and giving them to Esther, who snatched them both from his hands. 'I pay my debts! I always have. Heavy they were too, but I shouldered the burden. Yours is nothing in comparison. A blip. A footnote. In a few days, I won't even remember how absolutely you broke my trust.' She flicked through the chequebook frantically. 'How would *you* feel if people were conspiring to evict you from *your* house, huh?'

'Jane just wants you to be safe, we all do. You're here all by yourself, and it's getting harder and harder for you to do even the most basic things...'

'This is *my* home! I can do whatever I want. How. Much. For. Services. Rendered?' Esther snarled, over enunciating each word.

'I... I don't know....'

'I'll write this out for five hundred pounds, and we can draw a line under it.'

'*Five hundred pounds?*'

'You want seven fifty? A thousand? Perhaps I should give you a blank cheque and you can take what you want? And to think – I told you about Thackeray, let you wheedle it all out of me. You must have been telling everyone in the village and laughing behind my back.'

'I never did!' Bruno said, loudly. 'I wouldn't even search for him, because you asked me not to. Not *once.*'

'Yet the whole time you were secretly on my daughter's books... I honestly don't know what to believe, Bruno.' He leapt off the sofa and headed to the door. 'Don't you leave!' Esther screamed at him. 'I'm not giving you the satisfaction of saying the old miser on the hill didn't pay. Take this.' She ripped the cheque from the book and waved it at him, arm outstretched. '*Take it!*'

Grimly, Bruno stalked back over to her, took the cheque from her hand, and made again to leave. In the doorway, he paused.

'Thank you.' He indicated the cheque. 'This is going to help fix me.'

'What on earth are you talking about, fix what?'

'It's a place called Camp Change, and they have keynote speakers, and experts and group seminars.'

'Dear heart, a *camp?*'

'They teach you how to deal with feelings and control urges and thoughts... They can help readjust you.'

'What? This sounds like brainwashing, dear child. You can't change the fundamentals of who you are. You're being naïve.'

'I don't even *know* who I am. But I want to be *normal.* Someone who can have a family, and a life, and not hide all the time.'

'What did you say this place is called?' Esther picked up her phone, beside her. 'Camp what?' She started typing.

'No...' Bruno came towards her. 'I didn't... Don't...'

'Camp *Change*, I think you said. Dreadful name. Ah yes, here it is.' Bruno stood horrified. 'Dear heart, what am I looking at? All these smiling, vacant faces... This has a very sinister feel to it.'

'It's none of your business, please stop.'

'*You* can snoop and spy into *my* personal life, but when the tables are turned?' In a burst of fury, Bruno tried to snatch the phone from Esther, but she was too fast for him.

'Give it to me,' he yelled, his hand making contact with hers, the iPhone flying from her grasp and crashing to the floor with a crunching thud.

'Look what you've done!' Esther cried, as Bruno bent down to pick it back up. 'Give it to me,' she demanded, snatching it from him.

'Careful,' he warned, 'the screen is broken...'

Esther cried out in pain.

'It cut me!' she exclaimed.

'I told you, it's smashed!'

Esther inspected her hand. It was only a tiny cut, no more than a scratch really, but as they watched, it began to run with blood.

'Child, it's nothing. A comfort in some ways to see my blood's not as black as my heart.'

'Can I get you a plaster or a bandage?'

'Pass me that scarf over there, I'll wrap it around my hand.'

'I want to pay for the damage, it's my fault. Please take back the cheque.'

'Don't be ridiculous.' Bruno tried to give Esther the slip of paper, but she only batted it away with her bloodied hand. 'Take it, the money was hard-earned putting up with *me*. Now get me the scarf.' He scrambled to retrieve it obediently, and then she wrapped it around her hand. 'I've had quite enough excitement for one day.'

'Are you sure...? I'm...'

'It is time for you to leave.'

Folding the now slightly bloodied cheque, Bruno did exactly as she asked.

FOUR

ESTHER

She felt instant and catastrophic regret. Leaning heavily on her stick, Esther limped around the house, her hand still wrapped in the blood-stained scarf, feeling despair pour in, hot and suffocating. Bruno had betrayed her, yes – but was the punishment worse than the crime? Esther tried calling her neighbour Mary, but she was out. Dominic didn't pick up either. In a moment of weakness, Esther even considered ringing her daughter.

She had to apologise to Bruno, she must! There was something else too – she would tell him about the terrible place, Alberton Lodge. Even thinking the name made a shiver run down her spine.

After finally putting a plaster on the cut, which had mostly stopped bleeding – she hobbled to her address book, taking note of Bruno's street name and number, before fetching her keys from their hook. Esther couldn't remember the last time she'd had occasion to use them; it felt strange locking the front door from *outside*.

As she made her way around the house, Esther's eyes flittered nervously towards the downhill gradient of the driveway. *I've done it before*, she told herself, *I can do it again*. Of course, those other times were years ago, when she was in better health, before her stroke, and she had to practise many times to gain her confidence, even then.

Using the appropriate key, she unlocked the small external door to what would be the garage, if she had a car. Instead, it was a dumping ground for anything that Esther didn't feel like having in the house but couldn't quite part with – furniture to fix mostly, and books she was planning to rehome. Under a blanket, the 'popemobile' lay waiting, exactly as she'd left it. Jane had bought her the folding mobility scooter in the hope that it might make her more, well, mobile, but Esther had always felt awkward and exposed on the machine, eventually phasing it out, using her failing health as the final excuse. The big question was – would it still work?

If it didn't, at least she could say, with a clear conscience, that she'd tried everything. Esther shook her head, amazed at her own gall. Clear conscience, indeed. If the scooter didn't work, she'd shimmy down the slope on her bare behind if needs be. Fortunately, the scooter sprang to life when prompted, and once she'd remembered how to open the garage door – mercifully, that still worked too – she very carefully drove it to the edge of the sloping driveway. Esther practised squeezed the brakes, trying to jog her muscle memory. What if mice had chewed the wires, and they failed? In that case, she would get to Bruno's house considerably faster. The only alternative was to sit here and fester. *Tally ho* then, she thought, starting to inch herself down the decline, brakes clamped almost completely. With the beginning of momentum, there were no more decisions to make as gravity took hold. It was almost enjoyable, until Esther released the brakes slightly too much and she careened to the right, almost crashing into the shrubbery, regaining control just in time, and slowly, carefully making her way to the street below.

Any jubilation she felt was replaced with a sense of foreboding. Her driveway joined onto a small cul-de-sac, Mary's house the closest – and Esther felt invisible eyes staring at her from all other nearby windows. She was Frankenstein's monster, revealed. How long before the local children came to taunt her? Esther chided her own narcissism. *Nobody cares*, she told herself sternly, but still, as she trundled along the footpath, she recalled the feeling of being watched after her photograph was in all the papers – it wasn't fantasy then. Esther had loathed it, the twitch of recognition in someone's eyes, the spasm when they made the connection. One woman at the Post Office – Esther even remembered what she was posting, a Cranks recipe book to her vegetarian friend Marla in Paris, who was struggling with French carnivorousness – had exclaimed, 'You should be ashamed!'

'Should I?' Esther had managed in response, but she was so flustered she didn't lick the stamps properly, and perhaps they'd fallen off, because Marla's package never arrived.

'The nerve,' she mumbled to herself as she made her way further into the village towards Bruno's home, the scooter's motor whining. Esther could hear the traffic from the motorway too. Surrounded by a woodland barrier, she was insulated from it normally, but here it was a distant rumble, slightly menacing. Turning into Hedley Street, she spotted two workmen poking around a pothole. Esther considered the best way to pass them – should she cross the road and thereby avoid getting too close? No, that would signal fear. With her head held high, Esther made sure her speed was measured as she passed the workers, both men watching her unashamedly.

'Good morning,' she said, stiffly.

'Morning,' the older worker said, dropping the superfluous 'good'.

'No more rain today, I see.'

'None forecast,' the younger worker replied, rather sweetly.

He had a dimple in his chin. Esther had always had a weakness for a man with dimples.

'Let's hope the media can be trusted,' she sniffed, speeding the scooter up.

When she arrived at Bruno's address, Esther was surprised to see how small the house was. How many sisters did he have, two? Surely not a whole family in this little bungalow? All the homes on the street were the same size, though. Esther noted the windows appeared extremely well cleaned. The sound of the motorway traffic was a healthy roar now. She wondered what all those fumes must be doing to the lungs of these residents, without their own ancient woodland to screen the toxins.

Driving up to the front door, Esther was confronted with a step, forcing her to disembark from the scooter. She hadn't thought to bring her stick, so holding onto anything she could to steady herself, Esther managed to reach the door, knocking. It was Bruno's mother who answered, it must be – she had the same complexion, the same eyebrows, though much more manicured. She looked at Esther with recognition, she obviously knew who she was. Of course, everyone did. The mad old hen on the hill.

'I'm sorry to arrive unannounced,' Esther started, again the words much too crisp as they left her mouth. 'I wondered if your son was in?'

'Bruno's with his dad. They've gone to the town to pick up some groceries, and Bruno wanted to visit the bank, I think. Is there something I can help you with? I'm Tina, by the way – or you can wait for them? If you come inside, I can make us a cup of tea. I've just popped back from the salon, but...'

'I couldn't possibly impose myself on you. Oh, and by the way, thank you for those scones you sent over, they were delicious.'

Tina's cheeks reddened in almost the identical way Bruno's did whenever he was given a compliment.

'This lot usually make fun of my baking, so that's very kind.'

'They'll miss it one day, believe me. I envy you. A family. A business. A home. I used to think some of those things added up to a life sentence, but you don't know what a life sentence is until you've almost served one.'

Worry flashed across Tina's face.

'Is everything okay with you... and Bruno?'

'I wanted to leave him a message. Tell him... Tell him not to make the same mistake as I did. At one point, I had a choice to be in the fullness of life, or retreat, and I chose the latter. Shame binds us: it's the cartilage to the muscle of action; if it gets too tight, it stops us in our tracks. Tell Bruno I'm sorry. That I was wrong about everything else, but on this, I'm right. One more thing – ask him to search for Alberton Lodge. Will you remember, Alberton Lodge?'

Tina nodded, although she seemed taken aback by this stream of information. Before she could say anything though, Esther turned and made her way unsteadily back to the scooter. Her next worry was how to get back up the driveway; what if the machine didn't have enough oomph? She seemed to recall trouble with that in the past. Esther remembered the two workmen – the younger one with the dimples, that was her mark. She could ask him to give her a push if the motor wasn't quite enough.

Esther still felt uneasy about Bruno. Maybe she should have told his mother more? A thought reassured her – even with the newly broken screen, Esther's mobile phone was an extraordinary device, with canny powers.

And yes, she could always text.

FIVE

BRUNO

His mother was standing at the open front door when they arrived home, hands clasping each elbow, a strange expression on her face.

'How did you boys get on?' she asked, once they were out of the car. 'Sort your banking?'

'Yeah,' Bruno passed his mum and came inside, kicking his shoes off in the hallway, and placing down the bags of groceries he was carrying.

'What were you doing there, anyway?'

'Putting in a cheque.'

'For the window washing?'

Bruno made a non-committal grunting noise. He didn't want to discuss the logistics of banking a blood-splattered cheque – he'd been grilled for what felt like several minutes by the cashier, and there were long, muttered discussions between her and the manager before they agreed to process it. Dad hadn't helped matters – making poor-taste jokes about Bruno being an axe murderer, only slowing things further.

'I thought you said it was payment for your lessons?' his

father chimed in, plonking down his shopping bags, slightly out of breath.

'Don't carry the heavy stuff,' his wife reminded him. 'Speaking of – Bruno you had a visitor while you were gone.'

'Oh yeah, who?' Bruno replied as nonchalantly as he could, but his fight-or-flight muscles contracted.

'Esther.'

'What? She came *here*? How?'

'Drove down on a scooter.'

'By herself?'

His mother nodded. 'Esther wanted me to pass on a message, but for the life of me I can't remember what she said – it was a bit of a jumble, if I'm honest. I think you should call her, or head up there yourself – she seemed a little worked up.'

Although he made no outer show of concern, Bruno's mind was racing. What if Esther had revealed something about the camp, or worse – his reason for wanting to go there?

'I have to check on something first,' he replied, about to escape to his bedroom, when his mum called his name, making him turn again.

'One thing I didn't miss, Esther asked me to tell you about an Alberton Lodge? She said you should google it.'

'Okay, thanks.' Turning on his heels, he raced into the sanctity of his room, closing the door firmly behind him. Bruno noticed instantly something was different – a small pile of folded newspaper was sitting at the foot of his bed. He picked up the top sheet gingerly – he could tell it was old-timey simply from the quality of paper and ink. A memory of his dad on the car ride home mentioning 'Reg' and 'newspapers' came to Bruno now – he hadn't paid full attention, so wrapped up in his argument with Esther he'd been, replaying it over and over in his head. As Bruno turned over the page, the headline jumped out at him so viscerally, it almost made him drop it: THACK

IN SACK WITH MAN HATER FLACK. There was a photo of Thackeray looking angry – Bruno's eyes skipped down to the start of the article, but he stopped himself. Why should he invest in Esther's dramas any more? He needed to *focus*. Picking up the other papers, Bruno put them away inside his wardrobe, before booting up his computer. While it loaded, he wrote 'Alberton Lodge' in his phone notes – he was too conscientious to ignore the directive from Esther via his mother completely.

Next, Bruno checked his bank account – the cheque was sitting there but the money hadn't cleared. He admired the digits together on the screen, so handsome, so robust – before typing the Camp Change URL into the browser. Ignoring the smiling teen faces, he navigated immediately to the events section. There was a three-day course starting on the weekend – Bruno couldn't believe his luck, it was meant to be! The next one wasn't for another six weeks: he couldn't wait that long. His whole being yearned for transformation. There was no sign-up button, instead the website instructed him to email or call to book a place on the course. Normally, Bruno would always opt for the electronic approach – cold-calling people was not in his nature – but this was important, he didn't want his email to get lost in some inbox.

Bruno's phone vibrated, and he gave a surprised 'ha!'. When he looked, he could see it was a message from Esther. She'd never sent a text before.

i went to apologise please call met

Despite what had happened, Bruno felt a surge of pride that she was using the message function, but the glimmer was quickly extinguished when he recalled how angry she'd been when all he'd tried to do was help her.

Ignoring the message, he plugged the number on the website into his phone and called it.

'*Valor Enterprises Worldwide,*' came a man's high-pitched voice, when it was picked up.

'Oh-h,' Bruno stammered, 'I thought this was the number for Camp Change?'

'Yes, that comes under our programme umbrella. My name is Neil – how can I help you today?' There was something perky, if not slightly annoying, about the man's voice.

'I was hoping... um... is there space on the next course? I know it's in two days... but I... I wondered...'

'There is a place open.'

'Oh good, only – I'm waiting for a cheque to clear. It might take a day or two, but I really want to book the one this weekend...'

'No problem at all, as long as you have the deposit up front, we can sort all that out when you arrive. There is a no refund policy, however. Why don't you tell me a little about yourself, and I can enrol you over the phone? I'm just logging into our system now. Name, address and date of birth, please?'

Bruno rattled them off.

'And have family members asked you to come to our course?'

'No...' he replied hesitantly.

'That's great,' said Neil enthusiastically. 'You're arriving under your own steam. That's very promising. Are you connected with a church?'

'Not exactly.'

There was a clatter of keys.

'What are you hoping to get out of the course?'

'I just want to stop worrying about everything. I want to walk down the street and not feel like everyone is looking at me. I want to disappear.'

'Very brave. Can I take a credit card number?'

'I don't have one, will debit card do?'

'It's all plastic fantastic,' Neil laughed. 'We'll take the payment, and then you're locked in.'

'Oh good,' replied Bruno, and for just a moment he thought of Esther, of her face filled with disappointment after he'd told her of the camp, but he pushed this image away quickly.

'What's the main issue you're struggling with – homosexual tendencies, gender confusion or do you feel a lack in your core masculinity?'

'The first and the last, I guess.'

'Have you worn women's clothing?'

Instantly, Bruno thought of when he was a child, trying on his mother's dressing gown.

'No, not really.'

'Good to know,' Neil laughed as if a funny joke had been made. 'These homosexual tendencies of yours, have you acted on them?'

'Ah, no.'

'So, you're a virgin – but kissing, mutual touch, anything like that?'

'No.' Bruno tried to quieten his voice in case his mother was listening at the door. He felt very flushed all of a sudden.

'What about fantasies, dreams, things like that?'

'Well, maybe...'

'I'll tick occasionally then. Pornography?'

'I try not to.'

'I'm sorry to have to ask this, but have you even been sexually assaulted?'

'No!' Bruno replied vehemently.

'Again, I apologise, the form requires it. Good, good. That's about it, do you have any questions?'

'Does it work?' Bruno asked. 'The process?'

Neil laughed again; no, not a laugh, it was more of a 'bray'. 'I wouldn't be here if it didn't,' he answered. 'I'd be somewhere a lot hotter, that's for sure – and I don't mean Spain. Well, Bruno, you're booked in. I'll email you the travel details, itinerary and what you should bring. We look forward very much to meeting you.'

'Thank you, Neil. I'm excited.'

'We are too. Have a wonderful rest of your day.'

Bruno put down the phone and sat very quietly in a daze of mixed emotion, fighting every impulse not to call back and cancel.

'Coward,' he whispered to himself, the word elongated until it was almost a hiss.

He found it difficult to eat at dinner, his stomach was in such an excited knot. Daphne kept kicking the table leg and making the glasses shudder, which she'd apologise for, only to forget and repeat the process moments later. She was recounting a story about how the head had worn odd socks at assembly and the scandal this had caused.

'At least he was wearing any,' their dad said, loading lentil casserole onto his fork. 'I don't trust a man with naked ankles...'

His phone beeped.

'Filip,' reprimanded his wife. It was the family rule that phones were to be on silent during meals.

'Sorry, sorry... it's probably...' he went quiet, reading the message.

'You're not setting a good example, Filip.'

Bruno's dad furrowed his brow.

'What's this about you going to some camp, Bruno?'

Dropping his knife and fork on his plate, Bruno looked up, gobsmacked.

'Who texted you?' he demanded.

'Can I go to camp too?' Daphne pleaded. 'I have my own sleeping bag now and everything!'

'Why does he get to go to camp, and we don't?' Megan asked, scowling.

'Dad, who sent you that message?'

'Never you mind, son.'

'I do mind.' Bruno's face was bright red, he could feel his skin burning. 'That's my personal business.'

'Camp?' his mother asked. 'Like some kind of outdoor adventure thing?'

'Tell me who texted you,' repeated Bruno.

'First, explain what's going on.'

Bruno went to grab his father's phone. In the years before the cancer, his dad would have been too fast for him, but now his eye–hand coordination was much slower, and his son snatched it away easily.

'Give that back!'

Bruno was staring at the screen.

'*Esther?*' he cried, incredulously. 'Why does it say Esther?'

It was his dad's turn to be cagey.

'We swapped numbers.'

'When?'

'I walked up to the house and met her the other week. I like the old girl.'

'You didn't tell me about that,' his mum muttered, beside him.

'So, you asked Esther to spy on me?'

'It's nothing like that. She's lonely, I thought it would be good for her to have another contact.' He grabbed his phone back from Bruno. 'Now what's this camp? Esther seems to have a bee in her bonnet about it.'

'It's *none* of her business.'

There was another beep on his dad's phone. When his father checked it, his expression became even more serious.

'Girls, can you go to your room, please?'

'No, why – we never...'

'Go to your room!'

The girls were taken aback by their father's shouting. They froze, in shock, and then both stood up, eyes already welling with tears, and fled to their bedroom, slamming the door after them.

'Filip, was that really necessary...?'

But he wasn't listening to his wife. He was staring at his son.

'Esther seems to think you might be putting yourself in danger. Why does she have that idea?'

Bruno kept his eyes on his plate.

'She's a busybody,' he muttered, under his breath.

'What's this *camp*?'

'Filip, maybe we can talk about this once we've all cooled down...?'

'Esther says it's a place for *brainwashing*. What are you getting mixed up with, Bruno? If it's one of these radical groups you hear about on the news...'

'It's nothing like that. You wouldn't understand...'

'Enlighten me then.'

Banging the table with both fists, Bruno made all the cutlery jangle on the table.

'I'm trying to get better...'

'Better, how?'

'It's not like you can't have noticed...'

'What?'

'That I'm *different*. I'm not like the other boys at school. I've never had a girlfriend...?'

His parents exchanged a meaningful look.

'Bruno,' started his father, his voice instantly calmer, 'we love you. We love everything about you. *Everything*. I know there are things you're not comfortable with. Your mother and I both know. We were waiting for you to tell us when you were ready. We don't want you to change *anything* about yourself. Do you hear?'

Bruno kept his eyes averted.

'You don't understand what it's like.'

'Then tell us, we'd very much like to learn.'

'It doesn't matter now anyway. Everything's about to change...' As succinctly as he could, Bruno told his parents about the camp – about the breakthrough workshops, the healing circles, the transformative seminars, the...

'Look, son,' his father said in a measured tone while Bruno was still enthusing. 'Perhaps Esther's right to be sceptical, to me it sounds like one of those – what are they called – conversion therapy places?'

'Honey,' his mother said, 'if you want to talk to someone, we can get you a therapist or a counsellor. I know it must be isolating here... without other gay people...'

'I'm not...' Bruno sighed angrily. 'I'm not gay... I don't know, not completely... I'm not sure what I am... That's why I want to do the residential. It going to help me to process. The deposit's paid anyway and there's no refund. It's my money, I'm allowed to do what I want with it – and I'm not hurting anyone else. I don't want the girls knowing where I am, though.'

'Sweetheart, they're going to find out one way or another.'

'I'm not going to be the same when I'm back. I'll have *options.*'

'I don't know what they've sold you at this "camp", but it's not as simple as—'

'We'll see then,' interrupted Bruno, 'won't we?'

'You're as stubborn as your father.'

Filip glanced at his wife with a 'that's not helpful' expression.

'I know there's been a lot going on, with my treatment and money issues and everything. I haven't always been as present as I should be – I'm wiped out half the time. But that's all changing. We can go on a trip somewhere soon, just you and me. Have some quality time finally.'

'You can't just decide when you want to be a good father,' Bruno intoned, darkly. 'It doesn't work like that.'

'What do you mean?'

'All my life you made me feel like I wasn't enough because I didn't want to play football or watch football or talk about football, or rank the female newsreaders in order of hotness, or play "kiss, marry, kill" with the supermarket checkout ladies. Then you get prostate cancer, and do this huge one-eighty, but now I'm afraid you're going to die all the time – and anyway, it doesn't make up for all those other years. It can't.'

Bruno's mother let out a long exhalation, as if she was slowly deflating under the weight of her son's words.

'Believe it or not,' his dad replied, visibly shaken after Bruno's spiel, his eyes raw, 'I was only doing my best. I was trying to *engage* with you. My old man ignored me for the most part, that makes you feel like you're not enough, believe me. They don't give you a parenting guidebook, Bruno, but I know self-punishment when I see it, and that's what this camp of yours is. It's a smokescreen.'

'It's going to help me find myself.'

'All these empty catchphrases you keep spouting. Talk to *us*. Talk all night if you want to. You always clam up whenever we try.'

'Action speaks louder than words.'

'Not going to a place where they'll try and cure you, as if you're diseased, Bruno. That's not the right type of action.'

'You don't understand...' Bruno's eyes started filling with tears. 'If anything did happen to you, Dad, I'd be the man of the house. I'm doing this as much for the girls as I am for myself...'

'Oh, Bruno...' his father said, shaking his head.

'It's done now. And you can tell Esther to keep her nose out of my business – I'm never seeing her ever again.' Bruno stood up, pushing his chair back. 'The course starts on Friday.' His mum and dad protested in unison, but he ignored them. 'I'll take the train from Rugby. I'm not going to talk about it again.'

Bruno began to march to his room, when he heard a chair squeak, making him turn again. His father was standing, leaning on the table, perhaps to give himself more support, and his face was flushed. It was strange to see so much colour in him; he was usually so pale.

'You come back here and sit down,' his father yelled, his voice breaking. 'You live under our roof, and while you do...' and then he burst into tears. It was horrible to watch. His father hadn't cried during all of his treatment, or at least not in front of Bruno.

His mother placed her hand, very delicately, on her husband's shoulder, and he sank back into his chair.

'This isn't right,' she said, her face stony, 'but Bruno's an adult now. We must let him follow his own path, even if it's not the one we'd choose for him.'

'They'll get inside his head...'

'If we can't change his mind, what hope do they have?'

'I've let him down. Bruno's right.' He wept.

'Dad...' Bruno said, watching helplessly, as if he was a phantom, observing the scene without them knowing.

'You haven't let anyone down, Filip.' She addressed Bruno now, still frozen on the spot. 'Where is it, this camp?'

'On the coast. Great Yarmouth.'

'I'll drive you.'

'No, you don't have to...'

'But we're not keeping it from your sisters. There have been enough secrets in this family, all those months we didn't tell them your dad was ill. I want everything out in the open, do you understand?' Bruno considered challenging this but thought better of it. Instead, he marched to his room, but not before he heard his dad say, 'How did this happen, Tina?' And then, silence.

. . .

Bruno lay on his bed, watching ASMR YouTube videos as a distraction, and must have dozed, exhausted after the emotional adrenaline had worn off, because the next thing he became aware of was a gentle knocking. Sitting, he stared expectantly at his door, imagining his mum was about to come in, maybe with a cup of tea, but he soon realised the tapping sound was coming from his *window*. Bruno almost jumped out of his skin when he turned to see the face of Dominic smiling back at him.

'Why are you standing in our flowerbed?' asked Bruno in a hushed whisper, after he'd carefully opened the window.

'Just popping by to see how you are.' Dominic was wearing a long-sleeved T-shirt with 'Hitchcock Blonde' emblazoned on it in yellow fiery letters.

'You're crushing my mum's geraniums.'

'Can I come in?'

'No, *why*?'

'Just for a friendly chat. All will be revealed. Or I could go round the front, ring the bell, meet your folks...?'

'Fine, get in.' Bruno opened the window wider, and with surprising dexterity, Dominic levered himself inside, landing soundlessly. This was not his first time doing this, Bruno thought. 'Now tell me what you're doing here?' What would his parents think if they found Dominic in his bedroom?

'I've come to offer counsel.'

'Counsel – about what?'

'Going away to those brainwashers.'

Bruno shook his head in bewilderment.

'How does everyone know my business?' he hissed. 'You're a friend of Esther too, aren't you?'

'She's an acquaintance,' Dominic admitted, pushing up his sleeves. There were no pen-made tattoos on his arms today.

'Did she send you here?'

'I came of my own volition, but Esther *is* worried about you.'

'She needs to leave me alone.'

'I get it,' Dominic said, brushing dark hair out of his eyes. 'This village is a blip. There's no one of interest here, nothing to do. But when you meet other queer people, you'll take to them like a gay duck to homosexuality. You just need to get in the pond, if you see what I mean. Dip your toes.' He glanced around Bruno's room. 'Wow, your bedroom is intense.'

'What do you mean? It's a normal room.'

'*Aggressively* normal. It looks like it's been designed by committee. Way too neat and tidy, there's not a single representation of a human being, male or female, and is that a *Minecraft* poster?'

'I like it,' Bruno said, bristling. 'You really have to leave, Dominic.' He ushered him back towards the window. 'Tell Esther... actually, don't tell her anything. It was a mistake trusting her.'

Instead of moving to the window, Dominic managed to manoeuvre Bruno's desk chair around and sit in one evasive fluid motion.

'Look, I know sexuality's confusing,' he said, with a shrug, settling in the chair.

'How do *you* know? You always had sixteen girlfriends at school,' Bruno sighed and sat on the edge of his bed.

'Exactly, polyamory is not to be trifled with. I've also had my... hesitations... about where I fit on the Kinsey Scale on any given day. Where I fall on the sexuality spectrum. They're big questions for everyone, Bruno.'

'Not everyone.'

'Perhaps, but isolating yourself is not the answer. Extremism isn't either, unless it's a kink and consensual, then I'm back on board.'

'What *is* the answer then?'

'You have to find out yourself. That's the point. We're all different. It's a dance.'

Bruno stared at the floor.

'Maybe for you.'

'Hey,' Dominic scootered forward on the chair's wheels and touched Bruno's chin, making him jump as if he'd been zapped by an electric charge.

'What are you doing?'

'I was wondering... I don't know... Have you ever even kissed a guy before?'

'Are you even...?'

'Labels are so reductive, Bruno.'

'Oh, I see – Esther's basically pimped you out to me. You swoop in here, soften me up, and what – that's supposed to make everything better again?'

Dominic smiled mischievously. 'I mean, I am a pretty good kisser. Ask anyone.' He shook his head. 'I told you, I'm not here because of Esther. Not *just* because of her.'

'Why *are* you here then?'

'I like you.'

'Oh great, this is what I've *always* wanted. To be pity kissed by a bi-curious straight guy, while my parents are in the other room, twenty feet away. Have *you* ever kissed another man before?'

'I mean, I've thought about it,' replied Dominic. 'Academically. On inspection though, most of my impulses seem boringly conventional.'

'Why boring? – you're lucky. If you wanted to, you could get your HGV licence, and talk to the other drivers about, I don't know, boobs. Drinking pints, hauling loads, and discussing which boobs are the best.'

'You want to become a driver at the warehouses?' Dominic was aghast.

'No... but I want the option. Everything feels off when

you're not... normal. I can't even talk to the barber when I'm getting my hair cut. All they want to do is chat about sport. I can't fake it either – I tried for years with my dad.'

'I don't particularly like sport; it's not about sexuality.'

'It's a whole mess of things. You don't sit there thinking how you'd like the barber to lean in a bit more, how nice his cologne smells, what happens when he brushes your cheek with the back of his hand...' Bruno felt shocked at how open he was being.

'Hey, it's no picnic being straight either.' Dominic slapped his thighs with both hands. His fingernails were painted a chipped metallic blue today, Bruno noticed. 'The toxic masculinity, all the machismo, the posturing. Not being allowed to cry, or show weakness. Being judged solely on how much money you make. And now we're also supposed to use moisturiser and have a million followers, but if anyone catches you wearing mascara, there's hell to pay. At least *you* get an out.'

'So, you'd swap, if you could?'

Dominic considered this seriously. 'Sure,' he replied.

'No one would want this willingly.'

'Look, it's Whittleham. Go to London, or Sydney, or San Francisco. Anywhere but here.'

'I can't – my dad.'

'I'm sure he wants you to live your authenticity.'

'That's rich coming from you. I know you deal... illegal substances. How is that *your* authenticity?'

Dominic seemed caught out by this.

'Only pot,' he replied, raising a finger.

'That's not what I've heard.'

'Well, they're lies and slander.' Dominic clapped his hands once, and Bruno shushed him. 'Okay,' he said quietly, 'mushrooms and acid. But not anything stronger. Or addictive. I have my standards. Anyway, it's my family business, handed down from brother to brother.' He sniffed. 'Are you still planning to go to this brainwashing camp?'

'Incredibly, your pep talk hasn't changed my mind. And it's not brainwashing, it's re-education.'

'That's what they used to say in the old days. I watched a documentary about it – when homosexuality was illegal they'd send someone to an asylum, and they'd try to electrocute the gay out of them.' Dominic changed tack. 'Can you at least say goodbye to Esther first? It will break her heart if you leave without seeing her again.'

'She doesn't care about me.' Bruno folded his arms contritely.

'That's not true. She's one of the kindest people I know.'

Dominic's phone beeped.

'Turn it to silent, my parents will hear.'

'Alright, alright. Speak of the devil... Esther wants an update. WIL HE STILL GOT? All capitals.'

'She's texting you too?'

'I hold you personally responsible, she messages like a tweenager. It never hurts to have good spelling and punctuation. Right, I better skedaddle. Unless you want that kiss? Or some weed?'

'I'm fine on both counts.'

'Honestly, I think they might help you relax.'

'I don't do drugs.'

'They say love is a drug, my man.'

Maybe it was the corny way Dominic said, 'my man', with the playful arching of his left eyebrow. Or the intimacy of having another male in his bedroom. Or simply because his emotions were running high – but the next moment, Bruno's lips were pressing firmly against Dominic's. He had often wondered what it would feel like to kiss someone, if he would get it right, but Bruno quickly discovered instinct took over, his tongue, the movement of his mouth, the angle of his head. It felt good, like biting into a piece of fruit and realising it was perfectly ripe. But even though Dominic's lips felt good on his, Bruno was also outside of his body, staring at them both– the eyes of his parents, his sisters, a stranger – and *judging*.

'Mission accomplished,' said Dominic proudly when Bruno finally pulled away.

They both looked at each other. Bruno didn't know what to say, the elation and something sour – shame – was over-powering.

Dominic went to the open window and swung a leg over, so he was straddling the windowsill. 'Talk to Esther. Text her at the very least...'

'Maybe...' Bruno replied, as he gently pushed Dominic from the sill, and very firmly closed the window again.

The following two days were an excruciating exercise in controlled silence. Neither sister would leave him alone about the mysterious 'camp' he was going to, pestering Bruno merci-lessly and getting riled when he wouldn't talk. Between them, they tried everything – whining, teasing, complaining to their parents – their entire collective arsenal to get more information – but Bruno could be especially stubborn when he put his mind to it.

On the morning of his departure, battle lines had been clearly drawn. Daphne and Megan were aggressively ignoring Bruno, and the atmosphere was made worse by his father's wet eyes, and his mother's concerned expressions. As Bruno prepared to leave the house, both sisters were weeping in a heap on the sofa, and his dad was cleaning the kitchen for a second time – he'd even moved the fridge to scrub behind it – sniffing constantly.

'Guess you're going then,' was all he said before he hugged

Bruno. He was wearing the washing-up gloves, so he gripped his son with his elbows, hands free.

'Why can't we go tooooo?' wailed Daphne from the sofa.

'Can I talk you out of it?' asked his father, eyes bloodshot, from the bleach fumes – at least that was his excuse.

Bruno shook his head.

'It's so unfair!' Megan howled.

When Bruno went to kiss his sisters, they hid their faces under pillows, but as soon as he'd picked up his backpack and headed out to the car, he could see them at the window, watching mournfully and sobbing. In some ways, it felt like a fitting send-off.

Bruno's mum had been quiet all morning, and behind the wheel, she was no different. From Whittleham, it was a two-and-a-half-hour trip to Great Yarmouth: on the A14 to Newmarket, then the A11 to Norwich and the A47 the last twenty miles to the coast, where the camp was located. Luckily, it was dual carriage all the way. They barely spoke for the first hour, letting the radio fill the void between them. The sky was a metallic grey, and every now and then there would be a sprinkle of drops on the windscreen, but the rain they kept mentioning on the radio every fifteen minutes never materialised.

As the journey went on, Bruno began to feel more and more nervous. Several times he even considered asking his mum to turn around.

Trying to find ways to pass the time, he flicked through his notes app. Most of them were to-do's he could delete ('buy new squeegee') or random affirmations he'd stumbled across online, but didn't quite understand ('A leopard is stuck with his spots, unless everyone believes he's a jaguar', 'Work hard to not work hard, and reap abundance forever'). One of the most recent notes read simply: 'Alberton Lodge'.

Esther. He still felt bitter about how she'd treated him, but

Bruno googled it anyway, expecting a hotel from the name, but as he scrawled through the results, he realised 'the Lodge' was an old psychiatric hospital, which had closed in the 1990s. Why did Esther want him to see this? Was she equating Camp Change with an old asylum so he wouldn't go? That was a low blow. Maybe there was more to it than that, he reasoned. What if she'd been a patient?

'I don't know if I've ever told you this before,' his mum began, making him jump with surprise in his seat. Bruno braced himself instinctively for whatever was about to come, clicking off his phone. '...but my family and friends weren't thrilled when I first started seeing your father. It wasn't *him* – in their eyes, the people from Whittleham had a reputation.'

Bruno knew all too well from school the stigma, but he was surprised to hear it had come from his own relatives.

'Not Grandma and Grandad though?' he asked, in disbelief. Both Bruno's maternal grandparents had died when he was a child, but he remembered them fondly as being kind.

His mum was quiet for a second, as if deciding what she should divulge.

'They came around,' she replied, diplomatically. 'It did affect me though, what everyone thought. I actually broke it off with your dad for a few weeks, even started dating a local guy in Thornby.' Trying not to screw up his face, Bruno nodded passively, but it was strange thinking of his mum with anyone but his father. 'That other relationship was not good – he ended up being controlling, I was in a very dark place. I wouldn't wish that on anyone, but there was a silver lining, because it made me appreciate your father in a new light and ignore what anyone else thought when we got back together. I know sometimes you need to make a bad decision, to get to a better place. Even if it's a destructive one.'

She wiped tears away carefully, keeping her eyes fixed on the road. They sat in silence, Bruno wondering how to respond to this, until his mum turned up the radio, blasting a Tina

Turner song, as a handful of large raindrops splattered them-selves messily over the windscreen.

It was 12.41 p.m. when they found the sign for the campsite – they'd made it in good time, even stopping for some lunch. Bumping down a sandy road lined with tussocks of grass, they turned into a large car park, empty bar two other vehicles. After parking and turning off the engine, they stared at the holiday camp. It was both bigger and more dilapidated than Bruno had expected – a signposted office closest to them, a large hall build-ing, and wind-blasted cabins sprawling across the beachfront, some individual chalet style and others terraced together in rows, in various stages of disrepair. Except for a light in the office window, everything seemed empty and weather-beaten.

'How many people are coming?' his mum asked, nervous-ness in her voice.

'I don't know,' Bruno admitted. As they watched, a wiry man in chef's whites kicked open a door and marched around the side of the building.

'I'll come in with you,' began Bruno's mum. 'Make sure...'

'Thanks,' he countered, 'but I think I should do this on my own.' Beyond the buildings, he couldn't quite make out the sea. Usually, Bruno would want to run straight towards the waves, it was always a treat to be so near, but today the idea of all that water made him shiver.

Fetching his bag from the boot, parent and child stood in front of each other, more awkward than they'd ever been before. It was usually so easy hugging his mother, the most natural thing in the world. Now Bruno couldn't remember the correct way to *initiate* one. When they did finally hug, it felt stiff and awkward. Only the smell of her was reassuring, the mumsy aromas of hairspray and perfume – she was wearing the Calvin Klein he'd bought her last Christmas.

'We're here if you need anything,' she said, once they'd parted. 'I'll come pick you up again.' Bruno was trying everything he could not to get emotional. 'I'm sorry,' his mum continued, 'If we did something or didn't do...'

'You're great, I love you. This is about me.'

She nodded and rubbed his shoulder, her face crumpled in concern.

Slinging his backpack over his shoulder, he walked towards the office, turning to give a sober wave to his mother, now back in the car. He could just make her out through the windscreen. Why was she sitting there and not starting the engine? And then it struck him: she was crying.

Fighting every impulse to run back to her, Bruno turned and opened the office door. Inside, he was surprised to find it empty except for a desk – a piece of paper taped to it which read 'A courageous welcome!' – and a telephone. The only other thing on the table was a bowl of sweets, the sort Bruno's maternal grandmother would have when she was alive – dusty-looking, hard-boiled and unappetising. He wondered what he should do next. Remembering his mum waiting, he returned to the door, only to watch her driving off down the sandy road. Panic zipped through his veins.

'Hello?' came a voice behind him, making Bruno vault into the air. 'Can I help?'

There was now a short, middle-aged man standing behind the desk, bald except for wild, unkempt eyebrows that would have made his dad's – pre-chemo – seem manicured in comparison. A door was ajar at the end of the room, Bruno could now see.

'Yes... I'm here for the residential?'

'Welcome, you're early. Early is good, we like that! We don't often get early!' the man moved nimbly, opening the notepad he was carrying, and flicking through pages holding neatly ruled tables and meticulously scribed data. It struck Bruno as strange that a person with such wild eyebrows would have such neat handwriting. 'And you are...?'

'Bruno...'

'We spoke on the phone! I'm Brother Neil.' Bruno frowned, confused – had he misheard? Did he say *Brother* Neil? '*So* pleased you made it – you're in for an incredible few days. Really, it's life-changing. I'm jealous,' he chuckled. 'You can only begin this transformational work once.'

'Yeah, I'm... it's exciting,' Bruno replied without any enthusiasm.

The main door opened, and in came a red-haired man with what appeared to be his equally red-headed son, scowls on both their faces. Bruno had the impression they'd just had a skirmish outside – the boy's hair was messed up, and they were both slightly out of breath.

'I'll be with you in a moment,' Neil said, still rifling through his notebook. 'Bruno... Bruno... yes – here you are. Now, I have a note here to take an outstanding payment.'

'I only have a card,' Bruno replied, hesitantly, noting the lack of anything digital in the office.

'It's all plastic fantastic!' He'd used the same joke on the phone. Neil opened the drawer of the desk to take out a sleek white payment reader. Bruno had checked his account that morning, and the funds had cleared, but he felt nervous paying – he'd never handed over such a big lump sum before in his life. 'That's gone through, many thanks. Now if you head to the transformation centre next door...'

'Which building is that exactly...?'

'The hall,' Neil replied, his grin slipping momentarily.

Bruno locked eyes with the red-headed boy as he passed – he was short and stocky, a couple of years younger than Bruno perhaps, but he seemed jaded in a way that belied his age. His father's large pink hand was resting very heavily on the boy's shoulder, as if physically tethering him to the spot.

'Ah, Mitchell,' intoned Neil, as Bruno exited the office. 'Back again...'

Making his way to the next-door building, the hall he'd observed from the car, Bruno found it was set up inside with a whiteboard and a small circle of chairs at the far end. It was stuffy – the heating was on full blast, even though it was already a muggy May day outside. Bruno tried to open one of the windows, but they seemed sealed shut.

Since he was first, he considered which chair was best, deciding on the one at the four o'clock position. As he sat down, Bruno's phone beeped. Taking it out and turning it to silent – reception was terrible here, he noticed – he brought up the message. He expected it to be from his dad, but in fact it was from Esther.

hope you changed your mind, dearhart

He clicked off his phone without responding, just as Mitchell arrived, looking thoroughly fed up. Dragging his feet noisily, he sat in the chair furthest away from Bruno.

'Mitchell, is it?' asked Bruno, remembering his manners.

'Mitch,' the boy grunted, glaring suspiciously.

'Have you been to one of these residentials before, then?'

Giving a derisive 'tsk', Mitch nodded, before burying his head in his hands. At first, Bruno thought he'd upset the boy with his question, until he realised he was trying to sleep, resting his upper body on his knees.

Two others joined them over the next half an hour – a tiny, timid blond boy of maybe twelve who smiled apologetically as he walked into the hall with his shoulders up, as if perpetually flinching, and a lanky boy of about fourteen with longish brown hair, who walked with a swooping skip. Neither said a word when they arrived, taking their seats silently. Eventually, Neil bustled in, and Bruno panicked that this might be it – three boys, all younger than him, and bristly old eyebrows leading the weekend.

'There are a few people running late,' Neil explained, and Bruno felt instantly relieved, 'but I thought it would be good idea if we introduce ourselves. Let's go round and say our names and where we're from, shall we? Starting with you, Bruno.'

'I'm Bruno,' he repeated, redundantly. 'I'm from Whittleham.'

'How old are you?'

'Eighteen, nearly nineteen.'

'And what are you looking to get out of the next few power-packed days?'

'I want some tools to help me... you know, in the world... to make my life easier. No one tells you what to do, you get no guidance, right? So yeah, that's what I'm looking for.'

Bruno knew he was waffling; he was basically lifting what he was saying wholesale from what he'd read on the website – Esther would never let him get away with it, but Brother Neil did.

'Couldn't have put it better myself,' he said, fuzzy eyebrows raised approvingly.

The red-headed boy muttered something that sounded like an expletive. He was sitting up now, but barely, slumping almost out of his chair.

'Why don't you go next, Mitch?' Neil instructed, curtly.

'Do I have to?'

'It would be nice if you shared.'

'Nice would be running out of here and disappearing again.'

'Remember what happened last time?'

The boy nodded sullenly.

'How old are you please, Mitch? Let's not drag our heels.'

The blond boy giggled.

'Fifteen,' Mitch replied, with a heavy sigh.

Bruno was surprised – he appeared much older. They were children, all three of them.

'And why are you here, Mitch? Might I remind you pre-emptively, there's to be no swearing or lewd language of any kind. We don't want it getting back to Dr Allan, now do we?'

Mitch shifted uncomfortably at the mention of the doctor.

'I'm here to get better,' he muttered, at last. 'Because I'm... broken... inside.'

'Good, that's progress.' This last word from Neil slightly sibilantly – *ssss*. The man cleared his throat quickly. 'Together we can help you, Mitch. Isn't that wonderful?'

Everyone but Bruno nodded and mumbled varying degrees of affirmation.

'Neil, can I ask...?' Bruno began.

'Please,' Neil replied quickly, eyes wide. 'It's *Brother* Neil.'

'Brother Neil *Down*,' Mitch mumbled but audibly enough for everyone to hear, prompting sniggers from the two other boys.

'That's going in the book!'

Neil opened his large notebook from the office, and made a meticulous entry. Bruno tried to angle his head so he could see what else was on the page, but the writing was too small.

'So, um... what's the structure?' asked Bruno, when the focus was back on him. 'It says on the website that there will be inspirational speakers, are they coming tomorrow?'

'Dr Allan will be presenting in the morning, bright and early, don't worry.'

Mitch made a sound of annoyance or panic, it wasn't clear.

'And who is Dr Allan?' Bruno vaguely remembered reading about the doctor on the site but thought it better to play innocent.

'He's a *trained* psychiatrist.' Were there such things as untrained psychiatrists, Bruno wondered? 'He'll start on the first deep module tomorrow – before moving on to the assessment of parental relationship.'

'What does it have to do with our parents – isn't this about us being ga—?'

There was a sharp inhalation from Neil, cutting him off.

'We don't use that word,' he replied firmly.

'What do we use then?'

'Boys?'

'Same-sex attraction,' the three others spoke in flat unison.

'We have a dedicated treatment plan; Dr Allan will explain more tomorrow. Since you have so many questions, Bruno, maybe we should establish the ground rules.' Brother Neil opened his notebook. 'Any infraction of rules can mean a time of isolated prayer and fasting.' He read. 'Infraction of the rules includes improper speech, looks or touch.'

'What does "improper touch" mean?' asked Bruno, cringing at the phrase.

'The touching of two males, unless instructed to by a member of staff. It means, keep your hands to yourself.'

'Why would we touch each other?'

Neil's eyes gleamed.

'Isn't that the reason you're here in the first place? Because of physical urges? Doesn't it make sense to remove temptation while we are trying to find a solution for your transgressions?'

Bruno was beginning to feel flustered – it didn't help that the hall was so warm. Reactively, he began to remove his jumper, and as he did so, he felt the cooler air on his exposed belly.

'That's enough,' Neil shouted at Bruno, making him pull off the jumper in panic. 'You do not undress in public. Decorum.'

'It's hot, I was taking off my...'

Mitch started to shake his head, as if this was a warning. Brother Neil's face was red, and his eyes were becoming bloodshot.

'I know you're new here, Bruno, so I'm being lenient. But your resistance is an obstacle to growth.' For some reason, the word 'resistance' made Esther pop into Bruno's mind. 'Say, "I'm sorry, Brother Neil, for my infraction".'

'What?'

'Remember, if one of you gets a punishment, you *all* get given one.'

'That's not... you didn't say that before...'

Brother Neil gave a deeply unsettling grin.

'My mistake. Seems like we've gotten off on the wrong foot, Bruno. Might be worth us all completing a drill.'

The other boys groaned collectively.

They were all given a notebook and a pen, and instructed to write.

'When was the last time you experienced same sex attraction?' Neil asked, prompting everyone except Bruno to start scribbling. He paused, thinking of Dominic and their kiss and found himself blushing. He swallowed and started to write about Dominic climbing through his window. 'Give as much detail as you can. What was the weather like? What were you doing? What clothes were you wearing? What were your thoughts?' Bruno jotted down as much as he could remember, the crushed geraniums, the smell of Dominic's Brylcreem, how excited and revolted Bruno had felt. It all came flying out onto the page – it felt good to expunge the experience by writing it down.

'Now go back further, when was a time before?' Bruno instantly thought about when a Marks & Spencer's catalogue arrived in the mail, and he'd looked at the menswear section, and one particularly appealing male model with curly, ginger hair. He wasn't sure if he was attracted to the man, or wanted to *be* him. Perhaps it wasn't same-sex attraction, it was a desire to emulate? Maybe he only wanted to become a Marks & Spencer's model? Either way, it had made shopping for clothes in M&S particularly nerve-wracking. Bruno wrote all this down, the pen flying across the page.

Neil walked by, observing as they wrote. 'Doing very well, I see,' he commented to Bruno. 'You're getting the hang of it. That's what we like.'

'Thanks, Brother Neil.'

'Thank you, *Brother* Bruno.'

It was very strange hearing his name with this moniker, but he put it out of his mind and continued to write.

After almost two hours, they finished.

'Good work, brothers! Now we will be rewarded with an early supper before being shown to our quarters.'

'Why does he talk like he's in a Shakespearean play?' Bruno whispered to Mitch as they filed through the hall. The boy shrugged, but didn't say anything else in response, and Bruno felt the pang of rejection. Mitch seemed like the only one of the others with any grit. Three more attendees had arrived at the hall while they were journaling, all younger than Bruno, all meekly sullen.

They were led, Pied Piper-like, to a nearby dining hall, moths already fluttering noisily around the bare lightbulbs, even though sunset was hours away. Four squat trellis tables, and a metal bench in front of a partitioned kitchen greeted them inside. There came the clatter of utensils, and then the man in grimy whites whom Bruno had seen from the car came out carrying a large steaming pot and thumped it down on the metal table.

'Enjoy your meal,' announced Neil brightly, before turning on his heels to go.

The seven boys wandered to the pot in silence, picking up bowls and serving themselves.

'Yum, gruel for dinner,' said Bruno, rolling his eyes. At

school, he was always the quiet one, but in a vacuum, it seemed he became a joker.

The cook reappeared, carrying a large saucepan. He'd taken off his chef's jacket, and Bruno observed the pronounced bulge of the man's biceps, making him quickly look away, but aware the others were also appreciating the chef's arms. When it was Bruno's turn to serve himself, he found the meal was chicken curry, although it didn't smell as good as the ones at home; the aroma was of fat with only a hint of spice. Bruno was hungry, though – lunch felt like a long time ago – so he ignored his nose and heaped curry and rice into a bowl, as he considered where he should sit. He didn't want to choose a table only for everyone else to sit at another and make him a social pariah. He needn't have worried, as each of the boys had already moved to their own individual place at a table, barely acknowledging the others, so Bruno sat down at the least occupied table.

'Friendly,' he muttered under his breath, loud enough for the others to hear. Mitch glowered at him. 'What an afternoon, huh?' he said at normal volume.

'You haven't seen anything yet,' replied Mitch, darkly.

'I'm looking forward to it.'

'You sound like one of them. Are you a mole or something?'

The small blond-haired boy, who'd introduced himself earlier as Philip, hissed: 'We're not supposed to interact, he'll find out.'

'Who will?' Bruno asked. 'Are there cameras?'

He scanned the ceiling, but there was nothing but cobwebs, a few stray moths struggling in them futilely – the cobwebs reminded him of Esther's house, he realised, slightly wistfully.

'God will see it.' Philip hissed again. 'And then he'll tell Dr Allan.'

'I think He's too busy to watch us eating a curry.'

'That's what you think,' Philip said, removing what looked like a hair from his bowl daintily with his finger and thumb.

Bruno ate a spoonful of curry. It tasted exactly as it smelled – oily – and left a sludgy feeling on his tongue when he'd swallowed. The chicken was overly chewy too.

'Where's everyone from?' asked Bruno, trying one last time.

'They'll only make us do a drill tomorrow again as punishment,' replied Mitch, with heavy eyes. 'Any interaction, that's the rules.'

'We can't even talk?'

'It's to stop us having improper thoughts,' said Philip, as if he was reciting it.

'But we're only eating dinner...'

'You can still have improper thoughts while you're eating,' Philip corrected him with a disarming shrug.

'I'm definitely having *second* thoughts about this curry.' Bruno pushed his bowl away and the third of the original boys, the one with longer hair – Elliot, his name was – sniggered.

Giving up on any more fruitless conversation, Bruno checked his phone. There were four messages – one from his dad, wishing him well in a very formal manner, which wasn't typical, especially since the cancer; it was usually as if he worried each message might be his last. A lump formed in Bruno's throat, and he swallowed hard, tasting the oiliness from the curry again. Another message was from his sister Megan, which simply read: *Happy now?* One from his mum: *How are you settling in?* He replied to all three, with one-word replies: *Thanks!*, *Yes* and *Okay!*

The fourth message was from Esther:

Please tell me you are okay. I'm more than sorry.

Bruno was about to put his phone away without answering – quietly marvelling how perfect her typing was – until he imagined Esther's worried face, all alone in her big house. He wrote back:

I'm fine.

Ten minutes later, Neil returned, holding the bowl of dusty-looking sweets from the office. 'Dessert,' he announced, ceremoniously placing it on the table, to be resolutely ignored by all the boys. 'Once you've cleaned your dishes, I'll show you to the *sleeping quarters*.'

They trudged behind Brother Neil, single file and silently. The reed grass was wilder here – waist-height around the buildings – and the sandy ground was littered with sun-bleached plastic wristbands from some bygone festival, making this part of the campsite feel even more forgotten. Nearby seabirds circled in the overcast sky, but there was still no sign of the sea itself, no sound of waves even.

Bruno felt a tap on his shoulder. As he turned, Mitch had a finger over his lips.

'Keep walking,' the boy ordered in a whisper, Bruno obeying. 'He'll take our phones when we get to the cabins.'

'But I have to check in with my family,' Bruno hissed over his shoulder. 'My mum and dad will be worried if I don't.'

Mitch snorted, derisively. He had dark rings under his eyes, most likely the result of fast food and computer games, and too little sleep. Bruno's mum would be hard-pressed not to scoop Mitch up, if she met him, and feed him a bowl of vegetables.

'They'll blame it on poor reception. There's nothing you can do.'

Bruno had a sudden urge to start running. There must be dunes close by, he could hide there until it was dark enough to slink away unseen, but something stopped him, the same impulse override that made sure his body wasn't betraying his sexuality – limp hands, soft eyes, a weak posture – making him stand unnaturally rigid, when all his body wanted to do was *flow*. He'd paid all the money. The workshops hadn't even started yet. Did he want to be hypervigilant his whole life, if there were tools to be learned here, a solution even?

Slightly calmer, Bruno slipped his phone out of his pocket. Should he message his parents now, tell them he'd be out of contact? He felt a strong impulse to text 'I love you', but that would worry them most of all. And then it struck him: Esther's ancient flip phone! The one she'd given him was still in the pocket of his backpack...

Their 'sleeping quarters' were a row of connected cabins in a low wooden building, the flaking yellow paint bleached and blasted by the elements over many seasons. Bruno had worried momentarily about bunk beds; he'd never shared a room with another boy before, but fortunately, they were each given a single room, his assigned last.

'Your *boudoir*,' Neil announced, with a flourish of his hand, swinging open the cabin door. 'A breakfast buffet will be served at 7 a.m.'

'What do we do until then?' Bruno asked, peering inside, surveying the single bed that seemed far too small for him. When he'd last looked at his phone, it wasn't even 6.30 p.m.

'An early night gives you plenty of time for reflection and meditation,' Neil replied, curtly. 'You'll be let out of your rooms at 6.30 a.m.'

Bruno's forehead furrowed. 'What do you mean, "let out"?'

'The doors will be locked until the morning when you can take turns showering and brushing your teeth. It's for your own safety. The campsite is almost twenty-two acres, and we can't keep eyes on everything. Who knows what type of person is lurking?'

'Locked? What if I need to go to the loo in the night?'

'You'll find a chamber pot under your bed.'

'A what?'

'A ceramic container.'

'You want me to piss in a pot?' Bruno asked incredulously. Neil's face contorted.

'That's not the kind of language we employ around here.'

'What if there's a fire?' asked Bruno with genuine concern.

'We have processes to cover any eventuality. The main point is you stay *safe*.' Neil said this in a sing-song tone. 'I'll take your phone too, please, it's protocol.' Bruno hoped his protests sounded genuine. 'There's barely any signal,' Neil said, holding up a slab-like hand, 'so you won't miss much. Anyway, phones give you cancer.' At the c-word, Bruno inwardly lurched.

Sighing, he took off his bag, opened a side zip, and retrieved Esther's old phone, still there from the day she'd gifted it to him.

'This is yours?' asked Neil, amazed. 'It's older than I am.'

'My parents don't like us having smartphones,' Bruno explained with a shrug.

'Very wise. Although, you might consider upgrading. Phones have a shelf life, and this one might leak battery acid or contain asbestos. Mind if I have a rummage through your bag for any more electronics?'

Bruno tried not to seem rattled by this – he'd not thought to hide his actual phone, which was in the back pocket of his jeans – but Neil was already rifling through his backpack. Would he be forced to empty his pockets too?

'Done,' Neil replied, handing back the bag.

'Do you want to check my pockets?' Bruno asked, playing innocent.

Neil looked at him for the briefest of moments.

'I trust you,' he replied, patting Bruno on the shoulder affectionately. 'Not many of our attendees call to book themselves in here. That shows pluck.'

With that, Neil closed the cabin door behind him, the key in the lock clicking it shut.

Bruno stood, stunned for a moment. Surely he hadn't been locked in his room, like a prisoner, when he was *paying* to be here?

He remembered the window, but it wouldn't budge and the shutters seemed bolted. Sitting on the edge of the creaky bed, Bruno wrestled with what to do. He could make an SOS call, and both his parents would most likely arrive, enraged. Did he want to put his father through that stress? Bruno imagined the car ride home, the feeling of failure. All that money gone too. And there *might* be useful things to learn. The other boys weren't much in the way of conversation or company, but the programme started in earnest in the morning... He took out his phone, still unsure what to do. A message popped up on the screen as if it was waiting for him:

Dear hart, bloofy fingers, are you okay can't find the question mark

Bruno considered ignoring Esther; he was still furious with her after all, but a creeping sense of despair spurred him on to respond.

I'm okay. It hasn't really started yet, so I'm getting an early night for tomorrow.

Hope you're well, he added, politely.

Good, came the reply. *Please be careful with your mind, I like it just how it is*

Bruno chewed his cheek at this reply. Had Esther liked his mind when she was accusing him of meddling in her life?

I'm fine, he wrote back, *I have a Bible and chamber pot in my room, so I'm set* 😄

What is the name of the organisation you are at again, Im interested

Camp Change, he texted back, regretting doing so immediately.

And why do you have a chamber pot

Ignoring this, he started his own line of questioning, one which had been on his mind for weeks, but which he'd been too afraid to ask:

Esther, did you tell me you once worked with a band?

I did, I was there manager. Not a very good one, but they weren't a very good band, so we were a match.

Bruno paused, wondering whether to pull the trigger with his next question – unbeknownst to Esther, who carried on messaging regardless:

We toured around Europe in the late sixties, early seventies. I member, one night in Sofia, Bulgaria a fight broke out. A group of men had come from a pub next door and started making trouble. Dear heart, you haven't lived until you've seen a woman with a braid to the floor bash someone over the head with a bassoon.

Did anyone in the band play the flute? He typed carefully, before hitting send.

Why yes indeed, Genevieve my friend and lodger, was the flaunting

flay

it keeps changing the word so frustrating

flautist of the band. I've never heard a flute sound so melancholic. Or produce as much spittle. But why do you ask?

So, it had been Genevieve who had gone to the papers to sell Esther's story! Did she know this, wondered Bruno, should he tell Esther now? He was still contemplating what to do next, when she messaged:

Are you still there?

I am.

He decided to change tack. *I searched for the Lodge you told mum about.*

Oh good, although I had hoped it might cause you to question your decision to go to this camp. I also turned myself in to the hospital, willingly I might add, after all the stuff in the papers. It was a very dark time.

But you needed help, sounds like a good place to stay?

No. Esther wrote back bluntly. *It wasn't. When you're already wounded, it doesn't take much more to add scars.*

Bruno felt his heart starting to beat in his chest, locked up in this strange room – Esther's words touching a nerve.

And whats with this chamberpot? pinged his phone.

Unsure how to proceed, he took the easiest option – he ignored the message and turned off his phone completely.

SIX

ESTHER (19 JUNE)

At eighty-two years old, it was officially Esther's first experience of being ghosted.

She immediately thought there must be an issue with her phone, and turned it off and on again, as Bruno had shown her, but the message remained unanswered. Esther knew all about watched pots never boiling, but now she was learning that you could not materialise a response, however hard one willed it. To keep herself sane, she tried remembering the Gaelic name Thackeray had given her, even going to her library to see if any of the books there could jog her memory. There was a large section on Scotland, it took up most of one wall, and she thumbed through many of them, hoping something her eyes lay upon would be the trigger, but nothing. How frustrating was her memory.

Retrieving her phone (still no message), she tried searching online but she could not type the accented vowels needed, and that frustrated her even more, and so in the end she gave up, and went to bed in a terrible huff, having dreams of ceramic pots, and Bruno, reaching out to her, but never quite taking her grasp.

SEVEN

BRUNO (20 JUNE)

He was woken by a banging.

Sitting up groggily, Bruno struggled to remember where he was, but as soon as he did, he panicked there was a fire. Springing to his door, he found it unlocked, Mitch walking past in the hallway with his toothbrush in his mouth, a towel over his shoulder.

'Nice dinosaur PJs,' he commented sardonically, making Bruno quickly shut the door again. After changing into last night's clothes, he used the bathroom (he hadn't been able to bring himself to use the pot), showered, changed into a fresh outfit, and made his way to breakfast – he was starving.

The other boys were sitting in their individual sections again – one new addition, a scruffy-looking freckled kid bringing their numbers to eight – but slightly closer this time. Mitch and the long-haired boy, Elliot, were even quietly talking.

Fetching himself a massive bowl of cornflakes, milk and heaped sugar (even by his standards), Bruno sat down on a free table corner. His mind was full of Esther – the revelation about Genevieve seemed important in the harsh light of day, but it was impossible to know if this information about her past would help or be harmful. He remembered Esther saying: 'I'm the reason this happened. I did this to myself', but he wasn't even sure what 'this' was. If anything, he'd been too loyal. Bruno's mind went to the stack of newspapers in his closet – even in peak anger, he still hadn't read them. Talk about being nice to a fault.

He overheard two of the other boys talking quietly about 'Dr Allan', which snapped him back to his surroundings.

'Is Allan the doctor's first name or his last?' Bruno asked. No one answered, everyone chewing and staring sheepishly into their bowls. 'Maybe it's both,' Bruno continued, 'Dr Allan Allan? Or Allan Squared?' The smallest boy Philip sniggered, caught himself and shovelled more cereal into his mouth. 'Or maybe it's Al last name Lan?' They were dumb dad jokes, Bruno knew, but he pushed on with his barely mediocre stand-up routine. 'I'm going to call him Dr Al.'

'I wouldn't,' Mitch mumbled gravely.

The youngest boy squeaked another laugh.

'What's your name?' Bruno asked him, even though he already knew it.

'Pip,' the boy replied. 'Well, Philip. You should probably call me Philip. My mum calls me Pip.' He looked at his lap for a moment, and Bruno was afraid Pip might start crying.

'What's this Dr Allan like?'

'He's a genius,' Pip said reverently, and Bruno scrutinised the other boys for a reaction, but they were extremely careful not to show anything except powerful poker faces.

'I don't think I've ever met a genius before,' admitted Bruno, truthfully.

'He changed me,' offered Pip brightly, but there was something about the way he said this, as if he'd been told to say it, coached, that brought back Esther's phrase, *brainwashing*.

'How?' Bruno asked.

Mitch and the long-haired boy exchanged looks.

'You'll find out soon enough,' whispered Mitch, under his breath.

The main hall was set up differently this morning, the chairs no longer in a semi-circle but organised more formally into rows. This simple change made it feel more like a classroom at school, and Bruno shivered involuntarily. The Romani word *waffedi* – bad omen – came to mind, but he pushed it aside, sitting in the front row beside the long-haired boy, as Mitch, Pip and the others had already claimed the back seats. Misfortune was very much a part of Bruno's traveller heritage, superstitions around daily life and domestic rituals were common – he knew as a child that a smashed mirror was very bad news indeed – but he'd made himself unlearn these old stories, especially at secondary school. A smashed mirror was simply broken glass. There were no omens, good or bad. And still, as he sat, looking out the window at the overcast sky and towards the ocean he'd yet to see with his own eyes, the word came drifting back... *waffedi.*

Glancing down, Bruno noticed a bottle of water was waiting by the foot of his chair. That was a nice touch, as Esther might say, reassuring – proof they were in a seminar, not at school. His old classmates would have eagerly used the bottles as missiles, but here the boys sat silently, waiting.

And waiting.

Bruno turned his head occasionally to check if anyone was coming, but the other seven boys seemed completely motionless, their eyes glazed over in a trance. The only sound was the iron radiators ticking – why were they even on, it was already eighteen degrees outside? At one point, Bruno picked up his bottle of water, reading the label for something to do, and was about to take a sip, when he realised it was a month past its expiry date.

With nothing else to occupy it, his mind wandered to Alberton Lodge. Esther had gone there willingly. She always had a funny anecdote for any event in her life, but not this time. Camp Change was nothing like an asylum from the seventies, he reminded himself. *Don't let Esther's past affect the promise of your future.* It almost sounded like an affirmation he'd find online.

Finally, there was the sound of footsteps. The other boys seemed to sit taller, facing straight ahead, so Bruno followed suit. A man swept down the aisle of chairs to the already text-less whiteboard, spraying it with cleaner and wiping it in long strokes with a cloth.

His entire teen life, Bruno had worked fastidiously to keep his eyeline above a man's belt, but now he was presented with Dr Allan's pert backside as he manoeuvred around the whiteboard. Bruno glanced at the long-haired boy beside him and could see he was also transfixed.

'Here we all are,' Dr Allan said at last, turning and smiling at each of the seated boys in turn. He was handsome, Bruno noted with alarm, much more so than his grainy photo on the website, with preppy blond hair tucked behind his ears, whitened teeth popping artificially with the help of a tan, his fitted blue shirt failing to hide a worked-out chest. As the doctor surveyed them one by one, he held their gaze for an uncomfortable amount of time. Bruno was second, and it was as if Dr Allan had switched on a floodlight, making him shift uncomfortably on his chair, his cheeks reddening, armpits growing moist. Wriggling his toes, Bruno contracted his stomach muscles, bit his tongue – anything he could do to manage this strange, fixed grin that was aimed like a weapon. *Beware the smiling guard,* he thought, and again it sounded like something Esther might say. Fortunately, after what felt like an eternity, Dr Allan's tractor-beam smile moved on to Pip behind him.

'We are men,' the doctor announced in a stentorian tone,

once he'd finished eyeballing Mitch and the others. 'We have been fed an untruth, that we cannot *choose* our destiny. I am here to help us transform this lie.' The sheer energetic force of Dr Allan's words made Bruno's ears prick up. Now this was what he'd come for – a rousing keynote speech. 'Look at the eight of you sitting before me. Beautiful men. The sanctity of our being, our body, and especially our union with another, is an earthly privilege.' Dr Allan placed a hand on the long-haired boy, kneading his shoulder and making him cringe. 'But your parents have failed you. Let me hear it!'

'Our parents have failed us,' all the boys except Bruno parroted back in the flattest of monotones.

'They didn't mean to – no one is saying that – but your parents have let you down. Why else would you be here?' Bruno rankled at this. He didn't think his parents were to blame. 'Each of you is broken. You crave wholeness, I can see it in your eyes. That is my mission, to piece you back together. Are you ready?' Dr Allan placed his hand on Bruno's shoulder now, making him jump involuntarily.

The doctor waited expectantly.

'Y-yes,' stuttered Bruno.

'Good,' Dr Allan replied, slapping him on the back so hard, it knocked the air out of him. 'Let's have a one on one.'

'With me?' asked Bruno, glancing around at the others.

'Yes, you.' Dr Allan placed two chairs at the front, facing each other. As Bruno nervously took a seat, the doctor fetched a brown leather satchel from behind the whiteboard, taking out a black notebook identical to the ones Neil had instructed them to write in the day before.

'It's Bruno, isn't it?' He nodded. 'This is your first session, welcome. I've gone through the notes you made yesterday' (Bruno felt a pang of embarrassment – he'd assumed they were private) 'and I have a question. When did you decide to become same sex attracted?'

'I–I don't know.'

'Now, isn't that interesting?'

'I guess it's always been there?'

'Has it? Think back, Bruno. When was this false idea first sown?'

He closed his eyes, 'thinking', but in reality, he wanted to avoid the probing intensity of Dr Allan's stare. It was worse with his eyes shut, however – the room began to spin.

'When I started to notice other boys at school,' said Bruno, surprised at his own candour, as his eyes snapped open.

Dr Allan leant forward, unblinking.

'Noticed them, how?'

'There was a pull. When I was young – about seven or eight.'

'You had an appreciation for other males. That's natural, that's healthy. When did it become *abnormal*?'

Bruno winced at the word.

'When they realised I was different?' he replied, hesitantly.

'Explore this for me. Who are "they"?'

Bruno stared at his hands, and realised they were in tight fists.

'As a kid, sometimes I'd look at another boy for too long in class – they'd notice, and I was... bullied for it.'

'The other males picked up on an irregularity, and they attacked. That's what healthy cells do in the body; they fight abnormal cells.'

'I don't... I don't think I'm...' Bruno trailed off, not able to say the word.

'And yet, here you are.' Dr Allan smiled broadly. 'What's your relationship like with your father? He still lives at home?'

'Yes.' Bruno was feeling growing resistance. This was about his personal transformation, it had nothing to do with his parents. 'Dad's great.'

'A good man!' said Dr Allan encouragingly, opening the

notebook, and flicking through the first few pages. 'But he's been sick, cancer?' Bruno nodded mutely, horrified at seeing his writing in the doctor's lap. 'Cancer is when the sick cells win. When they are left unchecked. When the false idea, or the error, is not properly corrected. Do you understand?'

He nodded again, uncertainly. Surely Dr Allan wasn't implying he'd caused his dad's cancer?

'Did your father kiss you as a child?'

'I guess so...' Even as Bruno uttered the words, he realised it was a mistake. The other boys shifted in their seats; their intake of breath audible.

'That's interesting.'

'I had a normal childhood, a healthy relationship with my dad. He'd kiss me goodnight.'

'What do you mean by "normal"?'

'My mum and dad loved me.'

'And yet...'

'I'm here because I want to learn more about myself.' Bruno's voice was trembling, but he felt something rising inside him – frustration, anger.

'Very good. Most schools of psychiatry analyse childhood and the relationship with parents for vital prompts.' Dr Allan leant forward once again and clasped his hands together. 'I'm going to ask you something, and I want you to answer me honestly. Will you promise me that?'

Bruno nodded with even more hesitancy.

'Did anyone do anything inappropriate to you as a child?'

'No!' Bruno replied loudly. 'Absolutely not.'

'And yet, here we are.'

'Stop saying that,' Bruno replied angrily. 'It doesn't mean anything.'

'Where is this emotion coming from?'

'From you, from these questions.'

'I asked you to be honest with me.'

'I am. I was.' Bruno's face was burning, and he felt like crying.

'This is familiar, isn't it?' Dr Allan said to the watching boys. Bruno turned to see them all agreeing, cautiously. He felt like laughing, it was so stupid, their heads bobbing in unison. 'The great battle between our knowing and our unknowing. Because how else can we return to the place before the false idea? That place is home. Don't you want to go home, Bruno?'

'I do,' Bruno said, his eyes beginning to stream tears. 'I want to go home.'

Dr Allan grinned his big, perfect smile.

'Excellent. Then we can start.'

When they broke for lunch, Bruno was exhausted in a way he'd never experienced before. He felt heavy, like the sand that was everywhere had found its way into his pockets, his shoes, the folds of his clothes, weighing him down – he could barely eat, he was so tired. The other boys snuck concerned glances at him from their tables, Pip even asking Bruno if he'd like more juice, but it was all he could do to shake his head.

The weird lines of questioning, the looping back and around in logic, had tied Bruno up in mental knots. If his body was any indication though, something was happening. Dr Allan had spoken about *breakthroughs* in a reverential way. Maybe that's what was happening, he was breaking through – but into what?

Lying on his bed briefly after lunch, trying not to fall asleep, Bruno turned on his phone. Messages came through in quick succession – ones from his mum and dad, both wishing him well and sending love, making Bruno's eyes well up so much he could barely finish them, and thirteen messages from Esther.

Dear heart, what news on the Rialto? I hope they havent hooked you up to any polygraph machins yet. I was reminded of

Sent accidentally, I

Thums. All thumbs. As I was saying, I was reminded of my good friend

Really, this is getting ridiculous. Why do they make

Apologies, dear heart. My old friend, Albert Agee, who was a painter until he died quite suddenly in the eighties, he had AIDs you know, as a lot of them did, sadly. He used to say, nothing is left to waste in this great universe. We are spares and parts of the greater tapestry. This on his deathbeds, I've never seen a man look so content. It has stayed with me always. I am thinking of you hand felt I must share

Albert Finsk, not Agee. I don't know if that matters to you, but it would to him, I suppose. The old brain. Oh, where is that pesky exclamation mark again

Sent too quickly, but huzzah – I have found it!

!

I am just wondering if you received my messages, hoping I have not sent these ones wrong or to some other poor person. If you could just let me know dead heart

Albert Aspen, I don't know where I got Finsk from, I think he was my Dentist once!! It undermines the fact that he was a very close friend, but he was, I assure you.

Question, how do you find where you have sent

Ah found it. Ignore me.

Although he rolled his eyes at the sheer volume of Esther's messages, Bruno was glad she sent them. He was realising his family might struggle when he came back from the camp, with the new version of himself emerging, but he felt Esther could adapt, just like she'd learned to use her phone.

Messages received, he replied. *Everything going fine. Definitely change happening. Will tell you all about it tonight.*

The moment it was sent, Bruno regretted it. Why had he promised to report back to her? It was too late now.

Checking his social media and his email, out of robotic habit rather than interest, he noticed an email that looked like it was sent from Esther. He brought it up and saw that it had been sent at 3.29 a.m.

Dear heart, it began.

Forgive me for bombarding you again. I sensed that email is a better way to send longer form messages. If it's not, apologies. I have spent most of my adult life trying to keep my affairs private, so it is strange to want to share details, but I do. The dam is bursting. Terrifyingly. As I look out onto the darkness of the garden, I realise two things are absolute truths – you have never broken my trust and I owe you an explanation. I'm not sure if I can tell you everything, but I must at least make a start.

I loved a man who was well known and had aspirations. He loved me too, I feel sure of that. We wanted to build a life together, but we also desired to keep our worlds apart, to begin with, at least. It served both of us for we had very different

*worlds, but they were soon to crash into each other spectacu-
larly. It was my doing, my loose lips, I broke the vow, and then
every ugly truth came tumbling out, and I was vilified for my
part. I ruined his political career even before it had started,
brought scrutiny to his business, and... let's simply say, no man
or woman was left unscathed. My stay at Alberton Lodge
made matters worse, and by the time I left, I was a shell of my
former self. I hid away in Whittleham, known to be a refuge for
lifelong wanderers, and here I've stayed ever since, licking old
wounds.*

*What I can't quite put into words is the guilt I hold about
all those I have hurt. It is one thing to ruin your own life, but
another's?*

*Gloom, gloom, gloom. I am a ghost – no, a ghoul – no,
Thackeray once told me about a Scottish spirit, a type of High-
land banshee, called a 'weeper'. An invisible spirit in folklore
that foretells tragedy. If only...*

Bless you, sweet child, for reading these crazed ramblings.

Yours forever,

Esther

Bruno realised this meant the ban on googling Thackeray
was lifted, but he felt no desire to do so now. He didn't feel
anything, except numb. The afternoon session would start soon
anyway.

He hauled himself up off the bed, feeling almost as old as
Esther.

'How are we this afternoon?' asked Dr Allan brightly, hands
behind his back. No one answered. 'Who would like to start?'
Again, silence. The doctor's handsome features crumpled into

mock-hurt. 'I'm trying not to take this personally,' he scowled, 'but I'd hate to have to tell your parents you weren't cooperating.' There was a high-pitched straining noise behind Bruno, like the sound a young child might make if they wanted to get down from a highchair. 'Philip, excellent. Come on down!' Dr Allan said, as if he was on a gameshow.

Once seated on his chair, Pip's feet didn't touch the floor.

'In your notebook, Philip, you spoke about being harassed at school.'

'Yes,' Pip nodded enthusiastically, both arms crossed tightly across his chest.

'Can you elaborate on that for me?'

'What does elaborate mean?'

He really was very young, too young to be under the scrutiny of Dr Allan, Bruno felt protectively.

'Tell us how they teased you.'

Pip swung his legs.

'They call me names and things.'

'What kind of names?'

Shrugging his shoulders, Pip scrunched up his nose.

'You can say...' Dr Allan smiled.

Pip looked out of the window for a second.

'Mean stuff. Bad words.'

'This is a safe space,' Dr Allan said reassuringly. 'You also wrote them in your notebook, so I know them already.'

'Then why do I have to say them?' Pip asked, sounding slightly petulant, and Bruno thought, *Yes, Pip, that's it. Fight back* – before reminding himself that Dr Allan was trying to help him.

'By saying the names, we can start to start exorcise them.'

Pip flinched. 'I didn't say anything about demons,' he replied, looking rattled.

'Neither did I, Philip. Just the names. What do they call you?'

Pip shrank down in his chair.

'Pipsqueak,' he answered.

Bruno had to stifle a laugh; it was so wholesome.

'And...?'

'Pippa.'

'Why do they call you that, Philip?'

'Because I play with the girls.'

'That's right. You prefer their company.'

Pip seemed as if he was about to clarify something but changed his mind.

'What else do they call you?'

'You mean, the bad word?'

'Yes, the bad one.'

'Cigarette.' Pip hung his head in shame.

'And why do they call you that?'

'Because they'll get in trouble if they say the proper one – the word that starts with "f" and ends with "g" and rhymes with...' Pip thought for a moment. '...bag. Or wag. Or tag. So, they say "cigarette" instead.'

Mitch sniggered. Pip heard and turned, giving a goofy embarrassed smile that broke Bruno's heart, it was so unguarded. He could imagine what it must have been like for Pip in those playgrounds.

'And how do you feel when they call you that?'

'Not too bad,' Pip said, swinging his legs, one foot at a time, back and forth.

'How do you *really* feel?'

Pip swung his legs even faster.

'Sad. When I hear anyone say "cigarette", or I see one, I get this weird feeling. My hands go really cold, and I get pins and needles sometimes.'

'And why do you think they call you "cigarette"?'

'They don't like me.'

'Why not?'

Pip considered this with a furrowed brow.

'Because I'm different.'

'But Philip – don't you see? You were born *perfect!*'

'No, everyone says so – my teachers, the boys in my class, my dad...'

'You're not hearing *me.*' Dr Allan's voice grew louder. 'We have come with love and understanding to help you, Philip. To emancipate you from this false identity. You were created unspoiled, unflawed, in the exact mould of your father, me and everyone in this room. It's only when we cut ourselves off...'

'I try though,' said Pip with a sad chuckle, clapping his shoes together. 'There's nothing I can do. I'm hopeless.' He shrugged again, apologetically.

Dr Allan hissed. 'There is hope, Philip. There is always hope.'

'Maybe...' Pip's shoe clapping was getting louder, but he didn't seem to notice.

'You have to want to change. From your very soul.'

'I do, but then my dad says I'm not listening to him. And I had to do all those extra punishments because I bought a pink drawing pad instead of a proper colour like...'

'You're not focusing...'

'But it was the only one left, and anyway, I was going to swap with Bryony the next day because she had a green one...'

'Philip...'

'...but Dad doesn't want me talking to girls, which is weird, because how am I going to meet my wife if I'm not allowed to...?'

'Philip!' roared Dr Allan, picking up the water bottle next to him, unscrewing it and throwing water into Pip's astonished face. Bruno couldn't believe what he had seen. Water dripped down Pip's chin. He seemed as stunned as Bruno. He was frozen, his mouth ajar, feet still. The only sound was water dripping onto the floor.

'You see,' Dr Allan addressed the rest of the boys as if nothing out of the ordinary had happened, 'we get trapped in patterns. If we can't change them over time, they need to be broken. Thank you, Philip, you can return to your seat.'

Slowly, Pip stood.

'Good, progress,' the doctor said with a broad smile, as Pip, leaving a trail of wet footprints, made his unsteady way back to his chair. 'Who's next?'

EIGHT

ESTHER

Esther knew in the pit of her stomach that something was terribly wrong.

The moment she saw the delivery man balancing the two massive boxes in his arms, her logistical error was confirmed. She'd bought one – one! – 4-pack of handwash as an experiment to test out this 'online shopping', or so she'd thought. It was folly to even attempt it, she realised now, especially without Bruno's expertise and guidance.

'Where do you want them?' asked the delivery man impatiently.

'I'm afraid there's been a mistake,' Esther replied, as politely as she could. 'This is too many.'

'You'll have to fill in a refund form,' he informed her, dumping the boxes inside the hallway.

'Where do I get that?'

'Online. Once it's processed, they'll come and pick them up again.'

'But you're here now!' exclaimed Esther, politeness gone. 'They'll clog up the entrance. I can't move them. I'm in a wheelchair. What if there's a fire?'

The delivery man surveyed the hallway, hands on hips.

'Plenty of space if I stack them.'

'Yes, but what if they fall and crush me?'

This made him hesitate, but only for a moment.

'That'd be a different form,' he replied with nary a hint of a smile, as he returned to his van to fetch the other two boxes.

What was Esther going to do with them all? The online form seemed like it could be even more trouble – she might as well cut her losses. Esther tore into a box – her hands were strong and impervious from gardening, she thought of them more as mole's claws than human fingers – and discovered that there were four 4-packs of handwash dispensers inside. That made sixty-four all up. Esther had one bathroom and three separate toilets downstairs, and she could use one in the kitchen, what was she going to do with the others? Open a stall on the high street?

'Would you like one?' she asked the delivery man when he returned. After he'd plonked the boxes next to the first two, he inspected the plastic bottle closely.

'Can't,' he sniffed. 'I get eczema if I use regular soap. Too harsh on the skin. Drying. You want something with a better PA balance.'

'Now you tell me,' Esther said, thumping the box with her fist.

It put her in a horrid mood. She'd not only let herself down, but Bruno too by being the poor student. She still felt awful about everything – giving Bruno the money like that, practically shoving it in his face, was unforgiveable. At least he'd returned some of her text messages, even if they had run dry. Esther also felt a sense of unease about sending such a revealing email to him, she'd even searched to see if there was a way to 'unsend' it, but just like a real letter, when it was gone it was gone, with not even the possibility of intercepting the postman.

Most of all she was worried for her dear boy, interned in a

camp. How had this happened? But, of course, Bruno was stubborn. That was part of the reason Esther liked him so much.

Her mood was not improved by her daughter arriving.

'What are all these?' asked Jane, as she came through the front door.

'Hand soap,' Esther replied curtly, 'Take one. Or ten if you like.'

In the kitchen, her daughter boiled the kettle to make tea, opening cupboards that didn't need to be opened – snooping, Esther felt sure.

'I've had an offer,' Jane announced as she brought two steaming cups to the table, teabags still in them, Esther noticed disapprovingly.

'An offer on what?' replied Esther, her mind still on the handwash fiasco.

'What do you think, Mother? To go pick tulips in Holland. The house.'

'You're selling?'

And then she realised – of course, thought Esther.

'How have you had an offer,' she asked, tersely, 'when there's no offer to make?'

'Now, Mother...'

'Don't "mother" me.'

'A lawyer friend is looking for a place within driving distance of Coventry. They have three children, two girls and a boy. Surely, even you can see this place would be better utilised by a growing family.'

'Next, you'll be telling me the girls are adorable twins, with bows in their hair. *Utilising.*' She spat the word. '*I'm* utilising this house.'

Jane shot her a condescending look.

'This place is a form of self-punishment – it always has been...'

'It's my home, it's where I want to die.'

'Come now, it's not practical. Not in this draughty, ramshackle...'

Esther changed tack.

'How could this family of yours buy a house they haven't even stepped inside?'

Daintily, Jane picked up her teacup and blew on it.

'Potentially, they'd be interested in building something more *reliable*...' she replied.

'You mean, tear down this place, start again. That's why they haven't bothered to see it.'

'It's only a building, Mother,' her daughter's voice became shrill. 'And it's kept you locked away for years!'

Esther softened slightly. She remembered how hard she'd been on Bruno only recently, and the results of her harshness.

'I forget how difficult my life has been on you.'

'I don't care about myself,' Jane replied. 'I worry about you. Let me sell this place. We can buy you a lovely ground-floor flat with the money, with a much more manageable garden. Maybe even a place with a small greenhouse for you to tinker around in.'

Esther hesitated at this suggestion. She had always wanted to experiment with hothouse flowers in shades one might not expect – greens, blues, blacks.

'Do you know I have some very rare seeds somewhere still, given to me by the cousin of Salvador Dalí – Andalusian wild-flowers, if I remember correctly. Lizard orchids and bumblebee ophrys. They were a gift, well, an invitation really, but I turned him down on his advances. Kept the seeds though, I think they're in a packet in one of my old gardening books for safe-keeping. Most of them won't germinate after so long, but one or two might...' Esther was lost in thought for a moment. 'And what happens to all my belongings?' she asked at last.

'You mean all your hand wash?' Jane smiled. 'Storage. Or we can find a new home for things.'

'Sell them, you mean.'

'Mother,' Jane said, in her kindest voice, 'we must start thinking of the future. The *near* future. I spoke to the doctor, and he didn't give me any specifics, but he's worried about you. Your iron is low, your blood pressure lower still.'

'I thought he didn't give you specifics?'

'He's a family friend.'

'So much for patient confidentiality.' Esther frowned. 'Leaving here would eventually lead to an old persons' home. Death processing plants, the lot of them. To sit with a rabble of ancient men and women wetting themselves and dribbling. You can say many things about me, but I carry on. No, I'm all right up here.'

'You're incorrigible, Mother.'

'I'm afraid I am.'

They shared a smile, which was unusual for such two habitual adversaries.

'Oh, I almost forget,' Jane said, slapping her thighs. 'I brought you my old scrapbook. I kept everything you ever sent me at school – letters, postcards, envelopes, even wrapping paper and string on gifts.'

'You did?' Esther was amazed. 'And for so many years?'

'You're not the only hoarder in the family,' Jane replied, sardonically. 'I left it in the car. One second...'

She'd only just gone, when Esther's phone beeped.

It was Bruno. The message simply read:

I don't know what to do.

At first, Esther wondered if he'd meant to send it to her.

She'd discovered, much to her annoyance, how easy it was to misfire.

Are you alright dear heart? she messaged back, and waited.

'What are these, Mother?' her daughter asked on her return. She was not only carrying the scrapbook, but Dominic's spliffs were in the palm of her outstretched hand.

'You *have* been snooping,' Esther retorted, crossly.

'Are you buying drugs off those local men again?'

'You make it sound so sordid. Local men. They're boys.'

'How is that better? And it is sordid.'

'The weed is for pain relief.'

'What if it interferes with your medication? Does the doctor know?'

'Of course not.'

Her daughter sighed, thumping the scrapbook on the kitchen table, the joints dropped beside it.

'What am I going to do with you?' she huffed.

'Nothing, hopefully. Although, there's something I do need your help with,' began Esther, guardedly. 'A professional question.'

Her daughter sat taller, and made a *hmm* sound, to signify she approved of this.

'Hypothetically...'

Jane gave a '*ha*'. 'It's an inside joke in the trade,' she explained. 'People always say "hypothetically" when it has some direct correlation to them. It's the legal equivalent of "asking for a friend".'

'This *is* hypothetical,' replied Esther sharply, annoyed at being found to be so transparent. 'If a person, not me, wanted to leave land in a will, how would they go about it?'

Narrowing her eyes, Jane frowned. 'Are we talking about the garden?'

'No, I told you – do you think I'd be so asinine as to bring it to you so openly, if that was my plan?'

'True. In England, you can leave land to a trust, perhaps through a charity, like the National Trust. Trusts must be recorded with the Land Registry and pay taxes and so forth.'

'Could it be done anonymously?'

'Possibly, it depends when it was done. Not in the past twenty years, but potentially before that.'

'I see,' replied Esther, deep in thought. 'That's what I was afraid of. So, if it was set up anonymously, there would be no way of finding it through official means?'

'Any land in trust would need to be overseen by a solicitor, to make sure everything was above board, and not outside the scope of the law. You can't just fence a piece of land off when you die and tell people not to trespass.'

'Could I ask law firms?'

'You might, but I doubt they'd give you any information, unless you were legally entitled to it. We sure wouldn't. What is this all about, Mother?'

'It's nothing, you've been very helpful. Slice of apple cake? Mary brought some over.'

'It's nice to feel helpful, and not be the enemy for once,' and Jane smiled hungrily in a way that she used to when she was much younger, whenever her mother praised her for good grades (which, it had to be said, were frequent – the grades, that is, not the praising).

Feeling slightly more charitable, Esther even opened the scrapbook to peruse inside, her daughter sitting close beside her. There were class photos from the expensive private boarding school called Badminton that Jane's father had sent her to, all the girls in matching uniform. Occasionally it was a challenge for Esther to find her daughter in the mix, not because she didn't recognise her, but because all the girls looked very much the same. Each subsequent year the challenge became slightly easier.

'Oh, here you are,' Esther exclaimed, by the fourth one, tapping confidently.

'No, that's Samantha Granger. I'm there.' Jane indicated a slightly sullener girl on the next row. 'I remember, I'd just gotten my period; I was terrified you'd be able to see in the photo somehow.'

'Didn't we have the talk about things like that?' asked Esther, squinting with the effort of memory. 'My lot in London were constantly going on about menstrual blood.'

'No, we never did. It would have been too embarrassing.'

'I'm only embarrassed we didn't.' Esther patted her daughter's hand.

There were achievement ribbons, and academic certificates, and yes, many of the things her mother had gifted over the years – postcards, interesting foreign notes, European flyers from the band Esther managed – sent out of guilt, and love, and a sense of disconnect and duty. She had *tried*, Esther thought to herself. There were no prizes for trying though.

As they neared the final few pages, Jane glanced at her watch. 'I have to go,' she said, getting up and kissing her mother on the crown on the head.

'Remember to take a hand soap!' Esther called after her.

She checked her phone but there was nothing from Bruno. Outside, it was beginning to get dark, so she opened the kitchen door to smell the dusk before she turned on all the lights and attracted insects. Esther's sight and hearing may have dulled over the years, but her sense of smell seemed stronger. She breathed in earth and woodsmoke and the musky-sweet elixir of rotting leaves.

The phone behind her beeped angrily.

I don't like it here. I'm not sure it's a good place, Bruno had written.

Esther texted back:

Can I call you?

The answer came almost immediately:

No, the reception is bad. And they might hear.

What happened?

As she waited for a response, Esther could see the 'typing' symbol in the corner. She felt a profound connection with Bruno then, on his phone, in her dark kitchen with the door still wide open.

> *It's not what I thought it was. I was told it was going to be personal development to help me, what's the word, process stuff, but you were right. They do think we're broken. They are trying to fix us, but worse. I want to leave, but I also don't want to leave the other boys here with Dr Allan. They're all younger. It's really messed up.*

I'm sorry, Bruno added at the end.

Don't be sorry, dear heart. I just wish I could type as swiftly as you. Are you in physical danger?

There was a frustratingly long pause.
I don't think so, came Bruno's reply eventually.

That doesn't sound very reassuring. Anything but a resolute no is grounds for evacuation I'd say. You might be better help to your friends if you can first get to safety yourself. You don't want to go down with the ship, that won't help anyone.

There was no reply for a long while.

Have you spoken to your parents? Esther asked.
The response from Bruno came instantly:

*No, and please don't text Dad. I don't want them to worry, it
will knock his health. Promise you won't.*

*I promise, dear boy. But I am concerned. Should you maybe
call the police?*

That would be even worse. I'm tired, wrote Bruno. *it's been a
weird day. I'm going to sleep and see how things are tomorrow.
Thank you, Esther*

If you're sure?

I am, thanks again, goodnight

Esther put the phone down, but she felt shaken. A thought
struck her, and she picked up the phone once more.

What did you say the name was, of the doctor?

He's called Dr Allan.

What kind of doctor is he? Psychiatric?

I don't know.

Once she'd closed the kitchen doors tightly, Esther retired
to the library to start her research. Let's see who this Dr Allan
really is, she thought.

NINE

BRUNO

After sending the last message, Bruno slammed his phone onto his pillow futilely. He was furious at himself. The water-soaking session hadn't been the last time Pip was called upon during the day. Dr Allan never used the technique again; he didn't need to. Pip parroted back everything said to him. Esther was right all along. It *was* brainwashing.

Leaping off the squeaky mattress, Bruno started to pace. Of course, Brother Neil had locked the door – yesterday it seemed almost credible this was for their own safety, but now...

'Hey,' came a whispered voice.

Bruno glanced around him wildly, checking the door handle again (still locked) and the shuttered window – was he starting to lose his mind? – when he heard the sound again:

'Chill out. It's Mitch.'

'Where are you?' Bruno whispered back. *Under the bed?*

'There's a hole,' Mitch explained, and Bruno scanned the connecting wall until he found it, next to the chest of drawers, no thicker than a pencil. He knelt, and could see Mitch's hazel eye peering back through his scruffy red fringe in a very disconcerting way.

'Why didn't I see this before?'

'It was blocked with toilet paper,' replied Mitch. 'I wasn't spying on you, don't worry.' Bruno hadn't even considered the possibility of this until now. 'Found it on my first residential here.'

'How many have you done?'

'Three. For my sins.' Mitch chuckled dismally. 'My parents' friends have a son who came here, he's ex-gay now with a wife and baby. Doesn't stop him sneaking looks at me though.' Mitch glanced down; all Bruno could see was a mess of ginger hair. 'Met my boyfriend here, so that's one good thing to come out of this dump.'

'He was on the course too?'

'Yeah,' said Mitch, in such a flat tone, Bruno knew instinctively to change the subject. He'd had enough no-go topics in his life to be extra sensitive to recognising them in others.

'Was today normal, with Pip?' he asked instead.

'Oh yeah,' Mitch replied, more casually. 'Dr Allan usually starts with the smallest kid, to make an example in case anyone considers rebelling. I've given up. Each time I fight back or run away, they up my meds.' Bruno gave him a quizzical look. 'Downers,' Mitch explained. 'Makes your brain sludge. I take them twice a day; Neil watches me swallow them after breakfast, and I'm supposed to do it again after dinner, but sometimes he forgets, like tonight. Gives me headaches when I skip a pill, and makes me speedy, but I'll take that over the brain sludge any time.'

'Can't you tell someone they're drugging you?'

'It's all legal medication, and I have a track record. Erratic behaviour, self-harm, suicidal ideation.'

'I'm sorry, Mitch.'

'Thanks, but we're all in the same boat, aren't we? How come your parents waited so long to send you here? Have a girlfriend to keep them off your tracks?'

'My mum and dad didn't know about me until... recently,' Bruno replied. 'They're pretty supportive generally,' he added, instantly wishing he'd phrased his response better, it seemed insensitive after what Mitch had revealed about himself.

'Why'd they send you to Camp Dread then?'

'They didn't... I came here on my own.'

Mitch's hazel eye boggled.

'How'd you get the money?'

'Earned it myself.'

'You *paid* to come *here*?' Mitch disappeared from the hole, and there was the sound of laughter. 'You spent all your own money to get locked up in this nightmare with us?'

'Yeah, I know,' replied Bruno. He deserved this ribbing.

'Bet you feel stupid.'

'I don't know how I'm going to make it through the next two days. I want to get out of here.'

'Good luck,' scoffed Mitch. 'They're already super jumpy because there was supposed to be ten of us, but two kids pulled out. They told their parents some of the fun stuff here, like locking us in our rooms at night, and they bailed. My parents wouldn't care less, but Dr Allan's nervous. They don't want to have to file a missing person's report. Can't take the bad publicity.'

'It's like we're in prison.'

'At least in prison they get to watch TV. Do you know about the bunker? It's a cabin on the deserted side of camp where they put you for "self-reflection and fasting" if you make them angry – an isolation cell, basically.'

'They don't feed you?'

'Not when I was in there six months ago. It was freezing back then too. Want a mint?'

Bruno was confused. 'Aren't you locked in your room?'

'Through here, dummy.' A small white mint appeared in the hole. 'Get ready...' and with that, the mint was shunted through, Bruno only barely managing to catch it. Normally, he didn't like to eat anything that somebody else had touched (especially if they hadn't washed their hands, and Mitch didn't seem the most fastidiously clean person), but he didn't want to seem ungrateful, so he shoved it in his mouth.

'Thanks,' he said, the mint crunching between his teeth, the freshness of the peppermint tingling pleasantly.

'Don't mention it. When did you know?'

'Know what?'

The eye in the small hole widened.

'That you were "same-gender attracted"?' Mitch snorted at the phrase.

Bruno hesitated. It was still uncharted territory speaking so openly about something he'd kept buried in himself for so long.

'I suppose I've always known,' he began, carefully. 'I have two younger sisters, and when I was ten or eleven I thought I was different because I'd missed out on having brothers. Then I went through puberty and I realised it was more... complicated.'

'Oh, it's complicated, all right... Another mint?'

Before Bruno could answer, one came shooting through the hole.

'My dad saw me kissing my Bible camp bunkmate two years ago,' revealed Mitch, making Bruno immediately think of his kiss with Dominic. 'Dad couldn't make eye contact the whole drive home. Then we went to see a psychiatrist, there was medication, I started these residentials, the exorcisms...'

'Exorcisms? You're joking, right?'

'I've never been more serious in my life. Mint incoming.'

Bruno was faster at catching the missile this time.

'They think you're possessed?'

'I can't possibly be their son, so I must have a demon inside me. Sometimes I'm thankful for the pills. Takes the edge off my seriously fucked-up existence.'

'That's horrible, Mitch.'

'Yeah well, you're locked up in a cabin too, so I wouldn't count yourself exactly blessed. Wait until we get onto re-parenting tomorrow. That's when the real fun starts.'

'What the hell is re-parenting?'

'Hey, Bruno, that kind of foul language will land you in the bunker.'

'Oh, sorry,' he apologised automatically.

'I'm messing with you,' sniggered Mitch. 'Let's just say, hopefully Neil is wearing deodorant. One last mint for the road?'

It flew out, hitting Bruno in the face, but he managed to catch it on the rebound.

'Night, Brother Bruno,' the hole was filled by what looked like tissue paper.

'Night, Brother Mitch.'

Bruno sat chewing the mint, wondering what an anti-gay exorcism might entail, and not enjoying the mental image, when his phone buzzed on his pillow.

It was Esther.

I found something, read the message. *This Dr Allan is a real piece of work.*

TEN

ESTHER

Using the Google on her own took patience, but now Esther was becoming proficient with the mobile device, it yielded results. The thing that stymied her was where the cursor might go mysteriously and how to get it back when it inevitably disappeared. One had to focus all one's energy into the tip of the index finger and then tap the screen, in a gentle yet decisive manner, where you optimistically wanted the cursor to be – just once – and *voila*. Esther was also getting the hang of autocorrect (a doltish tool, in her opinion), the clicking on search results and what to do once she arrived at a website, steering clear of what she considered 'traps': white pages with no text, or error messages, or being spat somewhere against her will.

Sitting in the study with her third cup of strong tea, Esther was making some headway with this alleged doctor, when Filip messaged:

> *re: your quest, just had an idea. If land is sitting unoccupied and unbuilt upon, it usually enrages the neighbours? There's a plot on the outskirts of the village, guy keeps it for his horses to graze, always fighting with the houses on each side. If it's a*

piece of prime real estate, it might get written about in local papers too. People trying to get planning permission, or if a tree falls on a house from a trust or blocks a road – who's responsible? Locals can get v riled up. Just my ten pence worth.

Thank you, Esther typed back, *that's actually very useful.*

She tucked it away in her brain, to investigate later and returned to the matter at hand. There was the expected gumpf on the Camp Change website, how Dr Allan was a benevolent leader and wise man, but the rest of the Google results were surprisingly thin. Did Dr Allan not have his own website? That seemed to be par for the course – when she searched 'therapist' or 'psychiatrist' and then 'London', for example, hundreds of individual destinations popped up. Even to Esther's novice eye, it seemed like a strange omission.

She remembered then that there was a medical register, and sure enough, they too had a website. Esther still only had the doctor's first name or perhaps Allan was the surname? She typed it in the searching box, and three results came back, all females. She tried again with Allan as the doctor's given name, but now 441 results were returned. Esther needed a surname. On a whim, she tried searching UK criminal records, but it required both names. She sat back, flummoxed. *Think, Esther,* she commanded herself. How would you find out a person's surname in the real world? She might go to the library, ask them to help. Once upon a time, she may have searched the microfiche. That was it. She should search the online newspapers. Esther began with *The Times* (which, it didn't surprise her, demanded money to proceed), and then moved on to other available broadsheets, before turning to the tabloids. It was when she arrived at the *Daily Mail* that she made her discovery:

Married psychiatrist, 34, keeps his job after kissing male patient and telling him, my marriage is a sham.

A psychiatrist who began an inappropriate relationship with an adult patient won't lose his job. Dr Allan Tasker, 34, blamed his behaviour on his deteriorating marriage. In one of their weekly sessions, Tasker tried to kiss the male patient, known as Patient A, and suggested they meet at his house while his wife was away, a medical tribunal heard. No sexual encounter took place but Patient A later complained to bosses at the hospital in Devon, where the father-of-two worked as a consultant psychiatrist. At a Medical Practitioners Tribunal Service, Tasker faced being struck off after admitting misconduct but was suspended from practising instead for 18 months. The hearing was told the incidents occurred between September 2016 and March 2017 while the doctor's marriage was 'under strain'. He admitted he had been 'pushing the boundaries with Patient A and that it had become inappropriate'.

There were several photos of Dr Tasker; one was with his long-suffering wife, although their smiles both appeared genuine. He was conventionally handsome, in that tall gentile way, which made Esther dislike him even more – he didn't have to use his power to try and coerce the patient – he chose to. And to not get struck off the register! What was this world coming to?

Esther wanted Bruno out of the camp immediately, and her first impulse was to call Filip and explain all, but his ill health, and her promise to Bruno, made her pause. Dr Allan/Tasker was legally allowed to practise; it seemed that Patient A had been an adult, so there was no criminality. Maybe she should ring the police to be safe?

She started to wheel herself around the room, trying to

think of a plan. Bruno must know first as a priority. Esther texted him:

I found something. This Dr Allan is a real piece of work.

Bruno's response came quickly.

What did you find?

Dr Allan Tasker. Inappropriate relationship with a male patient. Struck off for 18 months, a few years ago.

Bruno messaged with the one piece of information she'd omitted.

Was the male patient an adult?

Yes, as far as I know. But how old, sixteen was technically an adult? Bruno was eighteen. *Do you want me to tell your parents?*

No. There was an excruciating pause. *Is he a real psychiatrist then?*

Yes, from what I understand hes legally practising. But hes probably on one strike and hes out. If you see anything inappropriate, anything at all, you could go to the police.

And if I found something, we could stop him doing these courses? Working with children? Once and for all?

Yes, but if that puts you in any danger...?

There are boys here who have had exorcisms – not by him, but people like him. It's so twisted.

I think you should leave, as sooon as your let out in the morning, slip away and get to a bus station, or find a taxi. Doesn't matter how much it costs, I'll pay the driver when you get here.

I don't want to leave the other boys. What will he do to them if I go?

You have to look after yourself first. Its no use being in danger, you can't help anyone then. If you were to get into trouble, Bruno, I'll never forgive myself. If anything happens, call the police. Promise me?

I will.

I'll look at more information, see if I can find anything else about him on line.

Said like a pro.

I had the best teacher, Esther messaged back, *one of the most patient and courageous people I know.*

I don't know how courageous I've been. I had it easy, and I didn't even realise it. Now it's time to step up.

Be careful.

I will.

Putting down her phone, Esther felt so very worried for Bruno. An emptiness gnawed at her, and she considered lighting up another of Dominic's spliffs, but Esther knew she wanted to be compos mentis in case Bruno needed her.

Music. She required music. There was an old record player

on one of the shelves in the library, so she plugged it in, and chose a record – to her surprise, she felt like some Debussy; normally, Esther found him too romantic, too pandering. As *Suite bergamasque* rang out in the room, she wheeled herself back to the table where her phone was. Picking it up, she opened the email app and started a new email without even one mistaken click.

Bruno's words rang in Esther's mind:

I don't know how courageous I've been. It seems I had it easy, and I didn't even realise it. Now it's time to step up.

And with Debussy filling the house with his tinkling keys, she began to write a heartfelt letter, one that was several decades too late.

Dear Olivia, it began.

Forgiveness does not come naturally to me. Perhaps I can blame this on my lineage – an eye for an eye, a tooth for a tooth – but my father was a mild-mannered gentile, and my mother's ethos was always kindness, unfashionably so. It was even detrimental to their business. They owned a shoe-making factory in East London, and once word got out that my parents would replace any damaged pair of their shoes brought to them, people ruined their perfectly fine footwear to get new ones. Chutzpah too, as some of the shoes were clearly never made at my parents' factory, but they replaced every single pair. The business was doing well, my father reasoned, they could afford it. I never understood their logic. It sent the wrong message.

Perhaps I have a bitter heart?

I wish I could ask for your forgiveness, but I don't know if I deserve it. I would state my case, but I doubt, once all the evidence was presented, that a jury would not still convict.

All I know for certain is, when I first met Thackeray I had no idea he was married. I understand what the papers said, how I was a wilful homewrecker – homewrecker, yes, but wilful, never. I didn't set out to destroy anyone's life, least of all yours. Small comfort, to you perhaps, is that I completely managed to ruin mine.

Any explanation I give feels like I am squirming on the hook, and this is exactly what has stopped me before.

She paused to wipe her eyes.

He was not wearing a ring. Thackeray never even mentioned he had children to begin with. There was a 'wife' but the information was murky, and he gave every impression he was divorced. Thackeray was careful never to actually lie, but he did skirt the truth. You might ask: Esther, why did you not ask more direct questions? You see, I was falling in love with him. I know that rings hollow, but it's the truth. I had my own reasons to keep things private, too; my circle in London would not approve of our pairing, so I only let a few trusted people in. And then came the revelation that he was still in the process of divorcing his wife, but it was complicated, with properties, the children, etc. Another half-truth because he had conveniently forgotten to tell you.

I understand, Olivia, from the time it all came out, that you had periods of estrangement from Thackeray during those years, living between Glasgow and Edinburgh, but you were still very much married. I don't know what his endgame was. To keep us both? For you to continue to be the mother of his children, and for me to be his...? It was messy. If he was alive today, that's what I would ask: why did you have to make it so complicated? And to run for mayor too, with the scrutiny that invited, hubristic.

Perhaps he might have worked some master plan – he was so confident in his abilities – if I didn't reveal our relationship in the most idiotic way. Thackeray and I were dining in London, and as I was powdering my nose, I started chatting to a delightful young woman, and she simply asked, 'Are you with Thackeray?' That was it. When we re-entered the restaurant together, his face was ashen when he saw us. Did I know who that was? No. A journalist, apparently, a real muckraker. Did I say anything? Now, this caused me to pause.

Again, these feel like excuses, not apologies.

I do wish for your forgiveness, I dream about it often, but I know the more difficult task is to grant my own. The idea sticks in my side even as I write these words. To forgive myself would be an emotional release, and I fear what would be left of me without this resentment, without this longing. Would I wake up tomorrow a new person? I find that simply terrifying.

Thackeray once said to me: 'Esther, love is the careful accumulation of happiness.' As a businessman and a capitalist that made sense to him, the collecting of people and things to create a delightful tapestry – an Eames Lounge chair here, a trip to Caprice there. He might define regret, therefore, as the careless accumulation of sadness. I have been careless but never with sadness. I've always remembered where I left it. Tonight, however, I am feeling reckless, and although I can't yet forgive myself, at least I sense the path. To thank for this, I have a young companion, who has stoked my curiosity and let me connect in ways I never dreamed possible. Ironically, he is in peril a long way off, and I feel powerless to help him.

Which is, I suppose, why am I reaching out to you. To stoke bravery.

I have not always been courageous in my life, but I have always been remorseful. Olivia, may you have found true forgiveness.

Esther

She cried for a short while, before saving the email in her drafts as Bruno had shown her. Was it cowardly to write from the heart, when you had no ability to send the words, she wondered. She didn't know Olivia's email address, or even if she was alive. Still, Esther felt *lighter* somehow.

Not yet ready to sleep, Esther wheeled herself back into the kitchen to find her daughter's scrapbook. She tested herself on the class photos – yes, now she could identify her daughter in almost every one, she realised proudly. Esther had not seen the final few pages, and when she turned to the last one, she gasped.

There, glued to the paper, was a postcard with Thackeray's large confident handwriting. The address was Jane's boarding school in Bristol, the date 18 August 1972. He must have sent it after their first meeting, which was very like him, to send a follow-up note, flowers even. After Esther had first met him, a hundred red roses had arrived the next day.

On the postcard, he'd written:

Dearest Jane, so wonderful to meet you, you are the spitting image of your mother, mo chridhe. Love, Thackeray

As soon as Esther saw the phrase 'mo chridhe' she recognised it instantly. This had been his Gaelic nickname for her. *My heart.* A term of endearment that was secretly theirs, in London, at least. She could recall the delicious shiver of ebullience it would send down her spine whenever he uttered the words.

It also triggered another, even more recent memory...

Taking out her phone, Esther opened Google Maps. Could she solve this mystery once and for all?

ELEVEN

BRUNO (21 JUNE)

He slept poorly, as if he'd lain awake with his eyes closed the entire night, but he *must* have drifted off, if only into the lightest of sleeps. When Bruno finally gave up the charade at dawn, he felt oddly energised, a buzzing all over his body as if he'd been drinking too much coffee. *This is what it must be like before a soldier goes into battle*, Bruno thought to himself, brushing his teeth, after being freed from his room by Neil.

'Who would like to start?' asked Dr Allan with his crocodile grin, at the first morning session. Outside, it was gusty, the sky was a cloudless cobalt, the sunlight lasering through the windows as hot as a heat lamp.

Bruno waited five seconds before tentatively raising his hand – he didn't want to seem too keen and make the doctor suspicious.

'That's what I like to see.' Dr Allan waved Bruno towards the empty chair beside him. 'You other boys take note.'

The hall creaked against the strong winds, as Bruno made his way to the empty chair at the front.

'You seem different this morning,' noted the doctor, staring at him in his uniquely intrusive way. Today Dr Allan was wearing a seafoam-green shirt with very faint horizontal stripes that made Bruno's eyes go funny if he looked at it too long.

'Do I?' he asked, trying not to give any more away.

'Has anything changed?'

'I suppose I've made a few connections,' Bruno replied coyly.

'Would you like to share them?'

Rubbing his knees, Bruno took a deep breath.

'I'm beginning to understand how secrets from the past can have a big impact on who we are today.'

'It's important to understand our history.'

'It really is,' Bruno agreed.

Dr Allan nodded, with a slightly quizzical look in his eyes.

'You have traveller blood, don't you?' The doctor crossed leg over knee.

'Uh, yeah... How did you know?' Bruno hadn't written about this in his notebook, he felt sure.

'I like to do background research on all my patients. Your village, Whittleham, is quite famous for its traveller roots. Which is interesting, as travellers are not usually known for putting down roots. Are you Irish or Romani traveller?'

'Romani,' Bruno replied.

'Both your parents?'

'My father.'

'I see. Makes a lot of sense. The added pressure to be masculine. Especially in such a machismo culture – or am I getting that wrong?'

'Machismo' was one of those words that Bruno really should know but didn't. His dad would of course though, and Bruno felt a pang of affection for him.

'There are a lot of misconceptions about travellers,' he replied, carefully.

'Such as?'

Bruno didn't want to be led down this path, to bring up all the discrimination and racism, in his schoolyard alone. He thought of Dominic again and how effortlessly cool he'd be in this situation – slouching on the chair, with his chipped fingernail polish, the gold wagon wheel around his neck reflecting the light...

'We're waiting.'

'I'm not gay because of my traveller roots.'

Dr Allan tutted. 'Remember, we use "same-sex attraction" in the therapeutic space.' He picked up the water bottle and unscrewed the top, taking a small sip. 'I'm interested by the fact that traveller culture tends to have strong masculine roles. Men are men.'

'But wouldn't that have protected me against... same sex attraction?'

'Not necessarily. When there is too much pressure, the child can act out. Perhaps your inclinations are a form of rebellion? Do you hate your father, Bruno?'

He spluttered. 'Course not!'

'Come now, who doesn't detest their father a little bit?' The doctor laughed, turning to the other seated boys, who gave an uncomfortable collective chuckle.

'I don't,' protested Bruno. 'I never have.'

Dr Allan removed a black notebook from the satchel beside him. 'Can I read you something I found interesting?' He didn't wait for Bruno to respond. '"*Sometimes it's like Dad is waiting for his real son to arrive. Like I'm a placeholder child. I'm always in the shadow of what a son should be, every time I'm not watching sport with him, or don't want to kick a ball around, or just want to be left alone in my room, I feel this incredible pressure, like a heavy grey cloud, crushing down on me.*" You wrote that?'

'Yes,' Bruno admitted, hanging his head.

'I'm pretty sure I'd dislike my father if he made me feel like I was being crushed alive.' Bruno continued to stare at the floor. 'The first step is to acknowledge the anger, to understand how it's twisted your sense of self into an unnatural form. Whether it was societal pressures, cultural issues, or simply bad parenting, they all had the same effect.'

'My dad is not a bad parent,' replied Bruno, in almost a growl.

Dr Allan folded his legs again, the other way.

'Tell me about your mother. Are you close to her?'

'I'm close to both my parents.'

Dr Allan lifted the notepad from his lap and raised his eyebrows as if to say: we both know that's not true.

'What was she doing when you were unable to connect with your father? Did she try to help?'

'It wasn't like that – she probably didn't even notice.'

'And yet you felt suffocated under her roof, feeling this rage towards your father. And your mother didn't step in, not once?'

'Sometimes she would tell Dad to lay off me, if he was winding me up about not wanting to watch the football.'

'She made excuses for you?'

'Mum could see I was getting – not upset, I don't want to say upset but...'

'It's very illuminating, the dynamic between you and your parents, don't you think? Aren't we seeing the connections here?' The boys nodded to varying degrees, Pip the most emphatically, Mitch barely moving his head at all. 'Anger towards the father, abandonment by the mother, an inherited culture that celebrates appropriate gender roles. Do you want to know what I think, Bruno?' The doctor tapped his chin with the pen he was holding. 'I doubt you're even same sex attracted. I feel your non-conforming was an act of rebellion against your parents, your family, and your society. To hurt them, the same way they did you.'

'But they didn't hurt me.'

'Then why are you here?'

Bruno swallowed the large lump which had formed in his throat. He looked around for his bottle of water, but he'd left it at his other chair.

Dr Allan began speaking coaxingly. 'Until you acknowledge that your parents hurt you, perhaps unknowingly – we're not blaming them – you won't begin to heal and step into your true wholeness.' He uncrossed his legs and leant closer. Bruno noticed that his breath smelled bitter. 'From my understanding, travellers have a very high marriage rate; it's almost unheard of not to get wed, otherwise you're shunned by the community. Wouldn't you like to give your parents grandchildren?'

Bruno fought back tears. He felt like he was outside of his body, as if he was still sitting on the other chair, watching from the audience.

'I want to try something, an exercise,' suggested the doctor, 'will you do that with me?'

Helplessly, Bruno felt himself nodding.

'I'd like you to take yourself back to a moment in your childhood, maybe when you were around eight years old, a happy time – it could be a picnic, or a birthday – have you found a memory?'

After a short pause, Bruno nodded.

'Can you share it with us?'

'It's my ninth birthday.'

'Describe what's happening with as much detail as you can.'

'I'm about to blow out my candles, and I can see everyone around me, my dad and mum, my grandma, my sister Megan – she was about five then – kids I was friends with. My uncle had come with his family from up north, it was the first time I'd met them.'

'It sounds like a lovely day. But you must have felt pressure too, all those eyes on you, their scrutiny?'

'I just wanted to eat the cake.'

The boys tittered, but they were silenced by a quick glare from the doctor.

'Bruno, I want you to push through the veneer of this memory.'

'What does veneer mean?'

'The skin, the outer layer. I want you to penetrate the true emotion of what happened, your true experience. Can you see your father; what is he doing?'

'He's standing beside me waiting as I blow out the candles.'

'Can you see his face?'

'No, I'm focused on the cake.'

The sensation of being separated from Bruno's own body was increasing as he reminisced.

'Does your father have his hand on your shoulder?'

'I guess so.'

'Everyone is waiting for you to blow out the candles. Their expectant faces watching, the uncle you want to impress, and yet, there's a knowing you can't. That you won't be strong enough. You're inadequate. Everyone will see the candle flames flicker uselessly, and they'll laugh.'

Bruno felt tears running down his cheeks.

'Dad will help me blow them out if I can't. That's what he used to do.'

'And why do you think he'd do that?'

'Because he's an adult and I'm—'

'Or maybe he knows you're not capable. He doesn't want to be embarrassed in front of his brother. Perhaps you took this pain, and you created a false self to hurt him in the same way his lack of confidence hurt you. Maybe you wanted to destroy him in the only way you knew how, to withdraw from the family, from living the one true path, to allow yourself to be corrupted with sin.'

Bruno's head was swimming. He realised he was inhaling in

short tight breaths, so he tried to breathe normally, but he couldn't remember how.

'Is he okay?' Bruno heard someone say, maybe Mitch, but by then the room was spinning and fizzing and fading and then...

...Bruno opened his eyes and found himself staring up at the concerned faces of Pip and Mitch, and the jubilant face of Dr Allan.

'We did it!' the doctor yelled, spittle falling from his mouth onto Bruno. 'You are on the path of righteousness; you are losing your grip on the darkness.'

'You alright?' asked Mitch quietly by Bruno's ear, and he nodded as best he could.

'Did you hurt yourself?' Pip's eyes were wide. 'You went splat on the floor.'

'Don't crowd around him, boys, Bruno is turning a corner. This is excellent news!'

'I remember the first time I fainted,' said Pip, 'I fell and hit my head. There was blood, everyone kept slipping on it.' He shrugged. 'It was a small cut too. It's weird to think there's so much blood in your body right now. All that liquid.'

'Sit him up,' Mitch commanded, and the other boys helped Bruno upright, steadying him so he didn't fall again. It was strange having them so physically close after they'd so carefully kept their distance.

'How does he do that?' Bruno muttered woozily.

'My dad says it's because he's a miracle worker,' Pip said brightly. 'I hope they have bread rolls at lunch today!'

Food helped. At lunch, the boys sat on their usual table corner, but as closely as they could, speaking more freely than they had before. When Neil came to check on them, they slid further apart, returning together once danger had passed. The boys were regaling Bruno with their 'breakthroughs' – moments they'd spoken in tongues, or fainted, or convulsed. Mitch was the quietest, only joining in to debunk the other boys when they became too animated.

'Pip, you did not see an angel.'

'I did! Dr Allan told me.'

'That was last summer during the hottest day of the year. It was heat stroke.'

'Wasn't,' Pip replied, belligerently. 'I saw the wings.'

Bruno chewed his food, not hugely paying attention to the others. He'd let Dr Allan take the power, get inside his mind – it was a horribly invasive feeling he'd never experienced before; even the memory made him shudder involuntarily.

No, this time Bruno would act faster.

TWELVE

ESTHER

Dominic finally answered his phone at midday.

'Hello,' he said in the gruff voice of a smoker only recently woken.

'There you are! I've been worried sick. I haven't heard hide nor hair from you.'

'I had a couple of days off work.'

'And you've smoked yourself into the abyss, I bet. It's not good for you.'

'Sometimes the abyss can be a friend.'

'None of that nihilistic talk, Dominic, it doesn't suit you. I need your help. It's Bruno.'

'How's the Brainwash camp going?'

'Not good. Not good at all.'

Esther briefly explained to Dominic the revelation she'd found on the doctor.

'Oh, man,' he cried, when she'd finished. 'How can I help? Name it.'

Esther wrapped the phone cord around her finger and let it spring back.

'Can you get us a car?'

'I can do you one better,' Dominic said. 'I happen to know the whereabouts of an available motorcycle.'

THIRTEEN

BRUNO

All the chairs were gone from the room when they returned from lunch. Dr Allan and Neil were talking in hushed tones by the whiteboard, and there was a stack of mats on the floor.

'Gather round, brothers,' Neil commanded, when he saw them. 'Take a mat, and let's make a semi-circle.'

At school, all the boys would snigger whenever a teacher said 'semi'.

Once they were seated on the floor, Dr Allan crouched down.

'We've made progress,' he said, 'but I want us to push through.' Bruno was sitting in front of him, with a direct view of his crotch. 'While you're having your re-parenting session, I want you to open yourself up to the experience, like Bruno did this morning.' He smiled at Bruno warmly. 'Mitch, why don't you go first?' He gestured towards Neil.

'Yeah, I've just had lunch... I feel pretty full and...'

'Don't make me ask twice...'

With a sigh, Mitch got up from his mat and moved towards Neil, who stood to greet him. There was something completely unwilling in Mitch's body language, as if he was bracing for a punch, but Neil only smiled. 'I won't bite,' he said.

'Good. Now, Neil,' Dr Allan said, bouncing on his heels, 'I want you to get into a comfortable seated position on the mat' – Neil did so – 'and Mitch, I want you to lie down, imagining this is your surrogate father. This isn't Neil, he's representing something much more important than that, no offence.'

'None taken,' Neil replied cheerfully.

'We are treating the psychological disturbance caused by defective fathering.'

Neil sat down on the mat, cross-legged, and Mitch knelt in front of him.

'How would you like to do this?' Neil asked.

'Ah, ah, ah, ah,' reprimanded Dr Allan, 'No talking, this must go beyond speech.'

Opening his arms, Neil beckoned Mitch towards him. Bruno watched in horror as Mitch leant forward and seemed to tackle the man around the waist. Neil wrapped one arm around the boy and stroked his back with the other. Bruno could barely believe what he was seeing – it was too intimate, and very shortly he would be forced to hug Neil, on a ragged gym mat, watched by the others. The thought turned his stomach. Suddenly, a strange spluttering noise could be heard. It took several seconds for Bruno to work out what it was.

Mitch was *crying*.

'No,' Bruno said, standing up quickly.

'Sit down,' commanded Dr Allan, with a wave of his hand, still hovering in his squat.

'This isn't right.'

'How could you possibly know what's right?' Dr Allan asked evenly. 'Are you a registered therapist?'

'No, but neither were you for eighteen months.'

'What did you say?' Dr Allan rose slowly off his haunches. There was something aggressive in the movement; it reminded

Bruno of a cat arching its back, hair on end, to appear more intimidating.

'Mitch, stand up, get away from him,' he commanded. The other boys were on their feet now, Pip looking warily at Bruno. Mitch stood up too, slowly, wiping his face, which was blotched and wet with tears. Neil was staring at Bruno, open-mouthed. 'I'm not comfortable with this.'

'What *you* feel comfortable with is precisely the problem,' Dr Allan replied, standing with his hands on hips. 'Re-parenting is a therapeutic process, highly regarded, to help undo the bad parenting you are currently displaying.'

'I had great parents,' said Bruno, his voice steely. 'And even if I didn't, hugging a grown man isn't going to stop me from being gay. Can't you see how ridiculous this is?'

'We. Don't. Say. That. Word.' There was so much force to the doctor's inflection, Pip winced and took small steps back.

'Yes, we do. *I* do. Or I should. I don't know why I was so afraid before. It's only a word. It doesn't change anything, not really, not inside yourself where it counts. And for the record, my dad was an excellent parent. When Toby Rackling teased me at school, Dad drove over to his house and made him apologise. Told me if the boy looked at me sideways, he'd wring his neck. Toby's dad is a loader in the warehouses too, big man, but Dad wasn't fazed. When I got my first bee sting, Dad carried me all the way from the park and put vinegar on it. He hugs me, hugs me all the time, in a good way. Not this twisted version. Do you even have any kids of your own?'

Neil seemed caught off guard by this question.

'No, but the therapy helped—'

'Quiet, Neil,' said Dr Allan, without taking his eyes off Bruno.

'It doesn't matter what your parents are like, what trauma you experienced. I was born like this, it's part of who I am. I've pushed it away for so long, pushed and pushed, as if it was easier putting all my energy into resisting instead of simply accept...'

'You're having a relapse, it happens!' the doctor yelled. 'You must trust me here.'

Bruno stared him square in the face.

'Why would I trust you, Dr *Tasker*?'

The doctor's eyes bulged. Bruno could feel the boys murmuring beside him, 'Dr *Tasker*?'

'Where did you hear that?' he demanded.

'A good friend told me,' Bruno explained. 'She found quite a few interesting things about you, Dr Tasker. All over the internet, I'm surprised the other boys don't know. Or their parents...'

Dr Allan Tasker took a deep breath.

'Neil, would you accompany Bruno to the retreat room? I feel he would benefit from some reflection by himself.'

'I'm not going anywhere,' replied Bruno, backing away towards the door. He had a clear path to it, and he was pretty sure he was going to be faster than lumbering sweaty Brother Neil. Dr Allan might be a sprinter, though.

'Yes, you will,' the doctor replied, calmly, 'otherwise there will be consequences.' Bruno continued to back towards the door. 'If you don't go, another boy will take your place. Philip.'

Pip squeaked in surprise at hearing his name.

'He didn't do anything.'

'Doesn't matter. When you sin, responsibility must be taken.'

'I'll run to a police station. I'll tell them what you're doing.'

'Run. We're not doing anything illegal.' Dr Allan gave his most unnerving smile. 'I'm a therapist.' His tone darkened. 'You are a troubled young person in my care.'

'You were struck off the register.'

'That was a misunderstanding, taken quite out of hand. And I was reinstated.'

'You had an inappropriate—'

'Neil, grab him.'

Both Dr Allan and Neil had been inching forward, and on the doctor's command they both raced towards Bruno, who turned, tripping over his ankle in his haste. He fell onto his hands, and before he could get up, the two men were beside him, each taking an arm roughly.

'Get off me!' Bruno yelled, but they had tight grips and they pulled him out of the hall, and through the desolate camp, his screams getting lost in the wind, even if there was anyone around to help. As they went further, the buildings became even more bleak – broken boards and smashed glass, one cabin with all the doors and windows missing, the interior blackened as if there had been a fire. Perversely, he could begin to hear the sea, even over the wind – it must be just beyond those dunes – and it made him think of holidays, and freedom, and cool water on hot summer days. He was drenched in sweat now, he'd do anything for a swim. To escape into the waves. Neil and Dr Allan dragged him all the way to a far cabin, the one that Mitch had warned him about, before Bruno was shoved forcefully inside, the door slammed behind him and locked with a 'thunk'.

Picking himself off the floor, Bruno felt stunned. He'd never been treated like that before, never manhandled against his will, but mostly he was worried for the other boys, if Dr Allan would punish them too, and so he banged on the door and screamed until his voice was hoarse. Only then did he remember his phone, but it must have fallen out in all the madness, or maybe it slid out of his pocket when he was on his mat, and a new wave of hopelessness hit Bruno. Because he understood that all his pain was of his own doing, and how he wanted to sit with his mum and dad as they hugged him, and he cried hot tears of frustration, promising himself, when he left this cabin, he would appreciate his life forever.

FOURTEEN

ESTHER

'That's it?'

'I didn't say it was exactly a Harley-Davidson,' deadpanned Dominic.

'You also didn't mention it was a rust bucket either,' replied Esther, archly.

Dominic struck the kick stand with his boot, but it didn't budge. He was wearing a raggedy T-shirt emblazoned with 'Stop the World, I Want to Get Off' over an even tattier black woollen jumper.

'Can't you find a car to borrow instead?' she asked, nervously. Her brother Cubby, rest his soul, had loved motor-bikes, and was forever having rows with their otherwise mild-mannered parents about riding them. In fact, he died in a boating accident of all things, when he was twenty-three – her heartbroken father raging at the funeral: 'Cubby should have spent less time on those bloody death traps, and more on learning to swim!' Esther wondered if she'd ever told Jane about her uncle's tragic end, or come to think of it, much about him at all.

'A car will take longer,' Dominic replied, giving the kick

stand another go, successfully this time. 'You told me time was of the essence.'

'Is it even roadworthy?'

'Yes,' replied Dominic, but he didn't sound convinced or convincing.

'How am I supposed to ride it, by clinging onto you?'

'Basically, but with the added protection of a large belt wrapped around us both.'

'You're joking?'

'You can always drive instead.'

'Not on your nelly.'

Esther wheeled up and inspected the motorbike more closely, which was a mistake, as she was even less reassured. The bike was older than she was. There was a spoke missing, it was rusty and the chassis appeared slightly warped.

'We can't take my wheelchair with me, trailing it behind. What happens when we arrive?'

'I can attach your walking frame to the back, the one that folds up. It's not ideal...'

'You can say that again. How do we flee with Bruno once we have him out of there? This is a rescue mission, remember?'

'We cross that bridge when we get to it.'

'No, this won't do. We'll hire a taxi from here.'

'Good luck getting one to drive you to the coast. They're funny about pickups in Whittleham at the best of times – think we're all going to do a dash without paying. Not that I have, of course...' Dominic grinned mischievously.

She eyed him keenly.

'Have you been smoking any of your wares?' she asked him frankly.

'Not today.'

'How long will the journey take?'

'About three hours. Are we doing it?'

Esther peered at the motorbike again nervously. She could

see the newspaper headlines now: *Petty Marijuana Dealer and Octogenarian in Ten Vehicle Pile Up*. It wasn't just the fear of an accident stopping her, it was the shame of being exposed, of being *seen*. For so long she'd hidden away up on the hill, that to move so quickly, to be around traffic and so many watchful people – it chilled her to the bone.

It had rained an hour ago too, excellent weeding weather with the soil newly moist.

'I don't know, Dominic. What would my daughter say?'

'You must have nerves if you're bringing *her* up as an excuse.'

'Noted,' Esther replied dryly. 'Can I think about it some more?'

'I have the bike until midday tomorrow, but I don't think we should drive at night, just in case I'm not good at handling motorbikes in the dark.'

'How many have you ridden before?' That should have been her first question.

'Let's just say I won't be entering the Paris–Dakar Rally any time soon. You said Bruno really needed us!'

'He does, but I want to get there in one piece. I suppose I'm afraid of failing him too. What if we're not the cavalry he wants or needs?'

'Act first, beg for forgiveness second. Always worked for me.'

'The innocence of youth,' Esther said, before the motorcycle fell over with a crash, fortunately not on anyone's foot.

FIFTEEN

BRUNO

It was getting dark. He'd finished crying, there were no more tears left, leaving him thirsty, as if he'd purged all available moisture from his body. Bruno guessed they'd bring him dinner soon – until he remembered Mitch telling him there was no food in 'the bunker' – but surprisingly, this didn't upset him any more. It couldn't; his sadness was already at rock bottom. Wiping his face with his sleeve, Bruno started to assess the cabin. It was the same size as his, but with a pitched roof and it smelled worse – of disuse, musty and slightly of cat urine. He tried the window, but of course that was fixed shut and there were bars on the outside even if he did manage to get it open. Bruno wondered who had attached the bars, if it was Brother Neil.

He switched on the light, but it didn't work. There was a Bible on the bedside table; much good that was to him with no light, and not that he felt in the mood to read, but at least it would distract his mind. Bruno so rarely had any time which wasn't filled by music, his phone, or television, and sometimes all three simultaneously. Now all he could do was think.

In the gloom, a memory began to form, of joining Facebook

when he was freshly thirteen. The platform was old news already, his schoolmates mostly ignored it, but Bruno's dad used the messenger to keep in contact with his brother, which intrigued Bruno. His uncle and his cousins – all of that side of the family really – had an element of mystery to them, seldom visiting, existing in the fringes of his life. Bruno connected with a cousin, who sent him an invitation to a private traveller group on Facebook, an inner sanctum, with talk of movements, news (mostly who was marrying whom), the occasional dark-humoured meme, and gossip. It was fascinating. Bruno felt he was gaining access to a part of himself.

Six weeks after he'd joined, someone in the group posted an innocuous photo of a teenager, standing in a field, his face partially turned away. He was gawky – half smiling, half bashful, a line of acne running along his cheekbone, and seemed so familiar, Bruno wondered if it was a cousin of his. The caption read: 'Looka this one'. Instinctively, Bruno understood what it meant. He didn't have to read the comments underneath, but although it turned his stomach, he forced himself to. 'Makes me sick,' said the first. 'Hope they disown him,' agreed the second. 'Do us all a favour,' came the third. More disturbing than the comments were the number of likes against each. The thumbs-up. The laughing emojis. In that clear moment, Bruno knew two things for certain – he was gay himself, and if it was ever revealed, it would make its way here, to this forum, and shortly after, to his uncle and all of his father's family. Bruno promptly deactivated his account and never logged onto Facebook again.

He stood, stunned by the memory. Had he supressed it or simply forgotten? Still racking his brains for an answer, Bruno crawled onto the bare mattress, ignoring his usual fear of dirt and bedbugs, and let the rusted springs take his entire heavy weight. He still hadn't told Esther about the Genevieve paper connection either, he remembered wretchedly.

Bruno must have fallen asleep. His mouth felt dryer than

ever, and it was pitch-black, a true darkness he couldn't remember experiencing before. There was usually always a light from *somewhere* – a laptop recharger, a Wi-Fi router, a lamp outside. He heard a rustling. Perhaps it was the wind. No, it sounded like a whisper. Sitting up, Bruno wondered if the lack of water was making him delirious.

'*Hey, Bruno.*'

It was coming from below the window. Jumping off the bed, Bruno headed down on hands and knees to investigate.

'Mitch?' he asked, almost expecting a tiny mint to fly through the air towards him. His stomach gurgled; he would gladly eat a mint.

'We don't have much time,' Mitch replied. 'I have to go back soon in case Neil does a check on us.'

'How did you get out of your room?' asked Bruno, amazed.

'You can thank Elliot for that.' Bruno almost asked 'who's Elliot?' when he realised it was the quiet, long-haired boy who mostly faded into the background. 'The kid's an escape artist. He's found a way of putting masking tape on a lock, so it doesn't quite catch. Afterwards, you can pull the door open with enough force. He jimmied all our doors at lunch.'

'Can he break me out of here?'

'No luck, this one has a padlock.'

A light twinkled, drawing Bruno's eye to the hole in the wall. Mitch must have a torch.

'How did you know this was here?' Bruno asked into the glowing cavity.

'I wasn't completely honest with you before,' confessed Mitch. 'I didn't just find the holes. My boyfriend Simon made them with a drill bit he snuck in.' Bruno marvelled at the resourcefulness of these boys, jimmying locks and drilling communication holes, realising how privileged he was never to be forced to learn these skills. 'Here, I have some cheese straws from dinner. I bet you're hungry.'

The light was obscured as one was pushed through the hole. Bruno snatched the cheese straw with his fingertips, and stuffed the savoury buttery goodness into his mouth.

'When do you think they'll let me out?' asked Bruno, finding it hard to swallow, his mouth still so dry.

'In the morning.' Another cheese straw came through.

'At least I won't die of hunger, thanks to you and Simon. Thank him the next time you see him.'

'I don't know when that will be. Simon's gone.'

Bruno stopped chewing.

'Gone where?'

'After the last residential, he ran away from home. Didn't even tell *me* he was going. His aunt and uncle are... well, they make my dad look like Parent of the Year, so I don't blame him. Simon hitchhiked down to London, I think. We never officially broke up, and he'll be in contact when it's safe, I'm sure. That's why you and I never stood a chance; sorry, Bruno.'

He smiled at Mitch's sweet bravado.

'Simon's very lucky to have you.'

'We're lucky to have each other. Want some orange juice?'

Bruno threw himself at the emerging straw with such force, he almost cracked his head on the wall. The juice was the best he'd ever tasted in his life, but it was gone far too quickly. It helped clear his head, though.

'Mitch, I need to get a message to a friend of mine called Esther. I think she can help us. Can you find a phone to use?'

'There's a phone box in the closest village, it's about half an hour away. I can wait until Neil's asleep and go then. What's her number?'

Bruno didn't know; Esther's number was always in his phone.

'Can you call directory assistance and ask for Esther Saul in Whittleham.' If Esther used to get spam callers, like she'd said, her number was likely in the directory. 'Make a reverse call, but wait a long time once it's ringing, because it can take her ages to answer.'

'What do you want me to say if I get through?'

'Ask for help – don't involve my parents though, Dad's still not well enough for the stress. Tell her to bring reinforcements, the police, or maybe her daughter Jane – that's really important. I'm not sure what Dr Allan and Neil are capable of, but I don't want Esther bearing the brunt.' A question popped into Bruno's mind. 'Mitch, if you and Elliot can get out of your rooms, why haven't you run away from the camp?'

Mitch gave a weary sigh.

'What's the point?' he replied. 'I'd never make it down to London, and it would just aggravate my dad. There's no such thing as freedom anyway, not when you're a kid. Final cheese straw?'

Bruno took the straw appreciatively, vowing on its flaky deliciousness to return every single one of these kindnesses as soon as he was free.

SIXTEEN

ESTHER (22 JUNE)

At 2 a.m., Esther thought she heard the phone, but it was too far away, and she was in a dreamed place, with Thackeray. He was covered in flour, and they were laughing. It was glorious. *Let it ring*, she thought sleepily.

Later still in the night, she awoke, worried – Esther had a sense that time was running out for her. That everything she had pushed down, down inside herself for so long was now bubbling up to the surface. It was Bruno, she realised; caring about someone again, and feeling the pain of loss and separation, it was bringing back the old hurt. Except there was no resolution for her and Thackeray. He was gone – there was nothing more to the story. And yet...

Esther brought up Google Maps again just to be sure she hadn't dreamed her discovery. *Mo chridhe* – my heart. Thackeray's declaration of love. She'd typed in 'chridhe' and one result had caught her eye instantly, to the north of Glasgow, a location called Cridhe Cruaidh. It meant 'tough heart'.

'Eureka,' she'd said, smiling at Thackeray's mischievousness. Why not call her a battleaxe and be done with it?

But perhaps this was coincidence? *Let's not forget reason and logic in the process*, she reminded herself. Remembering Filip's words, she typed Cridhe Cruaidh into the monopolistic search engine. Up came a small slew of local reportage and blog articles complaining about the plot of land, seeming to span several decades.

'Eureka and bingo,' Esther had said, eagerly.

And that was before she'd discovered the stones...

After she'd reassured herself, peering down on the foundations like the eye of God, she picked up her mobile phone and texted Dominic:

Let's go as soon as we can, the earlier the better.

At 8 a.m. there was a knock on the front door. Someone stood in the doorway wearing a helmet and motorcycle leathers. For a moment, Esther thought it was a delivery person (*not more hand soap!* she thought, fearfully), but then Dominic flipped up the visor.

'It's me,' he said chipperly. 'Your ride awaits.'

'Where did you get those clothes?'

'Borrowed them. Don't ask questions.'

'I know I said early, but I've never seen you before midday in my life.'

'As it happened, I fell asleep at seven last night watching *Twin Peaks*, which meant I had some very strange dreams, but I'm now wide awake. No weed in my system for over forty-eight hours, I could practically sign up to be an officer of the law.'

'Heaven forbid,' replied Esther. 'What am I going to wear, if you're all leathered?'

'Layers, and lots of them. It will be cold on the road. I have a spare helmet.'

Esther looked unsure for a moment.

'I don't know how I'm going to fare – my hip, sitting on such a wide seat, even if I am chained to you...'

'I thought of that already,' replied Dominic. 'Behold!'

He made a flourish towards the motorbike behind him, and Esther realised it had sprouted a sidecar.

'Where did that come from?'

'A more suitable carriage for m'lady, no?'

Esther was momentarily speechless.

'Won't we look like something out of a Marx brothers' movie?'

'If we're lucky. I'm a very good driver,' Dominic assured her.

'Very well,' Esther said with a sigh. 'Getting on these layers, though; it will take me an age on my own.'

'Would you like some help?'

'I thought you'd never ask. But you'll have to avert your eyes. I do not want to spoil the illusion of beauty and perfection.'

'You couldn't if you tried,' answered Dominic with a wink.

Once she was dressed – looking very much like the Michelin Man – and helmeted, Dominic guided her into the sidecar, covering her legs in blankets before buckling her in tightly. It was quite snug. When the motorbike roared to life, Esther had to stifle a cry – although would anyone hear it over the din and through her helmet? – but Dominic very slowly made their way down the driveway, making careful work of the Whittleham streets as well. Esther was beginning to think the journey might not be so bad after all, when they turned onto the A14 dual carriageway, and Dominic accelerated. The force was incredible, and to be so low to the ground at such speeds! Esther kept

thinking of the scene in *I Was a Male War Bride* where Cary
Grant, riding a motorbike with a sidecar, crashed into a bale of
hay. Except, instead of hay bales, there were articulated lorries
hurtling towards them.

Stopping several times because of her weak bladder, they
made their way towards Cambridge and then up to Norwich
before heading for the coast. Esther could smell the sea long
before she saw it – when was the last time she'd seen waves? she
wondered in awe.

The memory of travelling with Thackeray to Morocco came
to her as they sped on. From Marrakech they'd arrived in the
idyllic port town of Essaouira. Even the name was utterly
romantic – *Essaouira* – the sound of a gentle sea breeze, much
more evocative than Casablanca, they'd missed a trick there.
The medina was entrancing, their *riad* divine, the food glorious.
Thackeray would never usually touch weed – he didn't like
losing control – but he'd smoked some aromatic hash on the
oceanfront, and they'd laughed until their bellies hurt.

Had she known about his secret then? Esther wondered.
Did he make phone calls? Surely. But there were no mobiles
back then, no faxes even. When you were away, you were truly
gone. They might have been on their own planet, one filled with
joy, and light, and sweet mint tea. Was it wrong to have found
happiness, at the expense of another?

Once they arrived at their destination – a sandy car park
after an hour of continuous riding – it was a relief to take off the
stuffy helmet, although Esther now felt slightly naked
without it.

'What's the plan?' asked Dominic after he'd helped Esther
to her feet, untying the retractable walker from the back of the
bike and starting to set it up.

'We go in and make sure Bruno is all right.'

'What if he's not?'

'I cause havoc.'

'Nice,' Dominic said, grinning that most roguish smile, like a scruffier Errol Flynn. 'Are we ready to do this?'

'Let's. For Bruno!'

The place seemed deserted. It reminded Esther of a scene from *The Day of the Triffids* – a derelict British seaside resort where ominous things loomed, although she'd always imagined it might be quite fascinating to be consumed by a giant plant, enjoyable even, to her at least. And in the end, wasn't everyone fertiliser?

There was a sharp breeze, which would throw grit into their eyes, forcing them to shield themselves. Dominic wrapped a scarf around Esther's face, but this obscured her view, and she was trying to keep a lookout for her dear heart. It was slow-going as they limped towards the cabin marked 'Reception', and the pain in Esther's left leg was worsening, even with the walker, but she didn't want to worry her brave companion.

'Can I help you?' called a stout man who was striding very quickly to intercept them.

'My jolly good fellow,' Esther called to him jubilantly.

'*Jolly good fellow?*' asked Dominic under his breath in Esther's ear.

'Just go with it,' she whispered back. 'I do very much hope you can help me,' she announced at full volume, projecting her voice over a squall.

'Are you lost?'

'Constantly, but now I'm found. Was blind but now I... well, you get the drift. Is there a place we could sit? I'm afraid my legs aren't what they once were.'

'I'm afraid this is private prop...'

Esther's legs buckled underneath her. She'd meant to do it on purpose, but once her legs had been given the command, they added their own urgency to the proceedings. Dominic grabbed her shoulder, and the portly man ran up to take the other.

'I don't want to appear dramatic,' Esther said, with only a touch of *le théâtre*, 'but I might make a bit of a scene without a respite and maybe a glass of water.'

'Let's go into the canteen,' the man suggested, reluctantly. 'My name's Neil. Can I ask...?'

'Once I am seated, you may ask me anything, Neil – my hand in marriage, if you so wish.'

Even she knew she was laying it on thick. Several boys had come out of one of the buildings and were staring at the three of them warily, but there was no sign of Bruno.

The canteen was warm and smelled agreeably of toast and vegetable soup. Bruno was not inside here either. A trio of boys, all young, hung back watching intently as Esther was helped onto one of the benches. She leant on the crummy table, afraid that she might fall backwards again, very happy to be seated and out of the grip of sea winds.

'Outside,' Neil ordered the boys, and they vanished obediently.

'Can I trouble you for some water, kind sir?'

With a sigh, Neil walked over to where the lunch things were.

'Just go with my general direction,' whispered Esther to Dominic, once Neil was out of hearing range. 'We have to be careful, we don't know how strongly these people might react to our meddling. We may need to be smart about it.'

'Working smarter, not harder has always been my motto in life.'

'Good boy,' she patted Dominic's hand. 'When you get the chance, I want you to slip out and check the cabins. Ask those boys about where Bruno is. Something doesn't add up.'

'I'm on it.'

Neil was on his way back with a very full glass of water he kept spilling.

'Darn it,' he said each time.

'Never mind, as long as there's a drop left, and it's wet.' She took the glass thankfully – she was actually parched – and drained it in one.

'Also, could my handsome companion use your facilities?'

'Our what?'

'The WC.'

'Out there and to the right, past the yellow cabins,' Neil instructed, Dominic taking his cue. 'Now what exactly are you doing here? Has your vehicle broken down?'

'I wish it was as simple as that,' Esther sighed. 'It's about my grandson, Bruno.'

Neil's eyes grew big in their sockets.

'You're his grandmother?'

'His Noony, yes. I'm afraid I have to see him.'

'Couldn't you have phoned...?'

'Unfortunately, I have some very bad news. A death in the family. There are things much better delivered in person, as you might agree.'

'I'm so sorry to hear about your bereavement.'

'So am I, Neil – so am I.'

'Who died?'

Esther cleared her throat.

'Bruno's Nonny.'

'I thought you were his Nonny?'

'I'm his *Noony*. His Nonny is his other grandmother.'

'Isn't that confusing?'

'You don't know the half of it.' Esther shrugged, laughing.

'Bruno is out on a nature walk at the moment,' Neil said, threading his hands together on the table. 'But I'll make sure to tell him this terrible news as soon as he gets back.'

'Oh no, I must. Noony was a like a sister to me. It's tragic.'

'I thought you were Noony? And she was Nonny. The deceased?'

'I'm absolutely heartbroken,' Esther said, ignoring his question and scrunching up her face in what she hoped looked like desperate grief. 'I simply must see my Bruno.'

Neil looked about him nervously.

'Perhaps if you wait here, I can go see...'

There were angry yells from outside, and then Dominic, his arms behind his back, was forcibly brought inside by a tall handsome man in his thirties, who had a look of zeal in his eyes that Esther remembered from pictures of Nazi Youth. Ah, yes – she could recall the photo from the *Daily Mail*. The doctor...

'Get off me,' Dominic was yelling.

'Neil,' the taller man said, calmly considering the situation. 'I caught this thief snooping around the grounds, trying doors and windows.' He pushed Dominic, who caught himself on the table and gave Esther a look that said: 'Sorry, I fucked up'. The blond man scrutinised Esther. 'And who is this?'

'My name is Esther,' she said, trying to sit as tall as she could, but she felt very small in front of this athletically built man.

'It's Bruno's Nonny – I mean grandmother.'

Dr Allan and Neil exchanged a look.

'Do you know this ruffian?' the doctor asked Esther, bluntly.

'Of course, and he's no thief.'

'I was looking for the toilet, and this guy jumps me.'

'Looking for the toilet, were you? Why try the windows then? I'm afraid I'm going to have to ask the both of you to leave immediately. I'm very sorry, but the safety and wellbeing of our young charges is very important to us.'

Esther bit her tongue.

'Unfortunately,' she said, 'I must see my grandson. I have some very bad news.'

'His Nonny died,' Neil explained. 'His other grandmother. One's a Noony, one's a Nonny,' he added.

'I'm afraid as part of this residential programme, our young people are not allowed to have visitors. Now, if you'd please leave; I'd hate to have to call the police over a mix-up.' Dr Allan smiled at Dominic menacingly.

Esther raised her voice, enunciating as clearly as she could.

'If you don't let me see my grandson, it shall be *I* calling the police.'

Dr Allan appeared unfazed.

'Fine, we'll both call them. You can explain to the authorities why this was on your persons.' Dr Allan revealed a small plastic bag from his back pocket, full of weed.

'I've never seen that in my life,' Dominic said loudly. 'He frisked me, Esther,' he told her, 'basically stuck his hands down my pants. I forgot I had this one on me.'

'Esther... Esther... where have I heard that name before? It's not one you hear every day, and yet it's familiar. Of course, Bruno's notebook.' The doctor smiled. 'You're the old Jewish woman from his village.' Dominic gave Esther a startled look. 'What did you say you were, his grandmother? I think we can add attempted kidnapping to the possession of cannabis when the police arrive.'

Neil gave a loud gasp. 'You're not his N-Noon-N-Nonny at all!'

Ether realised they were caught. She couldn't even get up from her seat without considerable help. The two men, one stocky, one tall and muscular, were far too much for lithe Dominic to take on by himself. But most of all, she worried for Bruno – what if something terrible had already happened to him, and they were too late?

'Did you find him?' she asked Dominic point-blank, dropping all pretence.

'I asked one of the boys, he's locked in one of the outer cabins.'

'Interesting. I wonder how the police, or social services, for that matter, will feel about you incarcerating young people, especially as the wellbeing of your "young charges" is so important to you.'

Dr Allan grimaced, as Neil looked on nervously. 'Looks like we're at an impasse,' the doctor said at last, coolly. 'Maybe it would be best for everyone if you depart before any calls are made.'

Esther folded her arms.

'Not exactly a stalemate. Your name's Doctor Allan, am I correct? That's your legal practising name?' The doctor didn't answer. 'Your silence speaks volumes.' Esther indicated for Dominic to help her up. He nipped to her side and gently took her shoulder, getting her to her feet. 'Your full name is Dr Allan *Tasker.*'

Dr Allan clenched his jaw. 'What do you want?'

'To leave. With Bruno. Quietly. With no one going to the press. I wonder if the parents of those other children know what you've been up to? Not exactly practising what you *preach.*'

'Neil,' said Dr Allan in a steady voice. 'Can you get Bruno and bring him here for me, please?'

'Absolutely,' Neil replied, before running from the hall.

'Go with him,' said Esther, not taking her eyes off the doctor, Dominic following hot on the stocky man's heels.

SEVENTEEN

BRUNO

At the sound of the padlock, Bruno leapt unsteadily to his feet, unsure if this meant food or freedom. He'd managed to ration the bottle of water he'd received earlier that morning, only taking small sips, but his lips had never been so chapped, and he felt woozy, drunk even. Could you feel drunk from dehydration? His dad would know, Esther too. When the door finally swung open, he was greeted by the blotchy red face of Neil, eyebrows crazy as ever, but then someone else pushed past him. It took Bruno a moment to register who it was.

'Are you okay, buddy?' Dominic asked, taking him around his waist for support, or as if they were about to dance, Bruno feeling a strange fluttering sensation at his touch.

'Where did you come from?' Bruno asked, his voice hoarse, and seemingly further away than his mouth.

'Let's get you out of here, shall we?'

'My lips are dry,' Bruno complained as Dominic wove his hand under his armpit to guide him out of the cabin.

'They still look good to me,' Dominic replied, with a grin.

EIGHTEEN

ESTHER

Dr Allan had not moved a muscle, as he continued to watch Esther.

'I wonder who you are exactly,' he said evenly, at last. 'If I were to do my own investigation. Turn over a few of my own stones. See what scuttles out from underneath.'

'You don't scare me,' Esther replied, trying to stand her ground, but feeling vulnerable without Dominic by her side. The walker was a few steps away, too far, so she steadied herself with one hand on the table instead. 'I know a bully when I see one. Picking on children. You're the only thing scuttling out from under a rock.' Her knee wobbled, but she caught herself, putting more weight on her hand to stabilise her legs.

'Seems you're not in the best of health. I do hope you're not having an episode. I can give you something for the pain if you like?' The tone was mocking, Dr Allan was enjoying himself.

'I've been on this earth a good long time,' Esther replied, mettle in her voice, 'and I plan to stay here a little longer, if only to spite you.'

'You realise I'm *helping* these young people?'

Esther scoffed. 'You're betraying your own.'

'I'm nothing like them.'

'Thank goodness for that.'

The doctor sneered. 'What we teach here is adaptability. I haven't known you long, Esther, but I suspect that's never been your strong suit. I imagine your body has calcified along with your mind, stiffened by the resentments you've harboured, the ancient regrets. The world has always been against you. Am I right?' Esther didn't answer. She was finding it hard to maintain eye contact. 'You've come to the threadbare end of your tattered life, and you're hoping it affords you a vantage, but you've missed the lesson completely. Life is not about morals, and principles. It's about evolution. And you are a dinosaur staring down an approaching meteorite.' Dr Allan stepped forward until he was at the walker, gripping it with both hands, and leaning on it so much, it creaked under his weight. 'I allow these lost and desperate children a gift, one of belonging. True becoming. I give them back the love of their parents. Their peers. The sacred love of the divine. While you are nothing more than a *leech*.'

'Am I a dinosaur, or a leech?' Esther muttered petulantly. 'Make up your mind.'

'Leeches drain the lifeforce of their victims. That's what you're doing to these poor boys. Bruno feels sorry for you, he wrote about it in his notebook. You told him terrible, hurtful things, wounding him after he helped you – it's all in his writing. Do you think he'll forgive you? No wonder you came here, riding in on your white horse, anything was better than living with that guilt, with the responsibility of poisoning a young mind already clouded in confusion.'

'You don't know him,' replied Esther, earnestly. 'Or me.' It was getting so warm. Where was Dominic? Should she try and sit? Her leg was throbbing. 'Where is he?' she asked, her anxiety rising.

'He's gone, they're all gone. It's just you and me, Esther. We're having a reckoning.'

'It's nothing of the sort.'

'Wouldn't everything be better without you? What would the world miss exactly? You're only taking up space. It's almost embarrassing how you cling.' The walker groaned so much, Esther wondered if it would snap, and then where would she be? 'Is anything I'm saying untrue? Tell me, it's only the two of us. You can be honest. I promise I won't tell anyone.'

'I think...' she started.

'Yes?'

Esther rocked to one side but righted herself, clutching at the edge of the table.

'I think you're a fool if you imagine you can weasel into my head so easily.' She smacked the table with her hand, making the doctor flinch. 'All your watered-down psychobabble. Oh, I'll paint you a terrifying picture, *my mind as only I know it*. It's been churning away for decades, longer than you've even been *alive*. You speak of boys, as if you're not one yourself, doctor. Do you really think anything *you* could say would be a match for what's in here already?' She tapped the side of her head. 'Amateur,' she spat. 'Now if you give me back my walker, I'd like to be going.'

There was a shout behind her – Esther turned to see Bruno's magnificent beaming face.

'Dear heart!' she called, as he ran to envelop her in a careful embrace. They had never hugged before, she realised, and it was simply glorious. All pain melted away. 'You smell terrible,' she said, patting his back, 'what have they done to you?'

'I'll tell you when we're far from here,' Bruno promised. He began to sniff the air. 'Food!' he said excitedly, letting go of Esther and running to the trestle table at the back of the hall, grabbing slices of bread and stuffing them into his mouth.

Dr Allan had slipped away while they were embracing, Esther realised.

'Where's Dominic?' she asked but Bruno's mouth was too full. He slathered butter on a slice of bread, folded it and put it in his pocket before returning to her, and helping her with the walker. The pain in her leg was almost unbearable, but Esther pushed through, and outside, they were greeted by the three younger boys, hovering by the doorway, all wide-eyed and bashful.

'What are your names?' Esther asked them, as Bruno helped her shuffle past.

'Pip,' squeaked the smallest.

'Very good to meet you, Pip.'

The child gave the sweetest smile.

'I'm Mitch,' said the redhead, 'and this is Elliot.'

'They helped me,' Bruno explained, his mouth now empty enough to speak. 'We have to take them with us.'

'I wish we could, but we'll be done for kidnapping.'

She glanced up – Dominic was running towards them at a pace.

'They rang the police,' he yelled as he approached. 'When he first saw me checking the cabins. We have to get out of here.' Dominic joined Esther's other side, the boys trailing around the trio as she limped towards the car park as fast as she possibly could, which was not very. Sure enough, as they came towards the reception, they could see a police car parked beside the motorbike, a uniformed man walking beside Neil towards them.

Esther's leg buckled, Dominic catching her.

'Save the performance until they're closer,' he suggested.

'It's no act,' she wheezed. 'I have to sit.'

'Now? What if we carried you?'

'I need a moment. Please.'

The pain was overwhelming.

'This isn't part of your escape plan?' Dominic asked anxiously.

'I'm afraid not, dear boy.'

'Bruno, help her sit.'

She was gently lowered to the sandy ground.

'I'm sorry,' Esther was saying.

'Ring an ambulance!' Dominic called, or maybe Bruno.

At some point, the doctor must have slithered back, because she heard his voice.

'Let me look at her...' he instructed.

'Don't you touch her,' growled Bruno.

'Yeah – keep away,' Mitch joined in and soon the boys were yelling at Dr Allan, like crows trying to distract a predator from their nest.

Esther ran a hand over the ground. There was wild grass here, marram most likely, and she twirled several blades around her fingers and tugged, feeling the resistance of the roots in the sandy soil, tethered to the ground. The pain in her legs was almost unbearable now, a sharp stabbing, made worse by sitting, but there was no other option. She did not want to be carried or held aloft. She wanted to be here. Esther would wait until the ambulance people brought a stretcher, and that would be it, maybe the last time she was outside again. She'd be hospitalised, and if she didn't pick up some dodgy illness, her daughter would use it as an excuse to put her in a home, sell her house from under her, get rid of her possessions – it was all unravelling.

She glanced up at the men and boys around her – Bruno arguing with Dr Allan, as the three other boys yelled in agreement with him; the policeman asking her questions she couldn't quite grasp, repeating them loudly, so loudly she could feel his spittle on her face; Dominic, his face pale with worry, stroking her back, and she thought how funny it was to be here in a sea of so much maleness, how they felt they ruled the world, how sweet they could be and yet so harsh. She thought of her daughter and wondered the eternal question – had she ever been a good enough mother? Esther had fought so hard for the rights of women, but she'd resented the role of caretaker, and yet, those we care for eventually become ours. What a bright girl her daughter was. How hard-working. How selfless. And then Esther thought finally of him, the man-shaped shadow over her life, the one who had shamed her. No, that wasn't true, she had shamed herself: she must take responsibility for the pain.

Oh, the pain!

Esther pulled more blades of grass, and heard, or felt, the pop of the roots pulled clean from the ground, and it helped, knowing that though her legs and body might no longer be able to support her, these gardener's hands were still strong, hardier even than when she was young. Lifting her fingers to her nose, she breathed in the delicious smell of earth and grass, as the crows went *caw, caw* or maybe it was the boys – even more of them now, it seemed – or boys in bird clothing, their feathers catching the light, and sending shimmers down her spine, right to the core.

NINETEEN

BRUNO (5 JULY)

Two weeks, Esther had been in the hospital.

Bruno had visited her twice; the first time she was sleeping, and although the second time she was awake, she was groggy and barely present. Apparently, Esther was fighting a small infection, as well as the issue with her hip. It had been disturbing seeing her so frail, so grey, noticing the blue veins in her arms, and the tubes sticking out. It made Bruno want to run away.

'Dear heart,' she'd said croakily, as her eyes fluttered open, taking his hand.

He'd stood, eyes welling, smiling down on her, as she gently stroked his palm with her thumb, her eyelids half-closed. She said nothing the rest of the visit, falling in and out of sleep – she didn't have to, the occasional caress by her thumb was all he needed.

He went to her house every day, not exactly sure why. To check everything was fine for her return, he supposed. Bruno didn't have a key, so he sat on her front step, or with his back against the kitchen windows, or if it was sunny, on the grass. The weather was warming each day, the flowers starting to bloom in earnest, so Bruno spent mornings cataloguing the erupting blossoms, capturing the most beautiful ones several times a day, to show Esther later, documenting her hard work coming to fruition so she wouldn't miss out. In the afternoon, he might spend an hour identifying the images online, matching them with their alien-sounding names: Agapanthus, Zinnias, Bougainvillea, and rarer ones like Meconopsis, or the Himalayan Blue Poppy, which he initially wrote off as a weed. Until recently, Bruno would have felt self-conscious having so many pictures of flowers on his phone, he realised. At least that was one good development.

Often, when he wasn't working, Dominic would join Bruno in the garden, and they sat quietly together, as if they were in a waiting room. Although they rarely talked, sinking into a silence broken only by the sound of the birds in the trees overhead, or the wind in the branches, or a plane, Bruno had never felt more *in communication* with anyone. The position and shape of Dominic's body, where the toe of his foot pointed, how close his elbow was to Bruno's, the direction of his glances, everything. Of course, Bruno had been acutely aware of body language before, especially his own, making sure his wrists weren't limp, his gait was true, that his physicality didn't betray him. Now, it was different; playful, a conversation.

On the fifth, or maybe sixth day, Dominic sat closer to Bruno, so close that they were practically touching, and Bruno did not move away or counterbalance his presence by shifting position. The question of Dominic's sexuality remained, but it could stay that way – curious and unanswered. Bruno wanted to be braver, like he'd promised himself when he was locked in the cabin, so on the seventh day or perhaps the eighth, after Dominic inspected the rusted wheelbarrow, finding the new growth pleasing, and afterwards sat next to Bruno to take in the sun, Bruno let a hand – his hand – move onto Dominic's outer leg, and he left it there for what seemed like an eternity, expecting Dominic to brush it off, or ask him to remove it. Instead, Dominic placed his own hand on top of Bruno's, and they sat, purposefully touching, as a white butterfly skimmed past, and blackbirds dipped down from their branches to peck at the soil. At one point, Dominic began to stroke Bruno's wrist with his finger, and as the sun came out, Bruno wondered if this was possibly the most wonderful feeling he'd ever experienced.

One morning, on perhaps the tenth or the eleventh day, while Bruno and Dominic were holding hands, Bruno's head resting slightly on Dominic's shoulder, breathing in the sweet smoky smell of his neck, they heard a car pull into the driveway, and people get out, talking. Bruno and Dominic rushed, like two guilty boys, into the bushes without being seen.

Hidden by the foliage they watched, hearts racing, as three people walked around the side of the house to peer at the garden. It was Esther's daughter Jane, Bruno realised, with a man in a suit, and another more casually dressed in jeans – he seemed to be the one being shown around. Listening intently, Bruno could hear the suited man – an estate agent obviously – giving suggestions for landscaping, the taking down of trees to create more space and light, a proposed area for a new extended garage. He nodded at the rusted wheelbarrow, and must have said something funny, because the other two laughed, before walking back to the front of the house, unlocking the door, and going inside.

'What should we do?' Dominic asked. 'This place could go while Esther's still in the hospital.'

'I'm not sure,' answered Bruno, staring at Dominic's adorably crooked two front teeth. It was cold out of the sun, and he shivered. 'It's not Jane's house to sell, legally I mean.'

'She's a lawyer. Aren't there loopholes Jane could find? We have to tell Esther.'

'I will,' Bruno agreed, and perhaps trying to generate the needed courage, he leant in and kissed Dominic on the side of his face, and in the corner of his lips. 'Is that okay?' he asked, and Dominic nodded, kissing him back.

There were no complete thoughts, only snippets of sensation. The rustle of leaves. The smell of sun-warmed skin. A falling strand of Dominic's hair. The far-off sound of windows opening in the house. The brush of stubble. More breeze, the overhanging branches gently patting the tops of both their heads.

Eventually they stopped, still holding hands.

'I didn't know if you were...?' Bruno started.

'Straight? I think this proves I'm categorically not. I like kissing you is all I know. Is that okay?'

'If I get to kiss you again, then yes.'

They laughed. It was easy to be honest in the sanctity of Esther's garden.

On the twelfth day, Bruno received a text that made him whoop.

Dear heart, it read, *please forgive me. I'm afraid they wouldn't allow me my treasured monolith while I was hooked up to all those machines. Still a bit frail, but on the mend.*

Bruno shot back:

Can I call you?

Soon, I promise. But can you help me, I seem to have forgotten how to do a question mark again.

And then a moment later:

Ah, found it?

Esther's messages now held different weight, as if they were precious poems, and if Bruno couldn't sleep, he would go back and re-read old ones from her. Not the messages she sent while he was at the camp though, that was still too raw, but all the others. Bruno wanted to print them off and frame them, he couldn't really explain why – they seemed so full of heart.

Dinners at home had changed too. Bruno no longer took the evening family meal for granted – he now felt overwhelmingly grateful sitting at the table, not only for the food (yes, even the meatloaf), but also for the unconditional love of his parents, his beautiful baby sisters; even thinking about the cutlery, which had been his grandmother's – all that history! – would make his eyes well up. Bruno would catch his mother watching him apprehensively, and he fought the impulse to run around the table and hug her. How could he explain to them how lucky he was?

On maybe the eighth evening, they were eating vegan pizza – Bruno's gratitude was slowly fading each day, although he was fighting hard to keep it – when his dad made an announcement.

'Seems the doctors have given me the "all clear" to go back to work.'

'Not the "all clear",' his mum countered. 'Part-time. You still need to take it slowly.'

Filip brushed his wife's concern away with his hand, but then blew her a kiss when she continued to glare at him.

'Dad,' asked Bruno, 'can you see if there is any entry-level work coming up at the warehouses?'

Both parents glanced at each other.

'I mean, I can check,' his dad replied, carefully. 'But don't you want to wait a while? Let the dust settle. After everything that just happened...?'

Eight days ago, when Bruno's parents arrived at the hospital in Norwich, their faces were white as ghosts. Bruno and his dad cried in each other's arms, only his mum was able to keep herself together, stroking their backs as they wept. Tearfully, Bruno explained to them all about the camp, and in return, they held their son and told him – even if he didn't quite believe it himself – how brave he was, how Esther's health issues were not his fault, and that she was going to be fine.

His mum wiped her mouth with her napkin.

'I thought you weren't keen on the warehouses?' she asked, gently.

Bruno put down his slice of pizza, shook his head and shrugged.

'I need to start doing *something* with my life.'

'If Bruno wants to work there, you should let him,' piped up Megan. Since he'd come home from the camp, his fourteen-year-old sister had gone from his biggest critic to his most ardent defender. It was such a seismic shift, it only confirmed to Bruno the stress and worry he'd put his family under.

'Does he have to work at all?' chimed in his younger sister. 'He's been much nicer since he came back from the camp, he's playing games with us again and everything.'

'He has to go to work, stupid,' Megan replied. 'He's an adult. It's what adults do.'

'I'm not stupid,' Daphne bleated, petulantly. 'You're only mad because Lydia said mean things to you.'

'What about?' asked Bruno's mum, not missing a beat.

'She called me the b-word,' answered Megan, nonchalantly, 'because I wouldn't let her use my lip gloss.' Recently, Bruno's sister had taken to brushing her hair back off her face, and it suited her. 'After Dad was sick, I stopped sharing things because I don't want to bring germs into the house. But then Lydia said she wouldn't use my lip gloss anyway because it was a *gay* colour, and I told her gay used to mean "happy", and the b-word is a female dog, so I'm a happy female dog – who cares?'

'Wow, you really shut that down,' Bruno said, respect in his voice.

'Seems we have another logophile in our midst,' his mum added. Everyone looked at her in confusion. 'It means "word lover". What, your father's not the only person who reads those etymology books in the loo...'

'Is Dominic your proper friend now?' asked Daphne abruptly, pointing a crust at her brother, and peering at him through her spectacles. 'You were walking with him the other day...?'

'I think Esther's daughter is going to sell the house,' Bruno began, to change the subject, aware his cheeks were reddening. He'd told his mother – in confidence – that he was growing close to Dominic, and his mum had smiled, replying, 'I'd say this to any one of my children, gay, straight, male or female, please don't do *anything* without a condom,' which mortified Bruno so much, he had to hide in his room for an hour.

'Where will Esther go?'

'I don't know, she has loads of things, and she really loves her house. It's not practical for her to live there in the long run though.'

'Are you seeing Dominic later?' his mum asked, casually.

'Maybe, after he finishes work.'

'Mum, leave him alone,' Megan said with a smile. 'Can't you see he doesn't want to talk about his boyfriend?'

His dad choked on his pizza slice but recovered quickly – Bruno's suspicion that his mum had already leaked his news was confirmed.

'He's not my boyfriend, he's... a friend.'

'Who's a boy. That's what a boyfriend is!' chipped in his littlest sister, grinning.

It was moments like this when Bruno tried to remember the lives of the other boys, how their parents had forcibly sent them to the camp, drugged them like Mitch, caused them to run away or to live in constant shame. How he'd sat in the cabin, promising he'd never take his freedom or his family's acceptance for granted again.

'Actually, maybe he is a boyfriend.' Bruno's face was now pulsating with blood.

'That's what I said,' Daphne affirmed, matter-of-factly. 'Boys who are friends.'

'We're more than that – we're boys who kiss each other.'

His parents shared a covert grin.

Daphne frowned, considering this new information.

'You kiss? Like Mum and Dad?'

'Yeah... Because I like him, in that way.'

'Are you gay then?' It was so casually said, so devoid of any subtext.

'Yes.'

She nodded.

'How do you know about gay?' her dad asked, archly.

'I read this book about an elephant who had two mummies. And I don't know, sometimes you can just tell, can't you?'

'I guess you can,' her mum replied, trying to hide a smile.

'Is Dominic gay?'

'He is at least a little bit,' Bruno replied. 'Possibly bisexual.'

'What's that?'

'Maybe that's enough of the sexual talk at the table,' said his father.

'She wants to know – we need to talk about these things,' responded his mother.

'What if she brings it up at school?'

'Dad, what does bisexual mean?'

'Bisexual means greedy.'

'That's not helpful, Filip.'

'Then call me bisexual,' Daphne announced, animatedly, 'because I would like some more pizza, please!'

Bruno, Megan and his parents all struggled to stifle a laugh.

. . .

That night, Bruno received more messages from Esther. There was a slightly detached, dreamlike quality to them, and he wondered how medicated she was.

This place has allowed me to do a lot of thinking, dear heart

Is that a good thing? He'd replied. *I know I over analyse everything. Now I'm trying to put some of that energy into ending the conversion therapy place. Did I tell you I'm being interviewed by a PhD student next week about my experience?*

So many loose threads.

Bruno paused, had Esther seen his message?

Are you okay?

I want to say things, but I never can. About how I loved you all those years ago, how hurt I was. I carry the pain around with me always.

Bruno stared at his phone. She was obviously getting him confused with Thackeray – the man who had broken her heart. It felt too intimate.

I'm sure you didn't do anything wrong

I did. I ruined all our lives. Towards the end, I began to suspect you were not being exactly truthful, and yet I kept it to myself because I didn't want to lose you. What does that make me? I betrayed my principles.

Esther maybe you should sleep now. Everything is always better in the morning

Yes, dear heart, you're right. You were always right. I miss you, so very much.

I miss you too, Bruno replied truthfully, but not knowing if Esther meant him or not. His heart ached with worry for her – what if these were the last messages she ever sent him? If this signified the beginning of the end?

I love you

I love you too, Esther

And Bruno slipped into an uneasy sleep.

TWENTY

ESTHER (6 JULY)

She awoke, groggier than usual, and remembered why. Her hip had been troubling her in the night, more than it normally did, and a kind nurse had conspired with a doctor to really knock her out. Esther sipped some water from the bottle beside the bed and shimmied herself, painfully, to a sitting position.

A plan was needed, otherwise one would be made for her. She was feeling much better overall – last night aside – but Esther knew she wouldn't be allowed home as if nothing had happened, so it was time to make a contingency. The house was gone, ultimately, Esther understood that, but she wanted one last chance to say goodbye, to gather herself, and – well, other things – so that's where she must focus her efforts.

As the doctor arrived, Esther began to lay down her plan.

'How are you feeling?' Dr Rashid asked her.

'Much better, almost back to perfect health.'

Dr Rashid scowled, looking at her chart. 'It seems you were in some discomfort last night.'

'Growing pains,' Esther replied. 'Piffle.'

'Even so...'

'I was wondering when I might be able to leave this fine

establishment? I'm extraordinarily thankful to you and everyone here.'

'Well...' the doctor began, hesitantly, 'we need to talk to your daughter when she comes in today...'

'But is the consensus that I am being allowed to leave?'

'As long as you're well cared for. Has Jane spoken to you about support at—?'

'Yes, yes,' said Esther, 'I'm certain she cannot wait to see me back out in the world, and neither can I. There's life in the old girl yet.' She waved her fist in the air, making the tubes rattle, and causing a twinge of pain in her leg, which Esther was able to cover with a grimace.

'It's good seeing you in high spirits.'

'The highest. Ready to take on anything.'

'I wish I felt like that,' Dr Rashid said with a raise of her eyebrows.

'One just has to think positive!'

Dr Rashid shook her head in admiration. When she'd gone, Esther flopped back onto the pillows, exhausted by her performance.

One down, one to go.

'Are you wearing make-up?' her daughter asked a few hours later, on her daily visit.

'Just a touch of blusher on these very old cheekbones. I borrowed it from a nurse.'

'Aha,' replied her daughter cautiously, sitting in the chair beside the bed, and absent-mindedly rearranging the May flowering blooms in their vase – snapdragons, peonies and tulips, but no carnations as Esther abhorred them.

'What do you mean, "aha"?'

'I'm simply waiting for the other shoe to drop, Mother.'

'I'll cut to the chase then. I've been thinking...'

'I have thoughts too, maybe we can compare notes...?'

'I'd like to voice mine first,' insisted Esther, trying not to sound frosty. *Keep it light*, she reminded herself. *Remember what's at stake.* 'I know the house must be sold. I realise it's no place for a woman my age to live on her own. I appreciate you'd be put in a very difficult predicament – your aged mother, recently hospitalised, alone by herself. What if something were to happen again?'

'Yes... exactly.' Her daughter seemed surprised. 'Glad we're on the same page...'

Here it goes, Esther thought. 'I would like two weeks at the house to get my affairs in order.' Jane began to make disapproving sounds. 'Please, let me finish. There are things I need to organise, my whole life is contained there. You owe me that liberty. Obviously, in my current physical situation, I cannot be at the house alone – and I don't mean for you to move in, as kind an offer that would be. I also don't want a stranger in my house, not in my final days there – it would defeat the purpose of saying a genuine goodbye – but of course I will require some assistance, and so I would like Bruno to live with me to assist. I will pay him myself, so you don't even need to worry about that.'

'Bruno's the reason you're in hospital in the first place, Mother!' Jane's eyes were wide in horror.

'It's not his fault in the slightest. He didn't know I was to make my hairbrained journey.'

'I can't...'

'It will be perfectly fine. We are good together. He is a kind soul. Bruno will make sure I eat, call if any of the parts fall off my body, and will help pack up my most precious belongings before you ship me away to who knows where.'

'To live with me, initially.'

'A fate worse than death then,' Esther said, with a wry smile.

'Mother, I appreciate you being open to a discussion, but it's not feasible taking you back. The house is falling apart.'

'Nonsense – and I'm only asking for two weeks. All the doctors talk about giving me "dignity" to live my life. This will do exactly that. It's the very least you can do, after taking an estate agent to the house – and don't pretend you haven't.'

'Selling the house would only be to benefit *you*.'

'Until I croak. I'd hold onto the money fleetingly.'

'That's very unfair.'

This was true; Esther had lost sight of her plan. She lowered her voice conspiratorially.

'If you let me have this fortnight, I'll comply with every-thing – the selling of the house, the storage of my things, even a nursing home if it's what you see fit.'

'That's not even on the cards...' replied Jane quickly, only partially convincing. 'An inexperienced teenage boy – I'm presuming that you won't consider hiring a live-in nurse, or someone to drop by...?'

'You're correct, I won't consider it. Two weeks. It's all I'm asking.'

Her daughter gave one long, defeated sigh.

The moment Jane left, Esther whipped out her phone.

Bruno!

She typed so hurriedly, making so many mistakes, she had to delete everything the first go and start over. *Do I have an opportunity for you! How would you lik to stay at the Chateau Esther for 14 days and nights, all expenses paid, plus actual payment?*

It took roughly ten seconds before she received a reply:

Are you serious? Sign me up!

And with that, Esther's plan began to swing into action.

Two days later, Esther was discharged (her leg had given her more issues, but she'd bitten her tongue, knowing it would only delay her release) and Jane drove them back to her house, where Bruno was waiting.

'Go grab the wheelchair,' Jane called to him, throwing him the house keys to unlock.

'I never thought I'd be so glad to see this hunk of metal,' noted Esther, shortly after, as her daughter and Bruno heaved her gently into the chair and wheeled her inside.

'I've bought food, and I took the liberty of sending in a cleaner for a quick spruce,' Jane explained.

'To tidy up for the estate agent's photos, she means,' Esther said to Bruno, rolling her eyes.

The place did look extremely tidy, smelling of lemons, wood polish and bleach. There were fresh flowers waiting in the kitchen too – a bowl of sweet scented gardenias – and all the cobwebs were gone from the ceiling. Esther looked around suspiciously.

'I see the cleaners have moved things about,' she sniffed.

'We're going to have to go through everything eventually anyway,' her daughter replied with forced joviality. 'I'll leave you to it. Bruno, a word?' Obediently, he followed Jane back to the front door. 'I want you to call me if anything happens,' she said in lowered tones. 'Anything at all. Don't let her push you around. You're doing a vital job here, looking over the most important person in my life.'

'I can hear perfectly well,' Esther called from the kitchen. 'Shame on your lies.'

Her daughter rolled her eyes this time – they looked very similar when they did.

'Two weeks. Good luck. You'll need it.'

Bruno closed the door.

'Shall we have something to eat?' he asked as he re-entered the kitchen, 'or do you want to start the sorting straight away?'

'Oh, you can forget all about that,' Esther said offhandedly. 'That was just my cover story. We're not going to pack one jot...'

Jane's words rang in Bruno's ears.

'What do you want to do then?' he asked, nervously.

Esther smiled mischievously.

'Dear heart,' she said, 'my kind boy, we are going to *live*.'

Not long after that, Dominic arrived, like in one of those American movies where a party's thrown as soon as the parents leave.

'I thought you'd be pleased to see him,' Esther said with a wink, 'he tells me you've become very close.'

They were outside in the garden sunshine, a rug over Esther's knees, spirals of smoke rising, mostly from Dominic. Bruno made sure to sit well enough away, even though they were in the open air – he didn't want to be passively affected; he had a job to do.

'Doesn't really work that way,' replied Dominic, kissing him on the cheek affectionately, when Bruno explained his fear.

It was early July, and the foliage was deepening into a brilliant green hue that was both fecund and verdant – two words Esther had recently discussed over texts with Bruno's father, Filip. Everything seemed to be reaching for the heavens in thanks, from the long grass to the Dutchman's Pipe climbing its way up the side of the house via the drainpipe. Clover and buttercups had taken over the lawn, exciting the bees, who seemed beside themselves with all the abundance.

'Well, well,' Esther said, admiringly, watching the boys, 'the two of you – my dear hearts.'

'Hey,' Dominic protested, 'Bruno's your dear heart as well?'

'You are very different hearts, dear in your separate – yet equal – ways.'

'That's all right then.'

Dominic leant across and tried to take Bruno's hand, but he pulled away, still uncomfortable about showing affection.

'What are you going to do on your last few weeks of debauchery?' Dominic asked Esther, recovering from this slight. 'Your late-in-life Amish *rumspringa*?'

'I'd like to open all the windows and doors, and play loud music, and drink – you do drink, don't you, Bruno?'

'Sometimes.'

'Good.'

'And what then, after the two weeks?' Dominic asked, curious.

'We'll see,' Esther replied mysteriously. 'Oh, but that reminds me... Bruno, I've chatted to a lawyer, to see if there's anything we can do about your enforced stay at the *Maison de* Internalised Homophobia.'

'I'm still checking in with the boys every day online.'

'How are they doing?'

'The same. Not great but surviving.'

'We'll help them,' promised Esther. 'And closing down that camp is at the top of my agenda.'

For a moment, Bruno was silent.

'What if we do something that makes it harder for Mitch, Pip, Elliot or the others? If their families punish them?'

Esther was quiet for a moment too.

'We can offer lifelines, as best we can. They can choose to take them, or not – but it's infinitely better to have options than to have none.'

'I guess you're right. I keep thinking what an idiot I was to go there.'

Dominic squeezed Bruno's shoulder supportively.

'Don't spend any more time in remorse, take it from me,' said Esther. She took the joint Dominic was offering her. 'Life should not be dampened with regret but nourished with hopes and dreams.'

'That's beautiful,' said Dominic, exhaling smoke, 'who's it by?'

Esther shrugged. 'Don't know. I made it up.'

And they broke into laughter so strong and contagious that even Bruno joined in.

The cleaner had been upstairs too, and given the bedrooms a thorough once-over, so Bruno was able to choose any of them for his stay. The rooms on the first floor were all sparsely furnished with at least a bedframe, and a place to put clothes; the clutter and chaos on the ground floor avoided, being tucked out of Esther's reach. Bruno chose the bedroom with the best view of the garden, which coincidentally had the least amount of peeling wallpaper – a vintage magenta floral pattern that could have been in a museum – and then discreetly swapped the mattress to the upstairs one that seemed the least ancient.

Ultimately, Bruno would have preferred to sleep downstairs near Esther, in case he was needed in the night, but she wouldn't hear of it.

'I've been fine for decades, I don't need a nanny checking in on me now.'

Bruno gave her a look, but let it go.

Esther tactfully suggested that Dominic could stay the night too, if he so wished, but the boys decided against it. Bruno was skittish about sleeping in the same bed, and Dominic seemed to understand this. There had been plenty of change in both their young lives the past few weeks, and she was proud of them. Let the boys figure things out at their own pace.

When Bruno came downstairs the following morning, he was surprised to find Esther at the kitchen table with a steaming cup of coffee in front of her, scrutinising both her phone and the notepad she used during their internet lessons.

'When can we start again?' she asked on seeing him. 'There are new things I want to learn. I understand websites now, but I still have issues with anything transactional...'

Pulling out a chair, Bruno sat down. The aromatic nuttiness of freshly brewed coffee filled the air.

'Tell me what's going on?' he demanded.

'What do you mean?' asked Esther, looking up from her phone.

'Aren't we supposed to be sorting your stuff and packing? And why are you so calm about everything? Your daughter is basically selling the house and shipping you off, and you're sitting here sipping coffee. It doesn't seem like you.'

'Dear heart...' she began.

'Don't...' Bruno cut her off. 'I want the truth.'

Esther sighed. 'I cannot escape the obvious. I'm not well. This house is too big for me. You, of all people, should understand how much easier it is when you give up resisting. I wanted to engage in the world, that's the reason why I started these lessons. To connect. And it worked – it brought you into my life. You've opened my eyes to the potential of the digital era. It's an exciting place. I'm curious in ways I haven't been for a long time. Of course, before I'd be nosey about some fact or figure, and I would go thumbing away through my books, but now I see the internet as a vast treasure trove. These books, these things in this house, it's all "stuff". The lot of it can be boxed and stored in a dark room. But this,' she tapped her phone, 'is a collective consciousness. That's exciting. And I want to learn how to order a delivered pizza,' she added. 'I'm very interested in fresh, hot Italian food.'

Bruno stared at her carefully for a second more.

'Do you want to keep looking for the land?' he asked.

'Oh, no – I think I'm done with that for now,' Esther replied, with a tight-lipped smile.

'Okay,' Bruno replied, hesitantly. 'But before we start our lessons again, we need to have a serious talk.'

'That sounds ominous,' she deadpanned.

'It's about what happened to you... in the past.'

Esther took a deep, fortifying breath.

'Proceed, my dear.'

'When you were in the hospital, it scared me. I thought you might not... Doesn't matter now, but it spurred me on to find information which might help you. At least I was doing something productive while you were in there. I know you hate meddling, but this is for your own good. Plus, you came and rescued me, so officially I'm in your debt.'

'You owe me nothing,' she replied, earnestly. 'You have earned my loyalty ten times over.'

With the same focused energy, Bruno proceeded to tell her about Reg's story, of the woman with the flute case who'd come to sell her story at the tabloid.

'Genevieve!' Esther exclaimed. 'But why?' She sat with this information, racking her mind. 'I did always wonder with Genevieve... If she had *feelings* for me.' She looked up with her inquisitive coppery eyes, 'but that means...'

'It wasn't your fault. The story getting into the papers.' Mouth wide, Esther stared at Bruno, still processing. 'Speaking of newspapers,' he continued carefully, 'Reg had copies, and he lent them to me.'

'Of the ones I'm in? Do you still have them?'

He nodded. 'At home.'

'I see. So, you've read them?'

Bruno nodded again. 'They were horrible, the things they said about you.' Esther fought back tears. 'The way they attacked you...'

'*Genevieve*,' she said, shaking her head. 'I still can't believe it.'

'And here's the final thing,' started Bruno.

'There's more?' Esther said, with a sad chuckle, sniffling.

'I know this is a lot.'

'Let me take another sip of coffee.' Her hands were shaking slightly as she lifted the cup from the saucer. 'I'm ready,' she said after she'd returned it to the table.

'I found the phone number of Thackeray's wife.'

'What, how?' Esther was stunned. 'Olivia's alive?'

'Yes, she still uses Thackeray's last name, so I searched and found her Facebook page, and then I discovered she belongs to a book club in Edinburgh which has an online document with all the members' mobile numbers – it's probably supposed to be password protected. You should tell Olivia when you speak to her.'

'Why would I ever do that?'

'Because it would be good for you,' replied Bruno, bluntly. His dark brown eyes were focused on her with a kind intensity. 'If you're scared of snakes, the best way to get over your fear is exposure to snakes. I already know you're strong enough. You single-handedly took on Dr Allan.'

'Look how that turned out. Me splayed on the ground. What if you lop off one snake, only for two to grow back in its place?'

'What's the alternative?'

She saw his point. You could snake-proof your house as much as you'd like, but they could still slither into your mind, wriggle through your dreams...

'I'll take it into consideration,' Esther said, at last, 'but honestly, after all those revelations, I'm going to need a lot more coffee.'

The weather was turning wonderfully warm. For the next two days, Bruno flung open the doors and windows as Esther had commanded, so the house could drink in the sun. It also helped to air the dust, which the cleaner hadn't seemed to eradicate, but merely moved around or temporarily hidden. Esther and Bruno would sit together under the shade of a tree, usually Esther's favourite Golden False Acacia, which she called her Golden *Facetious*, so they could see their screen, but with their laps in the sun to warm their legs. Dominic would accompany them when he could, shirtless and regularly trouserless. Esther caught Bruno looking at his lithe naked body often – the boy seemed to be taking his time to approach the physical side of their relationship, but she hoped he'd hurry up before Dominic drifted away. Because as much as she loved her rogue, he was a drifter. He'd even drifted into homosexuality, and Esther worried that Bruno might eventually get his feelings hurt. But wasn't that life? – hurt feelings, one after the other? To be numb was to be cold, dead. In this glorious sunshine there was only thriving life, yearning, competing, fighting, but oh so alive!

In the late afternoon, on the second day, once the sun had gone in, Esther started her round of weeding. Dominic had joined Bruno for a late nap, and so she made sure to keep as discreetly far away from the house as possible.

'Genevieve!' she muttered to herself, for perhaps the thousandth time. The betrayal! Could her old friend really have been so vindictive? To throw Esther and Thackeray under the bus, like that? Possibly, came the answer, she was always a slightly funny one. All those years Esther had blamed herself completely...

Placing down the small pot she was patting with soil beside

her wheelchair, she took out her phone and stared at Olivia's number ensconced inside by the ever-diligent Bruno. It seemed unbelievable, after all these years, that by tapping one button on this device, she could be connected instantly to Thackeray's wife. Of course, that's how phones – even the regular kind, if you pressed enough buttons – had always worked, but mobiles were more personal. They lived *on* you, forever in your vicinity. Esther wondered where Olivia's phone might be, right at this very instant. Tucked away in a pocket? On a dresser? Already in her hand?

One press of a button…

With a shiver, Esther placed the phone on her knee, closing her eyes. Bruno was wrong, some things were better left…

A strange repetitive beeping was heard – like a muffled woodpecker's tapping. Unusual noises were never a good sign, this she'd already learned. Opening her eyes again, Esther could see the display on her mobile, in the shade of the mature rowan – trees once grown as protection against witches, she'd told Bruno on many occasion – was bright and active. What had she done?

As she picked up the device, her own face was staring back at her on the screen. It was such a shock she almost dropped the phone. Esther reasoned she must have opened the video by mistake; she'd done it before, many times by accident, but never with the accompanying noise. Before Esther could find a way to stop it, another woman's face replaced hers on the screen.

'Is that you, my darlings?' the woman asked, in a slightly quavering voice. 'Let me put my specs on, so I can see you better.' The face disappeared and reappeared wearing glasses. She froze. 'You're not one of my grandchildren.'

'No, I'm sorry.' Esther's heart was racing. 'I'm afraid my phone has a mind of its own…'

Olivia, for Esther could see her name written at the top of the screen, smiled.

'I do it all the time. Butt dialling.' Olivia peered more closely out of the screen. 'My apologies, but how do I know you?'

'My name is Esther Saul.'

'Esther... Esther... that rings a bell...?'

'I knew Thackeray.'

A twitch of recognition in Olivia's face then.

'Fancy that. I feel a strong sense of my younger self. She wants to call you bad names.' Olivia chuckled. '*Esther Saul...* You're alive then?'

'The last I checked. Although sometimes I wonder. Especially in the mornings.'

'Ah yes, the daily reanimation.'

Small talk. Esther was having small talk with Thackeray's wife – she could barely believe it. Olivia had only the faintest hint of a Scottish accent, as clipped as Esther's own. She had short grey hair, neatly coiffed, and inquisitive blue eyes. They could have been long-lost sisters.

'I have so many questions,' said Olivia, quickly.

'You do?' This startled Esther. 'I was afraid you wouldn't want to speak to me at all!'

'Why the heavens not?'

'Because of what happened... You said yourself, your impulse was to call me bad names, and I wouldn't blame you...'

'That was so long ago. Another *age*. The past is a mystery, and as you must know, fewer and fewer people can remember it. It's very frustrating. But you were *there*.'

Esther's voice broke as she spoke: 'I ruined your life,' she said, in almost a whisper.

'Come now, I think Thackeray and I did a pretty good job of that ourselves.'

'You don't hate me?'

Olivia frowned and pursed her lips, thinking.

'I did, for a long time. But I'm not that person any more.'

'You're being too generous,' Esther said, blinking back tears. 'I don't deserve it.'

'Do you have grandchildren?' Olivia asked. 'Or great grandchildren?' Esther shook her head. 'Ah,' Olivia said, knowingly, 'that's where you've gone wrong. I have five of the first and three of the last. Beautiful, every single one. When they're very small, they can be so naughty, and yet you forgive everything instantly. I say to them, "Don't you feel bad for pulling your sister's hair?" and they give these defiant little shrugs.' She chuckled.

'I want to lay all my cards on the table, Olivia. Your son Edward is angry with me.'

'Over the will? Yes, I remember Thackeray left a large parcel of land to an estate, and my son was furious.'

'He thinks I had something to do with it.'

'Does he?' There was a slight tightening in Olivia's face.

'I was never contacted when Thackeray died,' Esther assured her. 'Nothing was left to me, to my knowledge.'

'My younger son is very much like his father,' Olivia replied, 'he runs hot and cold. He can't understand why Thackeray would want land just *sitting* there, not making money. It infuriates him.'

'Way back,' said Esther, gently, 'Thackeray was building a house for... well... us.'

Olivia's face contorted slightly. 'Ah,' she replied, and the one syllable conveyed much. 'I was cocky. That still hurts.' She gave a tight-lipped smile and took a deep breath. 'I don't know anything about that, I'm afraid.'

'I've taken up too much of your time already...'

'You can't go!' exclaimed Olivia. 'What happened to you? Where have you been all these years? You slipped off the face of the earth! I thought about you a lot, after all the horribleness in the papers. That put an end to Thackeray's mayoral hopes. We weren't very happy together, but I was almost as ambitious as he was back then.' She snorted. 'I imagined myself as a politician's wife, Glasgow's answer to Jackie Kennedy.' Her accent was stronger as she said the famous first lady's name. 'That's why I couldn't stay mad at you, Esther – not in the long run. Thackeray obviously cared for you considerably, why else would he have risked everything? There I was, prepared to stay in a loveless marriage, for the children and to wear a pillbox hat on special occasions, but he threw it all away.'

'Sheer stupidity,' agreed Esther.

'In some ways, it might have been easier if he carried on with a secretary, because at least you can make excuses – they have everything you don't, youth or long legs or what have you – but you weren't a girl. You seemed like a woman I might have gotten along with, so that stung.'

'Thackeray never told me the truth – he said you were already divorced...'

'You believed him?'

'I did.' She paused. 'At least, I think I did.'

'Really?'

Esther was quiet for a moment. 'I wanted it to be true,' she said at last. 'I had ideals, about the world, and women, and the future, and when the scandal broke, it shattered everything. I'd become a betrayer, not only to you, but to my friends, to the cause. Everything I believed in.' Tears ran down Esther's cheeks.

'It makes me furious,' Olivia said, impassioned, and it was Esther's turn to flinch. 'Thackeray could have done more, said something, but instead he slunk off until it all blew over. It sounds like you had an appalling time. There was so much barely concealed anti-Semitism in the papers too, it was revolting.'

'Y-yes...' stammered Esther. She had not expected Olivia to be so on her side. It was almost jarring.

'I was married twice after Thackeray, and it put our

marriage into perspective. One always thinks of oneself as worldly and wise, until you age and get worldlier and wiser. If I had my time over, I would have helped my two sons deal with their sadness and anger better, I would have reached out to you again, when I didn't hear back the first time...'

'What do you mean "again"?'

'I called you,' replied Olivia matter-of-factly. 'I left a message with someone at your house. A woman, I remember she was annoyed because I'd tried several times, and she was rehearsing, a musical instrument.'

'*Genevieve*,' hissed Esther to herself. 'Did you call me before or after the newspaper story came out?'

'Before. I'd confronted Thackeray about his having an affair, and he told me about you, so I copied your number from his address book. I wanted to meet, to hash it out. To me, there was no reason we couldn't all continue within certain agreements – I told you I was ambitious, and to be fair, I was worried about the boys; the irony is I didn't want it spread everywhere. And then look what happened.'

'The person you left the message with, Genevieve, her name was, did you give her any details about yourself?'

'Only my name and number, I'm sure.'

'That was probably enough. I think she was the one to speak to the journalist.'

'What?! Why?'

'Jealousy.'

'This is ringing a bell. After it all came out, I remember Thackeray was harassed by some musician woman, she kept sending him love letters. It went on for many years afterwards. I know, because she wrote to me too, said terrible things.'

'Genevieve! The vindictiveness, after all those years I had to listen to her murdering that poor flute.'

'Love makes us do strange things, but even so – my word, what a strange woman!' The screen froze for a moment, as if punctuating Olivia's surprise. 'What of you – did you marry after all?' she asked, unfreezing.

'I have a daughter from my first marriage, but after Thackeray – it was difficult to find my place in the world.'

'That surprises me. Everything he told me about you, even everything I read, you seemed to have a real stake in things.' Esther blinked back tears again. 'I was right, you know,' Olivia gave a nod of her head. 'We might have become friends.'

'Thank you,' Esther said, trying to keep her voice even, 'you have no idea how much this means to me.'

'It's been a pleasure having you pop up on my phone. Thackeray always did have great taste in women. Take care of yourself.'

The screen went black, and Esther felt stunned, too emotional to cry even. Still dazed, she bent down to pick up another pot, but she vastly underestimated how heavy it was. In a moment, she'd tipped forward, fortunately onto soft earth, but the chair came down on top of Esther, and there she lay, literally eating dirt. Her first thought was, *how silly*, as she tried to right herself. When that didn't work, her only options were to lie there patiently or holler for help. She was considering if there was a third way, when Bruno – seeing what had happened from the kitchen – ran over to her. Esther was more embarrassed about the soil all over her face, and the fuss, than the fall, especially after her call with Olivia. She felt elated.

'You have to be careful,' Bruno scolded her, sounding very much like her daughter.

'Screw careful.' She spat out a blade of grass. 'What we need is a party!'

Bruno's entire family was invited, Dominic too, as was Mary, Esther's neighbour, whom Bruno had never met before, even though she'd been the one to place the advert in his mum's salon all those weeks ago. Perhaps the most surprising invitee was Jane.

'I owe it to her,' Esther explained, when the boys seemed visibly shocked by the news. 'Everything considered.'

'I think it's great.' Bruno nudged Dominic with his shoulder. 'Don't you?'

'Yes,' replied Dominic, cautiously. 'What an unexpected... treat.'

Tables were harvested from all over the house and put both in and outside the kitchen to give them options if there was rain, before being covered in blue washed cotton. Food and wine were ordered exclusively by Esther, with some guidance from Bruno, using apps on her phone (only one supermarket delivered to their catchment, and it was the priciest with a hefty delivery fee, but Esther didn't seem to care). She'd forgotten how much she enjoyed cooking, especially with her two young helpers at her command – Bruno, at least; Dominic mostly spent his time eating rather than assisting. Esther was careful to make easy dishes: salads full of herbs from the garden, tabouleh, roast summer vegetables, a pasta frittata recipe she'd stolen from a Venetian art dealer who had tried to sell her a dodgy 'lesser-known' Pietro Barucci. She also baked a challah, braiding the bread on the kitchen table before it headed into the oven to rise and brown wonderfully.

On the Saturday, Bruno seemed nervous about his family descending, the dear boys taking several trips into the garden to discuss things together fervently. Esther understood that introducing your partner to your parents was always nerve-wracking. Her father and mother had approved of her first husband, although they never grew to be particularly fond of him, tellingly – but they were both long dead by the time she met Thackeray.

Mary arrived first, to help with the setting up, taking Esther's cuttings and arranging them expertly into vases. Bruno seemed to like her instantly; she was quiet, but beneath her slightly matronly attire – a dull olive linen tunic 'party' dress, sensible stockings matched with black mary-jane shoes – she was a lot of fun. Jane descended soon after, brandishing a bottle of whisky. The first surprise of the evening for Esther was the sight of her daughter and Mary clinking shot glasses together.

Bruno's family arrived shortly afterwards, his sisters both shy to begin with, but soon running around the garden delightedly. Dominic, looking dapper in a denim shirt, was introduced rather formally to Bruno's parents.

'It's a pleasure to meet you both,' he said, quite rigidly for him, and Esther wanted to swoop in to ease the tension, although she had the clarity of mind to know it wasn't her place.

'We've heard a lot about you,' Bruno's mum said, smiling encouragingly.

'Seen you too,' added his father, 'at the shop. You're the noughts and crosses lad, right? I knew your dad.'

Dominic nodded uneasily. Esther knew mention of his father, who had run away to live with some other family, was a sore point.

'Wine?' she offered, tactfully. 'Everyone should have something to wet their whistle, for toasts at the very least...'

The evening continued to be full of surprises. When Esther sang the Shabbat and lit the candles, just as her grandmother would have done years ago, she noticed that Jane was watching with an expression of wonder, tears in her eyes. Bruno's mother and her youngest daughter Daphne sang a beautiful old English round together, called 'Ah, Poor Bird', the tune reminding Esther of the folksong 'Shalom Chaverim' – and then Bruno's other sister, a very pretty teen girl called Megan, serenaded them sweetly, but self-consciously, with a tune from someone called Taylor Swift.

'Now, the men!' shouted Mary, who'd perhaps had quite a few nips of whisky.

The men in question looked at their feet, except for Dominic, who stood up and did a marvellous, spontaneous jig, which started them all clapping.

The weather held, and it was warm enough, with the aid of a few blankets, to eat outside. Everyone marvelled politely over the food, and especially how Esther had sourced it all electronically herself, and she was able to tell the story of the hand wash – and remind them all to take at least two bottles each on their departure.

After a dessert of apple tarte tatin and thick cream – the combination of zesty sweetness and fat on the tongue absolutely perfect – Jane, Mary and Bruno's mother made coffees, while the children (Esther still thought of the two boys as children) played in the garden, Dominic showing the girls where all of the nests were.

'I'm going to miss this place,' Esther said quietly to Filip beside her.

'Bruno says you're moving on,' he replied. They hadn't touched on this taboo subject during their nocturnal texts.

'Something like that,' she agreed.

They watched as Dominic brought a curiosity in his cupped hands for Bruno to see.

'He's doing very well,' Esther said, nodding towards Filip's son. 'They both are. Those two are good for each other.'

Filip frowned.

'I'm pleased to hear it,' he said, but he didn't seem to be.

'You don't approve?' No use tiptoeing around the issue, she thought.

'It's complicated. After Bruno's experience at that conversion place, we want to be supportive. It sounds horrifying.'

'I can attest to that.'

He nodded solemnly. 'Things have changed a lot since he, you know, stopped hiding the truth about himself. We're all more relaxed – his sister Megan especially. It was like she was internalising his pain. And we're happy Bruno's found some-one. We don't want to be judgemental.'

'But...'

'Dominic comes from a family with a reputation. I don't want Bruno getting caught up with that. He still hasn't decided what to do with his life and I don't like the idea of him being held back.'

'I can vouch for young Dominic; he's a good egg.'

'I never thought I'd be worried about my *son* like this.'

Esther leant over and patted Filip's hand.

'You're doing very well.'

'And what about you, are you nervous about leaving here?'

'Nervous, no,' she batted the worry away with a flick of her wrist. 'I'm not scared of the world any more. I'm about to take a long journey, and the idea thrills me.'

'Your new place won't be nearby? Bruno will miss you – I will too.'

'We all have to go sometime.'

Their attention was drawn by a commotion; Megan and Daphne were being chased by Dominic, who it seemed was pretending to be a lion, and was roaring at the two girls, making them scream. Bruno was smiling from ear to ear as he watched them. He turned, saw his father and Esther staring at him, and his smile faltered for a moment, but quickly returned.

'You know, Filip, you once asked why they called me The Spitfire, and I promised I'd tell you another time. I think that day has come.' He leant in, intrigued. 'It's a little embarrassing, but not in the way I'm used to. Thackeray, you see, could be exceptionally romantic when he chose to be. In maybe 1973, we were at an air show in Edinburgh, and he paid one of the pilots to fly with a banner that read, "The Spitfire Princess, I love you". No one else at the show knew who the message was for, it was our secret. I must admit, it provided me solace over the years. When are we not looking for proof?'

'Constantly,' Filip replied, smiling fondly at his wife.

With some difficulty, Esther rose from her chair.

'Bruno? Dominic?' They stopped what they were doing, ran over to her obediently.

'Now?' Bruno asked.

'Let's begin.'

Dominic fetched a small barbecue from the closest shed, while Bruno went into the house, returning outside with a pile of newspaper and matches.

'Are we absolutely sure Reg doesn't mind us destroying his property?'

'He says it's fine,' Bruno assured Esther.

The sunlight was beginning to dim, the air was getting cooler and even more lushly fragrant.

'Then so be it.' She struck a match. 'Let's end this curse, once and for all.' Carefully, Esther lit the paper, and when the flame was big enough, she threw it on the barbecue to burn.

A spontaneous round of applause rang out.

Esther smiled at her generous guests; she wanted to drink in this scene, capture it in her mind's eye – her friends, her family, the house, the garden – for the very last time.

TWENTY-ONE

BRUNO (21 JULY)

When he woke the next morning, Bruno realised he might be in possession of one of his first-ever hangovers. His head throbbed, and as he sat up – much too quickly – the room spun. Moving more carefully to put on his slippers and dressing gown, he made his pilgrimage downstairs, floorboards creaking noisily at each step. Since his stay, Esther had slept in the study, 'so you know where I am and don't trip over me', forgoing her floor beds entirely. This morning though, Esther wasn't in the study, so Bruno checked the kitchen, but she wasn't there either. Nonplussed – she was probably in the garden pottering about already – Bruno started to make breakfast. As he opened the fridge, he recited the three names on a note he'd placed under an ancient fruit bowl magnet: *Mitch, Pip, Elliot.*

All the other boys had been picked up from the camp early by their parents – Dr Allan explaining there had been a security breach, and for safety reasons they were cancelling the rest of the residential, but not offering to refund the money, Mitch had noted wryly. Once they were home, Pip and Elliot found it more difficult to chat online, because their families closely monitored their computer usage and they weren't allowed phones, so only Bruno and Mitch were in daily communication. Together, though, they devised a plan to make it safer and easier for the two younger boys to join them – by signing up to the game Penguin World, they could all meet and chat as cutesy, cartoon bird avatars.

Their first order of business was to expose the good doctor, so Bruno sent the newspaper article anonymously to the other boys' home addresses. Much good it did him, Mitch complained, his dad would hardly blink if it was revealed the Taliban were leading the residentials. Bruno also took to the internet, dropping the *Daily Mail* link into forums about conversion therapy, and making sure that if anyone searched for 'Dr Allan', they would make the connection. Next week, Bruno was going to talk to a journalist who wanted to know what happened to him at the camp and might even write a story about it. This was a good development, but it made Bruno nervous too – was he ready to have his name out there, and outed, so publicly? Each time fear gripped him, he remembered how powerless he'd felt locked in the cabin. If the journalist wanted to publish his name, he would – especially if it helped the others.

After he'd finished breakfast and washed up his things, there was still no sign of Esther. Bruno walked through the house again, room to room, and when that yielded nothing, he checked outside, looking for tell-tale fresh wheelchair marks in the grass.

'Esther!' he called, starting to feel a needle of panic. Something was off.

He tried to recall the last time he'd seen her – she'd kissed him on the cheek goodnight before he'd stepped groggily upstairs.

What if she'd lost control of the wheelchair near the driveway? Bruno dashed down the path, still in his slippers, but found nothing. He considered going to ask Mary, but he wasn't ready to raise the alarm just yet. Esther did have a habit of sleeping in the strangest places, perhaps she'd emerge from a cabinet, or a broom cupboard and laugh at him for worrying? He ran back into the house to conduct another thorough search, yelling so loudly his voice went hoarse.

Half an hour later, he phoned Dominic.

'Esther's gone.'

'Gone where?'

'Disappeared. Her wheelchair's not here either. I've tried calling her, but it goes to answerphone.'

'Have you called Jane?' asked Dominic. He was working in the corner shop, the door buzzer kept going off in the background. 'Maybe she came and picked her up.'

Bruno hadn't thought of this.

'I'll ring you back,' he promised, hanging up and finding Jane's number.

'It's Bruno,' he said quickly, as soon as she answered.

'Is everything okay?'

From Jane's worried tone, Bruno instantly knew her mother wasn't with her.

'I can't find Esther. She wasn't in the house when I woke up.'

'She can't have gone far – although she was able to get to the coast the other day, I suppose. Is her purse there, her house keys?'

'I don't think so...'

It was then Bruno saw the note, written on crisp paper and sitting on the kitchen table, held in place under one of the jars.

Dear heart, it read in Esther's familiar handwriting:

I'm sorry to leave you, but it's the only way. I didn't want to make you complicit. Tell my daughter, it's my decision, I am still able to make those, you know. And that I love her. Thank

you, Bruno. For everything. Please really live your life, as I
have not always done. Much love, Esther

Bruno stood stunned, before remembering he was still on a
call with Jane.

'She's gone,' he told her. 'I think you should come over as
soon as you can.'

Jane appeared from her car, visibly flustered.

'I really could have done without this today,' she grumbled,
as she approached. Bruno wondered if Jane had a hangover too
– and if that was Esther's plan all along. 'The question is, how
did you let this happen?'

'Me?' replied Bruno, caught off guard.

'I thought you were here to keep an eye on her.'

'I did... I was... She left before I woke up.'

'And what time was that?' Jane held her keys in her fist as if
she was considering punching Bruno, maybe knocking out a
tooth or two.

'About 11 a.m.'

'Do you usually get up so late?'

'It was the party,' Bruno said, bristling. *You were here!* he
thought, annoyed, his temples throbbing.

'Fine, let's see what new mischief Mother has gotten herself
into.'

At the kitchen table, Jane inspected the note. She'd poured
herself a massive glass of tap water, which she was taking
substantial gulps from. The kitchen was still cluttered with the
detritus of the party: empty wine bottles (crowded around the
taller whisky bottle as if they were in a group hug), a salad that

wouldn't fit in the fridge, a messy stack of napkins, and Bruno noticed all the surfaces needed another good wipe.

'How can I be sure you're not in on this ploy?' Jane asked, once she'd finished reading. 'You help her escape and she writes this note to let you off the hook?'

'I didn't, I promise – I want her back as much as you do. She's only just come out of the hospital.'

'Did Mother seem out of sorts the past week? Was she morose?'

'If anything,' replied Bruno, 'she was happier.'

'That's not a good sign,' Jane noted, gravely. She made a strange gurgling noise, as if she was choking, and to Bruno's horror, he realised she'd begun to cry. 'I'm sorry.' She shielded her face with her hands. 'I was already feeling emotional after the party. Seeing Mother in her element, in such great form... I had a glimpse of our life *unlived*, if that makes any sense?'

'It does,' Bruno promised. 'Do you want a tissue?'

'I have one.' Sniffing, she found it in her pocket. 'I love Mother, I do. What if something *terrible* has happened to her?'

'It won't have, not yet. And I think we can find her.'

After Jane had rung the police to file a missing person's report (and was told they'd have to wait until Esther was gone for longer, even if she was old, vulnerable and had mobility issues, much to her daughter's irritation – Bruno would not have liked to have been on the other end of the call), she sat back down at the table.

'See here,' said Bruno, showing Jane his phone. 'When I was teaching Esther, I made a note of her logins and passwords, because – well, she'd forget what she did with them, and it saved time. If you give me permission now, I'll log in and we can check her activity.'

'Yes, yes, permission granted,' Jane said, impatiently. 'No time to start being coy.'

Bruno took a deep breath. Esther's daughter had all the directness of her mother, but with none of the charm.

'There's a transaction here,' he said once he was inside Esther's bank account. 'She recently paid for a chauffeur-driven car.'

'Why a bloody chauffeur?'

'Probably because regular taxis don't come this far out.'

'And if she's going to disappear, may as well do it in style. I like that on top of causing a huge inconvenience, and putting her life in peril, she's burning through my inheritance. Where do you think she's headed?'

'Scotland,' replied Bruno.

Jane was gobsmacked.

'But why?' she asked once she'd recovered.

'To look for Thackeray.'

'If that's the case, she's a little late...'

Bruno explained the search for house foundations – this seemed to make immediate sense to Jane; apparently her mother had been asking some land-related questions recently – and then showed her his screen:

'At 07.16 a.m. Esther made a purchase for £8.60 at the train station in Rugby.'

'That's not enough for a ticket to Scotland.'

'Esther knew I'd try to figure out where she went. Maybe she bought the ticket with cash to throw me off the scent – she always has some lying around the house. There's no confirmation email for a ticket in her inbox...'

'What was the purchase at the station then?'

'It looks like snacks for the journey.'

'Mother does like a Fry's peppermint cream on a longer car trip.' Jane gave a frustrated sigh. 'This whole thing's ridiculous.

Mother can barely walk, how is she going to get around Scotland by herself?'

'Esther's resourceful. If she puts her mind to it, she can do anything. Look, I can research which trains went north from Rugby this morning, and maybe we can narrow it down. Tell the police to keep a watch out for her? Esther's in a wheelchair, she's going to be easy to spot.'

'Then we've got her,' her daughter said, slightly menacingly, making Bruno wonder if he was doing the right thing after all. Perhaps he should have stayed quiet, and let Esther... No, he would never forgive himself if anything happened. They had to get Esther back, safely. He needed her.

TWENTY-TWO

ESTHER

With great care, Esther was assisted off the train by a station guard who had been waiting with a ramp.

'Please take this,' Esther instructed, when they were through the barriers, pulling one of the bottles of hand wash out of her handbag and presenting it to the bemused woman. 'It's my last one.' Esther had also given one to her chauffeur, who took no convincing to accept the gift, and the attendant helping her on the train at Rugby, who had to have the bottle thrust at him.

'Is there someone picking you up?' the station guard asked, concern in her voice, as she held the bottle to her chest. 'Or to help with your bag?'

'I do hope so,' Esther replied, scanning the busy station. Much had changed since she was last here; it had been modernised and reroofed, but she could still imagine Thackeray standing in his trench coat, waiting to collect her, delight in his eyes. At least once, they'd made it no further than the adjoining hotel, skipping down the concourse and into the biggest suite available. 'Can you tell me, is there a man here holding a sign with "Saul" written on it?'

'Seems so.'

'Excellent, if you could wheel me over, and put me in his charge.'

The handover went without a hitch, the driver Dan – with a lovely, crooked nose, perhaps he'd been a boxer? – whisking Esther to an awaiting vehicle.

'Straight to the hotel?' he asked, once they were both inside.

'Yes please, Dan,' she replied, cheerily.

To be in Scotland again, after all these decades! Esther was as excited as a schoolgirl. Her dash to the coast with Dominic aside, she couldn't remember when she had felt so free. Was there a massive pang of guilt over how she'd left Bruno, and her daughter – and trepidation about what was to come? Obviously, but she would deal with that tomorrow. Today she would embrace this sense of felicity.

'How does one open the window?' Esther called from the back seat, realising she'd become instantly posher in the span of a first-class train journey. *How does one?* – she sounded like the queen. Dan lowered the window automatically, and Esther was able to take in large gulps of air, feeling like a retriever with its snout sticking out, watching as the city whizzed by, the red buildings she remembered, amid the newer glass-fronted ones, many of them afflicted with varying degrees of vivid graffiti. The city seemed futuristic to her, in as much as she was in her own future, comparing it with recollections of the past, but perhaps all modern cities would appear strange?

The hotel was to be more understated than her lavish journey up had been. Esther felt it was prudent to take herself out of the city, especially if the police, or her daughter, were trying to find her. Esther knew they could probably trace her card, so she'd paid for the train ticket with cash, with plenty left to pay for the hotel tonight. After that... well... Things would play out naturally...

She pulled her nose out of the window.

'Dan, could we possibly take a short detour?'

'Where to?'

'Is there a place you'd recommend for a proper black pudding?'

'Oh aye, and they do a good cullen skink too.'

'Sounds perfect,' replied Esther. She hadn't heard of this culinary delicacy, but she couldn't wait to try it – despite the food on the train, her appetite was piqued, and she was famished for more.

Arriving at the hotel several stone heavier – a cullen skink had turned out to be a hearty haddock soup served with hefty chunks of the most delicious bread – Esther tipped Dan generously, once he'd kindly brought her luggage inside.

'You'll have to buy your own hand wash, I'm afraid,' she said, Dan smiling blankly in response.

The receptionist was a tall, quietly spoken man with horn-rimmed glasses.

'Could you tell me,' asked Esther, as she handed over the cash for her room, 'how I might go about finding farms to visit tomorrow? I'm thinking of taking a tour around the area.'

'I know pretty much every place around here,' the receptionist replied, clasping his hands together, 'and if I don't, I'm sure my mother can help. We have maps in our reading room too you're welcome to use.'

'And my room comes with Wi-Fi?' Esther had forgotten to check, she realised.

'It does indeed.'

'Good, I can't be doing without the internet, not even for a moment.'

'Oh, I seem to live on my phone.'

'Don't we all!' replied Esther gaily, before allowing herself to be wheeled to the elevator.

. . .

In bed later, she risked turning on her phone for the briefest of moments, and a million messages appeared like a seizure – ping ping ping ping ping!

From Bruno:

Esther, I can't find you (this did make her feel very guilty).

Where are you?

Are you outside?

If you don't ring me soon, I'm going to have to call Jane.

Found your note. I can't believe you went without explaining to me.

I'm telling your daughter everything. I'm sorry, but it's the right thing to do. What if you fall or get hurt?

From Dominic:

You're a scamp. It's chaos here after your break for freedom.

Text Bruno, he's worried.

From her daughter:

Please mother, don't do anything stupid. Anything else stupid.

We can discuss your living arrangements, if you were so unhappy you should have told me. It's not like you not to voice your opinions, so I'm left baffled.

Mother, please call. We don't want to get the police involved unnecessarily.

If you're dead in a ditch, I will kill you.

And from Bruno's father:

Esther, I've heard. I don't know if you're picking these up, everyone here is very worried. I know a while ago, I said if you were ever having one of those nights, I was here for you. Well, if you are, I am X

Just wanted to add, I had some very bleak times with the cancer. Dark thoughts. There are always days like that. But then there are those when the light hits differently, you know?

This last message affected Esther the most, her heart racing, hands trembling, and it took all her will to turn off her phone again without answering any of them.

Esther awoke early. Hotel rooms in the morning were always such a different beast from the ones you fell asleep in if you were only staying one night. All fantasy of luxury disappeared – the bed gave no more comfort, the view, however nice, was unnecessary. You were on borrowed time.

'Like life,' Esther muttered as she readied herself.

She was downstairs for breakfast (served with a traditional tatty scone) by 7.30 a.m., and afterwards, Esther wheeled herself into the reading room, lined with bookshelves, with newspapers, magazines and – ah yes – local maps on the table. A quick glance showed they held considerably more detail than the ones on her phone and what a luxury to—

'Hello, dear,' came a soft voice behind Esther, making her

jump. 'Sorry to startle you,' said the woman with gently lilting 'r's', who seemed in her late seventies. 'My son mentioned you might need some help looking for places to visit?'

'Ah yes, how good of you. Please join me.'

'I'm Margaret. Did you come up from England yesterday then?'

'I did,' replied Esther hesitantly – what if she'd been rumbled already?

'Rather you than me, to be honest. I get sore legs feeding the hens.'

'You keep chickens?'

'Aye, a coop out the back. You probably ate the eggs for your brekky.'

'I thought the yolks were a gorgeous colour, I mopped them up with my tattie scone.'

Margaret lowered her voice. 'When you work in the service industry, it pays to have a hobby you can exert some control over.'

'I suppose you can always wring one of the birds' necks if they annoy you?'

'Not so with guests.' Margaret chuckled. 'How can I help ye?'

Esther explained about Thackeray's suspected land, Cridhe Cruaidh, giving as much detail as she could.

'From everything you say, it sounds like it's up by the old Jamieson farm,' Margaret said with a nod.

'Can you show me where it is on the map?'

'Of course, hen. Right... here.' Margaret tapped the paper. 'Can I ask why you've come all this way to visit this wee spot?'

'Probably hubris,' Esther replied, 'possibly salvation.'

'Oh aye? That's quite a hill to climb then. If my memory serves, the road there is tight and I'm not sure if it's sealed. You'll have a hard time finding a taxi who'll want to risk it.'

'I must though.'

'We'll see what we can arrange for ye.' Margaret stood to go. 'Can I say – you have a wonderful energy about you. It's a pleasure to see. So many of our lot become mired in regret or worse – nostalgia – but you seem very sprightly.'

Esther felt genuinely tongue-tied by this compliment, and for some reason she wanted to give credit to Bruno.

'Thank you. I owe much of it to a young man who came into my life.'

Margaret chuckled. 'It's like that, is it?'

'Oh no...'

'Hen, there's no judgement here, believe me. The things I've seen here over the years. Good luck. I have a feeling you're going to find exactly what you're looking for.' Margaret winked and exited, before Esther could set her right.

The new driver was a sniffer, on average once every ten seconds. It was a form of water torture – and even when Esther offered him a tissue for his nose, he declined.

'I don't know if we'll fit,' he grumbled between sniffs. 'This road is for tractors.'

'Could you at least try?' asked Esther, her voice sounding horribly clipped in comparison. 'See how far we get?'

'What if I can't get out again?' the driver complained, quite rightly. 'There's nowhere to turn round.'

'I'll make it worth your while – with an additional tip.'

Grumbling under his breath, the driver nonetheless turned into the narrow lane.

It was a clear summer's day, the vast sky only streaked with a little cirrostratus, but breezier than Esther had hoped. They had driven for forty-one minutes – she'd set a stopwatch on her device – and covered twenty-five miles to the north of Glasgow towards the Fintry Hills. This felt physically correct now having made the journey – it was wild enough, and yet Thackeray wouldn't have wanted to be too far away from Glasgow, nor the connecting train station and airport, she reasoned. The countryside on the drive had become increasingly imposing, craggy hills like dozing giants, great swathes of conifer trees, the cows and sheep – and yes, lambs – appearing much smaller in the landscape, white, black or red specks against a deep tweed green. Esther wondered if the area might look familiar to her, having spent so many weeks poring over satellite views, but if anything, it felt unknowable; each time she moved her head, it seemed to shift and dazzle her with its glory in some fresh way.

'What are you doing up here?' asked the driver – he'd not told her his name – as they slowly made their way. 'No one out here...'

'That's what I'm after,' Esther replied, as brightly as she could, but it came out sounding brisk.

'I know what you mean – people are shite.' Esther smiled, but in fact she couldn't get into this sentiment. Bruno's face penetrated her mind again, like a sad puppy. 'All people do is step ova ya to get what the hell they want. Take my sister-in-law...'

But they were never to learn about the ills of the sister-in-law, because at that very moment, there was a loud crunching noise, followed by expletives from the driver (several Esther had not heard before) as he squeezed out of his side to look at the damage. She sat, worried about what to do. How could she even get out of the taxi here? There wasn't room. Inspection done, the driver squeezed back in and closed the door.

'How does it look?' Esther asked, worriedly.

'Not good. I'm going to have to reverse back.'

'I'm sure there's a place further up to turn around, it must come to an open area eventually...?'

'No way. I've scratched my paintwork.'

'What if I give you a thousand pounds?'

The driver was silent for a moment.

'Do you even have that kind of money on ya?'

'I do, it's all I have. And it's yours if you drive up a little farther.'

'How do I know you're not lying to me?'

'I'm not exactly going to ride and dash, am I?'

'True.'

He grumbled again to himself, but in a moment they were inching forward again.

'If we hit anything else,' he warned, 'that's it, game over.'

Esther sat, if not actively praying, then pleading to a higher being. Fortunately, they made their way up the hill and then down again in a back-to-front snaking 's'. On the next hill, the driver stopped and pulled the handbrake.

'We're here,' he announced, giving one long sniff. 'The path will take you to the top, if that's what you're after. Are you sure you'll be able to get back when you're done?' The driver didn't sound hugely concerned, which made Esther relieved. She'd worried she might have someone more chivalrous who wouldn't simply leave her in the middle of the countryside, on the side of the hill, but she needn't have – he couldn't get out of there fast enough. Once her wheelchair was ready, he plonked her (quite forcibly) into it, dumped her bag beside her, but then appeared sheepish for the first time.

'Ah yes, money,' said Esther, taking out twenty fifty-pound notes from her purse and presenting them to him.

The driver grunted, taking the money, with barely a thank you or a goodbye, before getting into the car again.

'What a charmer,' Esther said to no one in particular, as the vehicle moved off. It was instantly a relief to be away from all those sniffs.

After stowing her bag behind the stone wall running along the lane, Esther surveyed the hill. She could see a path of sorts, but it was steep and uneven. Behind her, sweeping farmland met even more hills, and beyond those the Trossachs, real mountains. Esther had never more felt like a speck herself. The wind whipped her scarf into her mouth as she stood gawping at the incline. There were trees about halfway up, and what looked like a cliff on the eastern side. But what lay at the top? There was nothing else for it, she decided.

Manoeuvring herself around so she was behind the wheelchair, using it for balance, Esther started up the slope. It was slow-going; her legs were still weak from being bedbound, but what she didn't have in calf muscles, she hoped she made up for with tenacity. She quickly realised that in this case, tenacity was just another word for wishful thinking. Out of breath already, she considered what to do, as the wind tried to strangle her with her own scarf.

To reach the top, if there was no other option, she would go on hands and knees, like the Greek Orthodox faithful she'd once seen, crawling up for their pilgrimage on the island of Tinos. Though they had a red carpet most of the way, Esther recalled, enviously.

What was she doing? She'd get herself killed. But really, what did it matter if she hauled herself up the mount with muddied hands and knees? There was no one here to see her, except perhaps God – and He'd seen Esther do some spectacularly foolish things over the years.

A twinge, thinking of Jane being told her mother was found filthy and alone on the side of a hill. But there was no dignity in death, wherever it was. Did Esther want to fade away strapped to a machine, or dribbling in a bath gown watching daytime TV? Or here, in the elements, under a great sky, the smell of peat so pungent it almost burned her nostrils?

Her legs were trembling now with each step, and she was only several yards up the hill. She needed a rest. Pulling the brake on the wheelchair, Esther sat herself down beside it. The view was breathtaking, the farmhouses and buildings gathering into civilisation to the West, more rolling hills to the East, these ones blanketed with trees, and the scrappy clouds were being overtaken by thick white painterly ones that seemed a little too conspicuously God's work.

'All this God talk,' Esther muttered. These thoughts were the very reason she was climbing this hill. To be rid of thinking, of worrying, of feeling like she could have done more. How many years did it take to comprehend life? Almost all of them, Esther felt despairingly, and yet she was no closer to *understanding* it.

As a distraction, she took out her phone from her pocket. She realised why people did this now – it always seemed so mindless when Esther saw people glued to their devices, but she finally realised that was the point. To *not* think. To gawk, aimlessly. Idiot vision in your pocket. She turned hers on, and like last night, it erupted in beeps and vibrations, like an annoyed pet that had been left without attention for too long. More messages from Bruno and her daughter. One from Jane stood out in particular:

We are coming.

Esther looked wildly around the hillside, imagining for a moment they might be staring at her.

Hitting reply, she began to type:

I'm fine, please don't waste your time, not any more than you have. You have been a wonderful daughter, I only wish I let myself know you better. I love you, dear.

Tears welled in Esther's eyes, but she fought them back.

Standing again was perilous, she was afraid the wheelchair might tip and topple down the hill, but once she had steadied herself, Esther was once more able to start the ascent. Her phone beeped several more times – darn it, she'd forgotten to turn it off – so she trudged on, ignoring it, but annoyed with herself; the robotic sound of the beeping was spoiling the natural ambience. She considered throwing the phone down the hill, but something stopped her. Perhaps it was the last vestiges of connection with the people she loved. Esther might talk a good game about being a loner, but it wasn't exactly true.

It was grim-going now, the hill growing steeper, but she was almost to the top. The view, when she arrived, took her breath away. It was on a flat-topped mount, with a steep drop to her right, and a smattering of trees, knocked askew by strong winds. Beyond the ridge, a valley sprawled below, and then came back up into the highlands. But what stopped her breath, more than the gorgeous view, were the stones. Esther recognised them immediately, the markers for a house that never was.

'Why build a home on a hill?' she'd asked Thackeray all those years ago. 'We'll blow clean off.'

'You've never seen a house I've built,' he'd replied with typical confidence.

'What if the hill erodes?'

'It's been there for centuries.'

'Everything crumbles eventually.'

'Oh aye, but this house will stand the test of time, you'll see.'

'Will it be big enough? I have so many idiotic things from my travels.'

'Room to spare, if I have to wrestle them up the hill myself.' He'd taken a long drag of his cigarette. 'Of course, I probably won't touch a thing, the boys will do all the heavy lifting,' he'd laughed. 'I'll take the fabrics and doilies.'

'They can be heavy too, if you have enough of them.'

'Do you want this house built, or are you finding excuses?'

'I do,' she'd said, and they both let the significance of those two words settle.

. . .

The wind whipped up, and it caught Esther and nearly made her sit down heavily on the ground, but fortunately, she grabbed the wheelchair handles for support. She was tired, tired of standing, tired of *everything*. She wanted to see those foundations, see them for what they were, with her own eyes, to know they existed, that at one point, not in the fabrication of her mind and memory, there was actual concrete proof Thackeray had loved her, and seen a future with the two of them.

Here it was.

Esther drew closer to the house that should have been hers, if the world had not gotten in the way. The stones had weathered, of course, and broken, but the shape of the building was there. The walls of the old sheep shed, the original building, could be seen too. Reaching the closest 'wall', which was a foot or so high, Esther steadied herself on the wheelchair and sat herself down. It felt good to have stone beneath her seat bones. She'd imagined this place for decades, wondered if it had really existed, seen it in dreams, and most recently, from a bird's-eye view. It felt like stone circles, as if she needed to say an invocation to break the spell, a ritual – the blood of a virgin, perhaps? 'Ha,' she laughed, with no mirth. She'd definitely not been one of *those* when she met him. If only she could speak to Thackeray, if the gods would grant her one more audience with him.

'Hello?' a man's voice called. 'Can I help you?'

Esther turned to see man in walking jacket and boots. He was gripping hiking poles, which she always thought looked rather daft – as if you were planning to ski, but with no snow.

'I'm fine, thank you,' she replied, curtly.

'Where's your companion?' the man asked. As he drew nearer, Esther could see he was in his late sixties perhaps, with white eyebrows, and a red ruddy face.

'My who?'

'I just thought... who pushed you up the hill in this then?'
He tapped the wheelchair with one of his sticks.

'No companion, just brute determination on my part.'
The man seemed surprised by this but didn't say any more.
'I'm Esther,' she said, sticking out her hand, because it felt
rude to be sitting on a rock on a hill, and not introduce
herself.

'Douglas. You not from around this way?'

'No, I've come far. Although, I was acquainted with the
man who made this,' she indicated the house boundaries, 'at one
point.'

'Oh, you knew Thackeray then?'

Esther almost fell off her rock.

'You did too?'

'Of course, the man's a legend round here. My wife and I
have lived by the beinn over there,' he pointed back the way
he'd come (Esther took 'beinn' to mean hill, but wasn't sure), 'for
the past forty-odd years. Me and the madam were both
teachers.'

'Did you ever meet Thackeray?'

'Several times; we weren't friends, but everyone knows
everyone around here.'

'He definitely did stand out.'

'Especially with all the controversy.'

Esther flinched: Douglas couldn't possibly know about her
past, could he?

'What do you mean?' she asked warily.

'Over this place.' Douglas gestured with his sticks. 'Even
when he bought it forty years ago, it was prime real estate, so
you can only imagine how much it's appreciated in price since
then. When he died, his son found out it had been left in a
trust.'

'To whom?'

'That was the thing, no one knows. It stipulated that the

land could not be built on nor sold in any major way. His son was furious, tried every trick in the book, but it was iron-clad.'

'Now, why would Thackeray do that?' Esther asked, fully aware she was leading the witness.

'A lot of folk have asked the same thing. Some say spite; he was not the most respectful of his neighbours, he had spats with a lot of them. Not us, mind, but we never wanted to buy it up from him. Or his son. Others say he wanted this place left as a natural reserve, but why not leave it to a charity? I have my own opinion...'

'Which is?' Esther replied, knowing on some level what Douglas was about to say next.

'Thackeray kept it for someone he loved. To make it an eternally sacred space. That's why he never wanted anyone to build on it, why he couldn't give it to his son. He wanted a gesture of his love, long after he'd passed.'

'But...' protested Esther, 'Thackeray was not a sentimental man.'

'All men are sentimental,' Douglas replied, firmly, 'we only find it difficult to show. And now, it sits here, unfettered by the passing of the years, wild, as everything gets bought up and built upon. That's why I come here on my walks. I always think of them, whoever she was, as a way of giving tribute.'

'That's beautiful,' Esther said, blinking back tears. 'I'm sure they appreciate it.'

'I'd best keep going, want to get my steps in and not lower my heart rate too much. I have lunch waiting for me at the end. Can I help you down the hill first? It's a steep one.'

'I'll be fine.'

'Are you sure?'

'I think I want to sit some more.'

'Can I give you my number, just in case you need a hand later? You could come and join us for lunch even, I'm sure my wife has made plenty, she always does.'

'That's very kind.'

Douglas took out his wallet, and handed her a card. It read *Douglas Fineman, DIY and Odd Jobs*. 'Ignore the description, I just do that for a bit of sport, I'm supposed to be retired, but you can't write "retired" on a business card, can you? I haven't given up on life and meeting new people yet.'

'I can tell. Thank you, Douglas.'

He smiled, continuing on his way, before turning round, 'You want to be careful of that drop,' he called to her, 'the cliff can catch you by surprise.'

'Thank you,' she called back, and watched him disappear over the ridge of the hill.

TWENTY-THREE

BRUNO (22 JULY)

They were driving at the exact legal speed limit, but it felt torturously slow to Bruno. Couldn't Jane break the law a bit, he wondered silently. This was unusual coming from him, Bruno was normally so law-abiding – but they might be running out of time... His phone was on his knee, allowing him to watch Esther's location ping on the Find My Phone app, but they were still some distance away. What if they couldn't locate her, or the signal stopped, or his phone ran out of battery? Even the countryside, interesting and beautiful though it was – and he was in Scotland for the first time! – flew by without any proper attention. Bruno's whole body, his whole being, was an arrow, pointing.

'I'm going to murder her,' Jane muttered bitterly, but they seemed to be tears of sadness in her eyes, not anger.

'We're going to find her,' replied Bruno, as much to reassure himself as Jane.

'And with her bad hip too. Has Mother ever told you how it happened?' Her knuckles were white as she gripped the steering wheel, he noticed.

'Only that she fell a few years ago.'

'She re-injured it then, but it was an old fracture.' Jane glanced at Bruno and then back at the road. 'After the stuff in the newspapers, Mother was clinically depressed – that's what you'd call it now, at least – she'd very publicly lost the man of her dreams, her London friends were less than supportive because they believed Esther had been fraternising with the enemy, it was all very complicated. Mother quite rightly needed some time away, so she booked herself into a psychiatric hospital...'

'...Alberton Lodge?'

'She's told you about the place?'

'It was one of the ways she tried to stop me going to Camp Change.'

Jane nodded and turned up the air con. It was getting warm in the car.

'Nowadays, they'd prescribe her antidepressants and perhaps some light yoga, but in the seventies, electroshock therapy was still popular. After one session, Mother was woozy, and she managed to roll off the gurney onto the floor, fracturing the bone in her hip.'

'Oh no.' Bruno covered his mouth. 'Poor Esther.'

'I wrote to Thackeray after it happened – that's what we used to do then, write letters to each other – pleading for him to go and see her, but all I got back was two lines: *I'm sorry. I made a promise to my wife.* What about his promises to my mother? I was so angry, I remember I kicked a dent in my bedroom wall. I liked Thackeray, I think most people did, he had charm to spare, but he was more about grand gestures than the real nitty-gritty of life. He wanted to become a mayor, but couldn't handle any personal scandal; he wanted to honour his wife, but he still fell in love with my mother; he apparently saved a huge expensive block of land in her honour, but he wouldn't go and visit her in the hospital when she was in crippling pain from a fall. Talk is cheap.'

'And life isn't nice,' added Bruno.

'No, it's often not. But do you know something, I'm glad Mother has you.'

They shared a smile.

'I think we need to turn down the next road,' Bruno announced, 'on the left coming up.' He toggled between Google Maps and the Find My Phone app. They also had a hand-drawn map that a guy at the car hire place had made for them, who had grown up near the Fintry Hills.

'This one? I'm not sure we'll even fit.' Nevertheless, Jane turned them into the lane. 'If we get one scratch on this car, hand on heart, I will absolutely kill her,' she promised, shaking her head in exasperation.

TWENTY-FOUR

ESTHER

The wind was getting even stronger – cutting right through her.

Thackeray *had* loved her after all, this was proof! Why not come to Esther when he could have though, instead of enshrining a block of land? No wonder his son had been so angry – in his eyes, Esther had not only stolen his father away from his mother, but wangled him out of his inheritance too, or at least a sizeable chunk of it. And Genevieve's duplicitousness, fuelled by her unrequited love for Thackeray, how had Esther not seen that? They had spent plenty of time together, the three of them, at the house in Swiss Cottage, or on trips; Thackeray was always generous.

A gust almost tipped her off the wall: the Scottish elements were not to be trifled with. Her bones would be chilled right through if she sat here on cold stone. Hoisting herself up into her wheelchair, Esther felt oddly light, as if the conversation with Douglas about Thackeray had changed her physically, released some heavy minerals in her body. Thackeray had protected this place for her – it was all but confirmed – and now she had returned, and in a way, they would be together forever.

Esther began to wheel herself towards the cliff edge; it was a dare mostly. Getting there was tough-going, even on flat ground, because of the long grass and the unevenness, a wheel snagging on a stone. Loose strands of her hair caught in her mouth and eyes, blinding her. Five feet from the edge, Esther risked a look down.

Do it then. Or be thankful for your life. No more complaining.

The ground below was maybe two hundred feet down, which would certainly do the job. Her bones must be as brittle as dust now; she'd smash into a hundred pieces. But with that thought came another. Bruno, and his newly minted brand of activism; how he had been so strident since coming back from the conversion therapy place, the shock of the experience mobilising him. Esther was proud.

Now sentimentality was taking hold.

She wheeled herself forward another foot. That was a mistake. She felt vertigo grip her immediately, and her impulse was to go back to safety. Esther wasn't exactly afraid of heights, but she'd never been so close to a drop. A blast of wind whipped her hair across her face, blinding her, just as a wheel hit a snag, and she lurched forward. *I'm actually going to fall!* thought Esther, panicked, as she clawed away the hair covering her eyes so she could see. Still blinded, she tipped forward and in that very moment, Esther knew in her heart that she wasn't ready to die.

As she felt herself start to plummet out of the chair, all the issues she thought it would solve exposed themselves as untruths – she could live quite easily anywhere, even with her daughter, Esther could survive without all the dusty stuff she'd accumulated, it was only holding her down like a weight. She wanted more dinners, more laughter, extra time with the people she loved. With the wind still slapping her hair across her face, she damned her stupidity. Esther realised Thackeray had not bought this land and frozen it in time as a memoriam to her – he'd done it because it gave him absolute control. Thackeray had tried to freeze her too, rejecting the real Esther and creating one to honour made from aspic. He'd wanted her to be the little woman, to hide her Jewishness, to cut herself off from her friends and everything she believed in, and she would not. But isn't that what she'd done to herself, enshrined herself on the hill? Severed herself from all the main arteries of life?

She called out in fear and anger, 'Help!' Esther didn't know how close she was to the edge, her hair was so much in her face – she was afraid to move in any direction. *Idiot woman!* she chastised herself. She clung to the ground for dear life, feeling both terrified, and never more happy to be living in all her many years.

If she couldn't get away from here, she would die of exposure by nightfall, that was certain. Death by misadventure.

It was then she remembered the phone. Of course! She rummaged for it in her pocket with one hand, still steadying herself with the other, holding on to a fistful of grass – much good that would do her if she did fall. The wonderful device, the shiny monolith, would help her: if she could call Bruno or her daughter, or ring the police, or – oh yes! Douglas, he'd given her his card! – but these hopes were dashed when she realised the phone was no longer in her pocket. Where was it? It must have slipped out when she was sitting on the rock, damn and blast!

She berated herself again, *idiot woman* scrabbling around on the edge of a cliff.

'Help!' she called again, frozen by fear. 'Please!'

Her name sounded in the wind, mocking her. *Esther*, she thought she heard the gale call.

But there it was again:

'Esther! What are you doing?'

With her hair in her eyes, she still couldn't see anything, but it sounded so much like Bruno, and her heart swelled, even if it was nothing but her imagination.

TWENTY-FIVE

BRUNO

Why was she not responding to his calls? Esther was on hands and knees and seemed to be crawling towards the edge of the cliff. She couldn't be trying to...?

Bruno called her name again. He'd sprinted all the way up the hill and was out of breath. The wind was so intense, maybe Esther couldn't hear him? He turned to Jane, only halfway up behind him, scrabbling as fast as she could.

'She's here,' Bruno called to her, and then raced towards Esther, feeling the burn in his calves and chest.

Esther was a flurry of fabric and white hair, swirling around her chaotically – he couldn't even see her face. This is how his parents must have felt, realised Bruno, when he stubbornly left for Camp Change – unable to stop someone you love from hurting themselves. He wasn't powerless though... Bruno's lungs were on fire... he could reach her.

He must.

TWENTY-SIX

ESTHER

A strong hand took hold of her and carefully helped her up and then back into the chair. Even before she could see it was Bruno, she knew it must be him from his touch – anyone else might have yanked her up, but not him, he guided her expertly.

'What are you doing here?' Esther spluttered.

'Rescuing you,' Bruno replied. 'Let's get you away from the edge.'

Esther felt the wheelchair reverse.

'Over by those stones,' she called, 'I want to see you.'

Bruno complied.

'Dear, dear heart, let me look at you.' Bruno squatted in front of Esther and she clasped his cheeks in her hands. 'I never thought I'd see you again, this wonderful face.' She continued to study it carefully, every pore. She kissed his cheeks, but Bruno pulled away from her touch, anger erupting in his expression.

'You left me,' he half yelled at her.

'I know, I'm very sorry...' replied Esther, shocked at Bruno's vehemence.

'What were you doing? You weren't really trying to... to go without saying goodbye?'

'Of course not, I just wanted to *see*. And I did! I'm an idiot.'

'You're not an idiot at all,' Bruno said, still furious, 'you're the most courageous person I know. I need you.'

'And I you, dear heart. I do. But how did you get here?'

'I set up an app to find your phone if it was lost. It showed me where you were.'

'So, the device saved me! Can you look for it? I think it fell behind that stone.'

Bruno searched, locating the phone in the grass where Esther had pointed. He passed it to her.

'Oh, you beautiful thing. Thank you, thank you.'

'Mother!' Esther turned to see her daughter, emerging up the hill, out of breath.

'Come here, come here!' Esther called, as Bruno turned the wheelchair. Daughter ran to mother, Jane collapsing into Esther's lap, sobbing. 'There, there,' said Esther, soothingly. 'You've done so well, for so long. I'm here now. I'm finally here.'

With Esther re-established back in her house – the potential sale given a reprieve for the time being – the burst of summer started to mellow into autumn. The low sun casting longer shadows through the branches, the deep leaf-greens beginning to turn. Apples and pears from the old fruit trees were ready to harvest, bulbs were to be planted and outdoor potted plants were to be slowly rehomed inside before the first frost.

When it came to romance, the blossoming was also beginning to falter. A first relationship was a lot of pressure to put on someone, and although Dominic was patient and kind, Bruno still had so many blocks. It was like he'd been given the keys to a house with no windows or doors – he only had to find his way in. His mum suggested therapy, but Bruno was put off by his experience with Dr Allan – he didn't want anyone else trying to get into his head.

'Can I be honest with you about something?' Dominic asked, one hot early September day, when they were lying in bed to escape the afternoon sun. The previous Thursday, Esther had declared summer over – the weather was to change irrevocably over the weekend – so they were all surprised by this late-in-the-season scorcher. *Global warming*, Dominic had sniffed, before diving into a lively debate with Esther about the appropriateness of her using the term, 'Indian Summer'.

'Sure,' Bruno answered, although – tellingly – his impulse was to flee from the bedroom.

Dominic propped himself up on an elbow. He was naked except for a pair of not-quite-white briefs that were a hand-me-down from his older brother. Secretly, Bruno found them sexy and gross in equal measure.

'I thought it would be easier being with a guy.'

Bruno ran this sentence through his mind several times, scanning it for implications.

'Easier how?'

'I don't know – that we'd share more of a sense of under-standing? Common ground. It's kind of sexist, actually.'

'You don't think we understand each other?' Bruno frowned.

'On lots of levels, sure,' replied Dominic, nodding. 'But I never know what's in your head. Not really. Like now, when you were looking out the window.'

'I was thinking about the camp advertised next month,' Bruno said, truthfully. 'If there's anything more I can do to stop it; and even if I did, about all the other conversion places out there, and the counsellors, and psychotherapists trying to "cure" these kids. Most don't advertise online, so I can't find them even if I wanted to...'

'Do you ever think...?' Dominic stalled.

'What? Tell me.'

'...that the best way to get back at them...' he bit his lip, his brow furrowed, 'is to – I don't know – *enjoy* your life?'

'I am,' protested Bruno. 'But that's not going to stop the bad things from happening.'

Dominic mumbled something.

'I didn't hear you,' replied Bruno, annoyance growing.

'Sometimes I wonder if your activism is another way to hide from yourself.'

Bruno gave Dominic an exasperated look.

'You think I'm *hiding*? That doesn't make any sense. I did that interview with the journalist. I'm constantly putting myself on the line...'

Moving onto his back, Dominic held both hands up.

'Forget I said anything. It was only an observation.' He rolled onto his side again. 'Let's go away, do something fun.'

'I can't leave Esther. Anyway, we have fun here – this huge house. The garden.'

Dominic gave a groan. 'You're turning into a recluse, just like her. Don't you want to go out drinking and dancing – be a regular teenager? And if you say Mitch, Pip or that other kid again, I'm going to lose it. They get all your attention, and I'm left with scraps.' He sat up suddenly. 'Honestly, I can't bear listening to myself. Do you know, when I was dating Jenna Scott in Year Eleven, she used to write me love poems? Multiple love poems a day.'

'Yeah, we all knew,' replied Bruno, dismissively. 'She used an online rhyming dictionary, they were terrible. Just because something can rhyme, doesn't mean it should.'

'That's not the point.'

'What is, then?'

'The poems proved she liked me.'

'You want me to write you bad poetry?'

'Perhaps. Maybe.'

'*Roses are red, Dominic is blue...*'

'If you're going to make fun of me, forget it.'

'I'm here in bed with you now,' Bruno placed a hand on Dominic's wrist, and rubbed it with his thumb, 'isn't that proof of how I feel?'

'Which is exactly what I'd have said to Jenna when she complained I wasn't raving over her awful poetry!'

Bruno laughed and patted Dominic's chest.

'You're used to having all the power, that's all it is. Being with me neutralises your male privilege.'

Rolling onto his back again, Dominic stared at the ceiling with wide eyes.

'Oh my God, you're right...' And then in a quieter voice, he asked: 'You're not just dating me as a sophisticated revenge ploy because I was more popular at school?'

'You're an idiot,' Bruno said, affectionately smacking his shoulder.

'So, you like me?'

'Of course, I like you.'

'You're not mad at me because I make you watch horror films, and then you're too scared to go to the toilet in the night?' Bruno shook his head. 'You don't worry I'm from a bad family?' Dominic picked at his cuticles. 'Or my selling of slightly illegal goods – that's not a deal breaker?'

'Nope,' replied Bruno, but he didn't sound as adamant as he could have. 'What did you mean before – about how I was hiding?'

Dominic let out a long sigh. 'You were in the closet for so long, worried about what everyone would think, but now you're so busy trying to save everyone else, you don't have time to be gay.'

'Do you want to do gay stuff now?' Bruno pinched Dominic's arm playfully. 'Is that where this was going all along? You were trying to get in my pants?'

Dominic screwed up his face.

'Those hideous grandpa boxers...?'

Bruno opened his mouth in mock horror.

'At least I'm the only person to have worn them!'

'Fast fashion is a real issue, Bruno.'

Barely able to keep a straight face, he rolled his eyes.

'Is it stupid?' asked Dominic, after a short silence.

'What?'

'Being in a relationship when we're still young? It's never going to work out, is it? Not in the long term. They never do.'

'My parents are still together, and they met when they were our age.'

'They're from a different generation.'

'What's the alternative then?'

Dominic shook his head.

'Something more than hooking up, but less than a relationship. There should be a word for it.' He turned, so he was looking directly at Bruno. 'I'm going to see about a packing job next week,' he announced, watching for a reaction carefully.

'Really?' This caught Bruno by surprise. 'You're always banging on about how the warehouses are a scam. How entry-level jobs are all about monitoring when you use the toilet and zero-hours contracts.'

'I can't stay at the shop my whole life – and you were considering working there a few weeks ago,' Dominic reminded him.

'I know, but...' *I came to my senses*, Bruno wanted to say. And now he was helping Esther. Or he hoped he was. It was becoming increasingly clear she needed more specialised care – a trained professional over a well-meaning teenager. Bruno was considering becoming a nurse, but to be honest, he feared any next step, especially one that would take him away from Esther. And Dominic, of course.

A fly buzzed in through the window noisily, and looped back around the muggy room, leaving the way it came. If there was something Esther's house needed, it was electric fans, especially here on the first floor.

'It's so hot,' observed Bruno, redundantly.

'The hottest.'

'Have you told your brother about us?' asked Bruno.

Dominic mulled over this question.

'It's none of his business who I'm with. He wouldn't care anyway. My old man's a different story, but that's the only benefit of being estranged...'

'Aren't you worried about people finding out online?'

'Not really. Should I be?'

Bruno shrugged.

'It's so easy for you.'

'What is?'

'*Being*, in general.'

'It might look easy, but I can tell you it isn't from the inside.'

Gently, Bruno traced his finger up Dominic's forearm.

'Maybe I will write you a poem,' he said, almost to himself.

'That would be nice, actually.'

Bruno huffed, flopping onto his back.

'I just want someone to tell me what to do with my life,' he moaned.

'Kiss me, and then go and check on Esther. I haven't heard her come inside from the garden yet.' Bruno gave Dominic a peck on his clammy cheek, and then jumped up from the bed. 'That's all I get?' asked Dominic, mock-offended. 'Bring me some water when you come back too.'

Pausing at the doorway, Bruno turned.

'Glass of cold water.' He was counting the haiku syllables on his fingers as he spoke. 'Hydrates the bisexual. Keeps his thirst in check.'

'Does it rhyme though?' called Dominic after him, as Bruno headed downstairs and towards the scorching heat of the garden.

Bruno found Esther in the shade of a small beech tree with a pair of secateurs, pruning a bush.

'Aren't you sweltering out here?' he asked when he reached her.

'It warms the bones. All great things come from warmer
climes; salsa dancing, jazz, curries, iced tea. Ooh, we should
make some iced tea!' She looked at Bruno. 'I thought you were
napping, dear heart? Too restless?'

'Sort of.'

'A lover's quarrel?'

'We don't really fight.'

'I've noticed that. Very modern.'

'Yeah.' Bruno sat down in the grass beside Esther's wheelchair, with his knees up, his wrists resting on them.

'I've always thought that's the most archetypal pose for a
teenager,' Esther said as she snipped. 'It's almost impossible to
do after the age of forty. The core strength goes. You make it
look so effortless.' Bruno glanced down at his body as if he only
just noticed he possessed one. 'It's not true what they say about
youth being wasted on the young. Youth can never be wasted.
It's an elixir, it really is. I can feel your youthfulness radiating
out from you. It's changed me. I'm making myself sound like
some kind of vampire, but youth emanates a kind of perfect heat
that can be enjoyed by everyone. I know you probably want to
grow up, and leave this time behind you as quickly as you can –
but it slips away so quickly in the night.'

'I don't know what I want,' Bruno replied sullenly. He
glanced up at the first-floor window where Dominic was
probably already dozing. 'It's me. I'm the problem.' Esther
waited for him to go on. 'When I was locked in that cabin, I
promised myself I wouldn't hold back any more... but it's not
so easy in practice. Maybe I'm just not supposed to be in
love.'

'Ridiculous,' Esther tutted. 'I know the smell of compost.
What's the real issue?'

Sitting up, Bruno let his knees fall to either side and took
hold of his ankles.

'I just keep thinking Dominic's the only guy I've kissed.

And he's not even properly gay. I always worry he's going to turn around and say this was all a joke, or a phase.'

'Isn't that a little unfair on him? He seems very smitten with you.'

Bruno was silent, staring at a patch of grass.

'I like him a lot...'

'But...' Bruno shook his head. '...you want to go and explore. Spread your wings.'

'No, I want to stay here,' he replied, 'with you.'

'Dear boy, please – we both know that's not healthy. You need to travel. First it was your father's illness, your sexuality, and then me. I think you're afraid of claiming your full potential. The world is a very big place.'

'What will you do?'

'I'm going to stop putting so many barriers up to my daughter. We'll sell this house. I'll move closer to her, in a little flat. I have some dues to pay. I want to get to know her – really know her – for the first time. It's a new beginning.'

'I'm going to miss this house.'

'Do you know, finally I don't think I will. Can I tell you a secret? I've always felt much more at home in the garden. Much less crowded with memories.'

'How do I know you're not bluffing again, and planning to escape?'

'The same way you changed when you came back from conversion therapy. There's no returning, not after you've opened your eyes.' Esther leant over and rested her hand on Bruno's shoulder. 'Be kind to Dominic, he's more emotionally delicate than I think either of us realise. I'm not saying stay with him for the sake of it. Perhaps it's kinder in the short term to follow your heart, wherever that takes you.'

'But I don't want to leave...'

'Oh pish, please,' Esther shushed him. 'You can always come visit.' She leant closer. 'There is something tenacious in you, Bruno, that I also see in myself. You have to listen to the small quiet voice inside yourself that's yearning. Let it be your guide. And whatever you do, if your heart snags on something, don't get stuck and mired in sadness, like I did. Promise me?' She squeezed his shoulder with her strong fingers.

'Okay, I promise.'

'Good, now shall I make us iced tea? I think the freezer has enough ice.'

'I can do it,' Bruno said, leaping to his feet.

'Goodness, you get up just like that? Gravity has other plans for me.' She yelled after him: 'Not too much sugar, remember. I'm sweet enough already!'

With the kettle on, thunderously loud – it looked like it was from a bygone steampunk era, and Bruno always had to ignore the limescale inside when he filled it – he sourced a lemon (donated from a tree from Mary's garden), sugar and checked the ice levels in the freezer.

His phone buzzed. He closed the freezer drawer and fished his mobile out of his shorts pocket. It was from the journalist:

The article has finally been green lit, Bruno read. *Dr Tasker and Camp Change is about to get a lot of unexpected publicity.*

Incredible! he typed back. He couldn't wait to tell Esther (Dominic's glass of water could wait, he'd have fallen asleep the moment Bruno left the bedroom anyway). When the kettle boiled, Bruno brewed the tea, sliced the lemon and added the ice as quietly as he could to the jug so as not to wake Dominic (much chance of that, he could sleep through anything). As requested, Bruno only added a few spoons of sugar because the doctor was a little worried about Esther's blood levels. After stirring the concoction gently, Bruno picked up the heavy jug, took two glass tumblers from the shelf and walked back into the garden. Esther had stopped pruning the hedge and was looking at something in the ground in front of her. Bruno enjoyed the way the grass felt under his feet, the sensation of the blades between his toes. As he drew nearer, he could see that Esther had dropped the secateurs beside her.

'Can you take this glass?' he asked, 'and I'll pour the tea.'

She didn't reply.

Bruno stood frozen, watching Esther.

'Dominic!' he called suddenly, backing away from the wheelchair. He had to put the jug of iced tea down, it was too heavy, and later he would remember how carefully he set it on the grass, conscious not to spill any. Esther's head was nodded to her chest. She might be sleeping, but no – he already knew this was different. Bruno touched her skin, she was still warm, and he tried to recall how to check someone's heartbeat. He remembered reading that when a person was very old, it was harder to find a pulse anyway. A mirror is what he needed – you held it under the nose, and the condensation showed their breath, he'd seen it in a movie. Where was he going to find a small mirror? He was about to run back inside the house, when he spotted Esther's phone, sitting next to her thigh in the wheelchair. When Bruno picked it up, it was relatively cool to the touch, and he held it under her nose.

There was nothing. He held it up to his nose, and the screen filled with condensation. Bruno tried on Esther again, desperately. His whole body was starting to sweat in panic.

'What are you up to, dear heart?' she said quietly, opening her eyes, and taking in the screen beneath her nostrils.

'Esther!' screamed Bruno, dropping the phone, and hugging her. 'I thought you'd gone.'

'Gone where? I must have fainted. It's this heat. They said it was going to change over the weekend, but you can't trust these meteorologists as far as you can throw them.'

'I thought you were dead!'

'Oh, well – that is rather unfortunate. Why were you trying

to feed me my device? Is there another function I don't know about? Resuscitation?'

'I was using it to see if you were still breathing.'

'That works, does it?'

'Not really, no.' He hugged her again, and over her shoulder, he saw Dominic appearing from the kitchen, still only in his underwear, bleary-eyed.

'You silly, wonderful, sweet boy.' Esther squeezed him tightly and then let him go. 'Let us begin anew, and never shall we forget the utter privilege of being in one another's company. Now pour me some iced tea, or I might actually keel over dead.'

Bruno obliged readily, glugging the liquid into a glass, the clink of ice ringing out throughout the garden in celebration.

EPILOGUE I

ESTHER (FOUR YEARS LATER)

Esther's *Aerangis fuscata* was giving her some strife. It was the watering; she couldn't quite figure it out. There was something mentally holding her back too – she still hadn't vanquished her own embarrassment at growing such delicate plants. Miniature orchids just seemed so *prissy*, especially the rare types she was now attempting to cultivate in the greenhouse. But they gave her so much joy. It was all Esther could do not to kiss each of them individually on their glossy leaves as she left at night.

The Brownish Aerangis was the orchid's common name, but that was deemed far too common by Esther, especially for such a sweet thing all the way from a rainforest in Madagascar, so instead she called it Libby. This too she was slightly ashamed about. Esther had given all her plants names. Never would she have done this out in the (comparative) wilds of the garden, but here in the gorgeous warmth of her very own hothouse, it was a hideously civilised place.

Every day, Esther still marvelled about how it had come to be. Three and a half years ago, while Bruno was still living in the house, he and Dominic had conspired with Jane to source one as the most thoughtful present ever conceived. Her daughter had become much more relaxed about Esther staying on here after the episode in Scotland. Perhaps 'relaxed' was over-egging it, but Jane seemed resigned to the fact that Esther's wellbeing was inextricably linked to the property and the surrounding garden. Interestingly, as soon as this change occurred, a chain of events was triggered. Jane, no longer in a constant struggle over her mother's locale, instead put her energies into her quality of life. Improvements were made to the house – rails were installed in the bathrooms, several ramps were added to make journeys in the wheelchair smoother, loose carpet was pulled up, and a special extra-firm, roll-up mattress was sourced so she no longer had to sleep directly on the floor. At about the same time as her daughter's change of heart, Esther discovered the delights of eBay. Like most addictions, it began at a leisurely pace. She only listed her first item – a French vase she'd never been hugely fond of because it was a gaudy orange, and therefore upstaged the flowers – to try the process of taking a photo on her phone, uploading it to the site, and setting all the parameters. When the vase sold, however (for the princely sum of £82.55 after a flurry of last-minute bidding), she was hooked.

'Can you sell *anything*?' she'd asked Bruno, zeal in her eyes.

Soon, Esther was trawling the length of the house. What began with dusty knick-knacks soon turned into furniture and rugs and anything not nailed down (and some things that were). The process delighted her – the weighing of the items, the posting online, the communication with potential buyers, and then the wrapping and sending – plus all the conversations with the postmen or women, and couriers. Esther loved the idea of all her unwanted (because really, what was ultimately wanted except a good conversation?) possessions finding new homes, new beginnings all around Britain, and often the world. Returning them, in a way, after momentarily borrowing them.

As the house emptied, it became more manageable, but also slightly sadder. The greenhouse was the answer to that, something new and delightful and full of life, and completely Esther's own.

She placed down Libby – fighting the impulse to whisper sweet nothings to her – and gazed out of the glass windows towards the kitchen. The doors were open, and a lunch rabble was forming.

After the surprise of the greenhouse, Esther had been much more amenable to her daughter's meddling, especially when it was clear she was going to be allowed to stay. The greenhouse was like a promise. Esther had accepted that a nurse would need to come, to help Bruno. And after her dear heart left Whittleham, the first nurse – her name was Aduka – became one of Esther's favourite people, and a dearest heart too. With the house empty again, and cleared of so much clutter, Esther began to aspire to use the house for *good*. As a halfway home, potentially for young homeless people, or young travellers who were not accepted in their families for whatever reason. Thus, she minted the idea with Bruno and Dominic, and then with Jane – who initially had a laundry list of reservations, but was willing to put them aside because hadn't she said that Esther was alone too often, and it wasn't safe? Surely, then, to fill the building with vibrant youngsters, to make the place a refuge, and a welcome home after decades of it being a fortress, was ideal.

'But, Mother,' Jane had said, in her most dramatic tone, during one heated conversation, 'what if you're murdered in your sleep?'

'Frankly, it will still be worth it. Much better than the slow decline of loneliness. And I'll be helping people, and they me. And if you like, I'll keep a steak knife under my pillow, so I can give as good as I get.'

'That is not reassuring,' Jane had chided her.

But miraculously, she had not stood in their way. Again, it was the changing of the tide – from Bruno coming into her life, to the loosening up of her possessions, to the arrival of wonderful Aduka, and then patient Magdalena when Aduka went home to Nigeria to start her own family. The house occupants had grown – first a deaf teenager who was having troubles with his parents, and then a traveller woman in her twenties who was leaving an abusive boyfriend – and of course there were issues, as there were with all families. Sometimes Esther wondered if she'd possibly made her life too difficult at her advanced age, but there was so much joy now, it spilled over into everything; the noise and the vibrancy, the deciding where in the garden or the house to eat, the transformation of rooms into more useful arrangements, the comings and goings of dear friends, and yes, family. And so many pairs of helpful hands, to move boxes (four years later, Esther was still selling strong on eBay; she had even become a premier seller), and large pots, and plant bulbs for the winter.

All this helped eased some of the pain when Bruno decided to leave. Of course, he must, she herself had encouraged it, but there was always a difference between what one said and later, what one *experienced* as a result. Naturally, Dominic was heartbroken, but again it was testament to their relationship, that no tenderness was ever lost between them, not then, not now. If anything, they seemed closer once the physical intimacy was gone, even after Dominic became engaged to Jenny, and the babies quickly followed.

Her dear heart, a lawyer in London. Esther had initially advised against the idea; she'd met many miserable lawyers in her lifetime, but Bruno had explained that if things were to change, he needed to be part of the system. That had never appealed to Esther – how could you be an activist and part of the problem at the same time? – but it made sense for him. And it was either become a lawyer, or a politician, so much better the lesser of two evils. She even helped Bruno's parents with the tuition fees, she wouldn't hear about an alternative. Esther had stayed very close to Bruno's dad, they'd messaged every week, and she was one of the first people he told about the cancer coming back, and how aggressive it was. Dear sweet Filip.

That was one of the downsides of life, the outliving of others. Esther had named an orchid after him of course, the handsome Cymbidium, or Green Orchid. Filip was sitting next to Thackeray. Again, it horrified her, the idea that the others would know how she was anthropomorphising these poor plants. Her relationship with the leafy Thackeray – a Common Twayblade, an orchid often found growing wild in Scotland, appearing 'erratically' according to one guidebook, and making Esther sigh, 'Well, that sounds like him' – had been a healing one, however. Esther could chat to him, fight with him, forgive him, ask him for forgiveness, all in the span of an afternoon.

Just then, Lori tapped on the glass door with her knuckles, holding a mug of what looked like tea in her other hand. Lori was a high-spirited, curly-haired 23-year-old girl, the big sister of the household now, and a far cry from the depressed young woman who'd arrived at the Manor House over a year ago.

'You're a dear,' Esther said, when Lori presented her with the steaming mug. 'How is everything going in the house?'

'We've lost the vacuum cleaner, but it will turn up.'

'It always does.' Except for one time when a very sweet drug addict took all the appliances and sold them for drug money. Collateral damage, Esther always told herself. Replacing the white goods occasionally was a small price to pay for all of this. How close she had been to the edge of that cliff! How thankful she was every day that Bruno and Jane had rushed to her aid.

'This one's lovely,' Lori exclaimed, picking up Libby in her pot.

Ah well, bite the bullet.

'Lori, I'd like you to meet Libby. She's an *Aerangis fuscata*. Libby, Lori.'

'It's a pleasure to meet you,' Lori said to the frustrating plant, reverentially giving the bloom a kiss on the petal.

Strangely, from that moment on, Libby the orchid no longer had any issue with water.

EPILOGUE II

BRUNO (NINE YEARS LATER)

He realised he was nervous. The meeting room wasn't ostentatious in any way; quite the opposite, it had a relaxed vibe, a small table with only four chairs, no screen, not even a telephone – he was used to long conference rooms with intimidating AV equipment and high-tech speakerphones, and everyone in suits all in a row. The posh-sounding blonde receptionist ('posh', from the Romani word for money, thought Bruno immediately, which triggered a memory of his dad – God, he missed him) had been lovely too. What was it then? Perhaps it was the fact he was at a charity, and instinctively, Bruno felt everyone here was better than him, because they were doing *good*.

After he'd completed a foundation course and then started his law degree at the University of Leeds, Bruno was adamant he'd become a barrister, so he could help people in court – it was obvious. Over the years though, he somehow lost his way: the path to becoming a barrister was hugely challenging and competitive, and the idea of wearing wigs and gowns in court put him off – maybe he could be more help behind the scenes? Graduating as a solicitor was no mean feat either, but when he started his qualifying legal work experience, he realised the reality of the job, especially at the beginning, was full of countless meetings, reviews of documents and soul-crushing admin; time recording, file referrals, archiving, the list went on and on. He was not helping anyone in the drudgery, least of all himself.

A tall man in his late twenties opened the glass door and entered the meeting room, smiling.

'Bruno, I'm Simon,' he said, sticking out his hand. He was wearing a white T-shirt, and a green hoodie, with black jeans, and although Simon was lanky, he moved nimbly, gracefully even.

'Good to meet you,' Bruno replied, standing to shake. His palm was warm against Simon's cool one.

'What brings you here?' asked Simon once they'd both sat down. He had a buzz cut, which accentuated his strong nose and jaw, Bruno noted, appreciatively.

'Yes, well...' Bruno cleared his throat. 'I've been following the amazing work you've been doing with homeless young people – I'm a donator too, so I suppose I'm helping keep the lights on,' he laughed, nervously. 'I trained as a solicitor, but I'm looking to segue into charity work, ultimately a paid role, but I'm more than happy volunteering to begin with.'

'Okay, great,' Simon opened the folder he'd brought with him, jotting down a note on a pad. 'I like your necklace, by the way.'

Bruno stopped fidgeting with the silver wagon wheel pendant, and let it drop against his clavicle. 'Oh this, it was a present. From my first love, actually.'

'He or she has good taste,' Simon remarked, warmly.

'Yes, *he* does,' Bruno replied, experiencing the small jolt of panic he always still felt when revealing his sexuality to anyone.

'Bruno's not a very common name... Can I ask you something?' Simon dropped his pen on his pad. 'Do you, by chance, know someone called Mitch Henderson?'

'Of course! Well, I did. We sort of lost touch. But for a while we were really close. How do you know Mitch?'

'We were each other's first loves.'

'Yes! Simon! Wow, Mitch told me all about you. Didn't you run away to London?'

Simon opened his arms. 'And here I am.'

'You survived, you made it?'

'Eventually, but it was hard-going. I slept rough for a year, which led me to this line of work. But I feel I know all about you too – Mitch used to give me updates whenever he could. You're *the* Bruno. He told me everything you did to help him and the other kids, and about how you got busted out of that awful Camp Change by a granny on a motorbike? Am I remembering that right?'

'Esther, yes! She was eighty-two at the time, and she's still going strong. Are you in touch with Mitch now? How is he?'

Simon's smile dimmed.

'Not great, unfortunately. Mitch has suffered a lot with addiction, over the years. All the stuff he went through as a kid. He's getting through it though – he's been sober for almost six months.'

'That's great news. I feel guilty for losing touch with him...'

'If it's any consolation, Mitch is an expert at disappearing. He's currently in Bristol, I can give you his new number if you like? I'm sure he'd love to hear from you.'

'That would be amazing.'

They were both sat grinning at the other.

'Right,' Simon said, at last. 'The charity. Where were we?' he seemed slightly flustered now too. 'I'm pretty sure something will come up. A suitable position, I mean. A role.'

'Can't wait,' Bruno replied with a broad grin, his left cheek dimpling.

A LETTER FROM DREW

Dear Reader

Thank you so much for reading *The Locked-Away Life*. If you did enjoy it, and want to keep up to date with all my latest releases, just sign up at the following link. Your email address will never be shared and you can unsubscribe at any time.

www.bookouture.com/drew-davies

What strange, unprecedented times. We've all felt like our lives have been locked away these past few years, I'm sure.

The main relationship in this story was loosely based on my connection with my grandmother, Mary. I was her tech support (not the only one though, she had a gaggle of us) and in lockdown, I spoke to her almost every day, and even helped her access Netflix. It was a revelation to her. Nanna gleefully told me one night she couldn't go to bed at midnight, because she was too busy 'binge-watching' *The Crown*.

She died a year ago – I almost wrote 'sadly', but Nanna was vibrant and hilarious right to the end, and ninety-four years is a great innings. She was also able to pack a surprising amount of Netflix in before she went. (Joking aside – she'd give me a clip round the ears for that one – I miss her, and hope she'd have enjoyed this book.)

The Locked-Away Life also centres on Bruno's experience at a conversion therapy camp. As of time of writing, conversion therapy – a dangerous practice that targets LGBTQ youth – is still legal in the United Kingdom, with the government dragging its heels on making the long-awaited law change and even then, refusing to ban trans conversion therapy. If you'd like to help, please email your MP. It would be much appreciated. More information can be found at banconversiontherapy.com.

Finally, if you'd like to leave a review, I'd be over the moon. As Esther might say, 'Eureka and bingo!'

Take care,

Drew

www.drewdaviesauthor.com

 facebook.com/drewdavieswriter

twitter.com/Drew_Davies

 instagram.com/drewdavieswriter

ACKNOWLEDGEMENTS

To my editor Christina Demosthenous, your kindness and encouragement during this writing process was epic. And to the whole team at Bookouture, including Sarah Hardy and Alexandra Holmes, my deep appreciation. Big thanks as well to Sally Partington, my copy-editor extraordinaire.

Thank you to my agent, Sarah Hornsley at Peters Fraser & Dunlop.

To Effy Karakantza – here's to the conversation in Athens that planted a seed.

Robert Dawson (robertdawson.co.uk) for help with the Romani words, and my cousin Tim Stanley for his semantic assistance.

To Kristen Bailey, for tirelessly being in the trenches with me.

And to the memory of my grandmother, Mary Davies (2021), and my two uncles – Paul Bridge (2021) and Peter Davies (2022).

Finally, thank you to Marios, who not only survived a lockdown with me, but even agreed to tie the knot after.

Printed in Great Britain
by Amazon